PRAISE FOR

STASI CHILD

'One of the best reads I've had in ages.
With its masterful intertwining of dual storylines and its
stark portrayal of life behind the Berlin Wall, this is
a cracking debut'
David Jackson, bestselling author of *Cry Baby*

'Deft, assured storytelling, a fascinating setting and a
compelling new detective – I was up late to finish it!'
Gilly Macmillan, author of *Burnt Paper Sky*

'Deep and dark, this debut is **utterly gripping**,
sucking you in straight from the get go . . . a corker of an
ending. Superb'
Nikki Owen, author of
The Spider in the Corner of the Room

'Young has recreated excellently the fear and paranoia
that permeated East German society . . . I really liked this
novel and **strongly recommend it**'
The Crime Warp

'If, like me, you have enjoyed the Soviet-based crime fiction of authors such as Martin Cruz Smith, William Ryan, Tom Rob Smith or Sam Eastland, this will prove itself an **absolute must-read** . . . Young has more than proved that his name will be one to watch in the future with this powerful, well-researched and intriguing thriller. A **highly recommended** debut'

Raven Crime Reads

'*Stasi Child* is a **deeply atmospheric** and haunting read . . . I love a novel that evokes so well a lost time and place, especially when mixing it up with an intriguing plot and strong characters. **Perfect**, really. The fact that *Stasi Child* is a debut novel makes it all the more remarkable'

For Winter Nights

'I was in awe whilst reading this novel. David Young manages to capture beautifully the sense of place . . . This is **a terrific crime read**; with its insight into a bygone era and a fascinating political slant'

Northern Crime

'Gripping. The personal and criminal elements are both immediately engaging and well paced. The threads ultimately coalesce to form an **astonishingly powerful** depiction of life in a totalitarian state and **the ending is stunning**'

Buried Under Books

David Young was born near Hull and – after dropping out of a Bristol University science degree – studied Humanities at Bristol Polytechnic. Temporary jobs cleaning ferry toilets and driving a butcher's van were followed by a career in journalism with provincial newspapers, a London news agency, and international radio and TV newsrooms. He now writes in his garden shed and in his spare time supports Hull City AFC.

STASI CH1LD

DAVID YOUNG

twenty7

First published in Great Britain in 2015 by Twenty7 Books

This paperback edition published in 2016 by

Twenty7 Books
80-81 Wimpole St,
London W1G 9RE
www.twenty7books.co.uk

A CIP catalogue record for this book is
available from the British Library.

Paperback ISBN: 978-1-78577-006-7
Ebook ISBN: 978-1-78577-005-0

1 3 5 7 9 10 8 6 4 2

Typeset by IDSUK (Data Connection) Ltd
Printed and bound by Clays Ltd, St Ives Plc

MIX
Paper from
responsible sources
FSC® C018072

Twenty7 Books is an imprint of Bonnier Publishing Fiction,
a Bonnier Publishing company
www.bonnierpublishingfiction.co.uk
www.bonnierpublishing.co.uk

INTRODUCTION

This novel is set in communist East Germany, the German Democratic Republic (in German the *Deutsche Demokratische Republik*, or DDR) in the mid-1970s, when the country had one of the highest standards of living of any in the Eastern bloc. At the time, with the Berlin Wall – or the Anti-Fascist Protection Barrier/Rampart as it was officially known in the East – firmly in place, few could have predicted the tumultuous events in 1989 which led to its dismantling.

The DDR has come to be identified with its feared Ministry for State Security, the *MfS*, more commonly known as the Stasi. But while the existence of the Stasi – and its network of unofficial informers – was known about at the time, its apparently bizarre methods and the huge number of people who worked for it only fully came to light *after* 1989.

Criminal investigations were generally the preserve of the People's Police (*Volkspolizei* or *VOPO* for short) and in particular its CID division (the *Kriminalpolizei* or *Kripo*). If a case had significant political overtones, then it would be taken over by the Stasi, which had its own criminal investigation department, its own forensic teams and so forth. Cases where the Stasi and *Kripo* worked together on the same team – such as the fictional one that follows – were rare, although there would often be liaison at a high level. However, many members of the *Kripo* were, of course, Stasi informers. And the People's Police was as much an organ of the state as the Stasi: its remand prison at its Keibel-strasse headquarters near Alexanderplatz in Berlin as equally hated as those of the Stasi at, for example, Hohenschönhausen.

A possible confusion for English-language readers is the police and Stasi ranking system, based on that of the army. A murder commission or squad – such as the fictional one here – would generally be led by a captain (*Hauptmann* – the equivalent of the UK's detective chief inspector), or perhaps – as in this case – a first lieutenant (*Oberleutnant*). This rank, that of my character Karin Müller, should not be confused with the much more senior lieutenant colonel (*Oberstleutnant*), one rank below colonel (*Oberst*).

For the sake of authenticity, I've retained the German ranks, and also the often monotonous communist use of Comrade (*Genosse/Genossin*) when addressing colleagues, particularly in the presence of senior officers.

D.Y.

1

The harsh jangle of a telephone jolted *Oberleutnant* Karin Müller awake. She reached to her side of the bed to answer it, but grasped empty space. Pain hammered in her head. The ringing continued and she lifted her head off the pillow. The room spun, she swallowed bile and the shape under the blankets next to her reached for the handset on the opposite side of the bed.

'Tilsner!' The voice of her deputy, *Unterleutnant* Werner Tilsner, barked into the handset and rang in her ears.

Scheisse! What's he doing here? She began to take in her surroundings as Tilsner continued to talk into the phone, his words not really registering. The objects in the apartment were wrong. The double bed she was lying in was different. The bed linen certainly didn't belong to her and her husband, Gottfried. Everything was more ... luxurious, expensive. On the dresser, she saw photographs of Tilsner ... his wife Koletta ... their two kids – a teenage boy and a younger girl – at some campsite, smiling for the camera on their happy-family summer holidays. Oh my God! Where was his wife? She could be coming back at any moment. Then she started to remember: Tilsner had said Koletta had taken the children to their grandmother's for the weekend. The same Tilsner who was constructing some tall tale at this very moment to whoever was on the other end of the phone.

'I don't know where she is. I haven't seen her since yesterday evening at the office.' His lie was delivered with a calmness that Müller certainly didn't share. 'I will try to get hold of her and, once I do, we will be at the scene as soon as possible, Comrade *Oberst*. St Elisabeth cemetery in Ackerstrasse? Yes, I understand.'

Müller clutched her pounding forehead, and tried to avoid Tilsner's eyes as he replaced the handset and started to get out of bed, heading for the bathroom. She wriggled about under the covers. It had been cold last night. Freezing cold. She'd kept all her clothes on, and her underwear now chafed at her skin under the tightness of her skirt. Before that, Blue Strangler vodka. Too much of it. Her and Tilsner matching each other shot for shot in a bar in Dircksenstrasse; a stupid game that seemed to have ended up with them in his marital bed. She could still taste the remains of the alcohol in her mouth now. She wasn't entirely sure what had happened after the bar, but just the fact that she'd spent the night at Tilsner's was something she knew she could never let Gottfried discover.

Tilsner was back now, proffering a glass of water with some sort of pill fizzing inside.

'Drink this.' Müller drew her head back slightly, grimacing at the concoction and its snake-like hiss. 'It's only aspirin. I'll make some coffee while you tidy yourself up.' The smirk on his unshaven, square-jawed face spoke of insolence, disrespect – but it was her own fault for letting herself get into this situation. She was the only female head of a murder squad in the whole country. She couldn't have people calling her a whore.

'Hadn't we better get straight there?' she shouted through to the kitchen. 'It sounded urgent.' The words reverberated in her head, each one a hammer blow.

'It is,' Tilsner shouted back. 'The body of a girl. In a cemetery. Near the Wall.'

Müller downed the aspirin and water in one long swallow, forcing herself not to retch it back.

'We'd better get going immediately, then,' she shouted, her voice echoing through the old apartment's high-ceilinged rooms.

'We've time for coffee,' Tilsner replied from the kitchen, clanging cups and pans about as though it was an unfamiliar environment. It probably was, except on International Women's Day. 'After all, I've told *Oberst* Reiniger I don't know where you are. And the Stasi people are already there.'

'The Stasi?' questioned Müller. She'd moved in a slow trudge to the bathroom, and now studied her reflection with horror. Yesterday's mascara smudged around bloodshot blue eyes. Rubbing her fingers across her cheeks, she tried to stretch away the puffiness, and then fiddled with her blonde, shoulder-length hair. The only female head of a murder squad in the whole Republic, and not yet in her thirtieth year. She didn't look so baby-faced today. She breathed in deeply, hoping the crisp morning air of the old apartment would quell her nausea.

Müller knew she had to clear her head. Take control of the situation. 'If the body's next to the anti-fascist barrier, isn't that the responsibility of the border guards?' Despite the reverberations through her skull, she was still bellowing out the words so Tilsner could hear down the corridor. 'Why are the Stasi involved? And why are we –' Her voice tailed off as she looked up in the mirror and saw his reflection. Tilsner was standing directly behind her, two mugs of steaming coffee in his hands. He shrugged and raised his eyebrows.

'Is this a quiz? All I know is that Reiniger wants us to report to the senior Stasi officer at the scene.'

She watched him studying her as she pulled Koletta's hairbrush through her tangled locks.

'You'd better let me clean that brush after you've used it,' he said. Müller met his eyes: blue like hers, although his seemed remarkably bright for someone who'd downed so much vodka the night before. He was smirking again. 'My wife's a brunette.'

'Piss off, Werner,' Müller spat at his reflection, as she started to remove the old mascara with one of Koletta's make-up pads. 'Nothing happened.'

'You're sure of that, are you? That's not quite how I recollect it.'

'Nothing happened. You know that and I know that. Let's keep it that way.'

His grin was almost a leer, and she forced herself to remember through the hangover muddle. Müller reddened, but tried to convince herself she was right. After all, she'd kept her clothes on, and her skirt was tight enough to deny unwanted access. She turned, snatched the coffee from his hand and took two long gulps as the steam rising from the beverage misted up the freezing bathroom mirror. Tilsner reached around her, grabbed the mascara-caked pad and hid it away in his pocket. Then he picked up the brush and started removing blonde hairs with a comb. Müller rolled her eyes. The bastard was clearly practised at this.

They avoided looking at each other as they descended the stairs, past the peeling paint of the lobby, and walked out of the apartment block into the winter morning. Müller spotted their unmarked Wartburg on the opposite side of the street. It brought back memories of the previous night, and his insistence that they return to his place for a sobering-up coffee – Tilsner seemingly unconcerned about his drink-driving. She rubbed her chin, remembering in a sudden flash his stubble grazing against it like sandpaper as their lips had locked. What exactly *had* happened after that?

They got into the car, with Tilsner in the driver's seat. He turned the ignition key, his expensive-looking watch shining in the weak daylight. She frowned, thinking back to the luxurious fittings in the apartment, and looked at Tilsner curiously. How had he afforded those on a junior lieutenant's salary?

The Wartburg spluttered into life. Müller's memory was slowly coming back to her. It had only been a kiss, hadn't it? She risked a quick look to her left as Tilsner crunched the car into gear, but he stared straight ahead, grim-faced. She'd need to think up a very good excuse to tell Gottfried. He was used to her working late, but an all-nighter without warning?

The car's wheels spun and skidded on the week-old snow that no one had bothered to clear. Overhead, leaden grey skies were the harbinger of more bad weather. Müller reached out of the car window and attached the flashing blue light to the Wartburg's roof, turning on the accompanying strangled-cat siren, as they headed the few kilometres between Prenzlauer Berg and the cemetery in Mitte.

The two detectives were still barely on speaking terms as they parked the Wartburg in Ackerstrasse, the street that bisected the two neighbouring graveyards of St Elisabeth's and Sophien parishes – both abutted by the anti-fascist barrier to the northeast. Tilsner nodded towards the entrance of the former, and Müller followed him through the gate, with its metal arch overhead. The cemetery, with dark headstones and monuments jutting up from a blanket of white, had a tranquillity at odds with the rest of the city. Green-winged angels guarded some of the graves, their once shining bronze turned verdigris after too many Berlin winters.

They walked to the area of the cemetery where the body lay. Stasi officers and border guards surrounded the girl's lifeless form, which was shrouded by a canvas cover. A man in a raincoat – who had been down on his knees, hidden by the headstone of a grave – raised himself to his full height. Under the coat, Müller could see a civilian suit, but from his bearing she guessed this was the Stasi officer mentioned in Tilsner's phone call. The man turned and smiled. He looked to be in his mid-forties, with fashionable sideburns and sandy hair worn slightly long. He could have passed for one of the West German news-readers that her husband Gottfried was so fond of watching, despite her protests.

She didn't recognise the man, but evidently he knew her.

'Comrade *Oberleutnant*. Thank you for joining us. *Oberst-leutnant* Klaus Jäger. I'm glad we were able to finally get hold of you.' He took her gloved hand in his and gave it a firm squeeze, before doing the same as he introduced himself to Tilsner. There appeared to be genuine warmth in the greeting. 'Please come with me a moment, both of you, and I will fill you in on some of the details.' He placed his hand lightly on her back and guided her and Tilsner towards a snow-topped wooden gazebo, where mourners no doubt sat in quiet contemplation of their departed loved ones. Müller attempted to look over her shoul-der at the body, but Jäger didn't seem interested in showing it to them just yet.

They sat in a row on a bench, sheltered under one side of the hexagonal structure, Jäger flanked by the two *Kripo* officers. Müller could smell his aftershave: it seemed to her an expen-sive, western fragrance. Her own perfume, she suspected, was pure Blue Strangler, forty degrees proof. She hoped he couldn't smell it.

Jäger gestured towards the taped-off area, where official photographers and forensic officers were busy at work. 'Nasty business. A girl. Mid-teens, we think.'

'Murdered?' asked Müller.

Jäger nodded slowly. 'We think so.'

'Murdered how, Comrade *Oberstleutnant*?' asked Tilsner. 'And why do you need the help of the People's Police criminal division if the Ministry for State Security is already investigating it?'

'Yes, why *is* State Security involved?' added Müller, before the Stasi officer had time to answer her deputy. 'Surely, *Oberstleutnant* Jäger, as the site is so near the Anti-Fascist Protection Barrier, this is a job for the border force?' She looked out beyond the activity around the body, towards the first wall of the barrier. There was rumoured to be a minefield on the other side, before a second wall – the whole thing stretching for kilometre after kilometre around the western sector. The stems of searchlights sought the heavens, spaced out every fifty metres or so like overgrown sunflowers. In the daylight, with the snow-covered graveyard in the foreground, it looked relatively benign to Müller, despite the occasional bark of patrol dogs. At night, it took on a very different character. But if its defences deterred *Republikflüchtlinge* – those who would risk an escape attempt to reach the West rather than stay and build a fairer Germany – well then, that was just fine by her.

Initially Jäger failed to fill the silence, but then gave a gentle laugh. 'That's a lot of questions, and I can't answer them all. What I can tell you is that you have been instructed by your superior officer, *Oberst* Reiniger, to assist me, at my request. And although, officially, I will be in charge, to all intents and purposes you will be the investigating officers. It may be a difficult case – you will have gathered that already – but it will be your case. Up to a point. I do not want the Ministry for

State Security's involvement widely known.' Jäger pulled both his raincoat sleeves up slightly, as though readying himself for work. 'What I can tell you is the reason that we are involved. The girl was apparently shot from the West – possibly by western guards – while escaping *into* the East.' The Stasi lieutenant colonel paused and looked directly into Müller's eyes. 'It is – I admit – an unusual scenario.'

Müller was aware of Tilsner, next to her, whistling through his teeth at this news. In shock, or disbelief?

'So she managed to scale one four-metre high wall,' asked Müller, 'cross the control strip, evade the dogs and the Republic's border guards, and then scale another four-metre wall – while being shot at from the West?' She hoped her incredulity hadn't become all-out sarcasm.

'That is the official – and preliminary – Ministry for State Security account of events. I have enlisted the help of yourselves, the *Kriminalpolizei*, to discover the identity of the girl, and to find evidence to support this account.' Jäger again held Müller's gaze, with a seriousness that made her give a small shudder. 'Should you find evidence to the contrary, I would suggest you keep such evidence tightly controlled. And bring it straight to me.' Müller nodded slowly. '*Unterleutnant* Tilsner?' he asked, turning to her deputy. 'You too understand what I am saying?'

'Of course, Comrade *Oberstleutnant*. We will maintain absolute discretion. You can be sure of it.'

Sighing, as though already wearied by the case, Jäger rose to his feet and beckoned them forward. 'I'd better show you the body. I warn you, though: it's not a pleasant sight. For reasons that will become obvious in a moment, identification will prove very difficult.'

Müller grimaced as she and Tilsner began to follow the Stasi officer. She didn't enjoy examining dead bodies at the best of times. That of a young girl – where identification would prove 'very difficult' – sounded particularly distasteful.

Ice and frozen snow crunched and popped underfoot as they followed the cemetery path back to the scene of the body, Müller stamping hard with each stride to work some blood and warmth into her feet. She lagged behind the other two, a sense of foreboding settling over her. Something here was awry.

The handful of officers from the various ministries parted to let the three of them get in close. Jäger gave a nod, and one of the men pulled the shroud away.

Müller looked at the body: a girl, face down in the snow. One leg apparently lacerated – by the barrier's barbed wire? – the other at a crazy angle to the rest of her body. Wounds in her back, evidenced by a blood-besmirched white T-shirt, partially showing through a top covering of torn, black material, which looked as though it had once been some sort of cape. She didn't appear to have been dressed for the winter weather. The regular pattern of the injuries suggested automatic gunfire, and the body was facing away from the protection barrier, towards the Hauptstadt. At least that fitted with the official account. She looked back towards the Wall, the searchlights, watchtower and the buildings of the capitalist West on the other side, adorned with their garish advertisements. From where exactly had she been shot? How had she managed to struggle so far?

'*Verdammt!*' exclaimed Tilsner suddenly, from his vantage point behind the girl's head. Müller watched Jäger raise his eyebrows, but there was no formal admonishment. 'There's no way we'll be able to identify that. The face is a complete mess.'

This time Jäger did intervene. '*Her* face please, *Unterleutnant*. She wasn't some inanimate object. And someone, somewhere, will be missing her. But yes, unpleasant. The cemetery gardener discovered her at dawn, but a stray dog had apparently got there first.'

Müller moved around to Tilsner's position, and saw what had provoked his reaction. Skin torn away from her chin to her eye socket. In its place was raw flesh, like a cheap cut of meat on a butcher's slab. The side of her mouth was open, but no teeth – just bloody, mangled gums. An animal couldn't have done that, could it? The sight – and the thought – was too much. Müller suddenly found herself retching, and quickly moved behind a gravestone, bending out of sight as the remains of last night's meal and vodka made a return journey out of her mouth. To try to hide her embarrassment, she started faking a cough, kicking snow with her boot to cover the evidence.

'Are you quite alright, Comrade Müller?' asked Jäger.

She nodded, avoiding Tilsner's gaze. Steeling herself, Müller looked back towards the body. It was then that she saw the girl's hand, splayed out in the snow. A teenager's hand, with pure, unlined skin. But what startled the detective were the black nails at the end of each digit. It was clearly supposed to resemble nail polish, but the coating had a matt, streaky appearance. Müller knelt down. Up close, she could tell the nails had been inked in, like a schoolchild might with a felt-tip pen. It was a sharp reminder of how young she was. Mid- or early teens. Someone's daughter. The same age as her own daughter would have been, if ... She stopped the thought. Her throat tightened again, her eyes moistened. She met Jäger's gaze. Throwing up had been bad enough, but she wasn't going to cry – not in front of a senior officer from the Ministry for State Security.

It took the arrival of People's Police forensic scientist Jonas Schmidt to lighten the mood. He was half-running – which was about as fast as he could manage – and panting, his flabby body threatening to burst out of his white overalls, with a brown kit bag swinging over his shoulder. Müller's stomach spasmed as the *Kriminaltechniker* stuffed the remains of a sausage sandwich into his mouth, wiping the grease from his face with the back of his hand.

'Many apologies if I'm late, Comrade *Oberleutnant*,' he spluttered through the food. 'I came as quickly as I could.'

Still not trusting herself to speak after her examination of the girl's body, Müller simply nodded, leaving Jäger to make his own introduction. As he did so, Schmidt made a strange little bow towards the Stasi officer.

'I hope we might be able to use the Ministry's own forensic laboratories, should the need arise, Comrade *Oberstleutnant*. Your facilities are so much better than those of the People's Police. Will there be any State Security forensic officers working with me?'

'No, Comrade Schmidt. This is now a police investigation. You will report to *Oberleutnant* Müller as usual. We have already photographed the body, but there are some other photos we need you to take.' Jäger looked up at the ever-darkening sky. 'And we'd better do it quickly, before it starts snowing again. First, let's go over to the platform.' Jäger gestured with his head towards a small temporary scaffold with a ladder alongside, which had been built next to the Wall – presumably by the border guards earlier that morning as part of the initial examination of the incident. They followed him towards it, careful to stay on the gritted tarmac of the pathway, stretching like a ribbon of liquorice through the otherwise pristine whiteness of the cemetery. Müller smiled to herself. Jäger might say this was a police investigation, but the way he was acting, only one person was in charge.

Jäger, Müller and Tilsner climbed to the top of the platform, followed a few moments later by Schmidt, now even more out of breath.

'Well ... this is a view ... you ... don't often see,' he said between gasps. 'Not without risk of ... getting shot.' Müller threw Schmidt a withering look, but Jäger merely smiled.

'Don't worry,' he said. 'The border guards know we're here. We have clearance. No one will be shooting anyone. At least not today. But last night –' Jäger stopped mid-sentence, and Müller followed his gaze to a building that looked like a rundown warehouse, on the western side of the barrier. 'Up there.' He pointed. 'Fourth floor. See the broken window?' Müller nodded. 'That's where the gunmen are said to have been shooting from.' She noted the slight equivocation in his words. He doesn't believe it either, she thought.

'Was it witnessed by our border guards?' asked Tilsner.

Jäger gave a small shake of his head. 'No. It's from the calculations of line of sight. And the blood patterns in the snow. Look there.' The Stasi officer pointed to the centre of the anti-fascist barrier's defences – between the inner and outer wall. 'You can see her footprints.' He gestured between the line of the two walls.

'How did she know that she wouldn't get blown up by a mine?' asked Müller, shivering as the wind whipped the top of the platform.

'I don't think you would give a lot of thought to that if you were being shot at and running for your life,' said Jäger. 'In any case, the strip isn't mined – that's all just an unsubstantiated rumour.' Despite the cold, Müller felt a blush warm her face.

'And the bullets? Or bullet marks?' asked Schmidt. 'Will I be able to get permission to go inside between the two walls to check there, Comrade *Oberstleutnant*? Is that why you needed me?'

Jäger snorted. 'No, Comrade *Kriminaltechniker*, it's not, and no, you cannot go inside the restricted zone.' He turned and gestured with his hand towards the side of the cemetery path. 'Your work is here. There are footprints, presumably hers, on this side of the Wall. Bloodstains as well.' Then he lowered his voice, although there was no one else on the platform, and the officers near the body were too far away to hear in any case. Müller wondered why. 'There are some tyre tracks too. Make sure you take photographs of those. Check them against any vehicle the church gardener uses.'

Müller was about to ask why, but then met Jäger's gaze, and received a look that made it very clear he didn't want to be asked.

When they got back down to ground level, Schmidt started busying himself with a Praktica camera, snapping shots of both the footprints and the tyre tracks. Müller and Tilsner wandered around the various graves together, as though the long-buried dead might give them inspiration about the girl's killing. Jäger meanwhile had returned to the scene of the body.

'I'm not sure how much of an investigation this is,' said Tilsner. 'It seems it's all wrapped up, and we're an afterthought.'

Müller shrugged. 'We'll just have to do the best we can. Did it look to you as though she could have been shot from that building?'

'What, the one over in the West? Maybe. It's plausible ... at a stretch.' He shaped some snow from the top of a granite headstone into a ball, and then threw it to the ground. 'But then to scale two walls, while injured, without our guards noticing? Were they all asleep? I very much doubt it.'

After a few minutes, they heard the breathless wheezing of a man behind them. Müller knew who it was without looking. Schmidt. 'What is it, Jonas?' she asked, as she turned around to be greeted by his florid features.

'I think … you should come … and look at this, Comrade *Oberleutnant*.'

Schmidt ushered them back towards the protection barrier and over to the tracks made by the footprints, some twenty metres or so from the taped-off area of the body. He knelt down in the snow, and gestured for Müller to do the same.

'Here, Comrade Müller.' He reached into his pocket, and pulled out an envelope. 'Look at this photograph of the girl's shoes on the body.'

Müller took the picture from the envelope, and frowned. 'Where did you get that from so quickly?'

Schmidt smiled and pushed the camera that was hanging round his neck towards her. It was smaller than the Praktica he'd been using earlier, and looked altogether cheaper and flimsier. 'It's a Foton. A Soviet instant camera. It might not look up to much but the results are just as good as from those American Polaroids. Anyway, look at the photo. Do you notice anything odd?' The photograph was a close-up of the soles of the girl's training shoes, still on her feet.

Müller shook her head slowly. 'No, Jonas, I can't say that I do.'

Schmidt passed it along to Tilsner, who held it up to shed more light from the leaden sky, but also shook his head.

'Alright. So you've had a look at the photo. Now look at the actual prints in the snow. Notice anything strange there?'

The two detectives bent over the line of prints, puzzled. Tilsner gave a long, slow sigh. 'Come on, just tell us. We haven't got time for games.'

Müller's face lit up all of a sudden. '*Gottverdammt!*' Then, in a whisper: 'Have you told *Oberstleutnant* Jäger yet, Jonas?' The forensic officer shook his head. 'Well, for the moment, please don't.'

Tilsner was still bent down, frowning at the prints. 'I don't get it. They just look like footprints to me.'

Müller pointed at Schmidt's photo. 'Look at her feet in the photo. She's got her shoes on correctly. Left shoe on left foot, right shoe on right foot.'

'Yes,' said Tilsner, the furrow on his brow deepening. 'So what?'

Müller gestured towards the actual prints in the snow. 'Look at those. Yes they're pointing in the right direction, as though she was shot running away from the Wall. But look at the shapes. The right-hand shoe has made all the left-hand prints, and vice versa. It's all the wrong way round.' She looked up at Schmidt, who was standing now, stroking his pudgy chin. 'What do you think it means, Jonas?'

'Well, I don't really know, Comrade *Oberleutnant*.' He smiled. 'I was rather hoping you two might tell me.'

'What it means,' said Tilsner, 'is that someone's disturbed the body. She was wearing her shoes the wrong way round when she was killed; maybe she put them on in a hurry if she was being chased. But whoever's disturbed the body hasn't noticed that, and when they put them back on, they put them on the correct way round.'

Now it was Müller's turn to emit a long sigh. 'That's the most obvious explanation. But not the only one.'

'What, then?' asked Tilsner, meeting her eyes.

'Best not talk about it here,' she hissed, flicking her head towards Jäger, who by now had noticed their fixation with the footprints, and was walking towards them. When he reached them he cleared his throat, and the two detectives rose from their crouching position.

'Anything of interest, Comrade *Oberleutnant*?'

'Oh, bits and pieces,' replied Müller. 'We were just checking the direction of the prints. It appears the preliminary findings are correct, that she was running towards the East, away from the protection barrier.'

'Yes, quite so.' Then he lowered his voice. 'Though I think you'll agree that there are discrepancies, and no doubt you've now noticed some of these. I don't want to go into too much detail here. But we need to meet tomorrow to go over everything.'

Müller watched Tilsner's face fall at the news his weekend would be disrupted. She wondered what else he had planned for his Saturday and Sunday without the wife and kids.

'Do you want us to come to the Ministry offices at Normannenstrasse?'

Jäger shook his head. 'It's better if we meet somewhere quiet.' As he whispered this, he glanced over at the other officers gathered around the site of the body, who seemed to be supervising its removal. 'I'll let you know in due course where that will be. Until then, keep any information strictly between yourselves.'

He shook hands with the three of them, and then strode towards the cemetery exit. Müller watched him depart, wondering what sort of a case they'd been handed. One in which a senior Stasi officer wasn't prepared to share information with his own Stasi colleagues. She looked up at the sky, and its ever-darkening clouds, then glanced at Tilsner. His sarcastic smile had been wiped clean: in its place, a look of apprehension, almost fear.

2

Later the same day.

The specks of white fell rapidly now. *Oberleutnant* Müller watched as the arc lights spaced along the Anti-Fascist Protection Barrier periodically highlighted the fall of the tiny frozen flakes, glistening in the shafts of light, before the blackest of nights took hold again. They needed to work fast.

As she went over the case in her head, her stomach rumbled. Hours without proper food – just a quarter broiler from the outdoor stand in Marx-Engels-Platz when they'd returned to the office earlier in the day. She could do with a good home-cooked meal. Would Gottfried have one waiting for her? That seemed unlikely after her night with Tilsner, and her failure to return to the marital apartment. At least this case was likely to feature in tomorrow's newspaper – and the story might give her the cover she needed.

A few paces ahead, Tilsner lifted the red-and-white tape and ducked underneath. The sweep of the searchlights periodically illuminated their path, but when their brightness moved away Müller was grateful for the torches they had brought. It wasn't the site of the now-removed body they were interested in, but the approach to it. The approach from the wall side of the cemetery, where Jäger had showed them the footprints and tyre tracks a few hours earlier.

Tilsner shone his torch along the path. It had only just started snowing again, so the tracks – their general outlines at least – were still relatively clear. And that was enough.

Forensic officer Jonas Schmidt had telephoned them at the Marx-Engels-Platz office some thirty minutes earlier – just as Müller and Tilsner were about to finally call it a day and return home, separately this time. The chance to delay her showdown with Gottfried had been something of a relief, despite the tiredness that weighed her down.

Schmidt had a theory about the tyre tracks, and needed them to return to the cemetery immediately. Now – alongside Müller – the forensic officer reached into his overcoat pocket.

A rustle of protective cellophane punctured the cemetery's silence, as Schmidt started jabbing his finger at one of the monochrome photos he'd taken earlier in the day.

'Here, Comrade Müller. It's just as I said on the phone,' he said, spitting the words out in his excitement. He flicked his torch between the photo in his hand and the tyre tracks on the ground. 'It's the pattern in the snow. They certainly don't match any of the tyres that would have been on the cemetery groundsman's vehicle. They're western tyres. Car tyres.'

Müller frowned, concentrating on the flashing torch beam. Why had a car from the West been in the cemetery, near where the girl's body had been found? As she mulled over the peculiarity of the case, she looked up and followed the beam of one of the searchlights. Her eyes tracked its movement to the southwest, along the line of the anti-fascist barrier, towards the entrance to Nordbahnhof S-bahn station – or at least to what had been the entrance. Now it was walled up, forgotten.

Müller rubbed her gloved hands together to try to keep the blood circulating in her fingers, and returned her gaze to the tyre imprints. 'We're not going to be able to see much detail now because of the new snow,' she complained to the *Kriminaltechniker*. 'Have you already checked the photos against the files at the lab? When you say a western car, can you pinpoint a make and model?'

'Yes, I went through all the files, comparing against each tyre pattern we have a record of. It took me several hours. As I say, it certainly wasn't a gardening vehicle. Definitely not a Trabi. Or a Wartburg, or anything from the Republic. Not Soviet either …'

Tilsner sighed in exasperation. 'Spit it out, Jonas. My bollocks and every other piece of me are turning to ice, and I don't quite understand why you've dragged us all the way back here if you've already worked out what car it was.'

Schmidt stood now, frowning, and shoved the photographs back inside his coat pocket. 'Well, that's just it. I've a good idea of the make, but not the model. That's why I wanted to come back and for you two to come with me.'

He got his torch out again and scanned it over the tyre tracks.

'Ah good! I wondered if that might help. Whatever it was, it had a long wheelbase,' he said. He gestured with his arm, sweeping the torch beam in an arc, like a mini-version of a barrier searchlight. 'See. You can tell from the width of the turning circle. In fact, a *very* long wheelbase. Strange.'

'What, like a truck or a bus?' asked Müller, conscious of her teeth chattering in the deepening cold.

'No, no. It was a car. Just a very long car. A limousine. And ... Hang on a –'

Müller shone her light at his face. All the colour had drained out of it.

'What, Schmidt? Come on, spit it out!' shouted Müller.

But Schmidt just shook his head. Müller could see the forensic officer was shaking. From the cold? Or from fear?

Schmidt started mumbling to himself. 'It can't be. It can't be. I must have made a mistake.'

Tilsner stepped closer. '*What* can't it be? What were you about to say?'

'Come on, Jonas,' cajoled Müller. 'Whatever you know you should tell us. Nothing can be so bad. The truth will out.'

Schmidt looked at the female *Oberleutnant* with pleading eyes. Then his shoulders slumped.

'The tyre marks are Swedish – as I said, I looked them up at the lab. A Volvo. They have a very ... a very idio ... idiosyncratic pattern.' He looked at them with desperate eyes, as if the significance were obvious. 'The car was a long-wheelbase Volvo.'

Müller was perplexed. 'So, a truck? I thought you said it wasn't a truck?'

Schmidt just stood shaking his head.

But for Tilsner the penny had dropped. 'Jesus!' he exclaimed. 'Jesus, Jesus, Jesus!'

'What?' shouted Müller, stamping her foot in the snow in exasperation.

'Do I have to spell it out, boss? A Volvo ... A limousine...'

Müller suddenly clutched her forehead. *Scheisse!* The images of official state parades with Volvo after Volvo of party bigwigs played through her head. If Schmidt was correct, it looked like an official car – a government car – had been here in the cemetery. Near the body.

Tilsner cupped her ear with his hand, lowering his voice. 'Karin, we have to talk to *Oberst* Reiniger. Immediately. We need to get him to take us off this case.'

Müller moved back slightly, staring into his electric-blue eyes, and gave an almost imperceptible nod.

3

Day Two.
Schönhauser Allee, East Berlin.

Sleep in her own bed came easily to Müller and the expected dreams featuring the mutilated face of the girl from the cemetery never materialised. But when she woke, she was initially disoriented to find herself alone. Gottfried, unsurprisingly, hadn't been waiting with dinner ready when she'd finally got home the previous evening, and he hadn't come back to share the bed.

Now a door slammed. She could feel his presence in the lounge, hear him banging in the kitchen, the crash of pans and crockery not unlike the din Tilsner had made the day before. These noises, though, had the extra force of anger behind each bang and clatter – a percussionist building to the climax of a dark musical piece.

Müller pulled the bedcovers over her head. If he came into the bedroom she would pretend to be asleep, hopefully putting off any confrontation until he was in a better mood. She turned on her side, pulling the blankets and sheets tight to her ears.

Then, the sound of a bowl or cup breaking on the floor convinced her that she would have to confront him now.

She slid out of bed, and into her matching slippers and dressing gown. Her toes luxuriated inside the lilac cotton – one of her few indulgences from the Intershop. Running her fingers through her hair as a makeshift comb, she moved the few metres through to the living room, sliding the slippers along the wooden-block flooring, too tired to raise her feet. She leant on the side of the doorframe of the galley kitchen, and watched her husband as he fussed around clearing whatever had broken with a dustpan and brush.

'I'm sorry for Thursday night,' she said. 'A particularly nasty murder.' She saw the day's *Neues Deutschland* lying on the worktop, which he'd brought back on the way from wherever he'd been. 'You might have seen it in the paper.'

Gottfried didn't respond or acknowledge her, but threw the contents of the dustpan into the bin, and then resumed his coffee-making, crashing the pan down on the hob.

'It took longer than we expected,' she said.

He turned towards her, folding his arms across his honey-and-brown striped pullover. The one his parents had bought him for Christmas. The one she hated – it made him look so old. The one he used to hate too. At the time, they'd giggled secretly with each other about the gift and how awful it was, his elderly parents' lack of fashion sense all too clear. His wearing it now sent its own message to Müller: a private rebellion.

'You were with him, weren't you?'

'Him? I don't know what you mean.' Faced by his silence, she found herself blabbering. 'It just got so late, I had to sleep over in the office. I didn't want to come back in the middle of the night and disturb you.'

He advanced towards her, his face red and blotchy. 'I don't believe that for a minute.' His wire-rimmed spectacles had slipped part way down his nose. 'I've seen the way he looks at you.'

'It's not what you think,' Müller protested, moving her hand towards his shoulder. 'And I'm sorry, I should have phoned. I missed you last night.'

He pushed her back.

'You do know very well what I mean. You're an attractive woman. Tilsner's always eyeing you up. I bet you finally fell for it. Was it good?'

'That's not –'

'Not what? There's no point lying, Karin. It's obvious something's going on. When did he first get into your knickers? When I was in Rügen?'

Müller sighed. It was futile arguing. He was the typical schoolteacher: always certain he knew best. Worse than that, a maths teacher – inhabiting a world where everything was right or wrong, black or white. She turned around and trudged to the bathroom, slamming – then locking – the door, and turned on the cold tap. Cupping her hands under the gushing, icy water, she splashed it over her face. She wasn't sure if she was washing herself, waking herself or trying to get rid of her guilty blush.

She hung her dressing gown on the back of the door, and slumped onto the toilet seat, head in hands. Where had it gone wrong with Gottfried? She remembered the frisson of excitement when they'd first met, playing 'chocolate kiss' at a family birthday party for his young niece. She just out of police college, trying to forget all that had gone on there, and he a newly qualified teacher. They'd joined in enthusiastically, feeding chocolate marshmallows to each other, until it had turned into an actual full-blown kiss, much to Müller's embarrassment, and much to the delight of the children present.

It was true: she *had* found herself more and more attracted to Tilsner, despite the fact that he had scant regard for his own marriage, and in the workplace was more often than not arrogant and insolent. When Gottfried had been away in Rügen – temporarily banished to the reform school after failing to instil his Berlin pupils with enough party zealotry – she had felt lonely. Drawn to Tilsner with his stubbly, craggy face and well-muscled body. And now Gottfried was back, well, it was no better. The few months in Rügen had aged him, transforming him from the overgrown student she'd first fallen for into a poor impression of a crusty old professor. And now he'd started attending those infernal meetings at the church. It was all just –

Gottfried hammered on the door.

'How long are you going to be in there?'

'I'm just starting my shower – maybe another ten minutes,' she shouted, above the hiss of the spray. 'Then we should talk.'

'I don't want to talk. I'm going out.'

'Hang on a minute –' Müller turned off the taps, hurriedly slipped the dressing gown back on and rushed out. She was just in time to see the apartment door slamming closed. She ran and opened it, and shouted down the stairs. 'Don't go, Gottfried. We need to talk.' But the sound of his footsteps continued downwards until the building's front door was crashed shut in turn, and she felt the vibrations in the banister she was gripping.

A door latch clicked to the side. Müller turned. Frau Ostermann's head peeked out. 'Is everything alright, Frau Müller?'

Müller pulled her gown tightly together, threw the woman a weak smile and sighed. 'Yes, yes, Frau Ostermann. Nothing to worry about.' The woman pursed her lips and clicked her door shut again.

Müller retreated to the sanctuary of the flat and walked to the lounge window, trying to see if she could spot Gottfried up the street. He'd already disappeared from sight. Instead, on the opposite side of the road, she noticed a white Barkas van. Letters on the side spelling Bäckerei Schäfer, a small private bakery near Alexanderplatz. Müller swallowed as saliva pumped into her mouth. A shower, the one she'd been about to have, then out to buy some fresh *Brötchen* rolls. Maybe the van would be selling some? That would fill her stomach, and cleanse the row with Gottfried from her head.

Thirty minutes later and she was actually out on Schönhauser Allee, but the bread van didn't appear to be selling anything. She set off at a fast walk, hoping the couple of kilometres to the office would energise her, overtaking families ambling along in the winter air. A girl of about ten suddenly bumped into her, dodging her brother's snowball. Müller smiled, but inside she felt a sharp pang of loss and guilt. Children with their parents, playing happy families, just as the Tilsners had been doing in that pose at the campsite. Something she and Gottfried would never be able to do.

4

Nine months earlier (May 1974).
Jugendwerkhof Prora Ost. The island of Rügen,
East Germany.

Someone near me is crying. Awful sobs that make me want to join with them. *Mutti!* She has to leave. They're taking her away. I'm trying to pull her back, but I seem to have no strength in my arms, as though I'm just a small child again. I look down at my hands and realise they *are* a little girl's hands. Still I try to cling on, but her fingers slip through mine. Why are these men pulling her away? She lives with me and Oma, here on the campsite, in our flat above the reception. This is where she belongs, running on the beach, with our matching red hair blowing about in the wind. Don't go! Don't go! I need her. I plead with them. She reaches out for me, but something is holding me down, stopping me from helping. With all my strength, I break free and run out onto the stairs after them. But they've disappeared. And something's wrong. These are the stairs at the *Jugendwerkhof*, at Prora. Where has our little white campsite house gone? I turn around in panic to get back into the flat, but the same giant men are there and are trying to take me away too. I want to run, but something's holding me down. Covering me. It's heavy and I can't breathe and –

I wake. Sweating. Heart thumping in my chest. I throw the heavy blanket aside, and take deep, deep breaths. The nightmare recedes, but the crying is still there, those same awful sobs. I turn and I realise it's Beate, in the bunk next to mine. I gather my nightdress about me, recoiling from the smell of my unwashed body, and climb from my bed into hers, drawing the blankets around us. I stroke her jet-black hair, sweat-drenched like mine. I try to be as quiet as possible, not wanting to wake the other girls in the dormitory, but with these triple bunk beds and their creaking metal frames, I know that's unlikely.

'Shh. Shh. Beate, it's OK. It's OK,' I whisper as I wrap my arms around her slight body, my own larger frame dwarfing hers. 'Please stop crying. Every night you are crying. You've been like this ever since the field trip. What's wrong?'

'I can't tell you,' she whispers between her sobs, as I stroke her back, marvelling at the way I can feel the bones under her skin, not covered by the layers of fat that I know hide mine.

'Why not? I'm your friend. I won't repeat it. I won't tell anyone else. What are friends for if we can't share secrets?'

The noise of Beate's crying and my whispering starts to wake the others.

'Shut up, Behrendt. Just shut up and get back to your own bed!' hisses Maria Bauer, the dorm leader. 'And you, Ewert. Stop your snivelling. Both of you get back to sleep, otherwise we'll all get put on extra work duties.'

Beate quietens, responding to Bauer's bullying threats rather than the comfort of my body next to hers, but I stay there. In her bed. My fingers tracing the indentations of her spine. Counting the bumps. Stroking her hair. Wondering why every night it is like this.

Then suddenly footsteps outside the dorm door. Louder. Closer.

The bolt of the lock is thrown back.

Light on.

I try to jump back to my own bunk, but too late. Frau Richter's huge frame fills the doorway, her eyes trained on me, as I'm frozen half-in, half-out of Beate's bed, shielding my eyes from the bare electric bulb above.

'What's all this noise coming from here? *Jugendliche* Behrendt! *Jugendliche* Ewert! Get back to sleep immediately. Behrendt, get back in your own bed – and see me in my office tomorrow morning, straight after breakfast.' She clicks the light off again. 'And I do not want to hear another word from this room otherwise it will be even more serious.'

The door slams shut, the bolt is locked. I climb slowly back into my bunk, turn away from Beate and listen to the waves of the Ostsee below, crashing onto the beach. I think of Mutti. Of Oma. Of better times far away from *Jugendwerkhof* Prora Ost.

I do sleep, and when the morning bell rings I almost forget why this overwhelming sense of dread is hanging over me. As the girls start to put on their work clothes, I dawdle and move towards the window. I pull myself up, tensing my arms against the grey-painted iron bars that fill half the frame, and on tiptoes I peer out over the top of the grille to the Ostsee below. The beach stretches to left and right for kilometre after kilometre, but so, I know, does this building. I know it all too well from our anti-fascist lessons. How this was supposed to have been Hitler's seaside playground for his workers. Tens of thousands of them in these grey, forbidding walls. But tens of thousands of them who – if it had ever been completed – would have been able to look out on a beautiful seaside scene. To splash in the water, play in the sand, things that are now just memories to me.

'Irma!' shouts Beate behind me. 'Come on. We'll be late. After last night we don't want that. Richter's already got it in for you.'

I turn, retrace my steps to my bed and start pulling on my clothes.

As I take my usual place next to Beate at breakfast, I realise that my plate is empty. Everyone else's plate has its usual contents: roll, sausage and cheese. I see bully girl Bauer smirking at me at the head of the table. I look towards Frau Schettler, who's still finishing putting out the plastic cups full of margarine and jam. She will help me. She's one of the few friendly adults. Her and the new maths teacher from Berlin, Herr Müller. He usually has a kind word for me.

I put my hand up to attract her attention. 'Frau Schettler. My plate is empty.'

She looks at me apologetically, then raises her eyes to a point somewhere behind me. I turn to follow her gaze, and there is Richter.

'You should know by now,' Richter says, 'that the roll, cheese and sausage are a privilege. A privilege unique to this establishment. A privilege lost for bad behaviour.' She reaches over to the other bread basket, the one with the stale sliced bread in it, and passes it to me. I shake my head. She slams the basket down on the table. 'Very well then, *Jugendliche* Irma Behrendt. But I fear your strong-willed nature will be your undoing. It is many hours until lunchtime. Many hours of hard work in the workshop. But it's your choice. And remember. My office. Straight after breakfast.'

Bauer sniggers at the end of the table. Beate lays her hand gently on my arm to console me. But it will take more than that. I hate this place. And I hate Richter too.

As the others head off towards the workshop, I trudge along the corridor towards deputy director Richter's office. I purposely try to walk as slowly as possible. To delay the meeting. To try to rile her. Eventually, though, there is no option but to knock on the obscured rippled glass set into the white-painted metal door.

'Come!' she calls, and as I enter, she gets up. 'Ah, Behrendt. I was beginning to wonder what was taking you so long.' She puts on her jacket and straightens herself in the mirror, adding some lipstick and powder to her face. 'I think it's time for a little discussion about you. Follow me!' She marches down the corridor briskly, and I almost have to run to match her strides. I know where we are heading.

Richter raps on the grey metal door. I hear Director Neumann's voice asking us to wait. There are the sounds of lowered voices inside: his, and a female voice that's familiar.

The door opens. I gasp as Beate comes out, touching her hair, fiddling with the buttons on her work shirt. I start to ask her why she's here, but Richter grabs my arm and drags me into the office before she can reply. In any case, Beate seems reluctant to meet my eye. Richter virtually hurls me in front of her, and then pushes me forward to stand in front of Director Neumann's desk.

'*Jugendliche* Behrendt. I'm getting a little sick of seeing you here. What have you to say for yourself?'

I stay silent, looking down at my work shoes. Richter grabs my chin and forces my head upwards so I can't avoid Neumann's ravaged face, feeling that instinct of revulsion I know I shouldn't show as I look down from the black eyepatch to the distorted, blotchy flesh below. 'Answer the Herr Director,' she barks.

'I don't know,' I say, meeting his one-eyed gaze levelly. 'I do not know what I have done wrong.'

'Well, Behrendt, that is simple. You were found by Frau Richter in another girl's bed after lights out. That's against the rules. You know that very well.' Neumann rocks back on the legs of his chair, fiddling with his eyepatch with one hand, while clicking the end of his pen with the other. I let the noise fill the silence for a moment.

Click, click, click.

'Well, girl?' he says finally. 'Have you lost your tongue?'

'No, Herr Director. I was simply comforting Beate. Nothing more. She was crying. I was afraid she would wake up the other girls. I was just doing what any good citizen would.' I hear Richter tut and sigh behind me. Neumann places his pen down on the table and folds his arms across his stomach.

'The thing is, Behrendt, that Frau Richter and I have received reports that this has been going on a lot, that you're in *Jugendliche* Ewert's bed virtually every night. Is that correct? Is it some sort of perverted teenage love affair?' I wonder who's been snitching. It's not hard to guess. No doubt it had been Bauer. She and Richter are as thick as thieves.

I try to justify myself. 'Herr Director, I just –'

Neumann interrupts me with menace in his voice. 'Is ... that ... correct?'

'Yes, I've been in her bed sometimes, comforting her, but it's not –'

I'm silenced by Richter slapping her hand over my mouth from behind. I try to bite into her flesh, but she wrenches my arm up behind my back until the pain forces me to relent. She puts her mouth right up to my ear. 'You're an insolent pig. And now you'll learn your lesson.'

Neumann bangs his hand down on the table. 'Stop your insubordination, *Jugendliche* Behrendt. Bring her here, Frau Richter.' Richter pulls me by my hair, the unruly red mat of curls that I hate so much, and then forces my body down so that my face is pushed flat against Neumann's desk. I hear the sound of Neumann unbuckling his belt. Please God no, not that! I've heard the stories from the other girls, but please, not me! My thighs clench tightly together, as though the muscles are acting on their own. But then another sound, a swoosh of leather sliding against clothing, and I risk a glance upwards as Neumann draws the belt from around his trousers. He wraps the buckle end three times around his wrist, and then flexes the tongue, a gloating expression on his face.

'*Jugendliche* Behrendt,' says Neumann. 'You will spend the next three days in the bunker in isolation to teach you the error of your ways.' I start to sob, alternately crying out and trying to breathe in as Richter forces my face back down on the notepad. 'After that, you and Ewert will be split up into different dorms. She is a bright girl and obedient. We don't want unruly elements like you leading her astray. Do you understand?'

I continue to cry. 'Answer the Herr Director!' shouts Richter.

'Do you understand?' Neumann asks again. He slaps the belt in a whip-like motion on the table, millimetres from my eyes. It snaps like a bullet shot.

'Yes,' I sob. 'Yes I understand.'

He lashes the belt against the table again. The tip whips my nose, sending pain shooting into my head. 'Prepare her please, Frau Richter.'

I struggle against their hold, but they're too strong for me. Richter starts to lower my work trousers. 'No, no!' I scream. 'Please don't. I'm having my –'

Richter silences me by cracking the palm of her hand against my cheek. The sting is nothing compared to my humiliation and shame. I screw my eyes shut and push my face into the table, trying not to let them see.

'Five lashes!' shouts Neumann. And then, with his mouth right up against my ear, he hisses: 'This will teach you. And if you cry or struggle, the punishment will be doubled. Understand, *Jugendliche* Behrendt?'

I repeat the words of a few moments earlier, between my sobs. 'Yes, Herr Director. I understand.'

5

The chief forensic pathologist's office at Charité Hospital felt over-crowded to Müller. She'd filed in along with Tilsner and Schmidt, following after Jäger, who – despite what he'd said in the cemetery – seemed determined to take control of proceedings and had for some reason postponed his one-to-one meeting with her. Müller had tried to push for a prompt autopsy, but the Stasi lieutenant colonel hadn't seen fit to disrupt his weekend, so they were only getting underway now, on the Monday morning.

Jäger gestured to the three officers to stand at the back of the room while he occupied the chair in front of the desk, behind which sat three men in a line: one in civilian clothes, flanked by two in medical overalls.

It was the man in the civilian suit that spoke first, eyeball-ing the Stasi officer opposite him. 'You do realise that this is totally irregular, *Oberstleutnant.*' He banged his hand down on a fat grey-covered volume on the desk. 'The Order on Medical Post Examinations has been in force since 1949. It makes it quite clear that in cases of suspected unnatural death the only officials present at the autopsy should be myself as the Attorney for the Mitte district of the Hauptstadt, together with the chief pathologist and a certified doctor.'

The standoff intrigued Müller. She watched Jäger nod across the desk at the attorney. 'I'm fully aware of the provisions of the OMPE, Comrade Seiberling,' he replied evenly.

'Well, you'll understand then that the only people I will be allowing into the mortuary room to witness the legal autopsy will be Professor Feuerstein,' the attorney gestured to the grey-haired man to his left and then mirrored the gesture to his right, 'and Doctor Wollenburg, who was on duty at the Charité Hospital when the corpse was first brought in and who was the certifying doctor who performed the initial external examination. The only others present will be myself and the mortuary assistant.'

Jäger's answer came after a moment's consideration. 'That's entirely understandable and would be reasonable enough in normal circumstances,' said the Stasi lieutenant colonel. 'However, these are not normal circumstances.' Müller watched him reach into his inside jacket pocket and draw out an envelope. He opened it, placed the contents on the desk and rotated it for the attorney to read.

'You'll see the signature here.' He reached across the desk and traced his finger under a blue ink scrawl. 'Comrade Erich Mielke. Colonel General Mielke.' He smiled convivially at the attorney. 'I think that will be all the authorisation we will need for me – and my People's Police colleagues – to attend your autopsy, don't you agree?'

Seiberling repeatedly flattened out the sheet of paper with the side of his hand, as if stunned that the Minister for State Security had any opinion whatsoever on his autopsy. There was a moment's silence as he considered his options, but Müller knew he didn't really have any. 'I see,' said the attorney, finally, nodding. 'Comrade Mielke himself.' As Jäger had a moment earlier, he ran his finger under the signature, almost reverentially. 'That is of course a different matter entirely,' he said, speaking as though to the document rather than Jäger.

'I'm glad you're in agreement, Attorney Seiberling. Comrade Müller here,' he gestured towards Müller, 'is in charge of the investigation on behalf of the Mitte *Kriminalpolizei* and she will be present, as will her deputies, as will I.'

The attorney sighed, then Müller watched him rise from his chair, open a beige metal cupboard and take out protective clothes, masks, gloves and shoe covers. He pushed them over the desk towards Jäger.

'You'd all better put these on, then,' he said. 'We'll start right away.'

Inside the autopsy room, with its pervasive smell of disinfectant, the mortuary assistant brought the girl's naked body on a wheeled metal trolley from the cooler. Initially, Müller was surprised that the woman was able to lift the body onto the autopsy table without assistance, then noticed her well-muscled forearms. It was something she was glad to see: women at every level supporting the Republic, something that would never happen in the West.

As the detective looked down at the girl, she had to fight not to turn her head away. The face had had some of its lacerations partially repaired and displayed a waxier, paler appearance than when Müller had previously seen it close up, three days earlier in the graveyard. This gave the body a more human touch, but the toothless gums, the empty eye sockets that the dog had presumably attacked first, in its ravenous need for nourishment ... Müller found herself averting her gaze, concentrating instead on the girl's hands, just as she had three days earlier. Unadulterated white skin, and the pathetic attempts to mimic nail varnish.

Professor Feuerstein clipped a miniature microphone to his apron, and fixed the jack into a small dictation machine which he then slid into his pocket. 'You will all get my full report in due course, but I will make comments and record them as I progress the autopsy, which I will then review at a later stage. But feel free to interrupt and ask questions.' Müller found the pathologist's tone soothing. He seemed less stuffy and rule-bound than Seiberling.

'Do you have the photographs from the scene?' he asked Schmidt. The *Kriminaltechniker* handed over a bundle of cellophane-wrapped black-and-white photographs. Feuerstein and Wollenburg busied themselves pinning them to an adjacent noticeboard. The spread of photographs – images of the girl's body taken from various angles – reminded Müller of the things that didn't add up. She found herself thinking about the tyre tracks. The irregular shoeprint patterns in the snow. The apparent intended direction of the girl – on the surface a failed attempt to cross into the East, but one that Müller suspected had been staged.

Next to the board, on another table, the girl's bloodstained clothes and shoes had been taken out of evidence bags and laid out on a plastic sheet.

Feuerstein snapped the protective rubber of his gloves and moved across to the autopsy table. He looked down at the girl's face, then at the *Kriminalpolizei* detective. 'Do you have any further information as to the girl's identity, Comrade Müller?'

Müller had been holding her breath for moments at a time, trying to keep the stench of disinfectant from her lungs. 'At present, no,' she replied. 'We will in the coming days cross-check against all reports we have of missing girls of a similar age, but so far we've only made an initial check of the files.' Feuerstein nodded.

The mortuary assistant placed a body block under the nape of the girl's neck, exposing the underside of her chin and pushing her chest upwards. As the autopsy progressed, Feuerstein made regular comments into the dictation machine, and occasionally bounced questions off Wollenburg, questions that always seemed rhetorical. Seiberling, meanwhile, was being ignored. The exchange in the pathologist's office with Jäger had – Müller surmised – rendered him as good as impotent.

Feuerstein used a magnifying glass to check the body millimetre by millimetre. To Müller's untrained eye, he appeared to be paying most attention to the eye sockets of the girl's mutilated face, to her neck and fingernails. The wounds in her back seemed of little interest.

He gestured to Müller and Jäger to look more closely at the neck.

'Do you see these marks? This abrasion here?' Feuerstein traced his finger above the girl's skin, in a slight curve. 'These are most likely caused when the victim tried to prevent some sort of trauma to her neck. The marks are from her own fingernails as she desperately fought for air. And look here.' Feuerstein had gently pulled down the girl's left eyelid, which still remained intact above the ravaged socket. Müller could see a pattern of tiny red spots. Feuerstein pointed to them with his other hand. 'They are petechiae – minuscule haemorrhages in the skin.' He pulled the eyelid back again. 'The eyes, of course, are no longer present. And I will comment on that in my final report. If they had been, I would have expected to find petechiae there too, in the conjunctiva.' He then gestured to the girl's neck. 'You would usually, in these cases, see bruising here as well – but occasionally not, and this is one of those rare occasions.'

Müller was conscious of Schmidt's belly pressing into her back, the smell of whatever variety of wurst he'd just eaten invading her nostrils.

Suddenly he spoke, a confused note in his voice. 'So you're saying she was strangled. And yet there are no obvious marks on her neck, other than from her own fingernails?'

'Exactly,' confirmed Feuerstein. 'If she had been killed with some sort of ligature then there certainly would have been. But I would deduce she was strangled with someone's forearm. A muscular, but fleshy, forearm – hence the lack of bruising. By the time we have completed the autopsy, I would expect to have found – by X-ray and dissection – fractures to the laryn-geal skeleton. In other words, damage consistent with manual strangulation to the cervical spine.'

Müller's brow tightened in confusion. 'But what about the wounds to her body?' she asked, pointing at the photos on the noticeboard that Schmidt had taken at the scene. These clearly showed what looked like bullet wounds, in a regular pattern, across her back. Feuerstein gestured to the mortuary assistant. The woman and pathologist combined to turn the girl's body over.

'Yes, there are bullet wounds,' Feuerstein said. 'But, Dr Wollenburg, perhaps you can explain to our colleagues why we are certain these were not the cause of death, even before we complete our investigation.'

The blond doctor stared directly at Müller as he began his answer. She dropped her gaze back to the girl's body, trying to concentrate on what he was saying, rather than his angular good looks.

'Yes, there are lesions consistent with bullet wounds,' said Wollenburg. 'But even when the body was first brought to me, it was obvious that these were inflicted *after* death. Several hours after, in fact. There's a lack of haemorrhaging from the wounds. Yes, they were from an automatic, or semi-automatic, weapon. The pattern implies that.' He moved over to her clothes. 'There is a significant amount of blood on her outer clothing, but much, much less on the T-shirt she was wearing under her top. In other words, the blood was applied from the outside.'

'What do you mean, *applied*?' asked Müller.

'Well, to put it another way: *faked*. Very clumsily faked, so I would guess it was something that was done in a hurry. It *is* a bloodstain. But we've tested it – it's not human. The pattern is inconsistent with a bullet wound, and inconsistent with having seeped, flowed or pumped from within her body. It was thrown on her top later. The blood is from an animal – we believe it's feline.'

Seiberling, who'd been standing quietly in the background, now moved forward and addressed Jäger, who'd been listening to the explanations by the pathologist and doctor without comment. 'So you see, *Oberstleutnant* Jäger, it doesn't look like she was shot from the West while trying to get into the East at all. That story in *Neues Deutschland* was obviously wrong. I don't think there is any requirement for you four to be here for the remainder of the autopsy.'

Jäger himself said nothing for a moment; Müller found the silence unnerving. When he did finally reply, it was in the same quiet, measured voice he'd used throughout his exchanges with the attorney. 'I don't think we should jump to any conclusions, Comrade Seiberling.' He turned to Müller and held her gaze. 'I'm sure that *Oberleutnant* Müller will examine all the evidence in her usual thorough fashion, and will arrive at the correct conclusion.' There was no real menace in his tone, yet Müller understood it as a veiled threat. Then Jäger turned back towards Seiberling. 'And you're right, of course. We can leave now confident that you will provide us with a full and detailed report. But please don't suggest to us what our conclusions will be. That's not really your job, is it?'

He then reached across the girl's body on the mortuary table and tapped Professor Feuerstein's miniature dictation apparatus. 'You'll make sure you send me a copy of the recording of your autopsy notes, won't you, Feuerstein? And our other conversations.' Feuerstein clicked the machine off, and Müller watched Seiberling's face fall as he realised his verbal sparring with Jäger was all recorded on it.

The pathologist smiled. 'Of course, Comrade *Oberstleutnant*. Of course.'

6

Day Five.
East Berlin.

An S-bahn train rattled overhead. In the temporary offices of the Mitte Murder Commission – shoehorned into a railway arch below Marx-Engels-Platz station – Müller watched the contents of her overflowing in-tray battle gravity as it shook with the vibrations. She lifted a folder off the top of the pile, opened it and began turning the pages.

On each page there was the picture of a girl, first name, family name, address, date of birth, height, hair colour, eyes, shape of nose, comments about teeth and then details about other distinguishing marks. She'd been through the entire file at the weekend, and now here she was, starting her day doing the exact same thing again. They had to be seen to be doing something – and perhaps there was a detail she'd missed. The trouble was that all these girls were missing from the Hauptstadt and neighbouring *Bezirke*, and none of them seemed to match with the girl whose mutilated face she'd last seen on the mortuary table of Charité Hospital. And, if the official explanation for the case was correct, the girl wouldn't be found in the missing files of the Republic in any case, because she'd come, allegedly, from the West to the East. Müller sighed, and banged the olive-green folder shut.

'Werner!' she shouted through the side office door. 'Come here a moment.'

Through the dividing window, she watched her deputy stretch at his desk in the main office, pick up a file of his own and then lope towards her, as though deadlines were something to which *Unterleutnant* Werner Tilsner didn't have to adhere. All very well for him, the handsome bastard, thought Müller. But he wouldn't have Stasi *Oberstleutnant* Jäger or police *Oberst* Reiniger breathing down his neck and wanting answers every five minutes.

'What can I do for you, Comrade Müller?'

Müller felt herself blush at Tilsner's sham subservience. '*Karin*. Just call me Karin when it's us two. Or boss if you insist. I've told you that enough times.'

'Of course, Comrade Karin.'

'And you can cut that out too. What's that you're holding?' Müller pointed at the forest-green file embossed with gold lettering that Tilsner carried in his left hand.

'Missing girls.'

Müller frowned, and tapped her own differently shaded green file. 'But I've already got that file here.'

Tilsner placed his file on Müller's desk, and rotated so she could read the writing on it. The gold-embossed emblem of an eagle – flexing its wings like some unlikely avian bodybuilder – told her all she needed to know. It was from the West.

'How did you get this?'

'I didn't. *Oberst* Reiniger got it for me.' Müller tried to hide her annoyance – why had Reiniger given it directly to Tilsner? It should have come to her. Tilsner was unfazed. 'He's on the Inter-Berlin police liaison committee or something. It's his pet project. Willy Brandt started it – part of his reaching out to the East –' Tilsner rolled his eyes, and smirked.

Müller began leafing through the file. Other than a few more colour photos and better-quality paper, it was remarkably similar to its DDR equivalent. 'Is this just for West Berlin?' she asked.

Tilsner walked round Müller's desk and drew up a chair next to her. She felt his thigh touch hers. She didn't move her leg away, and found to her annoyance that she could feel the heat rising in her face. 'No,' he replied, with a slight smirk. 'The whole of the Federal Republic.'

Müller placed the two files side by side and squeezed each in turn between her thumb and forefinger. Then turned and looked questioningly at her deputy. He shrugged. '*Republikflüchtlinge*. That's why the file for one city is as big as the other for a whole country. Although I'm surprised there are so many. I thought there was some sort of agreement where the younger ones got returned to their parents or guardians back here.'

'Presumably only if that's what the parents want. Anyway, the Federal Republic is not a country – it's a fascist anachronism.'

'Yes, yes, whatever,' said Tilsner, leafing through the West German file. 'The question is: is she here?' He tapped the open western folder. 'Or here?' He pointed at the olive-green eastern file. Then he turned and eyeballed Müller. 'Or do we have no record of her at all?'

'We'll just have to go through them all systematically,' said Müller. 'Let's cross-check her physical details with the entries in each file.'

'I need something to help me along the way first. Elke!' Tilsner shouted out into the main office. Student detective Elke Lehmann looked up from her desk. 'Two coffees, please, for me and *Ober-leutnant* Müller here. Quick as you can. Two sugars for me, one for the *Oberleutnant*.' The girl started busying herself with tins and mugs at the side of the room.

'I see you've got her well trained, Werner, but she's supposed to be learning about police work, not making coffee.'

Tilsner shrugged and smiled at his superior. 'She's happy to do what I want.'

Müller glanced at the side of her deputy's face as he began unclipping the pages of missing girls from the West German folder. Strong chin, hint of stubble and fierce blue eyes. I bet she is happy to do whatever he wants, thought Müller, then chided herself for the ridiculous flash of jealousy.

Another train went through the station overhead, and Tilsner swore when the pile of papers he'd taken from the file fell to the floor from the table's rattle. '*Scheisse*. Can't they get us a proper office?' They collected up the pages and files and moved out together to the outer office. Müller crossed to the long side table, moving the empty coffee cups and textbooks.

'So where do we start?' asked Tilsner. 'Height? Hair colour? Eye colour?'

'We don't know her eye colour. We can't even check for dental records.' Tilsner grimaced at her reminder. 'Let's take all the pages out, divide them into piles and just work through them like that. We could maybe start with age. We know from the pathologist that she was between thirteen and seventeen years old. Maybe we should add another year's leeway each side and discount any of the girls under twelve or over eighteen?'

Tilsner nodded, and they began leafing through the pages of each file, collecting a pile of rejected girls who didn't meet the age criteria.

Elke approached with the two cups of coffee. Tilsner took a sip from the one he was offered and recoiled in disgust. 'Elke, what the hell is that?' The girl reddened and dropped her gaze.

Müller sipped from her own cup. It *did* taste disgusting, but she simply said, 'Thank you, Elke. Just ignore him. He got out of the wrong side of bed this morning.' She immediately felt a pang of guilt – *his* marital bed, the one she had sullied with her presence, clothes on or not. Tilsner grinned at her, as though he knew what she was thinking. Then he pushed his mug to one side and left it there.

They continued shuffling through the papers until they had been through the whole pile. Evidently teenage girls were the most likely to be reported as missing, because the reject pile was actually smaller than that of those who met their age criteria.

'What next?' asked Tilsner.

'Height?' suggested Müller. 'How tall was she? About a metre and a half?'

Tilsner got his notebook out of his pocket. 'Just over. It says here 1 metre 52. That's what the pathologist put in his report.'

'OK, so she could have grown if she'd been missing a while, and if she was young enough. So we still can't discount girls who were shorter when they went missing.'

'But we can reject taller ones, because she won't have shrunk. Everyone over, say, 1 metre 55 for starters.'

They divided the pile in two, and worked through it, pulling out the papers of any girls over their height limit.

'That's helped,' said Tilsner. He fanned out the three reports he had left. 'How many have you got?'

She spread them out on the table. 'Just seven.'

The details of ten girls to look through. They spread the ten pages out, side by side, along the table. Müller went along flattening each with a sweep of her hand. Then she returned to her own office and brought back two black-and-white photographs of the girl – one taken at the scene where the body had been discovered, and the other from the autopsy report. She took the autopsy photo first, showing the girl's face after the pathologist had done his best to repair her injuries; the result didn't look particularly human. She moved it – left to right – along the table, pausing above the details of each girl and comparing photographs. None looked like even a distant match. She did the same with the photograph taken at the scene. That was more difficult because of the obvious facial injuries. Again nothing.

She sighed and turned to look at Tilsner. Her deputy was staring trance-like at the photos.

'What is it?' she asked.

He took the original photo from Müller, the one from the cemetery, and held it – almost reverentially. 'It's this picture. It just makes me so sad. It's how I felt at the cemetery as well. You know –'

'What?'

'That she could be Steffi, my daughter, in a few years' time.'

Müller nodded, not trusting herself to speak. She'd felt the exact same thing at the cemetery and in the autopsy room.

'Steffi's six now. A little curly-haired fireball. Full of energy. I can do no wrong in her eyes. But in less than ten years, well ... she could end up like this.' Müller could see his eyes moistening, his hand shaking slightly. It wasn't the Tilsner she thought she knew. His devil-may-care mask had slipped, if only for an instant.

'You were telling me the other night that family life doesn't agree with you.' She laughed, trying to lighten the mood. 'Or was that just your usual chat-up line?'

Tilsner snorted, and tossed the hair back from his forehead. 'No. It wasn't. It's true. I got married too young, didn't I? When Koletta fell pregnant. We'd both just turned twenty. That's no age at all. And then Marius came along straightaway; it just felt we didn't have the time to live our lives. He's the same age as this girl. But it's always the girls, isn't it? Always the girls who end up like this.'

He continued to finger and stare at the photograph. Then his face creased into a frown as he picked up the autopsy photo.

'Hang on,' he said, his voice suddenly animated.

'What is it?'

Tilsner put the photo back on the table above girl number six. Then he got some scissors and started cutting round the face of the girl from the autopsy, and then did the same for the report for missing girl number six.

'I hope you know what you're doing, destroying evidence like that,' said Müller.

'They're only copies. But look!'

He pointed excitedly at the two photos, placing them side by side, having cut the hair from the picture of each photograph.

'Don't you see? It looks like the same girl. Only the hair is different.' He placed the cut-out faces back in the surrounding frame of hair, making the photos complete again. In the missing report, the girl had a large mass of blonde hair. In the autopsy photo, the hair was dark, short and straight. Müller examined the photos closely. Tilsner was right, up to a point. There was a resemblance, although – given the injuries – she wasn't as sure that it was the same girl.

'East or West?' she asked.

Tilsner picked up the piece of paper and read the address. 'East,' he said. 'Friedrichshain.' He read the report on the girl. 'Silke Eisenberg. Suspected of wall jumping – but, as usual, it was the other way, escaping to the West.'

'Perhaps she could have gone there, but then attempted to return?' suggested Müller.

'Well, anything's possible – if pigs had wings,' replied Tilsner in a deadpan voice.

Müller sat down on a chair next to the table, exhausted, even though it was still early in the day. Checking out this girl's home address was all they had to go on. It wasn't much, but at least it was a start.

7

As Müller and Tilsner arrived at the Eisenberg family's apartment block in Friedrichshain, Müller found herself wanting to shield her ears from the furious clanging and crashing of building noise. The dust and smell of new cement and render made her want to cover her mouth and nose, reminding her of her childhood and the post-war rebuilding of destroyed homes. They picked their way to the block mentioned in the missing persons' file, careful to stay on the wooden duckboard – the only way of safely negotiating the mess of mud and melted snow between the two buildings.

Opposite the Eisenbergs' block, another concrete high-rise was emerging from the ground, seemingly expanding upwards metre by metre as Müller watched. It reminded her of her nephew's *Pebe* toy set: the gift she'd given him at the family Christmas at her mother's guesthouse in Thuringia the year before last. He'd constructed a modernist high-rise from the interlocking plastic bricks in just a few hours, while the adults digested their festive lunch. Now here, grown-up workers from the workers' and peasants' state were building the socialist dream in its full-scale form. But while that filled Müller with hope for her country's future, the memory of the Christmas gift was a source of guilt. This year, she hadn't been back to the family home in Oberhof – the Republic's answer to St Moritz – and she knew her mother, sister and brother would feel she'd let them down. Müller had claimed she was too busy with work, but –

She stopped the thought, and hung back as Tilsner rang the entryphone buzzer. He jabbed on the button repeatedly, shouting into the mouthpiece to no avail.

He turned towards Müller and shrugged in exasperation, then tried pulling on the locked front door.

'A few months old but knackered already.'

Just then, above the construction din from the opposite block, Müller simultaneously heard and felt footsteps on the wooden duckboard behind her. An elderly lady approached – weighed down by shopping bags – the timber slats wobbling under her shoes. The woman pushed away wisps of pure white hair from her lined and leathered forehead, tucking them under the red-and-white polka-dot scarf that was wrapped tightly round her head.

'Are you from the neighbourhood committee?' she asked Müller. 'This is what I was talking about.' The woman gestured at the muddy mess underfoot. 'It's no good building us new apartments but not sorting out the roads and footpaths. If I fell off, I'd probably drown in that mud. Still, at least you're here now.'

Müller withdrew her *Kripo* identification and showed it to the woman. '*Oberleutnant* Müller. *Kriminalpolizei* Mitte. We need to get into this apartment block. Do you live here? The entry system doesn't seem to be working.' Müller pointed to where Tilsner was still pulling at the door and jabbing buttons at random.

'Nothing works properly here,' said the woman. 'That's what I said in my written complaint. I can let you in, but will you try to make sure they do something about it in return?'

'It's not the job of the criminal police to respond to petitions, I'm afraid, Citizen –'

'Keppler. The name's Keppler.' She shuffled towards the door with her bags, placed them down on the muddied wooden boards and then fumbled in her pocket for the door key. 'Who is it you're looking for anyway, dear?'

'The Eisenberg family. Flat 412.'

'Ah yes. Same floor as me.'

'You know them, then?' asked Müller.

'I do. And I could give you some interesting information.'

Müller eyeballed the woman with what she hoped was her best stern expression. 'Then you should. Withholding information from the People's Police –'

'...is a very serious matter. I know that, officer. I hope, in return, you might mention the terrible state of the footpaths.' She waited for some response from Müller, but the detective continued to fix her with a glare. Eventually the woman continued without any assurance in return. 'Something fishy is going on there if you ask me. She's kept herself very private since her daughter disappeared, and her husband ... well you probably know all about him anyway. But she'll be in, there's that at least. She never goes out these days.'

'And what about Silke, the daughter?'

'Well they've reported her missing, haven't they? Look, posters everywhere.' The woman gestured with her eyes to the wall of the lobby, and Müller saw the exact same photo from the file, this time as the centrepiece of a missing person's poster, offering a 1,000-mark reward. 'They're making out she's been abducted or something, but it's obvious where she's gone.'

'Where?' asked Tilsner.

'Where do they all go? To the West, of course. Watch all their western TV programmes and get silly ideas. She was always a bad one.'

'What do you mean?' asked Müller.

The woman leant down to pick up her shopping bags. 'I'll tell you on the way up,' she said. 'Can your young man give me a hand with these? There's no point him pressing those buttons, because the lift doesn't work either.'

The three of them laboriously climbed the four floors, with Tilsner taking both her shopping bags. On the way, in between regular stops to get her breath back, Frau Keppler extolled her theory that Silke Eisenberg had been mixing with the wrong sorts. Having sex with boys. Then men. And then with money changing hands. Frau Keppler's view was that she'd simply crossed the Wall to earn more money in the West's lucrative red-light districts. She divulged the information in an ever-quieter voice. By the time they were at the fourth level she was virtually whispering into Müller's ear, between regular rasping intakes of air.

'You do realise what you're alleging, Citizen Keppler? *Republikflucht* is a very serious crime,' said Müller, matching the elderly woman's whisper. '*Republikflucht* and alleged prostitution.'

The woman gestured with her eyes to the door to apartment 412. 'You'll see, dear,' she whispered. Tilsner handed her the shopping bags. 'Thank you, young man,' she said, this time at full volume.

As Frau Keppler retreated down the corridor towards her own flat, humming a tune as she went, Müller rang the Eisenbergs' bell.

The door opened a few centimetres, and half of a woman's face appeared, bisected by a security chain which prevented the door opening fully. 'Who is it?'

Müller held up her *Kripo* ID. '*Kriminalpolizei*. We're here about Silke.'

The woman made no initial move to undo the chain or open the door further. 'What about Silke? She's not here.'

Müller sighed. 'We know that, Citizen Eisenberg, but we may have some information about her. Could you let us in, please? This is a criminal investigation.'

Now it was the woman's turn to sigh. A strange reaction, thought Müller, unless what the old woman had alleged was true. The chain jangled as Frau Eisenberg freed it, and Müller and Tilsner stepped into the brightly painted hallway of the flat. The woman looked out of place amongst its neatness. Mousy hair, unwashed greasy housecoat and, more importantly, a look in her eyes that didn't suggest she was expecting to receive some bad news about her daughter.

Müller held out her hand. '*Oberleutnant* Müller, *Kriminalpolizei* Mitte. And this is *Unterleutnant* Tilsner.'

The woman wiped her hand on the back of her housecoat, before accepting Müller's handshake. 'Marietta Eisenberg. I'm Silke's mother.'

'And where's her dad?' asked Tilsner.

The woman snorted. 'You should know more about that than me.'

'What do you mean, Frau Eisenberg?' asked Müller.

'I mean I don't know where he is. He was arrested three months ago, just before Silke went missing, but I don't know where he's been taken. You lot won't tell me anything.'

Müller looked quizzically at Tilsner. He shrugged. 'We don't know anything about that, Citizen Eisenberg,' she said. 'And if he'd been arrested by the *Volkspolizei* we *would* know, I can assure you.'

'It wasn't the police who took him. It was the Stasi.' Müller frowned. Perhaps they should have checked in with Jäger before coming here.

'Well then, I'm sure they had good reason.' It was a little cruel, but Marietta Eisenberg had rubbed her up the wrong way. 'I'm sorry for what's happened to your husband. But we're here to talk about Silke – can we sit down?'

Silke's mother ushered the two detectives into the lounge. Müller was impressed as she took in the decor. The woman's daywear might have been dirty, but her apartment was spotless – and full of the latest gadgets. A telephone, television, expensive-looking parquet flooring and a tasteful range of fitted wood-veneer cupboards and bookshelves. It was how Müller imagined a flat in West Berlin might be furnished.

'I know what you're thinking,' said Frau Eisenberg. 'How does a family whose husband has been arrested by the Stasi afford something like this?'

'It *is* a lovely flat,' said Müller, swallowing her curiosity, 'but it's no concern of mine. Shall we sit?' She gestured to the beige corduroy sofa. Out of the corner of her eye, she saw Tilsner in the kitchen, riffling through cupboards and drawers.

Eisenberg kept darting glances towards Müller's deputy. 'Does he have authorisation for that? For going through my things?' she asked.

'Don't worry about *Unterleutnant* Tilsner,' said Müller. 'The fact we're from the *Kripo* is the only authorisation we need, Frau Eisenberg.' Then Müller turned more conciliatory, and laid her hand on top of Eisenberg's. 'We simply need to find out as much as we can about Silke. You see, a girl has been found.' Müller studied the woman's face, watching for her reactions. There was apprehension, perhaps fear – but no real surprise.

'Really?'

Müller nodded, but kept her hand clasped to Eisenberg's. 'But it may not be good news, I'm afraid.' This was the bit Müller hated: telling a parent that the police believed their child was dead. 'A girl's *body* has been found.'

Eisenberg stared at her in apparent disbelief. At the same time, Müller was aware of Tilsner now having moved out of the kitchen and the lounge, and towards the bedrooms. She didn't think Frau Eisenberg, in her distressed state, had noticed.

'We're not sure it's Silke. For your sake, I hope it's not. But we need you to look at a photograph to see if it is her. Can you do that for me?'

Marietta Eisenberg looked crushed. Her husband in some unknown Stasi jail. And now her daughter, having been missing for months, was possibly dead. 'Where was the girl's body discovered?'

'In the Hauptstadt. In Mitte.'

'The Hauptstadt?' asked Eisenberg. 'In the East?'

'Yes, of course.'

'But –' The words died in Eisenberg's mouth.

'But what, Citizen Eisenberg? Is there something you want to tell me?'

'N-n-no. I … I … it's just –'

'What?'

Frau Eisenberg held her head in her hands and stared at the floor. 'Nothing,' she mumbled. 'Nothing.'

Müller started to pull the photograph of the girl from her pocket, when she heard a shout from inside the flat.

'Boss!' screamed Tilsner. 'Come here, now.'

Müller jumped up from the sofa and hurried in the direction of her deputy's voice. It was obviously a girl's bedroom. Pink everywhere. With posters of western rock groups and pop stars on the wall. Müller recognised Mick Jagger with his pouting

lips, David Bowie with his orange hair. On another wall, Free
German Youth and Pioneer certificates and posters, from earlier
years when Silke's aspirations had apparently followed the party
diktats for model socialist children.

Tilsner was at the girl's bed, the drawer of the bedside cabinet
open. He held a letter in his hand. 'The mother should have hidden this a bit better. Putting it in the girl's own drawer probably
wasn't the most sensible move.' He passed the letter, envelope and
enclosed instant-camera photo over to Müller. Müller looked at
the photo first. It was colour, something hard to come by in the
Republic. But what was interesting was it was a self-shot photo of
Silke in front of the main entrance of the KaDeWe department
store in West Berlin. She looked at the western postmark on the
envelope. From just three days earlier – after the murdered girl's
body had been found. She raised her eyes to Tilsner's.

'So she's in the West. And alive. Our body by the Wall is not
Silke Eisenberg.'

'No, boss. Not unless someone else posted it after she was
killed. And while that's possible, it seems unlikely. So we're no
further on.'

They heard sobbing behind them, and both turned. Standing
there in the doorway, Marietta Eisenberg looked both upset and
alarmed. As well she might, thought Müller. Her daughter may
not be dead, but she was guilty of *Republikflucht*. And if Marietta
Eisenberg had helped her daughter to flee to West Berlin, then
it wouldn't merely be her husband enjoying the hospitality of a
Stasi jail.

8

Gottfried Müller knew that he was breaking a promise to his wife, but justified it by reminding himself that she'd broken an even more important pledge: her marriage vows.

Each of Gottfried's strides up Schönhauser Allee was more like a stamp of frustration. He could have caught the U-bahn but he needed the air and the anonymity of the street, rather than being glowered at by some matron across an underground train carriage.

Gottfried could feel his glasses slipping down his nose as he strode on. He pushed them back into place, and then waited at the red pedestrian *Ampelmann* sign outside Dimitroffstrasse U-bahn station; Wartburgs, Trabants and Ladas poured more of their fumes into the choking night-time smog. Since he'd come back from Rügen everything had been a hundred times worse than before he went. At first he'd been quite keen on the idea of a few months by the Baltic coast in the reform school. That was until he'd actually seen the conditions. But even there, he'd felt calmer, as though he could actually make a difference, even if it was just a question of trying to cheer up the children and show them some kindness.

Gottfried decided to walk up Pappelallee – it would be quieter. He needed to calm down before he reached the church. Saturday's argument with Karin still rankled. That she'd chosen to stay out all night rankled even more. He could tell she was lying, so he in turn felt no guilt coming here now. All previous bets were off.

With his head bowed, he almost failed to spot an elderly woman weaving her way through the patches of snow on the pavement. She stumbled, and he reached out to hold her and prevent her falling, thinking how frail and light she felt – and realising that the left arm of her coat was empty, just fabric hanging down limply. The woman nodded her thanks and carried on her way, but Gottfried stopped a moment. It was a timely reminder there were people worse off than him. He watched the woman's back as she shuffled off, the coat arm flapping as she went. Was she too old for a prosthesis? Or was it her badge of honour? Older citizens with missing limbs from war wounds or bombing injuries had been a common sight when he was growing up in Berlin. That and the huge number of angry single women who'd fly off the handle at the slightest schoolboy provocation. Women widowed and aged before their time by the ravages of war.

He glanced at his watch, pulled his coat up around his neck and speeded up his strides. If possible, he wanted to be a few minutes early for the meeting. Pastor Grosinski might be able to offer some useful advice on how to avoid the collapse of a marriage. Although perhaps he and Karin would just be better off letting nature take its course.

Approaching the entrance to the church, Gottfried stopped again for a moment. He tilted his head back slowly, letting his eyes pan upwards, admiring the building's red-brick solidity and the green patina of its copper steeple, disappearing through the smog haze into the moonlit sky. It appeared to have survived the war's bombs and bullets better than the old woman he'd almost bumped into.

As he walked up the steps to the church's front door, some fractional movement or flash in the corner of his eye made him turn and peer up at one of the windows in an apartment block across the road. There was a man in the shadows, holding something. Watching from the second floor. His face looked remarkably like that bastard Tilsner, Karin's deputy. The man moved away from the window. Gottfried wondered for just an instant whether he should run across the road to the apartment and confront him. But then he shook his head, turned and entered the church. It almost certainly *wasn't* Tilsner, just someone who looked a little like him from a distance. *I need to pull myself out of this – I'm becoming obsessed.*

9

Day Six.
Plänterwald, East Berlin.

Müller pulled the collar of her overcoat up around her ears, and then wrapped one lapel inside the other to try to keep out the cold. The brisk walk from Plänterwald S-bahn station had temporarily increased her internal body heat, but now – waiting by the unmanned ticket office of the Kulturpark – the icy morning air seemed to be eating into her bones. Although Jäger had said he wanted to meet somewhere quiet, she hadn't quite expected it would be the Republic's only amusement park: closed for the winter, empty and covered in snow. The day, time and venue had been in a typewritten sealed note on Ministry for State Security official paper, delivered to her in person at Marx-Engels-Platz by a motorcycle messenger. That was strange enough in itself, but disturbingly Jäger had also asked her to make sure she wasn't followed. On the S-bahn, she'd thought for a moment that a man in builders' overalls had been doing just that. He'd got on at Marx-Engels-Platz, in the same carriage, and although she'd tried not to look at him, she got the impression that he was occasionally checking on her. But Müller was the only passenger to alight at Plänterwald, and she chided herself for her paranoia.

She hitched up her coat sleeve and glanced at her watch. Five past ten: he was five minutes late already. She pulled the sleeve back, dug her hands deep into her coat pockets and then turned, scanning the approaches to the park. No one – not a soul. Not even the sound of birdsong to disturb the near silence.

Then a clang of metal, from where she hadn't expected, the entrance to the park itself, and there was Jäger, in casual clothes but carrying a briefcase, accompanied by a man she didn't recognise, wearing the uniform of the VEB – the state-owned enterprise that ran the park.

'Sorry I'm a little late, *Oberleutnant*. The caretaker, Comrade Köhler here, isn't used to visitors at this time of year, and I had to go and track him down. He's going to take us somewhere private for our meeting.' Müller gave a small nod, as the caretaker gestured to her and Jäger to follow him through the turnstiles.

As they entered the park, Jäger's eyes met hers. 'You look frozen stiff, Comrade *Oberleutnant*.' He patted the front of his sheepskin jacket. 'This is what you need for weather like this.' Then he pinched the sleeve of Müller's grey-green overcoat, rubbing it between his finger and thumb. 'Not a People's Police overcoat.'

Müller laughed. 'I wish I could afford one, Comrade *Oberstleutnant*. I expect the salary of police first lieutenant is slightly lower that that of a Ministry for State Security lieutenant colonel.'

Jäger smiled a knowing smile. Not everything was equal in this socialist state of workers and peasants, thought Müller, but it was still a fairer world than on the other side of the anti-fascist barrier. She could tell that from Gottfried's infernal western news programmes and their never-ending reports of strikes and workers' disaffection.

The snow here, on the outskirts of the Hauptstadt, hadn't melted into a muddy morass of sludge like that next to the Eisenbergs' apartment block in Friedrichshain. With colder temperatures overnight, their footsteps crunched along the path, making enough noise almost for a whole column of People's Army soldiers, even though there were just the three of them.

As they turned a corner, Jäger pointed to the swan boats lined up on the banks of the lake, out of action for the winter. 'Have you been here at the height of the season, *Oberleutnant* Müller? My children love it.'

'I don't have children, *Oberstleutnant*. And no, I haven't.' The admission was accompanied by a sharp stab of regret, and then the sudden memory of the murdered girl, lying dead in St Elisabeth's cemetery. That girl wouldn't be coming to sample the rides of the Kulturpark anytime soon either.

They lapsed into silence for the rest of their walk behind the caretaker, Jäger appearing embarrassed by the exchange. Müller saw they were heading towards the park's iconic Ferris wheel. When they reached it, the caretaker took a set of keys from his pocket and opened the control room.

'We're going to get a free ride,' said Jäger. 'I hope you've a good head for heights.' Müller nodded. She wasn't going to admit that she hadn't. 'Not to mention a sterner stomach than the other day at the cemetery.' Although his teasing was gentle, Müller felt her cheeks flush at the reminder.

The electric motor hummed into action as Köhler started up the mechanism, the groaning grind of un-oiled metal slowly replacing the sound of the wind rustling through the trees. Müller counted six cabins go past, before Jäger held up his hand for Köhler to bring the ride to a stop. The cabin selected by Jäger swung gently on its hinges as he opened the safety bar and stood to one side to let her in. They sat down opposite one another; Müller felt her stomach lurch as Köhler released the brake. As the giant wheel slowly began to turn, Müller watched the Stasi officer run his fingers along each edge of the cabin, then peer under each bench seat.

Jäger raised his head to look straight into her eyes. 'This is my usual meeting spot for quiet talks,' he explained, 'and so our agents have checked it over already. But you can never be too careful, and what we have to discuss is quite ... sensitive, shall we say.'

Müller nodded, hunching down into her coat as the cabin climbed and the temperature dropped. She risked a glance out at the city, and instantly felt queasy. She shouldn't. She was a mountain girl. Well, if the hills of the Thuringian Forest could really be called mountains. The mountain girl who'd never had a head for heights. Who'd been a promising winter sports athlete at school, until...

She stopped the thought. Tried to pull herself together, and focus on Jäger, who seemed oblivious to her fear.

'The full autopsy report has some interesting findings, things I didn't want to discuss in front of Tilsner and Schmidt – at least not until I've gone over them with you.' He drew out a folder from his briefcase, and then rose to join Müller on her bench. The cabin rocked with the sudden movement, and Müller kept her eyes to the floor to avoid reminding herself how high they were. She knew that under her gloves her knuckles would be turning white as she gripped the end of the wooden seat ever tighter. They seemed to have reached the apex of the wheel now. Its forward motion had stopped, and the cabin settled into a gentle swing from the wind and the residual energy of Jäger's decision to play musical chairs several hundred feet above ground. Was he deliberately trying to unnerve her?

Jäger had clearly noticed her look of terror. 'Are you alright, Comrade *Oberleutnant*? Perhaps this location wasn't such a good idea. I must admit, I usually come here in the summer months. I didn't realise it would be so windy.'

Müller breathed in deeply. 'I'll be fine,' she lied, her stomach feeling as though it was about to drop out of the bottom of her body.

The Stasi lieutenant colonel nodded, and opened the folder. 'The pathologist, Professor Feuerstein, has come to some startling and slightly awkward conclusions.' He turned a couple of pages. Müller found herself once more wanting to avert her eyes from the photograph of the girl's mutilated face, but that was the page Jäger had settled on. 'You see the smooth, almost shiny, melted appearance of the skin here, right at the side of where much of the face has been torn away?' Müller squinted at the photo, and to the section Jäger was tracing with his finger. 'It's the result of coming into contact with a strong acid. In this case sulphuric acid, from a car battery.'

Müller frowned. 'She'd been in some sort of accident, then? Or are you saying this was done deliberately?'

'Feuerstein doesn't comment on that. To be honest, he doesn't have to. He believes the skin came into contact with the acid post mortem.'

'So, deliberate? To hide her identity after she'd been killed?'

'Almost certainly, I would think.' Jäger nodded.

'And what about the injuries to the rest of her face? Were they caused by a dog, as you were saying at the cemetery?'

Jäger shook his head, and gave a slow sigh. 'No. You can probably guess. Her face was deliberately ripped apart, after acid was thrown onto it. And her teeth were pulled out, one by one, with iron pliers.' Müller gave a small gasp and raised her hand to her mouth. 'Feuerstein found rust residue on her gums.'

'That poor girl. So whoever it was tortured her first?'

Jäger again moved his head slowly from side to side. 'No. The teeth were again pulled out post mortem.'

'Someone has gone to great lengths to prevent identification of the body.'

'Exactly,' said Jäger. 'And that is going to make your job exceedingly difficult. Because that is exactly what you, Tilsner and Schmidt need to do. Find out who this girl was. That's what I want you concentrate on. And we need to be careful not to publicly challenge the official version of how she met her demise.'

'But clearly, Comrade *Oberstleutnant*, you cannot still believe that she was shot by western guards as she was trying to escape to the East?'

Jäger said nothing for a moment, so that all that filled the silence was the screeching of the cabin, as it gently swayed backwards and forwards. Like the screams of a girl, thought Müller.

'That is still the official account of her death,' Jäger said finally, a flat note in his voice. He reached into his inside pocket and drew out an envelope, 'This authority for your missing person's search may help you.' He pulled out the sheet of paper and showed it to Müller.

She frowned. 'I don't need the approval of the Ministry for State Security for a missing person's search.' And why, if Jäger didn't want them to be tracking down the girl's killer or killers, was he so keen that the body should be identified at all? Surely the Stasi would be better off drawing a line under everything?

'That's true,' admitted Jäger. 'But look at the signature.' Müller saw it had been signed by Erich Mielke, just as the authorisation had been at the autopsy. 'It may prove useful to have this in certain circumstances, *Oberleutnant* Müller. It will also serve as a reminder ... about the limits of your permitted inquiry.'

'And those limits are?'

'To concern yourselves with the missing person, the girl. Rather than the perpetrators. Though I dare say –'

'What, *Oberstleutnant*?' prompted Müller.

Again the Stasi lieutenant colonel paused, as though for effect. 'I dare say that in searching for the girl, the evidence you uncover may be useful to me. Should we at any stage wish to challenge the official account.' He turned and stared directly into her eyes. 'But that will be for me – and me alone – to decide.'

Müller found herself shivering, as much from the implied threats as from the cold. Now she had become used to the rocking motion of the cabin, she risked a longer view of the Berlin skyline, stretching for kilometre after kilometre but dominated by the television tower in Alexanderplatz, looking from this distance a little like a hypodermic needle. The *Fernsehturm*: symbol of the Republic's progress. Yes, it was a small country but it was focused on the future, making its mark, not inward-looking and money-obsessed, or reliant on manufacturing cuckoo clocks for tourists like some western states.

She turned back towards Jäger, who was still leafing through the autopsy report, and risked another question. 'But presumably my team is at liberty to pursue any and every lead that might help us to identify the girl?'

Jäger slapped the autopsy report on his lap, and glowered at her.

'I don't want to have to repeat myself, Karin. There's a good reason why I, as a senior officer in the Ministry for State Security, have been assigned this case.'

'Can you tell me what that reason is?'

There was a flash of anger in his expression, which he quickly attempted to hide.

'No. Not at present. It's enough for you to know that it's a sensitive inquiry, and for you and your team to respect the limits that I've outlined.'

Müller turned away again, and fixed her gaze on the dizzying vista of Berlin, far below. She swallowed.

'Did you want to hear what Tilsner and I have discovered so far?'

Jäger raised his head, and then shrugged. 'Is it the fact that the vehicle tracks in the graveyard were from Swedish tyres, or that her supposed footprints were so badly faked that whoever did it couldn't tell his left from his right?'

Müller felt her face burn from a mixture of embarrassment and anger. Was he toying with them? 'It appears that you're already aware of all the discrepancies, Comrade *Oberstleutnant*. Are you sure you need the help of the People's Police? Tilsner wants us to request to be taken off the case.'

The Stasi officer held his hands up. 'Sorry. That was unfair of me. You are vital to this inquiry. I chose you personally. I need a competent *Kriminalpolizei* team to gather and record evidence, and do that independently of the Ministry for State Security. So please, do not think your efforts will be in vain.'

Müller snorted dismissively.

'I can understand your reaction,' said Jäger, closing the file. He returned it to the briefcase, and then stood and waved at Köhler to restart the motor for the downward journey. Müller tightened her grip on the bench again as the cabin pitched forwards. 'But I'll tell you something that I hope will make you want to continue to help me. Feuerstein says in his report that the girl was sexually active. But also that – from evidence of bruising around the genital and anal region – she had been raped and abused before she was strangled to death.'

Müller slowly exhaled. As Jäger paused, the memories flooded her brain. Memories from her time at the police university that she had tried again and again to forget.

Jäger suddenly reached out with his arm to touch her knee, sensing something was wrong. She felt herself curl away. 'Are you alright, Comrade Müller? Your face is rather pale.'

'Is it?' she asked, aware of the slightly vacant note in her voice. 'It's probably just the motion of the Ferris wheel.' She forced a laugh. 'Perhaps I don't have a head for heights after all.' The small lie had been found out.

The cabin was almost back at ground level, and she could see Köhler's silhouette in the control hut. Jäger cleared his throat. 'There is one more thing I must tell you; just so you're aware of the kind of person we're dealing with. The nature of the bruises indicate that the final rape was committed at approximately the same time as the bullet wounds were faked in her back, and her face and mouth were mutilated.'

'At the same time?' asked Müller, incredulously.

Jäger slowly nodded. 'Approximately. What is certain, says Professor Feuerstein, is that the last rape was committed post mortem.'

Müller closed her eyes and let her lungs fill slowly. Now she knew why she wouldn't be supporting Tilsner's attempts to get them moved off the case. Now she knew why she was prepared to search in every corner of the Republic to find the identity of the girl ... and – despite Jäger's warning – the identity of her killer.

10

Nine months earlier (May 1974).
Jugendwerkhof Prora Ost, Rügen, East Germany.

I wake with a start, banging my head against the roof, coughing and choking. My second nightmare in as many days fades, and I realise I'm still in the *Jugendwerkhof*, in the isolation cell nicknamed the bunker. My punishment just for trying to comfort my friend. I don't regret it, don't regret trying to speak up in front of Neumann and Richter, even though my arse still stings from where he beat me, the bastard.

The bunker is somewhere all of us usually try to avoid – one of their weapons for keeping us in line. No heating, so it's bitterly cold. No light, so it's in semi-darkness. And not enough space to stand. I'd been dreaming about Mutti, Oma and I having a lovely *Grillfest* on the beach in front of Oma's little white campsite house. Then Mutti and Oma's faces had transformed into the hated ones of Richter and Neumann. Now, straightaway, I realise that one thing from the dream is real: the smell of burning. Smoke is coming through the narrow slit – a lousy excuse for a window. I pull off my jumper, banging my wrist on the bunker's roof in my haste, and stuff the woollen material into the gap in an attempt to keep out the fumes. I know what's happened. There is a pile of kindling next to the cell. Some of the girls like to throw lit cigarette butts from the window onto the wood, saying they want to try to set fire to it and suffocate any occupant of the bunker. I'd always assumed it was just a joke. I'd never realised how terrifying it would be to be the girl trapped inside.

'Help me! Please!' I cry. My heart thumps in my chest. Despite the cold in the bunker, I feel sweat pooling under my armpits.

I am lucky, though. Someone does hear my cries. Footsteps. Running. Then a splash and hissing, as someone throws a bucket of water on top of the kindling before the fire can take hold.

'Are you OK, Irma?' says the voice, which I immediately recognise as a friendly one: Herr Müller, the maths teacher who arrived earlier this year from Berlin. 'I'm sorry for that. It will be OK now. It's out. And I'll have words with Director Neumann and Frau Richter to ensure those responsible are disciplined.'

I stifle a snort.

'You don't believe me?' he asks.

'I believe you will say something, sir. But they won't act on it. They're probably pleased. It's part of the punishment.'

'That can't be right, Irma. Anyway, what are you doing here?'

'What is anyone doing here? In the eyes of the authorities we've all done something wrong.'

I see Herr Müller's hand now, pushing my woollen jumper aside. He's holding an apple. I grab it eagerly. 'Thank you,' I say, and almost feel like crying at his small gesture of kindness.

'I meant why are you *here*?' he asks again, lowering his voice in case others are eavesdropping. 'In the bunker?'

'I was caught in bed with Beate in the dorm. Every night she's crying, but she won't tell me what's wrong. I was just comforting her.'

'I understand,' he says. 'You're all here together, but it can still be lonely. And now you're in the bunker, are you alright? It seems a terribly cruel punishment for something so trivial.'

I hold the apple in my right hand, and then rub my wrist with my left where it banged against the bunker roof. 'It's OK,' I lie.

'It's not OK, Irma,' he says, whispering now through the window slit. 'Children shouldn't be locked up like this.'

I realise what he's saying is dangerous for him. If it is a trap, what worse trouble could I get in? Where is worse than the bunker at *Jugendwerkhof* Prora Ost? 'If you think it's so wrong, why are you working here?' I ask him.

'You think I have a choice?'

'No,' I say. 'I don't suppose you do. I don't think anyone truly wants to work here.'

'Maybe Richter.' He laughs softly. 'But no, I certainly do not want to work here, but they have difficulty attracting staff ... I was accused of not giving sufficient weight to political teaching at my school in Berlin. And, as my wife is a leading detective in the *Kriminalpolizei*, the authorities weren't too impressed. So they sent me here. Temporarily, so they say, as long as I keep my nose clean.'

'You shouldn't be whispering to bad girls in the bunker then.'

'No, probably not.' A pause. 'It would be nice to leave though, wouldn't it?'

Is he trying to trap me again? 'Leave? Leave Prora Ost?'

'Not just that,' he says, his voice still lower so I have to strain to hear.

This is dangerous talk. I know better than to respond. Maybe Neumann and Richter are outside too, listening to my every answer, and maybe Müller is on a fishing expedition. Fishing for would-be *Republikflüchtlinge*.

'You know where the furniture from the workshop goes?' he asks.

'No. We're never told. I just assumed it was for government bigwigs. Something like that.'

'It's not. It goes to a new shipping terminus they've built at Sassnitz.'

Most of the girls wouldn't even know where Sassnitz was. But I do. I'm from Rügen, born right here on the island. Sassnitz is a pretty little town, with a lovely fishing harbour. I remember going on boat trips from there as a child. With Mutti. With Oma.

'And do you know where it goes after Sassnitz?' he whispers. Now I'm sure he's trying to trap me. To get me to say something to incriminate myself. And I thought he was one of the few decent teachers. He ignores my silence and continues his whispering. 'It goes to –'

He stops abruptly, mid-sentence. I hear two sets of footsteps. His, moving away from the bunker, and another person's, moving towards his. Then I give an involuntary shiver as I hear Director Neumann's voice.

'Comrade Müller. What are you doing here?'

'I was just taking a short smoking break, Herr Director.'

'Smoking? I didn't think you smoked.'

'I've just taken it up. Stupid habit, really.'

I hear him cough, as though to reinforce his lie. Then I hear Neumann sniffing. 'What's that burning smell?'

'It was my cigarette butt,' Herr Müller replies. 'I accidentally threw it on the kindling pile here – nearly started a fire. But it's out now.'

'Yes, well, we don't want any fires, do we? Please keep far away from this area in future. We have had occasions where teachers here have started talking – or even worse, passing food – to children in the bunker. I wouldn't follow their example if I were you. That is, if you ever want to get back to your regular job in Berlin.'

'No, Herr Director. Thank you for the advice.'

I hear them both walking away, and curse Neumann's interruption. What had Herr Müller been about to tell me? Where did the furniture packs from the workshop go? It was almost as though he was deliberately planting something in my head. I try to shake the thought away, and concentrate on counting off the remaining hours in the bunker. I wipe the apple on the sleeve of my top and bite into it, savouring the explosion of juice.

11

Müller ran her hand repeatedly through her blonde hair. She was waiting for *Oberst* Reiniger in her office, having only just got back from the Kulturpark Ferris wheel. Tilsner sat by her side, twirling a pack of Juwel cigarettes and occasionally tapping it on her desk.

'So what did Jäger say?' he asked.

'I'll fill you in fully later. But basically he wants us – no, he's *instructing* us – to treat the case simply as a missing person's inquiry. He has no interest in us actually finding the killer – or killers.'

'I doubt very much that it's disinterest,' said Tilsner, pulling one of the cigarettes out, then placing it in his mouth without lighting up. 'Just as we've got someone sitting on us, telling us what to do, it's probably just the same for him.' His words came out half-slurred, almost like a ventriloquist's, speaking as he was with his lips clasped round the filter. She studied him for a moment. He seemed nonchalantly confident about the ways of the Stasi.

'So why are we meeting Reiniger?' he continued.

Müller shrugged as she watched Tilsner strike a match, put it to the end of the cigarette and then take a long drag. She could not help but notice his abrupt change of topic – plainly he did not share her dismay. She waved the smoke away. Ever since she'd given up at police college, she hadn't shared his tobacco habit – and hadn't missed it. 'I didn't ask for the meeting, so I've no idea.'

Tilsner exhaled a perfect smoke ring, watched it rise slowly to the ceiling and the S-bahns overhead and then leant back on two legs of the chair. 'Ah. Sorry. That might be my fault. I did get in touch with him this morning with my thoughts. Saying that perhaps he might like to consider taking us off the case. I thought that was what you wanted?'

She narrowed her eyes at him. 'You should have cleared that with me first. Anyway, I've changed my mind.'

'You've changed your mind? Why? I certainly haven't. The whole case is a mess. The last straw for me was when I took Frau Eisenberg to the mortuary this morning and she confirmed what we already knew. That the murdered girl isn't her daughter. We've got nothing to go on, and we're getting nowhere. I want out.'

Müller sighed and shook her head. 'It's not your choice, Werner. And in any case, isn't that what detective work is all about? Actually doing the legwork and finding the evidence, even if it's not staring us in the face? What I'd like to know is who's leaking information to Jäger? He seems to know all about the tyre tracks, and the fact they're Swedish. And about the footprints almost certainly having been faked. Do you think it's Schmidt?'

Tilsner shrugged, and tapped the ash from his cigarette into his now-empty coffee mug, the gesture revealing once more his expensive, western-style watch. 'Who knows? It could be anyone. The *Kripo* is full of unofficial collaborators. My money's on Elke; she makes a bloody awful cup of coffee, and it wouldn't surprise me if she learnt that in Stasi school.'

Müller mouthed a silent 'ha ha' at her deputy's feeble joke, and then stood to attention as *Oberst* Reiniger knocked on the glazed door and entered. Schmidt trailed behind him in his ubiquitous white laboratory coat, chewing the remains of one of his regular snacks. Reiniger ushered them to sit, though Müller noticed that Tilsner had barely made the effort to get up anyway.

Like Schmidt's, the material of Reiniger's uniform stretched and strained around his middle as he sat down and brushed imaginary fluff off each of the three gold stars on his silver epaulettes. As a colonel, he was nominally more senior to Jäger. But they all knew that Jäger – as a leading officer in the Stasi's investigation branch, Department Eight – held the real power.

He linked his fingers across his straining midriff, and then rotated his thumbs around one another. 'So, Karin ... I think you need to fill me in on what we have so far. *Unterleutnant* Tilsner here is of the opinion that you don't have enough leads, and that we should leave it in the hands of *Oberstleutnant* Jäger. Do you agree?'

Müller shook her head, then cleared her throat of Tilsner's cigarette fumes. 'I don't think that's a choice we have, Comrade *Oberst*. I admit we don't have much to go on, but *Kriminaltechniker* Schmidt here has made some significant progress already.'

'But are we any closer to identifying the girl?' asked Reiniger.

'No,' interrupted Tilsner. 'The woman I took to the mortuary –'

Reiniger sighed. 'I was asking *Oberleutnant* Müller, not you.'

Müller glanced at Tilsner's reddening face and had to stop herself from smiling.

'So, Müller?' asked Reiniger again.

'No, but I gleaned some extra information this morning from the autopsy report.' The fact that it had been handed to her by Jäger wasn't anything the other three needed to know. 'The girl was sexually active.'

Tilsner snorted. 'Not that unusual for a teenage girl.'

'Go on, Comrade *Oberleutnant*,' prompted Reiniger.

'Well, not only was she sexually active, but she'd been raped. And not only had she been raped, but she'd been raped post mortem.'

'*Scheisse!*' exclaimed Tilsner, stubbing his cigarette out angrily in the bottom of the coffee cup, almost as though he wanted to twist it into the face of the killer. It hissed in the dregs. Across the table, Müller saw Schmidt's face grow suddenly pallid, much as it had that first evening in the cemetery.

'*After* she'd been killed?' asked Reiniger, as though in disbelief.

Müller nodded.

Tilsner leant his head on his hands, elbows resting on the desk. 'So you're saying we're dealing with a necrophiliac?'

Müller shrugged. 'Possibly … Or perhaps a murderer who simply spotted an opportunity. A pretty sick murderer …'

'So is there any way uniform can help you, Karin? You're a small team and … well, you're fairly new to the job.' He didn't add '*and you're a woman, and a young one at that*'. But she'd heard enough similar comments since her promotion to know that was what he was thinking. She felt herself bristle at the implied put-down. But perhaps he *was* just trying to be helpful, in his slightly clumsy, patronising way. Perhaps he could tell how much this was all affecting her. He almost certainly didn't know the full reason why.

'I think we need a rigorous check on known and suspected sex offenders, starting in Berlin. But perhaps taking in neighbouring districts too. Maybe even in the whole Republic, if there's anyone we know of that –' She paused. What sort of person was a necrophiliac? A pervert? A madman? 'If there's anyone of that persuasion.'

Reiniger gave a slow nod. 'I can certainly get officers onto that. We don't have to connect it to this case, if you're worried about Jäger thinking we're going beyond the missing person brief. It can simply be an operation to check on the movements of sex offenders. No one's going to object to that. What else have we got?'

'There's the felt-tip pen ink. Jonas, you were going to get in touch with the pathologist and examine that, weren't you?' Müller eyeballed Schmidt.

'Yes, I haven't quite had a chance to do that yet. But there are these …' Müller watched him start to reach into his briefcase, and while Reiniger's eyes were trained on what the forensic officer was about to pull from his bag, Müller shook her head at Schmidt and mouthed a 'no' across the table. She knew he was going to start talking about the tyre marks, and didn't want him to. Not in front of the colonel. Schmidt caught her look. 'Well actually, that's not quite ready yet either,' he said, replacing the folders. 'If that's the priority, I'll get onto the felt-tip pen ink straightaway.' He made to stand, but Müller motioned him to sit down again.

'So what exactly is the relevance of this ink?' asked Reiniger, his frown betraying his bemusement at Schmidt's apparent change of heart.

'Her fingernails had been inked in,' explained Müller. 'I think it was an amateur's attempts to make it look like black nail polish.'

'*Black* nail polish?' asked Reiniger. 'That's unusual.'

Tilsner snorted. 'Kids these days. They get up to all sorts.'

Müller ignored her deputy, and instead answered the colonel. 'I agree it's unusual, but not unheard of. It's the sort of thing I used to do as a child on *Walpurgisnacht*.'

'But *Walpurgisnacht* is still several weeks away,' said Reiniger. 'Surely it can't have been anything do with that?'

Müller shrugged. 'I agree, it seems unlikely. Nevertheless, the ink is a lead. Your officers may be able to help us with that, Comrade *Oberst*. I was wondering if you could detail people to find out which state-owned enterprises make felt-tip pens in the Republic, or whether any are imported. There must surely be only a few manufacturers.'

Tilsner huffed. 'Yes, but millions of pens. Thousands of shops. I can't see how that's going to get us very far.'

The colonel gave Müller's deputy another withering look, and then started to rise from his seat. 'We can try to help with that, *Oberleutnant*. And if there is anything else, be sure to call.'

'I will certainly do that, Comrade *Oberst*. Your help is appreciated.'

'He's a stuffy old fart, isn't he?' said Tilsner, once the colonel was safely out of earshot.

Müller smiled. 'Maybe. But he's offering to help, so why look a gift horse in the mouth? We can get Elke to liaise with the People's Police uniform officers on both the sex offenders search and the felt-tip pen manufacturers.'

'So what will we be doing?' asked Tilsner.

Müller raised her eyes towards Schmidt. 'Jonas? You wanted to show us something. Sorry about earlier, but if – as I expect – it's about the tyre marks, I'm not sure I want to share that with the colonel at this stage. It's bad enough that Jäger seems to know.' She searched Schmidt's face for any sign of embarrassment, any giveaway that he might have been the source of Jäger's information.

Schmidt moved all the coffee cups to one side, and then reached into his briefcase and littered the table with a series of photographs and photocopies of tyre tracks and patterns. 'I've made negative prints of the tracks from the scene of the crime. That way the pattern shows up more easily.' He pointed at two of the negatives. 'These are the two key photographs. Notice anything?'

Müller studied all the sheets. And then pointed to three of them: the two negatives and one of the photocopies of tyre patterns. 'These three,' she said, smiling. 'They match. In fact, they're an exact match.'

'Precisely, Comrade Müller. Precisely. This,' he held up the matching photocopy of a tyre pattern, 'is a pattern from a Swedish tyre made by the Gislaved tyre company. The firm's named after the town where the company was formed, approximately equidistant from Gothenburg and Jönköping.'

'Swedish tyres. That confirms your theory from the scene,' said Müller, reaching for the cup the forensic officer had moved to one side. She took a sip and then spat it back into the cup. It was stone cold.

Schmidt nodded. Tilsner, too, looked impressed with Schmidt's work.

'And not just that. Gislaved is the main supplier for Volvo cars.'

Tilsner slapped Schmidt's back, making him splutter. 'Well done, Jonas. So that's that sorted – we know that Volvo supplies cars to party bigwigs and the Stasi.'

Schmidt screwed up his face. 'It's not as simple as that, unfortunately.'

'Why not, Jonas?' asked Müller.

'Well, although the Republic uses Volvos for official functions, the stretch limousines – well, they're customised, adapted Volvos. Volvo don't actually manufacture a long-wheelbase limousine themselves.'

'Why's that a problem?' asked Müller, frowning.

'It's like camper vans,' said Schmidt. 'A lot of vans in the Federal Republic are based on a Volkswagen van body, but not all of them are sold by Volkswagen. They have their coachwork built by another specialist firm. It's the same with the Barkas vans over here, and it will be the same with the Volvo limousines. There's no guarantee that the tyres they leave the Volvo factory with will still be on them after the bodywork has been completed.'

'So who adapts them?' asked Tilsner.

Schmidt spread his arms out on the table, palms upwards, in a gesture of apology. 'I haven't managed to find that out. And I've tried blowing up the various photos of official state parades, but I can't get a clear enough image of the tyre pattern on the vehicles to be of any use.'

Müller frowned. 'So what can we do, Jonas?'

'Well, what I have discovered is that there's a central garage where all the official cars are serviced, and stored when they're not in use. It's in Lichtenberg. Near Normannenstrasse –'

'– near Stasi headquarters,' said Tilsner. 'How are we going to get in there? Shouldn't we discuss it with Jäger? He might be able to get us the information we want, without us having to do anything underhand.'

Müller vigorously shook her head. 'No. I don't want to involve Jäger this time.'

Tilsner shrugged. 'OK. But I don't see how we're going to talk our way into this garage without his help. It will be closely guarded, won't it?'

'Yes.' Schmidt nodded. 'But overnight there are fewer guards – in the early hours, sometimes just the one.'

One guard. If Schmidt was right, thought Müller, perhaps some sort of diversion might be a way of getting into the compound, and surreptitiously taking photos of the car tyres. She remembered the document signed by Mielke, which she still had in her inside pocket. That might help, but it wouldn't be of any use on its own. The guard would be sure to insist on phoning his superiors to check its authenticity.

'Isn't the whole of the area around Stasi headquarters a restricted zone?' asked Tilsner.

'Yes,' said Müller. She turned to the street map of the Hauptstadt, pinned to the office wall. 'Where exactly is it, Jonas?'

Schmidt stood and pointed to an area just east of Normannenstrasse.

'So that's just outside the restricted zone,' said Müller. She rubbed her chin. What Schmidt seemed to be suggesting was horribly risky. If any of them were caught it would be the end of their police careers – at the very least.

12

Later the same day.

Over the next few hours, Müller, Tilsner and Schmidt had discussed their possible options, with Müller eventually concluding that any scheme to try to trick their way into the limousine compound was far too risky. They were all party members, they were all working for the state. Müller wasn't prepared to put all three of their careers, their futures, in jeopardy. Nevertheless, she was determined to get the information they wanted without making the direct approach to Jäger favoured by Tilsner. Although she didn't voice her fears aloud to the others, Müller at the back of her mind had the suspicion that this whole case might be some sort of elaborate set-up by the Stasi lieutenant colonel. Any attempt to cross-check whether a government limousine was involved in their case had to be made in absolute secrecy.

A plan began to formulate in Müller's mind when she started asking Schmidt if there was a way, other than directly taking photos of the tyres themselves, that they could verify their design, and therefore pin down their make and rule them in – or out.

'Well, we discovered the vehicle in the cemetery was on Gis-laved tyres through the imprints in the snow,' Schmidt replied.

Müller stared up at the pictures of the tyre prints, pinned to the noticeboard in the Marx-Engels-Platz office, thinking hard.

'The trouble now,' said Tilsner, 'is that a lot of the snow's melted. Certainly the roads are all clear in the Hauptstadt. So that's not going to be much good.'

Müller continued to fix her gaze on the tyre pattern photos, an idea forming in the back of her mind. Then she turned.

'We don't need snow,' she said. 'What we need is sand.'

Once Müller had outlined her idea, Schmidt and Tilsner had worked to set it up. Schmidt quickly established a fortuitous con-nection. Although the limousines were stored in a compound near the Stasi HQ at Normannenstrasse, they were serviced and cleaned in an industrial zone just off Siegfriedstrasse – still in Lichtenberg, but further east, and outside the Stasi-controlled zone. On the same business estate, there was a depot of the VEB Autobahnkombinat – the state-controlled motorway construc-tion company – currently involved in building an autobahn from the Hauptstadt to Rostock, on the Ostsee coast. Trucks loaded with building materials regularly moved between the depot and construction site. And the freshly serviced and washed limou-sines for state officials also regularly travelled between the depot and the Normannenstrasse compound. Usually in the evening, or at night, to avoid the traffic and prying eyes.

The next piece of the plan was implemented in a phone call received at Marx-Engels-Platz by Elke, the student detective.

Enthusiasm bursting through every pore, she rushed through to Müller's side office to tell her the news.

'Comrade *Oberleutnant*,' the girl gushed. 'I've just received an anonymous tip-off you may need to know about.'

Müller pretended to finish working on some documents on her desk, then looked up at the trainee, trying to appear bored and disinterested.

'What about, Elke?'

The girl brandished a piece of paper full of notes towards Müller. 'It's an allegation that some members of the VEB Auto-bahnkombinat are involved in a black market operation. Smuggling western contraband hidden in their construction trucks, under loads of sand or gravel, to villages and towns north of the Hauptstadt – along the route of the planned autobahn to Rostock.'

'Was the caller a man or a woman?' asked Müller, trying not to break into a smile as she examined Elke's handwritten account. She knew full well who the caller was. 'Did he or she have any sort of accent, anything which might help identification?'

'Well, it was a man. He had a very rough, muffled voice. But quite a strong accent. Low German. Northern.'

Müller pictured Tilsner putting on his best regional accent, speaking with his hand over his mouth or through a handker-chief to disguise his usual tones. He'd insisted Elke wouldn't rec-ognise him. He was right.

'Thank you, Elke. This would normally be a matter for the uniform division, but it sounds interesting. If you're not doing anything else, why don't you contact the operator and see if you can trace where the call was made from?'

'I've already done that, *Oberleutnant*,' said Elke, the pride clear in her voice. 'I thought it would be from somewhere up north. But it wasn't. It was from a call box here in the Hauptstadt. In Mitte. Near Alexanderplatz.'

Probably from outside one of Tilsner's favourite bars, thought Müller. But Elke didn't appear to suspect anything.

'That's good work, Elke.' Müller picked up the girl's handwritten notes and put them in her pocket. 'I'll pass these onto the uniform division. I think we're a little too busy with the murder investigation to look into it ourselves. But well done.'

The only remaining thing to do was to use the anonymous call, and Elke's account of it, to persuade Reiniger to authorise a spot check – and if necessary the temporary confiscation – of one of the construction trucks. Schmidt would try to discover which one was likely to be transporting suitable sand.

Standing nervously in front of his office desk, Müller could see the suspicion in Reiniger's expression. But he nevertheless agreed to sign the necessary form of authority.

'I hope you're not bending the rules here, Karin.' Then he lowered his voice. 'And if you are, make sure you don't get caught. I don't want any of your shit left at my door. Understand?'

Finding a suitable truck proved easier than Müller expected – Schmidt seemed to have strange contacts everywhere. She and Tilsner had tracked it along Siegfriedstrasse, and then – with the Wartburg's siren blaring and blue light flashing – pulled it over in Herzbergstrasse. The driver and his mate protested their innocence, but once Müller made it clear that they would be arrested if they defied Reiniger's signed order, they calmed down. Müller insisted she and Tilsner would explain the situation to the motorway construction company, but that they would have to confiscate the vehicle to check its contents thoroughly, grain by grain.

They were in the truck now, driving slowly back towards Lichtenberg for the second time in the space of a few hours: their first visit had taken place the previous afternoon, to check that the slightly hare-brained scheme at least had a chance of success. The next significant movement of limousines from the service depot on the industrial estate to the storage compound was due in a few hours' time – and would be under cover of darkness. Müller and Tilsner were heading there now in the tipper truck, with Schmidt following behind in the unmarked *Kripo* Wartburg. Both vehicles with just their sidelights on to try to make sure they didn't draw attention to themselves down the wide boulevards of the eastern part of the Hauptstadt. Müller glanced to her left in the lorry's cab, where Tilsner had his hands gripped to the IFA W50 tipper's steering wheel, shirtsleeves rolled up despite the winter weather. He seemed all too at ease in what ought to have been an unfamiliar role. There was a lot to her handsome but mysterious deputy that she still hadn't fathomed.

The wide avenues they were driving down were the scene of the parades that had played in her head at the cemetery. She recalled the most recent: celebrating the Republic's twenty-fifth anniversary, the previous October. Müller had stood at the edge of the crowd, filled with a sense of pride about what her small country had achieved, watching the massed ranks of People's

Army soldiers on their synchronised march, followed by party and government leaders – in Volvo limousines. Now, that pride was replaced by a sense of foreboding. Karl-Marx-Allee, and its monolithic wedding-cake-style buildings, held a much more sinister air in the semi-darkness of weak street lighting. Were they doing the right thing? It felt slightly treacherous. But then she remembered the mangled face of the girl, and what had happened to her in the hours immediately before and after death. If anyone from the government or party was involved in *that*, well, they deserved to be brought to justice and shamed.

Schmidt had provided them with their disguises – the hard hats and overalls of construction workers – together with diversion barriers and lanterns from the People's Police's supply depot, which they'd thrown on the back of the tipper truck. They needed to work quickly, closing off a section of Siegfriedstrasse between two junctions and putting up the diversion signs. Schmidt had established that a convoy of limousines would move between the two bases tonight, and had even pinned down an exact time. Müller didn't ask him how he'd obtained the information. She wasn't sure she wanted to know.

Traffic was thin at this time of night, and the drivers of the few vehicles that did reach their makeshift roadblock simply followed the signs for the alternative route. Closed-off roads were a daily occurrence in the Hauptstadt, so they didn't arouse suspicion.

Tilsner manoeuvred the tipper truck to one side of the road, crunching through the gears, making Müller want to hold her hands over her ears. He didn't seem such a confident driver now.

Once in position, all was silent, other than a beeping sound from inside the truck's cabin.

'*Scheisse!*' he exclaimed from the open driver's window. 'I can't get the back to tip up.'

Müller climbed up to the cab to try to help.

'It should be this lever,' said Tilsner, forcing it forwards, the strain etched on his face. 'But it's not working. Any bright ideas?'

Müller leant over to the driver's side and glanced around the cabin controls. She could smell Tilsner's all-male scent, his masculinity somehow accentuated by the workman's overalls. His square-jawed face thrown into sharp relief by the weak street lighting. His breathing laboured from the effort of trying to force the controls to do what he wanted.

'I've no idea,' she said. 'Not really my strong point.' She moved across to the passenger window, unwound it and leant out. 'Jonas! Come up here a moment.'

She helped pull the weighty forensic officer into the cab, his face flushed with the effort of climbing up. Tilsner demonstrated the problem.

Schmidt immediately laughed. 'You won't get anywhere that way. Here.' He pushed a red lever – one that neither Müller nor Tilsner had noticed – to one side. 'You have to release the safety catch first, like that. Now try again.'

This time – amid the scrapes and scratching of poorly oiled metal rubbing against metal – they could see the back start to lift.

'Drive forward at the same time,' said Schmidt, squeezed onto the front passenger bench next to Müller. 'That way you'll spread out the load better and there'll be less spadework for us to get everything ready.'

The roar of the diesel engine competed with the whoosh of the sand as it slid off the back of the tipper and onto the road below. There was a sudden fresh smell of aggregate dust combined with sweet diesel fumes: it reminded Müller of the Ostsee holidays of her childhood, and later when courting Gottfried. Beaches, harbours, pleasure boats. When the world had seemed a much more straightforward place.

With the load of sand emptied, Tilsner brought the rear of the tipper truck to the horizontal, then manoeuvred the vehicle – with more gear-crunching – back to the opposite side of the road. Now one side of this section of Siegfriedstrasse was blocked by the truck – the other by a partly flattened pile of sand. The three police officers worked with the shovels and brushes they'd brought with them to fully level off the sand pile.

Müller glanced at her watch. *Scheisse!* Only five minutes before the convoy was due. If the cars came early, or if they didn't finish in time, there could be trouble.

'Hurry it up. Both of you,' she shouted. 'We've only a couple of minutes left.'

Tilsner pulled Schmidt's shovel out of his hands. 'You're doing more harm than good. Anyway, you need to get into position.'

The forensic officer ran up the road towards the entrance to the industrial estate, stopping every fifty metres or so to get his breath back. Once in position, he waited for the convoy of limousines to emerge as Müller and Tilsner frantically finished smoothing out the layer of sand.

Müller looked at her watch again. The limousines should be here now, but still no sign. She kept her eyes trained on Schmidt further up the road, but as the minutes ticked by, he still hadn't given her the agreed hand signal.

Another ten minutes passed. At last she saw the *Kriminaltechniker* raise his arm. The cars were underway.

She quickly removed the barriers from their section of the road, placing them instead across the side streets that until now had been the diversion route. The only way for the limousine convoy to proceed now was over the layer of sand.

As the long-wheelbase cars approached, Tilsner and Müller began to shovel sand from the side of the layer back into the rear of the truck, to give the impression they were clearing up a spillage.

The first driver stopped as he passed, unwinding his window and shouting at Müller as she held a hand up to her eyes to protect them from the headlights of the following vehicles.

'What the fuck's happened here?' he shouted. 'We've just cleaned these cars. We don't want sand all over them.'

Müller shrugged in apology. 'I'm sorry. Our load tipped off accidentally. We're working as fast as we can to clear up.'

She could see the man roll his eyes, his face highlighted by the beam of the car behind. She knew what he was thinking. *Women working as construction workers.* Like many East German men, he probably thought that they should be at home doing the housework. But that wasn't the way it happened. The female workers and peasants of this little country played a full role. The driver and his ilk would eventually learn to accept that. Müller began to shovel again, directing her anger into scraping the aggregate from the road surface as the car moved off.

Tilsner, following their pre-arranged plan, moved slightly further into the sand-covered side of the road with his shovel as the second limousine was about to drive through. It earned a beep from the car's horn, but achieved what Müller had planned. The car had to swing further round, making new tyre prints rather than following the same tracks as the first limousine.

They repeated the same trick for the third and final car of the short convoy. This time the driver not only blared his horn, but shouted in anger at Tilsner. 'Get out of the way, idiot. You'll get run over.' But the policeman held his ground, and the scheme had succeeded again. The limousine driver had to mount the kerb on the far side, but the driver's side tyres made a third distinct set of tracks.

After the three limousines had disappeared around the corner towards Normannenstrasse, Müller and Tilsner put the diversion signs back in place, and Schmidt arrived at a half-run, panting.

'Sorry, only three cars, Comrade *Oberleutnant*,' he said apologetically. 'Maybe they only service and clean the limousines that have actually been used in the previous week.'

'Don't worry. It's better than nothing, Jonas. Well done for getting the information. Take your photographs of the tyre imprints, and then let's get out of here before anyone realises what's going on.'

13

Nine months earlier (May 1974).
Jugendwerkhof Prora Ost, Rügen, East Germany.

My three days of isolation are over. Last night I was back in the dorm, and thankfully, despite their threats, Neumann and Richter haven't separated me from Beate. Last night she slept well for once.

I've survived the bunker. I try to remember that saying from school: 'that which doesn't kill you makes you stronger'. I think that's what it was. I feel stronger for having got through it, even though my task in the workshop today is considered physically the most demanding. It's packing. Packing and carrying. But although it's the most tiring – because of the heavy lifting when the boxes are ready – I still prefer it to the drilling and cutting workshop, which is just so boring, and it's easier to make a mistake and get into trouble. Here, the precision-cut strips of wood and chipboard have to be carefully placed into the cardboard boxes interleaved with protective paper, and then sealed and wheeled out of the factory to the yard and loaded onto pallets.

But going where? That's what intrigues me now. Herr Müller had been about to tell me, I was sure of that.

'Get a move on, Irma. Stop daydreaming. You don't want to be sent back to the bunker now, do you?' The admonishment comes from Frau Schettler, who supervises the packing room after her breakfast shift. But she's smiling as she delivers it, so in return I knuckle down and speed up. Kitchen cabinet door, left side, right side, cabinet back, shelves, top, bottom. And don't forget the corrugated paper between each layer, or the plastic bag of fixings. Then tape up the box and load the forks of the trolley. It's repetitive, dull, but you can't go wrong, really. Another self-assembly kitchen unit safely despatched. Frau Schettler is generally kind, and she has a soft spot for me, treats me a bit like a naughty daughter. I look up at her, grin, and she smiles back in return.

One reason I feel happier today is I actually got the full breakfast this morning. The whole works. Fresh bread roll, sausage and cheese. Richter was right about that. Working on a full stomach *is* better.

I notice Schettler going into the office to check something. I look to my left and right – Mathias Gelman one side of me, Bauer on the other. Both seem to be concentrating on fulfilling their packing quotas. I take the chance to glance at the small pocket book Herr Müller gave to me at breakfast time. 'It's to help you with your studies, Irma,' he'd said. I pull it out of the front of my knickers – no one would look there, I hope. *A History of Rügen*. A strange book to give me. I flick through the pages, not really understanding why a maths teacher would give me a local history book. Then I spot Schettler returning with some papers, and quickly hide the book away.

'What was that?' a male voice asks.

I turn my head and realise Mathias has seen it. Heartthrob Mathias. Every girl's dream. That's the other advantage of the packing room. You get to meet boys. The only chance in Prora Ost – other than at mealtimes. That's why Beate likes it too. She will be so jealous I'm here next to Mathias – I've seen the way they look at each other. I think she's sweet on him. Maybe he's turned her down? Maybe that's why she's crying all the time? Perhaps I have a chance with him.

'It's just a book.' I feel myself blushing under his gaze, as I realise I'm being disloyal to my friend. And what would Mathias Gelman ever see in me, anyway?

'What book?'

'Oh, just something Herr Müller gave me at breakfast. A history of Rügen. He knows I'm a local.'

'A local yokel from Rügen,' snorts Mathias.

I punch him on the arm. 'Don't make fun of me, Mathias.'

'Why do you want a local history book if you're from the island? Don't you know it all already, you local types?'

'Oh, just piss off,' I say, and turn back to my work.

But Frau Schettler has seen the exchange. 'Behrendt! Gellman! Come here. Now.' We leave the packing bench and move forward, the book chafing between my legs. I try my best to look shame-faced. But Mathias keeps his head held high.

When we're next to her, she lowers her voice so the others can't hear.

'Look, Irma, I like you but you're making things difficult for me. Director Neumann and Frau Richter will be watching you closely, monitoring your output, and if you're found to be slacking it will be back to the bunker, or worse.'

'You've been in the bunker? Wow,' says Mathias, as though I've done something hugely impressive.

'She's just got out, Mathias. So you can help her. Don't start chatting to her or distracting her.' She looks at him sternly, but there is a softness behind her frown. 'And maybe if you get ahead of target, you could help Irma catch up?'

Mathias nods, and smiles at me. We go back to the packing bench.

'You're lucky I didn't tell on you,' he whispers, first making sure Schettler isn't looking. 'You owe me one.'

I don't dare to read Herr Müller's book in the dormitory. After the close shave in the packing room, I wait for a chance to go to the communal toilets before we're locked up for the night. In the dorm, there is just a bucket to sit on, and the stench of piss and shit is ever-present, stinking out our dreams; but here in the washroom, the toilet cubicles do have doors. I take the book out as I lower my knickers, first examining the folds of my lower stomach. They sting from where the plastic cover has been rubbing against my skin. I'm still too fat, I know that, even though the food in the *Jugendwerkhof* is often so revolting. I know I have to do something about it, but Oma always used to feed me up, perhaps to make up for the fact that she felt Mutti didn't pay me enough attention. And once you start eating too much, the habit's hard to break. Even in somewhere like this.

I quickly skim through the book, knowing that Richter or someone will come knocking on the door if I spend too long in here. I turn each page carefully; I don't want the rustling of paper to alert anyone. Much of the book's content is familiar from school lessons in Sellin – the way the island has been under different rulers down the years. The West Slavic Rani. The Danish princes of Rügen. Swedish Pomerania. The unfinished, then abandoned, town of Gustavia, built by King Gustav IV of Sweden. And then this place, Prora – Hitler's intended holiday camp in the Nazi era – now a concrete monstrosity filled with army construction workers at one end, and the *Jugendwerkhof* at the other.

All very fascinating, but, as Mathias said, I know all this already. I begin to close the book, and just as I do so I notice a pencil mark in the margin, highlighting the section about Gustavia. The word Sweden is underlined too. I flick through again, excited now, the pages fanning cool air on my face. I spot one more piece of highlighting in the margins, right near the end of the book, in the section on DDR local history. It's about the construction of the new port at Sassnitz. Once again, a mark in the margin, and the word Sassnitz underlined. A third time I flick through, back to the front of the book. Checking there is nothing else. But those are the only two marks in the margin. The only two words underlined. *Sassnitz*. And *Sweden*. Herr Müller's message to me.

I realise the book is dangerous. If I can understand the message, so would Richter or Neumann. I flush the toilet, rearrange my clothes and put the book back where it was in my underwear. As I exit the cubicle, I look left and right. No one else is here. I glance round the corners of the room, up to the light fitting. There's nothing that looks like a camera. I quickly check the corridor. Empty. Then I go back to the washroom and over to the window, trying to prevent my footsteps being heard on the cold hard floor. It's barred, but I can still open it. I take the book out and slide it along the ledge, out of sight. No one will be able to link it to me anymore. And as long as a gale doesn't blow, it should just stay sitting on the ledge day after day, week after week, the rain slowly turning it back into pulp.

14

February 1975. Day Seven.
Schönhauser Allee, East Berlin.

Bright winter daylight filtered through the blinds of the apartment's lounge windows, warming Karin Müller's face, coaxing her awake. Müller yawned and stretched, rubbing the dull ache in her back, the result of sleeping scrunched up on the sofa. It had been the early hours of the morning when she'd finally got back to the apartment, and so she hadn't wanted to wake Gottfried. She'd used her old People's Police coat and the tablecloth as blankets. She couldn't face another slanging match.

Her back spasmed as she rose from her makeshift bed. The flat was shrouded in near silence, the slow ticking of the mantelpiece clock and her own breathing the only sounds other than the usual traffic noise outside. Where was Gottfried? She assumed he'd be asleep in bed when she'd got in, but hadn't checked. And now she saw the bedroom door was open, and the room itself empty. Was he trying to play her at her own game? Or was this something worse? She felt her heart rate increase, and returned to the living room. His coat, scarf and gloves had gone from the peg. Had he been here at all? Then, on the dining table, she spotted a torn-off piece of paper:

Karin. If you can't be bothered to let me know where you are, then perhaps it's best if you don't know where I am either, but at some stage we're going to need to talk. If it's divorce you want, you're going the right way about it.

The writing was not in Gottfried's usual neat schoolmasterish script. Instead it looked like it had been scrawled quickly, angrily. What exactly was he up to? And where had he gone?

Müller returned to the bedroom, looking for clues there. The bed was unmade but had clearly been slept in. Her side still pristine; his with the covers thrown back and the pillow at an angle. She looked at the wedding photo on Gottfried's bedside cabinet. The beaming smiles showed how happy they'd been. Where had it gone wrong? Were his suspicions about her and Tilsner the result of some sort of guilt on his part? Though she had to admit to herself they were perhaps justified given the way she'd acted so stupidly that night in Dircksenstrasse.

If he had anything to hide, where would he hide it? Probably not in the flat. But she opened his bedside drawer in any case. There were a few papers. She riffled through them. Most were to do with the school. She read the original official warning which had led to his 'exile' at the *Jugendwerkhof* in Rügen, a period that seemed to have changed him so much. He'd apparently supported a boy who had withdrawn from the communist youth movement, grown his hair and started a rock band. The boy had been referred to a youth court – there was nothing further about what had happened to him. But for Gottfried, the recommendation was that he should spend some time teaching within the Republic's children's-home system: that in participating in the re-education of youths into fully fledged socialist personalities, some of that re-education might actually rub off on the teacher himself.

Müller sighed and replaced the letter. Perhaps she hadn't done enough to support him, but in playing the rebel – or at least the supporter of rebels – he'd put her own position at risk. She had another quick look through the papers. Nothing of interest, except a pamphlet about the meetings at Gethsemane Church.

Thankfully, though, there was no evidence of another woman. Frau Eisenberg had kept Silke's letter from the West in the girl's bedside drawer, but Gottfried, she knew, would be a lot cleverer than that.

She glanced around the room, her eyes drawn to the top of the wardrobe. She dragged the bedside chair towards it, then stood on the seat and stretched her hand up to reach along the top surface, hidden by the wooden profile above the doors. At first, she could just feel her fingers sliding through the dust and dirt, and then they clawed something. A small cardboard container, about four centimetres square. Müller lifted it down and examined it. *Mondos Luxos* spelt out in gold lettering, on a vivid purple background. Sweets? Pills? She frowned, and flipped the small packet over. Immediately, the instructions on the back ended her confusion. A condom packet. *Condoms? He knows I can't –*

She stopped the thought, as realisation dawned. He didn't need condoms for making love to her, but these obviously weren't intended *for her*. Müller panicked, her heart racing. She climbed back onto the chair, and began scrabbling about the top of the wardrobe again. Maybe he *was* the guilty party all along. The guilty party deflecting the blame by attacking someone else, by making insinuations about her and Tilsner. It was one of the oldest tricks in the book: one of the first things she'd been taught in police college.

The college. The vile memories of *him*. She tried not to think of his name, tried to forget, but she couldn't – he was with her day after day, and had been for the last fourteen years. Walter Pawlitzki, her lecturer at the People's Police college. He'd been her mentor. She'd looked up to him. And then...

Scrabbling with her fingers, Müller suddenly remembered why she thought the top of the wardrobe was such a good hiding place. Because she'd used it herself before, to conceal a small object. Not cardboard, but metal. It didn't take long for her to find it. She picked it up, stepped off the chair and opened the wardrobe door. It was something she shouldn't do, she knew that. An addiction she tried to fight, but that, at times like this, she could not resist.

She jiggled the tiny key into the locked bottom drawer in her side of the wardrobe. Her drawer. And then she opened it.

There were two sets of clothes, neatly stacked, on the left and the right. The tiniest clothes possible. Baby blue and white on the left. Baby pink and white on the right. The male–female cliché. She resisted the temptation to take the clothes out and unfold them. That was only for when it got really bad. Instead, she contented herself with stroking the top of each pile of material, left and right, and wondered what might have been, if things had turned out differently.

Then she closed the drawer again and locked her memories away.

The Bäckerei Schäfer van was still there, although when Müller closed the apartment block front door, and lined her eyes on the street light on the opposite side of Schönhauser Allee, she realised it had moved a few metres. The vehicle no longer obscured the foot of the lamp post.

She set off at a fast walk towards the centre of the Hauptstadt, following her usual route towards Marx-Engels-Platz, then turning towards Alexanderplatz and the television tower. The bread van preyed on her mind: when she got back to the office she would ask Elke to look into it: how could a private bakery, which by definition was only permitted a handful of employees, afford to have a delivery van sitting mostly idle outside her apartment block? It didn't make sense.

The police building on Keibelstrasse was a warren of small rooms and corridors. Having shown her pass, Müller set off to try to locate the forensics lab. She'd been here enough times before, but still usually managed to make at least one wrong turning. The corridors seemed to close in on her.

Müller finally located the correct door for the lab. She saw Tilsner hunched by Schmidt at his desk; evidently he'd only just arrived – and with shadows under his eyes, he looked as tired as she felt.

Schmidt was fiddling with his camera, squinting at the top. 'I just want to make sure it's wound through properly,' he explained. 'We don't want any mishaps.' Finally, he nodded in satisfaction, extracted the fully wound film roll, and then placed it in an envelope. 'Come on then, you can both come into the darkroom and see what we've got.'

Müller glanced both ways to see if anyone might be listening. 'Is it secure, Jonas? There won't be any of your colleagues in there?'

'It's fine,' replied Schmidt. 'I've booked it out for the next couple of hours.'

After processing the negatives and hanging them up to dry, Schmidt started using the first of the celluloid strips to produce black-and-white prints, gently bathing the photographic paper in a shallow layer of developing agent as Müller and Tilsner watched. He moved the tray from side to side, taking care not to spill any of the liquid as it rippled over the paper.

As Schmidt swirled the liquid, the image of a tyre impression captured in the layer of building sand gradually started to appear. He worked his way through the photographs.

'What do you think, Jonas?' asked Müller, unable to handle the silence.

'Well, I'll have to check with a magnifying glass once the prints are dry. But look.' He held up a photocopy of a tyre pattern he'd brought into the darkroom with him. 'This is the

Gislaved pattern, on this photocopy. Look at these angled grooves. Very distinctive. And then look at the photographs.'

Müller and Tilsner both craned their heads over the developing tray as Schmidt used tongs to move a print from one bath of agent to another.

'Fixing agent,' he explained. Müller pulled back slightly from the acidic, vinegary smell. But she could clearly see what Schmidt meant. There were none of the same distinctive patterns. Whatever make of tyres were on the cars in the government compound and service area in Lichtenberg, it didn't appear as though it was Gislaved. If their small sample of three limousines represented the entire fleet – and since all three were the same they had no reason to believe it didn't – none of these cars had been at St Elisabeth cemetery. They'd hit another dead end.

15

Back in Marx-Engels-Platz, Tilsner and Müller sat opposite each other in her side office. Through the glazed window, Müller could see Elke talking into the phone, presumably checking up on the bakery.

Tilsner rested his elbows on the desk, and gave a slow sigh. 'We don't seem to be getting very far.'

'Slow steps, Werner. You know that. I still think those tyre tracks are significant.'

'At least we now know it doesn't seem to have been a government car.'

Müller nodded, then frowned. 'Which means the likeliest explanation is that it's a car from West Berlin. No citizen in the East can afford a Volvo. By now, we should really have asked for the details of all vehicle movements at the crossing points.'

'Let's just go to the checkpoints now. Ask to see the files. Jäger will be able to give you the necessary authority. Give him a ring at Normannenstrasse.'

Müller felt herself biting her bottom lip. She didn't want to involve Jäger more than necessary, but Tilsner was right. She picked up the receiver and began to dial.

Grenzübergang Friedrichstrasse. She knew it was called Checkpoint Charlie in the West. They parked the Wartburg in a side street a hundred metres or so before the crossing, and then went the rest of the way to the East German checkpoint on foot.

As they walked, Müller leafed through the authorisation documents that Jäger had provided. One of his minions had biked them to Marx-Engels-Platz from Normannenstrasse less than an hour after she'd made the phone call. The southerly wind that had been thawing the snow suddenly lifted the key piece of paper from her grip and deposited it in the gutter. Tilsner leant down, fished it out and then wiped it with his sleeve. He checked none of the ink or the signature had smudged. 'No harm done, except a bit of road dirt. Lucky for you.' He winked at her. She glowered back.

Checks were carried out by a strange combination of Stasi officers and border guards. That was why Jäger had the authority to send people to look through the books, and why they'd been able to get permission so quickly, rather than waiting for the Republic's usual cumbersome red tape to take its course. His immediate agreement to her request had been a little surprising, and Müller was still unsure as to the Stasi lieutenant colonel's exact motivation. On the one hand he was forever outlining clear parameters they shouldn't cross. Warning them. But at the same time, he seemed to be opening doors for them to dig deeper and deeper, whatever the consequences. She wondered again about the risks they took to get the tyre prints – might Tilsner have been right, that they could just have asked Jäger?

As they entered the checkpoint, Müller glanced up the road, past the barriers, to the bustle of West Berlin beyond. She wondered if it really was as glamorous as the adverts on western TV made out. Or were *Der schwarze Kanal*'s accounts of strikes, homeless unemployed begging on the streets and ruthless greedy bosses nearer to the truth?

All the border guards were busy. Most were frantically shouting to each other, running to and fro as the weekend rush of tourists began; others had their heads buried in paperwork. Eventually, Müller found the senior officer and showed him their authorisations, and they were led to a side office with several volumes of files, divided into each day of the week. They split them up, three each. Tilsner showed no eagerness to take the seventh, so Müller added it to her pile. She looked over Tilsner's shoulder. Spread in front of him were the files for the Saturday, Sunday and Monday. Müller's four covered the remaining period up until the previous Friday, when the girl's body had been discovered.

They began to check through them. Müller found her eyes scanning down the columns rapidly, discounting all the Mercedes, BMWs, Opels and Volkswagens that made up the majority of the entries. She moved from column to column, page to page, file to file.

'No Volvos,' she said to Tilsner by the time she was about halfway through.

'No. Same here.' He scanned down the list. 'Mercedes, VW Beetle, Opel Kadett ... All West German. We're talking about a pin in a haystack here.'

'Are we sure, if it was a *customised* Volvo, that the border guards would even recognise the make?' asked Müller.

'I think so,' Tilsner replied, looking up from the lists for a moment. 'Even if some of them aren't the brightest brains our Republic has ever produced. Volvos have a very distinctive shape and front grille.' He turned his attention back to the files. 'Here's a Chevrolet. Makes a nice change, but it doesn't help us.'

Müller tore her eyes away from him and busied herself in her own file, still without a Volvo in sight.

'Hang on a mo. Here we go, boss. A Volvo. Swedish plates, Swedish male driver. Danish female passenger.' Tilsner noted the details. 'But it was just a regular saloon model, a 144.'

Müller was nearly at the end of her own four files. She still hadn't found a single Volvo.

'And here's another. But again, a saloon. Danish plates, this time.' Tilsner noted that too, then continued scanning his final file, until he shut the folder with a resigned expression. 'That's it. Two Volvos. What about you?'

Müller shut the cover of her final folder. 'Nothing.' She sighed, and got to her feet, picking up the files and carrying them back to the checkpoint's main room. They were going to have to go through this exact process at another five or six crossing points. And, at the back of her mind, was the thought that perhaps – after all – the tyre tracks had no connection with the girl's death.

They decided to work anticlockwise around the zigzag barrier that enclosed the western sector. In any case, the next nearest *Grenzübergang* in the other direction, Heinrich-Heine-Strasse, was mainly used by commercial goods vehicles. Schmidt had been insistent the tyres belonged to a long-wheelbase car, rather than a van.

At Invalidenstrasse and then Chausseestrasse they failed to find a single Volvo in the files. Their next stop was Bornholm-erstrasse – between the districts of Wedding in the West and Prenzlauer Berg in the East.

From the queues on the western side of the barriers, Müller could already tell that their search had more chance of succeed-ing here. Again, she sought out the senior officer. This time it was a stocky woman in an army major's uniform, permed and dyed blonde hair straggling messily from under her cap.

'This is very irregular,' she said, as she fingered Müller's *Kripo* ID. She ushered the two detectives to sit on the opposite side of her desk as she peered at the authorisation from Jäger, and lifted the telephone. 'I shall have to check with the Ministry.' Müller watched her dial and wait for an answer, and then listened as she explained the circumstances. The name that seemed to do the trick was that of Stasi *Oberstleutnant* Klaus Jäger. The answer the major got when she read the name down the phone immediately changed her attitude. Now there was nothing she couldn't do to help Müller and Tilsner, getting the relevant files herself for the two detectives and letting them use her own desk to check through them.

They divided the files – covered in the similar olive-green cloth – the same way. Müller took Tuesday to Friday; she gave Tilsner the ones for Saturday through Monday. But, just to relieve the boredom, Müller worked through hers the opposite way. Starting with the last page of the Friday file, and then working backwards, eyes scanning from entry to entry, car to car, pages turning regularly. The rustling of the paper was almost drowned out by the near-constant shouting of the guards checking waiting vehicles outside.

The breakthrough didn't take long. 'Here, Werner,' Müller said, the excitement in her voice causing the major to look round quizzically. 'Look.' She traced her finger under the entry in the file for the Thursday night – eight days before the girl's body was found. She watched Tilsner's face as he read the entry. 11.47 p.m. A black Volvo limousine. A West German male driver and a West German male passenger. Even if these were the murderers Müller couldn't believe that they would have used their real names. Almost certainly they would have had fake IDs. But now they had the registration number. They had the make of car. And – in the 'extra information' column – something else. According to the log, the driver and his passenger were making their journey to the East to attend a friend's wedding, and this was supposedly the bride and groom's luxury transport.

'What do you make of that?' asked Tilsner. 'Perhaps they did just come over for a wedding. Perhaps it's not the vehicle we're looking for.'

Müller frowned. 'Possibly. But the timing would be too much of a coincidence.' She stood up, straightened her clothing and smiled at her deputy. 'I think this may just be it. The breakthrough we've been searching for.'

16

Day Seven.
East Berlin.

Events unfolded rapidly once they'd radioed back their information from the Wartburg to *Kriminaltechniker* Schmidt. It wasn't strictly forensic work, but Müller knew Schmidt's assiduous methods were the best way of pinning down the car via its West Berlin registration plate. She just hoped that the suspects – if they had used false IDs – hadn't used false plates too.

They'd only just got back to the office in Marx-Engels-Platz and started their coffees – which Tilsner had ordered from Elke despite her previously undrinkable effort – when the phone in Müller's side office rang. It was Schmidt.

'They did use fake plates, I'm afraid. That registration plate corresponds to an Opel Kadett in Charlottenburg.'

'How did you find that out?'

'One of my *Kriminaltechniker* friends from Weissensee applied to go to the West last year. His West German mother was ill, and she needed a relative nearby, so they let him go. He helps me out now and then.'

Müller took a sip from her coffee. Thankfully Elke had used the genuine expensive coffee this time, as instructed by Tilsner. She glanced across at her deputy. 'What's he saying?' he mouthed, silently.

She ignored him, and instead continued her phone conversation with Schmidt. 'So does that mean we're no further on?' asked Müller.

'No. I've got something really interesting, Comrade Müller. I wondered if the wedding story might have a grain of truth in it, so I asked my friend to go out and get a bridal magazine. They're very popular in the West for women who are planning their weddings. You can imagine the sort of thing, *Oberleutnant*: glamorous pictures, models in white dresses, adverts for catering companies –'

Müller had no need to imagine. She'd seen the adverts on West German television programmes, but didn't want to reveal that to Schmidt.

'Well, the magazine had an advert at the back for a limousine company, and one of their offerings is a black Volvo. But as I told you the other day, Volvo don't actually manufacture limousines, so that seemed a little odd. I got my contact to get in touch with Volvo car dealers in West Berlin. They confirmed it was impossible to order a limo from Volvo, but – and here's the interesting thing – they'd heard that this wedding hire company had one on their books.'

She watched Tilsner tapping his fingers ostentatiously against the desk. He always claimed Schmidt used two words when one would do.

'Carry on, Jonas,' she said into the mouthpiece.

'This limousine seems to be quite famous in West Berlin, at least among those who are interested in that sort of thing. Apparently it wasn't imported, but constructed and welded together from the front and back of two Volvo saloons. So, in effect, it's one of a kind. Anyway, I got my West Berlin forensic officer contact to check with the car hire company on the phone. It was hired out nine days ago – the Wednesday – on a three-day cheap midweek rate, and returned on Friday afternoon. It was needed for a ceremony in the West on the Saturday. What was a little odd is that it looked as if it had been steam-cleaned – even though cleaning is included in the hire rate.'

Müller grinned. 'Good work, Jonas.' She could imagine Schmidt smiling proudly at the other end of the line.

'Thank you, *Oberleutnant*.'

'But if the car has been thoroughly cleaned, then even if we did somehow manage to get hold of it, there may be no forensic evidence left.'

'That's possible, of course, *Oberleutnant*. But in my experience they always miss something.'

Müller nodded thoughtfully. 'And what about the victim's clothes? Any luck with those, Jonas?'

'Not yet, *Oberleutnant*, but I'm still waiting for some of the lab tests to come back.'

'OK. Well, let me know when you have anything more.'

She put the phone down and then relayed to Tilsner the half of the conversation he'd missed.

'We're going to need to get hold of that car,' he said.

'How? We can't just go over there, hire it and bring it back, and we can't ask the West Berlin police for help. There's never been a joint East-West police operation in the entire history of the Republic, despite *Ostpolitik*.'

Tilsner looked dubiously at her, then took a long gulp of his coffee. He leant back, savouring it, and then folded his arms across his chest. Müller watched the muscles flex under his shirt, then chided herself silently.

'We can't go there, but the Stasi can. They're already there.'

'What do you mean?' asked Müller.

'Oh, come on, Karin. You know as well as I do that there will be Stasi agents at every level in the Federal Republic, and especially in West Berlin. One of them could help us. You just need to give your friend Jäger another ring.'

Müller sighed. This was becoming a habit, but she nevertheless picked up the receiver again. She was less sure than before that he would support their request. Was this a step too far? One word from the Stasi officer, and they would almost certainly be taken off the case. But they needed to get hold of that limousine.

With a shaky finger, she slowly dialled Jäger's office at Normannenstrasse.

17

Nine months earlier (May 1974).
Jugendwerkhof Prora Ost.

Beate has disappeared, and none of them will tell us where she is. When I tried to find out from Richter before lights out, she slapped my face and told me not to be insolent. That it was none of my business.

So I lie here, unable to sleep. Moonlight filters in through holes in the blue curtain material, casting ghoulish shadows about the room from the metalwork of the bunk beds. I look across at the bottom bunk next to mine, where Beate would normally be, but it has been stripped. Folded sheets, blankets and pillow neatly arranged at its foot. Without Beate's body shape in the way, I can see further across, to the next bunk bed. Bauer. Lying there snoring. But to be fair to her, she seemed as worried about Beate as I was before lights out, trying to back me up in my confrontation with the detestable Frau Richter. To no avail.

My mind races. I imagine all sorts of things happening to Beate. There has to be a reason why she cries every night. I can't believe that it's simply because she's locked up here in Prora Ost. Yes, it's awful, but until all this happened – until the nightly tears – Beate seemed to cope with it all well enough.

I find myself twisting my messy red hair into even more knots. I know I shouldn't, but I can't help it. I turn away from Beate's bed and instead look at the pinpricked, moth-eaten curtain, and try to count the shafts of moonlight. I usually find the sound of the Ostsee waves calming, lulling, but tonight each wave seems to echo through my head – each crash on the sand prevents me from slipping into sleep. Is the sea trying to tempt me, to remind me of Herr Müller's thinly disguised message in the history book? Maybe the sound of the waves is the sea talking to me, luring me to break free. As far as I know, no one has yet managed to escape from Prora Ost.

The underlined words from the book dance before my eyes. Sweden and Sassnitz. Sassnitz and Sweden. The two words almost being spoken aloud by the surf as it crashes on the sand. A link. A route. But I have no idea how to use it.

No one has ever escaped from Prora Ost.

Sleep did come eventually. It always does. But as daylight replaces moonlight at the curtain's holes, I make no effort to get up. Eventually Bauer comes over and shakes me, but there is no malice, no vindictiveness in her actions. She is just trying to make sure I'm not late, so that Richter has no further excuse to punish me. She, too, is worried about Beate. Maybe I have misjudged her.

At breakfast, I get my first clue. Beate's place is empty, and I whisper my question about my friend to Frau Schettler. She looks at me kindly, takes my hand and holds it for a moment, and then frowns. 'Beate is unwell. In the sanatorium.' As she says it, her eyes are looking at the floor, and I feel this is not the whole truth. 'Perhaps she will be better by this afternoon, and back in the dorm by tonight.' She releases my hand quickly, and I see her eyes look over my shoulder. I turn. It's Richter. I make my way quietly back to my place at the breakfast table, a gap next to me where Beate should be.

I'm in the packing room again this morning – I feel so rotten that I don't think I could have coped with anything else, despite the harder work. I look at the rota on the wall for the next month to check I've got my usual shifts, hoping they coincide with Beate's. I trace my fingers down the columns but I seem to have just three shifts in the packing room instead of my usual ten. The others will be in the workshop, which I enjoy far less. *The bastards!* No doubt that is another of Richter's or Neumann's ideas. Further punishment for Behrendt, they probably thought. And what's more, there's only one shift where mine coincides with Beate's. That's if she's even recovered by then. It's an extra evening half-shift in the middle of the month. The 22nd of June. The date seems familiar for some reason. I move my finger across to see who else we'll be with. Mathias Gellman. So it's not even as though I'll get a chance to chat with Beate. She will only have eyes for Mathias, and he for her, the way it's always been recently. Mr Perfect Mathias, with his looks of a western pop star or footballer. And that thought triggers my memory. The 22nd of June, when West Germany plays East Germany in the World Cup. Mathias will hate to miss that. I wanted to watch it too. Now I *know* they are punishing us.

I move to my workbench, getting ready for the routine of kitchen door, left cabinet side, right side, back, shelves, top, bottom. But I look at the components to pack, and I look at the size of the box. Everything is bigger, like it has all been magnified, and we have a sheet of new instructions. I look across at Maria Bauer, who, like me, is fumbling with the various pieces. Frau Schettler sees our confusion and walks over.

'Beds,' she says. 'We have a new order.' I look at the parts again, and the larger shapes of veneered chipboard and timber start to make sense. A headboard. Bed slats. Bed posts. All in clean, functional lines. I guess this is the sort of thing they like in Sweden.

Schettler sees me biting my lip as I survey the huge piece of cardboard which – when folded as per the instructions – will form the box that all the pieces will fit into, like a giant 3D jigsaw. 'Yes, they are big boxes, Irma,' she says. 'When each is complete and loaded, it will take at least two – maybe three – of you to lift each one onto the trolley. If you need the help of one of the boys, just raise your hands.'

By the end of the day I know I will be exhausted. I begin to regret my eagerness to work in the packing room. But after a day doing this, at least I should be so drained that sleep will welcome me, whether Beate has returned or not.

I have an hour's free time before dinner when I end the shift. I drag my feet, one in front of the other, as I trudge back to the dorm. It's as though someone has added hundreds of tiny lead weights to the insides of my work trousers.

It's the shouting that alerts me. Richter – a scared note in her voice. Telling someone not to move. To hang on. I have never heard Frau Richter scared before. I run towards the noise and find myself in the exercise yard at the back of the building. Richter is there, and Neumann, their faces staring upwards at an acute angle. Neumann is holding Mathias tightly, as though to stop him intervening in the drama.

I follow their line of sight.

A body.

Clinging to the wall, on the narrow ledge that runs under the fifth-floor windows. The floor of our dorms. The highest point in Prora to prevent us escaping. Beate's arms and legs stretched, like a spider with four legs missing, precariously attached to the vertical surface. The drop is twenty metres, thirty. Maybe more.

In an instant, my tiredness evaporates. I race past Richter, Neumann and Mathias. Richter tries to put an arm out to stop me, but I have found an inner strength and I wriggle from her grip towards the stairwell. Another teacher is there, Herr Küfer, stopping everyone from entering. I just put my head down and charge into him, my head aiming for his stomach, my hand for his groin. At the moment of impact, I squeeze his balls, and as he doubles up in pain, I thrust through the doorway. By the second floor I'm already out of breath and feel a stitch in my side, but I force myself on and up the remaining three flights. I'm nearly knocked over by Bauer and another girl coming the other way, carrying a mattress.

There is another teacher at the entrance to the washroom, but it is Herr Müller. He doesn't try to stop me. 'Be careful, Irma,' he shouts as I race past. 'Don't do anything stupid. Don't put yourself at risk too.' But he knows that pleading with me is useless.

I reach the toilet window and open it. There are bars across the lower half, but I lever myself up with my arms, get a knee on the window ledge and climb up, then stick my head out.

Beate has her eyes shut tight, face to the wall. One hand – her right, furthest from me – is grasping the downpipe, and the other is groping along the wall, stretching millimetre by millimetre, trying to reach this window – the window where I am. I can hear her breathing. Shallow breaths, rapid. Frightened breaths. I try to stretch my arm to reach hers, but I cannot.

'Beate,' I whisper.

She opens her eyes. I see her chin and lips trembling, the fingers on the hand nearest me shaking. 'Irma. Oh, Irma. I couldn't do it. I wanted to jump. I got on the roof, and they caught me and took me to the sanatorium, but I got out. I was going to try again, but now I'm scared. I don't want –'

'Shh,' I say. 'Shh. You're safe now. You'll be able to edge back along here. I'll talk you through it. You'll be OK. Remember, we all love you. Mathias loves you.' My own skin feels clammy, and I am breathing rapidly like her. The skin on Beate's face is white, almost translucent, and across her perfect bone structure it looks like the skin of an angel. An angel without wings. I climb to the second rung of the window bars, hook my feet under and stretch still further out of the window. My heartbeat pulses in my ears. 'Just try to move very slightly towards me. Try to stretch,' I say.

She does. Maybe a centimetre. Then freezes. 'I can't! I can't let go of the pipe. I'll fall. Oh, Irma.' I see the tears welling in her eyes. I stretch too, but our hands are still some fifteen centimetres apart. I look down. I shouldn't have. It makes me feel giddy. I see Richter and Neumann. But they are silent now. Children continue to pile mattresses on the floor. Army soldiers from the base next door arrive with ladders. They test them against the wall in turn, but all are too short to reach.

'You can do it, Beate. *We* can do it,' I say. I loosen my right foot from under the iron window bar and move it to the top rail. Now only the toe of the boot on my left foot is holding me, but freeing my right leg allows me to twist further, stretch my arm out further. I can see the beads of sweat on Beate's brow as she stretches in turn. And then we touch. But that is all we can do. Touch our fingers together. I am stretching every sinew in my arm. It will go no further. I try moving my right leg again so it is completely out of the window, digging it into the ledge. The manoeuvre gives me a few extra centimetres. I clasp Beate's hand.

'Just gently edge along towards me,' I say. 'I've got you. You won't fall.'

She tries. I see her clenching her eyes closed with the effort, her grip on my hand so tight it sends shooting pains down my arm. I'm now balanced half-in, half-out of the window. But suddenly her foot nearest to me slips. She makes a grab the other way, to grasp the downpipe again.

The movement pulls me fractionally. I claw at the window with my free hand, but my right leg loses its footing, sliding on something. *The pulpy mess of Herr Müller's history book.* I realise I'm about to take Beate down with me. 'Let go,' I scream. Her grip loosens, just in time.

I scrabble with my left leg, trying to hook it back under the window bar.

Too late.

Balance gone. Slipping. Falling. Arms windmilling against a rush of air. Thinking. Of Sassnitz. Of Sweden. Of freedom.

Of what it will be like to die.

18

Jäger used his usual method to arrange his next meeting with Müller. A motorcyclist delivered a telegram to the Marx-Engels-Platz office instructing her to be at the Märchenbrunnen – the fairy-tale fountains in Friedrichshain People's Park – at eleven o'clock prompt.

It was easier to get to than the Kulturpark. Perhaps, thought Müller, that first meeting was intended to unnerve her; to show her his power. Inadvertently, he'd probably disturbed her more with his second choice of locale. The fountains held a special significance: it was where she and Gottfried had returned to time and again when they were first dating, when she had just finished police college and he was a trainee teacher. One of the things that attracted her to him was the way he'd known – without it being spelt out – that her air of melancholy spoke of a deeper wound. The way, in their meetings in front of the statues at the Märchenbrunnen, he'd taught her to laugh again, to enjoy life. On their second date, he'd surprised her with a gift of a miniature witch's house from *Hansel and Gretel* – edible, of course. Little touches like that had allowed her to smile again. The dark cloud of her past wasn't addressed, other than for her to admit – when Gottfried knelt down and proposed that summer in front of the fountains – that they would never be able to have children. She'd seen the sadness in his eyes, but he'd just held her tightly, and let her shed her tears on his shoulder.

The tram to Friedrichshain suddenly moved off, jostling her into the middle-aged man sitting next to her. She tried to smile an apology, but he stared fixedly ahead, his chin sinking into the fleshy rolls of his neck, and his arms flopping like rabbit paws on top of his briefcase. Was that how Gottfried would turn out in a few years? Greasy hair centre-parted, and with a vacant, defeated expression?

They'd finally been in the flat together at the same time last night, but not in the same room, and not speaking. He'd arrived back after she'd gone to sleep, exhausted and depressed by the slow progress of the case. By the time she'd got up, he'd already left his makeshift bed on the sofa, and exited the apartment. His note from yesterday morning had said they needed to talk, but neither of them seemed to be prepared to make the first move.

The barked announcement 'Volkspark Friedrichshain!' jolted her from her daydream, and she rushed for the exit before the doors swung closed. The fresh air – or East Berlin's excuse for fresh air – was a relief after the smoky atmosphere inside the tram. She stood for a moment by the tram stop, pulled her make-up mirror from her coat pocket and opened it. The eyes staring back at her were bloodshot with dark circles underneath.

The Märchenbrunnen looked transformed in winter: nothing like Müller remembered from her visits with Gottfried all those years ago. The eleven-arch arcade still dominated the fountains, but the pools themselves were blanketed in white and the fountain pumps had been closed off to protect them from ice. Snow White, Sleeping Beauty and all their fairy-tale friends were hidden away under hollow cubes of wood, each one topped by its own snow-covered pitched roof. The only figure on show was Jäger himself, who'd cleared snow away from the low wall at the front of the fountain complex, and was huddled there in the same sheepskin coat he'd worn at the Kulturpark.

'No new coat yet, Comrade *Oberleutnant*?' he asked her, with a warm smile.

Müller grinned back. 'I told you, Comrade *Oberstleutnant*. Not on my salary.'

Jäger gave a small laugh. 'Maybe I should recruit you? But that will depend on the outcome of this case.'

'And will I have any say in the matter?' asked Müller, taking her seat on the wall next to the Stasi lieutenant colonel. She tucked her overcoat under her to protect her skirt.

Jäger chuckled. 'Perhaps. But more importantly, how are your inquiries progressing, and why did you want to see me?'

'Well, as you know, we're at a dead end in terms of identifying the girl. There's nothing that's a match in the missing-person's files. Well, other than the girl we already ruled out from Friedrichshain, and some possible girls from the West – but we have no way of chasing up those leads.' Müller paused, and searched Jäger's eyes for a flicker of a clue, but he wore his best poker face. 'We're examining her clothes, of course. And uniform officers from the People's Police are trying to pin down exactly what sort of ink was on her fingers. They're also checking the movements of known sex offenders, particularly ones with a predilection for –'

'You don't have to spell it out, Karin. In fact, I'd prefer you didn't. I get the gist.'

The use of her first name briefly derailed Müller's train of thought. 'But we have made significant progress with the tyre tracks. I know it might seem at first glance to be a bit of a wild goose chase, but I feel if we can locate the car that was at the scene, then possibly we may find new clues to help us to identify the girl.'

He frowned. 'I'm not sure that is the way forward. It risks the danger of your taking the investigation in the direction which I've already warned you you cannot.'

Müller held his gaze. 'It's solely my intention to try to identify the poor girl involved. I've already given you my word about that.' Müller knew she was lying to him, lying to herself. But she got the feeling that for all his protestations, Jäger wanted this case solved just as much as she did. In *all* respects. 'There is, however, a serious problem,' she continued.

Jäger sighed. 'And what's that?'

'As you're aware, our inquiries show that those tyre marks are from a Volvo … a Volvo limousine. Our first thought was that perhaps it was a car linked to senior officials in the Republic.'

Jäger cocked his head to one side quizzically. 'But you've discounted that, I take it? And how exactly did you discount it?'

'Through our inquiries.'

Jäger frowned. 'I hope those inquires didn't involve the faking of a tipper truck losing its load of sand in Lichtenberg?' Müller felt her face redden and her heart rate increase as Jäger challenged her, his eyes locking onto hers. She didn't answer, just dropped her gaze. 'I heard about the incident,' said Jäger, more gently. 'I knew immediately it was you and Tilsner. It was a very stupid thing to do. If you wanted to check that information you could simply have asked me. I want to make it clear to you that if you exceed your authority, if you break the rules, then the consequences for you will be very severe. You already know this is a sensitive inquiry, otherwise the Ministry for State Security would not be involved. So be careful.'

'Yes, Comrade *Oberstleutnant*,' she said, shamefaced.

Jäger's face relaxed into a smile. 'However, I did find it quite amusing. Now, there was something you wanted to ask me, and you still haven't.'

Müller nodded. 'It concerns the limousine. Once we'd established it was unlikely to be from the East, we checked at the crossing points to see if any suitable vehicle had crossed from the West.'

'And did you find one?' asked Jäger.

'Yes. There was one that crossed the night before the girl's body was found at *Grenzübergang* Bornholmerstrasse. Two male occupants, allegedly taking the limousine to a friend's wedding in the East, but it was travelling on fake plates.'

Jäger sighed. 'So does that mean we can't trace it?'

'Well, we think we may have located it. We're only aware of one in the whole of West Berlin. It's owned by a wedding hire company, so –'

'So you want me to authorise, or arrange, an operation to recover that vehicle?'

Müller nodded.

'That's possible, of course. But it will be difficult. I will have to –'

Jäger suddenly pinched her arm through her coat. She was about to ask him why, then saw a man in a leather jacket approaching them. He looked as though he was going to come right up to where they were sitting on the fountain wall, but then diverted, to walk round behind them, through the arcade at the back of the fountain. When she was certain he was out of earshot, Müller asked: 'Do you know him?'

The Stasi lieutenant colonel nodded slowly. His face looked ashen.

'He's a Ministry for State Security agent. From Department Eight. My department.'

'Your department?' asked Müller, her voice laced with incomprehension.

Another nod from Jäger. 'It was a message to us, or rather to me. I did warn you, Karin, that this could get complicated.' Jäger sighed, and started to get to his feet. Müller did the same, slapping the back of her coat to get the snow off, and to try to force some warmth back into her frozen thighs. 'From now on,' he said, 'be very careful about ringing me. Just wait for me to get in touch. Do you understand?'

Müller nodded twice in assent, then looked over the Stasi officer's shoulder to the arcade, where the agent still lingered. The fairy-tale fountains had now taken on a far more sinister air.

19

Day Nine.
Marx-Engels-Platz, East Berlin.

Waiting in the office for Jäger and Tilsner to arrive, Müller wiped the sleep from her eyes. In the reflection of her face in the compact mirror, she noticed her finger shaking. Too many late nights, too much vodka and too much arguing with Gottfried.

After the meeting at the fairy-tale fountains, Jäger had worked fast, summoning her to a briefing at the Marx-Engels-Platz office at eight o'clock in the morning.

The door to the main office crashed open. It wasn't Jäger, but Tilsner.

'What are you doing here on a Saturday?' she asked. 'I thought you were spending the weekend with Koletta?'

Tilsner smiled enigmatically. Then the door swung open again before Müller had a chance to quiz him further; there was Jäger, looking as fresh and fit as he usually did, and nothing like she felt.

'Morning, both of you,' said the Stasi *Oberstleutnant*. 'I trust you slept well?'

Müller hadn't, but she nodded all the same.

'I've got the necessary authorisations for the operation, but securing the manpower was more difficult.' Jäger pulled up a chair at the long table under the noticeboard and urged the two detectives to do the same. Müller watched him glance up at the photographs of the girl's body which were pinned on it, before he gave a sad shake of his head and reached into his briefcase. 'I was hoping that the Main Intelligence Directorate – with which I have close links – would have been able to supply us with agents to go over to West Berlin and secure the car. They're the foreign intelligence specialists and would have had the necessary experience in operating there. Unfortunately, at such short notice, they couldn't spare anyone.' He passed over two sets of documents. 'So you two will be going.'

Müller frowned at Tilsner. Neither of them had experience operating in the West. But her deputy simply shrugged and smiled as Jäger continued. 'These are the authorisations you'll need to show at the Republic's checkpoints.' Then he reached down into his bag again, pulling out two small forest-green booklets. 'And these are your West German passports.'

Müller saw the same eagle, flexing its wings, as there had been on the Federal Republic's missing persons' file. She read the accompanying words: *Bundesrepublik Deutschland Reisepass*. She picked hers up and flicked through it. A People's Police ID photo from a couple of years ago had been used as the passport photograph, presumably taken from her police file. She looked at the name: *Karin Ritter*. Then did the same with Tilsner's: *Werner Trommler*. She felt a sense of relief. At least they wouldn't have to pose as a married couple.

Jäger seemed to have read her thoughts. 'No, you're not married.' He laughed. 'But you are about to be. That's why you're hiring the limousine. For your wedding.' He met her eyes. 'So you will have to pose as a couple. Is that going to be a problem?'

Tilsner laughed. 'Of course not, Comrade *Oberstleutnant*.'

Müller scowled.

Jäger handed each of them an envelope. 'Some West German marks. You'll need them to go shopping for things for your wedding and forthcoming marriage – and also to pay for the car hire and a deposit. But don't get any ideas. Everything will need to be accounted for with an expenses form, and everything will need to be brought back to the Republic. The items you buy will be useful for our agents when they're operating abroad in the future. Each envelope has a list of what you should buy, and where from. Please don't deviate from it.'

Under Jäger's watchful eyes, Müller opened her envelope and read the list. Specific brands and shops were typed out. Müller felt herself blush as she saw the list of women's underwear she was expected to purchase – along with prices which would have bought ten times as many items in the East.

'How long will we be staying in West Berlin?' she asked Jäger.

'One day only, I'm afraid. That should be enough time. You will however have a hotel room in which to freshen up. And – before you ask – you will have separate rooms.'

'So we're not allowed to get some practice in before our wedding night?' Tilsner chuckled.

'It's not a joke, *Unterleutnant*,' scolded Jäger, his voice as close to anger as Müller had yet heard. 'This is a serious operation, and seems at the moment – in the absence of any leads to identify the girl – our best hope of securing some evidence, something, to build up a clearer picture about her.'

'My apologies, *Oberstleutnant*.'

Jäger, his face serious, nodded in acknowledgement. 'You'll be travelling in a Mercedes owned by the Main Intelligence Directorate, on false West German plates. Try not to get involved in any traffic accidents or anything like that, or it may blow your cover. Drive carefully and slowly. Don't be seduced by the extra power it has compared to your usual Wartburg. One of you will have to drive the Volvo limousine back to the Hauptstadt tonight, and the other will need to drive the Mercedes. Are you both OK with that?'

The two detectives nodded. Müller was a nervous driver, and always let Tilsner take the wheel whenever possible. He could have the limo, and she would drive the Merc. She wasn't looking forward to it.

'And you will be wearing western clothes, appropriate to your status as an engaged couple about to be married. I have the clothes in a bag in my car outside which I'll give you in a moment. We checked your sizes from your personnel files. Again, they're borrowed from the Main Intelligence Directorate. It goes without saying that we'll need them back at the end of the operation.'

Müller glanced at Tilsner. He looked unperturbed: clearly it didn't bother him as much as it did her that the Stasi appeared to have unfettered access to her *Kripo* employment record. But then there was his watch, the other luxury items she'd noticed in his apartment. He had access to extra money from some-where. Was it from working on the side for the Ministry for State Security? It would explain why they'd been allowed to go to West Berlin without an obvious Stasi chaperone. Jäger's protestation that there were no agents available had rung hol-low. Perhaps there was one available, and he was accompanying her: People's Police *Unterleutnant* Werner Tilsner.

20

Nine months earlier (May 1974).
Jugendwerkhof Prora Ost, Rügen.

I hear the sea, the waves crashing, and in my head I'm at Oma's campsite house in Sellin. She's whispering to me. Telling me it's time to get up. My eyes open. She's there at my bedside, but seems so much older. I try to raise my head. She shushes me. And then I remember. I am not a little girl at Oma's. For some reason she is here visiting me.

A woman in a white coat enters: a nurse with an array of medicines on a metal tray.

'She's awake,' says Oma. The nurse walks over and takes my pulse, then urges me to open my mouth and places a thermo-meter under my tongue. My head feels as if it is full of cotton wool. I can't really get my thoughts straight. I glance towards the window and see the bars. They trigger a memory.

Suddenly I'm pulling the thermometer out of my mouth. I throw it to the floor and begin shouting, crying. 'Beate. Beate. I tried to save her. I really tried, Oma.' My grandmother strokes my head, as the nurse prepares an injection. 'Where is she?

Where is she? She's not dead, is she?' Then a pinprick in my arm as the nurse holds me down. My head feels heavy. Someone answers my question but it doesn't register. I try to ask them to repeat themselves but the words won't come. A deep, drugged sleep pulls me under.

Another voice at my ear I recognise, but this time I don't want to open my eyes. I try to turn away from the voice, but hands move my shoulders back round.

'Irma, we need to talk to you.' The detestable voice. Richter's voice.

I open my eyes and realise I'm not at Oma's. I'm not in hospital. I'm in the sanatorium of *Jugendwerkhof* Prora Ost, and in my vision is the face of Frau Richter. Behind her, on a chair in the corner of the room, is her one-eyed, scar-faced boss, Director Neumann.

'Where is Beate?' I ask her. I'm surprised how weak my voice sounds. 'Is she safe?'

Richter nods. 'The fire brigade managed to bring her down.'

I'm so relieved that I can feel tears welling up. I try to fight them back by thinking of something else. I try to move my legs, wiggle my toes. Everything seems fine except the fog in my head that won't let me think clearly. The elation of knowing that Beate has survived is tempered by the knowledge that both of us are still caged in this hellhole.

Neumann stands up now, so both he and Richter are in front of my eyes. 'You are alright, Irma, but what you did was very stupid. Your friend survived, but no thanks to you. You could have killed yourself and her. That's a very serious matter.' The words soak into my cotton wool brain, producing no reaction. All I care about is that Beate is alive. I try to turn away from him, but Richter pulls me back. 'Now, we are prepared to overlook all this, just this once,' he says. 'But you must never tell anyone about what happened. As far as your grandmother or anyone else is concerned, you simply had a fall when you were acting the fool. I don't want to hear anything about Beate's prank. Ever. Do you understand?'

He is trying to blame me, trying to make me feel guilty. But his main concern is that nothing about Beate's state of mind should get out to the authorities. Higher authorities than him. For the first time, I've some sort of hold over Richter and Neumann. I wonder if one day it might come in useful.

'I understand, Herr Director,' I answer in my most fawning voice. I see Richter smile. It's not a pretty sight.

I seem to be spending more time asleep than awake, but as the pain in my head and body clears, I realise there is no point giving anyone the impression I'm fully recovered. I still have to wear a neck collar, but they tell me that is a precaution. The sooner I'm completely well, the sooner I will be back in the daily grind of the workshop. I have only Richter's word that Beate is alive, and I won't believe that until I see it with my own eyes. I don't even understand how I survived with just a jarred neck and bruises.

My next visitor is another teacher. Herr Müller.

'Thank you,' I say to him.

'For what?' he asks.

'For the b—' His eyes dart to the side urgently, and I see the nurse sitting there and manage to stop mid-sentence. I don't think she notices. 'For coming to see me,' I say.

He grins. 'I'm glad I've got the chance,' he says. 'That was a very, very stupid thing to do. Brave, but stupid.'

'I still don't understand how I survived.'

'We saw you about to fall, and we also saw that Beate had grabbed onto the downpipe. We'd piled up mattresses under Beate's likely trajectory. Literally a few seconds before you fell, the fire brigade had readied their rescue net. They managed to move it a couple of metres under you. You still fell very heavily onto it. But the doctors say there is no lasting damage. You'll be fine.'

'Thank you,' I say again. He seems such a kind man. A bit bookish. A bit owlish. I still cannot fully understand why he is here working at Prora Ost.

'Unfortunately, I'm going to have to leave you now, Irma. I hope you and Beate will be OK.'

'Leave? You've only been here a couple of minutes.'

He smiles again. 'I didn't mean right now. I can stay a bit longer. What I meant was I'm leaving the *Jugendwerkhof*. Apparently, Neumann has recommended to the education authorities that I've seen the error of my ways and am a reformed character.' He lowers his voice. 'I think he just wants me out of the way. More trouble than I'm worth, which suits me fine.'

'I will miss your kindness. There's not a lot of it around here. Will you miss us?' I ask.

'I'll miss you, Irma. And Beate. Maybe one or two others. But to be honest, I shall be delighted to be back in Berlin. I'm a city boy at heart.'

He leans over, as though to kiss me goodbye, and as he does so, he whispers in my ear. 'Don't forget what it says in the book,' he breathes. 'I'm sure there's a way.' Then a small chaste kiss on my forehead, and he's gone.

21

February 1975. Day Nine.
East Berlin.

As they headed north through sparse Mitte traffic, the smell of the leather upholstery – together with Tilsner's extravagant use of aftershave – made for a distinctive aroma in the Mercedes. Müller savoured it. It made a change from the smoky redolence of lignite smog: the trademark odour of the Republic. The roads as far as the *Grenzübergang* Bornholmerstrasse and the Bösebrücke bridge were familiar to them both. After that, Müller would be map-reading their way through West Berlin, towards Schöneberg and the wedding car hire company.

As they approached the checkpoint, Müller saw the dyed-blonde major from Thursday's visit walk towards the Mercedes. She looked at it disapprovingly, as Tilsner scrabbled for the button for the electric window.

'Good morning, Comrade *Major*,' said Tilsner. It brought a smile from the frosty blonde officer.

'Good morning, *Unterleutnant*. The Ministry for State Security has approved your passage through, and we will be expecting you on your return. Do you know what time that will be tonight?'

Tilsner looked towards Müller, raising his eyebrows.

Müller leant in front of Tilsner, towards the open driver's window. 'I think it will be around one in the morning, Comrade *Major*. Something like that anyway. It's all detailed in the authorisation that was telexed through to you by the Ministry for State Security.'

The major gave an almost imperceptible nod of her head. 'Good. We will be waiting for you. Good luck.' With that, Tilsner hit the window switch and the glass rose silently and smoothly. He pressed the accelerator, and the car glided away. Müller dreaded to think how many more marks this car had cost than the Wartburg.

Müller looked out of the windows, comparing what she saw with her own eyes with what was marked on the map. They could have almost been anywhere in the Hauptstadt. The only difference was the style of street signs, more cars and trucks, and the actual makes of those cars. The ever-present Trabants, Wartburgs and Ladas from the East were nowhere to be seen.

By the time they reached the wedding limousine hire company in Schöneberg, Müller had reappraised her snap judgement that the West looked pretty much like the East. Their route had taken them to the west of the Spree, swinging further west through Tiergarten, and then – just to see first-hand what they'd already seen in the photo of Silke Eisenberg – Müller directed Tilsner on a small detour to take in the exterior of the Kaufhaus des Westens. Tauentzienstrasse reminded her of the Paris boulevards she'd seen on western TV and in magazines, the throng of Saturday shoppers making her feel almost claustrophobic, even though they were safely ensconced in the comfort of the Mercedes.

Tilsner took one hand off the wheel to point out of the windscreen towards a high-rise building with a revolving silver emblem on top. 'The Europa Centre, commonly known as the Mercedes Building. That's the Mercedes logo spinning round.' To Müller it looked ostentatious, unnecessary. A symbol of the economic power of the West perhaps, but also a sign of the West's glorification of business and the business of making money.

Ignoring the road signs, Tilsner made a U-turn, so they could have another look at the KaDeWe from the southern side of the street. Müller marvelled at all the fashions in the window displays. She remembered that the KaDeWe was on the list of required shops they had to visit. She felt something akin to excitement, and then chastised herself. Those who could afford all this – who had they trampled on to reach the top of their businesses? At least east of the protection barrier, for all the shortages, they were trying to build a fairer way.

Once they had reached Schöneberg, the hire company was relatively easy to find and all the documentation was ready for them to sign. Tilsner showed his fake papers and handed the salesman the hire amount and deposit in Deutschmarks from the envelopes Jäger had given them. He did it all with the smoothness of someone who was used to this level of duplicity, betraying none of the nerves that Müller herself felt. It reinforced her suspicions of earlier that morning. There was far more to Tilsner than met the eye.

Her deputy was wearing gloves just in case the previous hirers had left fingerprints, but as it was winter, that didn't attract the suspicion of the hire company staff. Müller very much doubted the person – or people – they were hunting had been stupid enough to leave prints. But maybe – if the murdered girl had still been alive by the time she was in the car, *if* indeed she had ever been in the car – they might find something to establish her identity.

She reluctantly climbed into the driver's seat of the Mercedes, and then followed Tilsner and the limousine out of the car park, after first warning him to drive slowly. After initially struggling with the unfamiliar gearstick and controls, she managed to keep pace with him round the ring road, before turning east at Westend. They cruised along Spandauer Damm, then Charlottenburg Palace emerged on their left. Müller risked a quick glance away from the road when they stopped at the traffic lights. It was a symbol of great wealth, of privilege, of everything the Republic was fighting against, but as she turned into Schlossstrasse where their hotel was situated, Müller had to admit the palace – with its central copper-domed tower, red-tiled roof and wing upon wing of sumptuous cream stone – was a beautiful building. Whoever had commissioned it, privileged or not, certainly had good taste.

In the hotel, things took a strange turn. They'd agreed to have a couple of hours' rest before setting off to buy the items on Jäger's shopping list. Müller's room looked out onto Schlossstrasse, and the angry repeated beep of a car horn drew her to the window. She edged back the curtain a fraction, and saw the Volvo limousine pulling out of the space where Tilsner had parked it. For an instant, she wondered if it was being stolen. She knew rates of car theft were higher in the West – or so *Neues Deutschland* claimed. But then she recognised Tilsner at the wheel, laboriously trying to manoeuvre his way out of the space. That was what had attracted the ire of other drivers. Where was he taking the vehicle, and why? Was she wrong about his loyalty to the Republic – could he even be using this as an opportunity to defect?

She picked up the hotel phone and asked reception to put her through to Tilsner's room. No answer. She wasn't expecting one.

She decided the best policy was to say nothing. If he wasn't aware she knew he'd slipped away, it might be to her advantage. Turning away from the curtain, she moved to the bathroom and ran a hot bath – adding dollop after dollop of bubble bath. Müller slipped out of her new western clothes, the ones Jäger had given her from the bag in his car, enjoying their silky feel on her skin as they fell to the tiled floor. She smiled to herself. Some decadent western luxury, it was what she needed.

22

As he'd gone to get the newspaper, Gottfried had noticed the bread van parked on the other side of the street. It had seemed out of place. And the name of the bakery was unfamiliar.

He'd already been exhausted by the constant rowing with Karin. Now it felt as though his whole world had disintegrated. He'd meant to get up early, to see her off and perhaps mend some proverbial fences. Instead, she had left on her secret weekend mission without saying goodbye, and he hadn't woken. The row would now fester in her mind, just when he needed her most.

It was about ten minutes later, when Gottfried was settling down to do some school marking, munching on a fresh *Brötchen*, that all hell broke loose. A hammering sound on the apartment door made him look up in shock.

'Who's that? What's going on?' he shouted, through a mouthful of bread. In the back of his mind, he already knew. His transfer to Rügen had been a warning. A warning he'd ignored.

As he got up to move towards the door to open it, he realised he didn't need to bother. With a splintering sound, the door burst open and half a dozen leather-jacketed men surrounded him. Pinning his arms. Cuffing his hands behind his back. Ignoring his frantic shouts and questions, and dragging him down the stairs.

'What are you doing?' he screamed. 'My wife's a police officer. She'll report you to the authorities for this.' As soon as the words left his mouth, he realised his threat was empty. For all he knew, Karin may have been already aware that this was going to happen. May have even ordered his arrest. It was a frightening thought.

One of the thugs yanked his cuffed arms further up towards his shoulder blades. The pain pulsed into his head.

'Keep quiet, citizen,' he hissed into Gottfried's ear. 'If you know what's good for you.'

Despite his desperate situation, Gottfried still found himself checking that no neighbours were watching as he was forced across the pavement towards a Barkas van – similar to the bakery van but a different colour, a different company name on the side. He didn't want anyone to see his shame, his humiliation.

The aroma of fresh bread from breakfast was still in his nostrils, the taste on his tongue. But they were instantly replaced by the smell of piss and shit as he was bundled inside and forced into one of several tiny holding cells in its rear.

The door to the cramped cell was slammed shut. Seconds later, he heard the engine roar to life. He was being taken somewhere. He just didn't know where, or why.

23

Day Nine.
West Berlin.

Oberleutnant Karin Müller found herself sweating inside her new western clothing provided by Jäger as she browsed the KaDeWe's shoe department. The skirt was wool, the blouse silk, the knickers and bra cotton – natural, expensive materials. On her, they just didn't feel right. Like a painting in an incongruous frame. And it didn't help that the heating inside the department store seemed to be on too high. She looked down at the fur-lined winter boot that the male assistant was levering her left foot into. Almost 300 marks' worth of footwear – the pair cost virtually the same as Müller's weekly wage.

'Would madam care to take a walk? Perhaps look at them in the mirror over there? They suit you very well.' Müller reddened at the man's compliment, but played the part and walked towards the full-length mirror. She was glad Tilsner wasn't here to add to her discomfort; they'd agreed to meet up later in the hotel in Charlottenburg, and meanwhile he'd gone to the sports department to buy some Hertha Berlin football paraphernalia from Jäger's shopping list.

She fussed with her hair in the reflective glass. It was hanging limp and greasy. Then her eyes moved down to the boots. Black suede, ending just below the knee, with grey fur turnovers. Over her shoulder she could see the assistant, waiting eagerly.

'I'll take them,' she said, smiling. The man returned her smile, but there was something about his that seemed unctuous and false. He just wanted the sale, she thought. That's what it's all about here.

Müller lay back on the hotel bed and stared up at the ceiling. She couldn't help feeling something was badly wrong when she'd been able to enjoy – if that was the right word – an afternoon's shopping in West Berlin's most iconic department store, while the dead girl she was supposed to be trying to identify lay in the cooler of the Charité Hospital mortuary. Could they, should they, be doing more in the Republic? Knocking door to door, on every apartment with a teenage girl the right age? But that would be a Sisyphean task. Reiniger and Jäger would never authorise such a campaign.

There was a rap on the door. Müller jumped up and opened it to find Tilsner dressed in various blue-and-white striped items. She ushered him in.

'Do you like it all? I've got the figure of a footballer, don't you think?'

Müller laughed at the too-tight replica Hertha Berlin football shirt. 'No, I don't.'

Tilsner attempted to flex his pectoral muscles. She just shook her head. He looked ridiculous. A blue-and-white knitted hat and striped scarf completed the ensemble. 'I feel a bit disloyal.

I'm a Dynamo fan, after all. I'd better not show Marius. I don't want him transferring his affection to a western club.'

Müller sat on the bed and said nothing. It was well known in the Hauptstadt that Dynamo was a Stasi-backed team, Mielke's pet project.

'So, what are we going to do to while away the time?' asked Tilsner. She watched him look at all her shopping bags. 'Shall we give each other a fashion show?'

Müller shook her head. 'No, let's not bother. I'm tired.' She rubbed her stockinged feet and then lay back on the bed again. 'I thought I might get some sleep, then we could perhaps go out and get something to eat?'

Tilsner shrugged. 'OK.' He laid his hand gently on her nylon-clad leg. 'You wouldn't like me to lie on the bed with you?'

Müller rolled her eyes and sighed. 'No, Werner. Just forget about that. I'm married. You're married. I'm your boss. You're supposed to be my deputy. Let's just keep it all straightforward. OK?'

Getting to his feet and stretching, Tilsner moved towards the door, and then met her eyes. 'OK, Karin. Have it your way.' He opened the door and slammed it behind him.

Müller let her head fall back on the pillow, and closed her eyes.

The strained atmosphere between the two detectives continued into the evening. Perhaps a pre-marriage tiff was authentic, and Tilsner had certainly lapsed into a morose sulk. When it came to paying the bill, they realised that between them they barely had enough of Jäger's cash left.

As they left the restaurant, Müller looked up at the neon advertising signs, flashing with false bonhomie, and the Mercedes building's star. It rotated amid a fluorescent glow, casting eerie flickers into the night sky.

Back in Charlottenburg, they packed their respective purchases into the limousine and the Mercedes.

'Will you be OK driving the Mercedes at night?' asked Tilsner, a sullen note in his voice.

'I'm sure I'll be fine. I'll follow you. Just don't go too fast and keep a look out in the rear-view mirror.'

They began the return journey, car horns sounding regularly as Tilsner attempted to negotiate the traffic. Müller kept as close as possible to the rear lights of the Volvo. It was all very well driving an unfamiliar vehicle in the daylight, but it was already well past one in the morning. She knew the Hauptstadt would be virtually traffic-free by this time, but here in the West it was still surprisingly busy. Jäger had been mistaken in his insistence that it would be quieter after midnight.

Soon after they turned onto the ring road at Westend and began to head north, Müller got the sense that they were being followed. The headlights of the car behind were on full beam, alternately coming right up to the rear of the Mercedes and then dropping back again. She tried to ignore them, and flipped the tab on the rear-view mirror to its anti-glare position.

Then the car behind pulled out, and she was conscious of it directly alongside her, so close that it felt as though the two cars would touch at any moment. Müller took her foot off the accelerator slightly. The car alongside did the same. She risked a glance across. There was a man with sunglasses, gesturing at her to pull over. It didn't look like a police car. She tightened her grip on the steering wheel, trying to stop her hands shaking. She was determined to ignore the other driver and just concentrate on the Volvo's rear lights.

Suddenly a crash. The other car had buffeted into her, and she felt the Merc's steering wheel torn from her grip. Müller fought to control the unfamiliar car. Then another crash. She saw sparks flying. Heard the groans and grinding of metal tearing against metal. The Merc's wheels slid, whiplash threw her forward and her body jolted against the seat belt. Then … nothing. Just the hiss of the radiator.

Disorientated, Müller switched off the engine. She felt pain from her left breast where the seat belt had cut into it, but otherwise seemed unhurt. She opened the driver's door and climbed out. Immediately, she was dazzled by onrushing cars, blaring their horns but failing to stop. She flattened her body against the side of the car and then edged round to the front. Steam rose from under the bonnet. Müller tried to investigate the passenger side but the car was wedged tight against the crash barrier, the front wing dented where it had hit. Tilsner and the other car had already disappeared to the northeast, around the ring road. No sign of either of them. She looked the other way: blue lights and sirens in the distance. *Scheisse!* Then she realised a vehicle was pulling into the hard shoulder behind her. She shielded her eyes from the glare, momentarily blinded, and thinking in that split second that she now knew exactly how a rabbit in the headlights felt. Paralysed. Thinking that perhaps she should run, rather than stay and meet her fate.

'Are you OK, Karin? What happened?'

It was Tilsner! She ran forward, and crushed him in a hug.

'Thank God!' she said. 'I thought the others had returned.'

'The others? What do you mean?'

'You didn't see the crash?'

'No. I just realised that you'd stopped following me. I thought I'd better double back and check you were OK. Are you?'

Müller was conscious that he was patting her, rubbing her back. It was the first time she'd known him to touch her in a platonic way. She breathed in deeply.

'I think so,' she replied, finally. 'But I'm not sure about the car. Someone deliberately forced me off the road. It was terrifying. You didn't see them? A black car? A man with sunglasses?'

He shook his head. 'I'm afraid not.' He looked at the Mercedes doubtfully. 'We need to try to move it before the police spot us, even if we have to tow it back with the limo.'

Tilsner asked her for the keys; she gestured with her eyes to indicate they were still in the ignition. He climbed in, started the car and then shouted from the door. 'Mind out of the way. I'm going to try and reverse.' She heard him rev the engine, then a groaning sound, and finally the tearing of metal as he forced the car away from the barrier. Well, most of the car. Part of the wing had come free and was still stuck at the roadside.

He climbed out, yanked the torn-off metal away from the barrier and then put it in the car's boot. 'It's still driveable ... I think.

Do you want me to drive it and you take the limo? Only this time don't have any tangles with imaginary assailants.'

'I wasn't imagining it – they tried to force me off the road. Who do you think it was?'

'I don't know. Look, if you want, I'm happy to say I was driving. I get on well with Jäger. We know each other from way back. He won't hold it against me.'

Müller said nothing, but gave a small nod.

After a few near misses, Müller successfully negotiated the limousine to the Bösebrücke and the *Grenzübergang*. The western police just waved them through. On the eastern side, the dyed-blonde major was nowhere to be seen. But when Tilsner – ahead in the mangled Mercedes – flashed their authorisation, they were immediately let through.

Müller felt a definite sense of relief as they entered the Hauptstadt. This was home. This felt right. The after-effects of shock from the crash were lifting. It was somehow less tense away from the freneticism of the West.

By the time they had delivered the limousine to Schmidt at police headquarters and debriefed Jäger over the phone about the Mercedes, it was nearly two in the morning. Müller wondered if she ought to go straight back to the Schönhauser Allee apartment, and try to make her peace with Gottfried. If she let the tensions between them fester then a break-up was inevitable. Was that what she really wanted? To throw away her marriage? She glanced at her watch again. The trouble was, given the time, he would be fast asleep and in no mood to be wakened. She couldn't face another argument.

Müller made up her mind. She asked Tilsner to take her back to the office in Marx-Engels-Platz. It would be the emergency blankets and pillow from the cupboard, then an early start. She would work the Sunday. The way things were, it seemed easier than returning home.

In the office, she allowed herself one reminder of the West. She piled the shopping bags on the long table, under the noticeboard, and then lifted out the large shoebox that contained the boots. She opened it, and peeled back the protective tissue paper. Then she removed one boot, and caressed the fur-lined top, as though stroking a cat. A small touch of luxury. Then she looked up at the photographs pinned to the noticeboard. The dead, nameless girl. The girl without teeth. The girl without eyes.

Müller dropped the fur-lined boot as though it was infected.

24

Day Nine.

The near total blackness and smell of urine and faeces closed in on Gottfried Müller. The movement of the vehicle jolted his body from side to side, up and down, the bile of panic and nausea rising in his throat. He made to reach with his hand to try to cover his mouth, fighting with the steel cuffs that chafed at his wrists. But there wasn't enough room to move.

Taking a long breath of the putrid air, he tried to stand from his contorted half-sitting, half-crouching position, but gave up as his body pressed against the walls, the floor and the roof. It was like being in an upright, foreshortened coffin, a space less than a metre square in width and depth, and perhaps a little over a metre and a half high.

He thought of Karin. Was his arrest – if that was what it was – connected with their fractured relationship? Had she finally had enough of his accusations of infidelity and reported him to the authorities for anti-state activities?

Already it felt like they'd been driving for hours, his sense of direction destroyed by turn after turn. Acceleration, deceleration.

Stop. Start. Banging him around like the contents of a washing machine drum, with no way of seeing outside to check where he was. From the length of the journey, it must be somewhere far from Berlin.

Light! Blinding, piercing white light, but he had no way of shielding his eyes. The vehicle had stopped, the doors opened, the smell of diesel and exhaust neutralising for an instant the odours of out-of-control body functions.

'*Raus! Raus! Hände hoch!*'

Guards in East German military uniforms were manhandling him, jabbing him, forcing his arms upwards. Still in the Republic, then. The journey had seemed so long, so disorientating, he hadn't been sure – thinking perhaps he was being taken as far as Poland, as far as the Soviet Union. He tried to keep his hands raised in front of his face to protect himself from the glare of row upon row of strip lights shining on dazzling white walls. They were in some sort of garage.

Then the guards were pushing him in the back, ignoring his questions, as they manoeuvred him through an iron-grilled door. A red light in an empty corridor. He was shoved into a cell, the clang of metal on metal, and then maximum darkness.

What have I done? What am I supposed to have done? Shout it out! Tell them!

'Guards, guards! I demand you tell me why I'm here!'

No response. Not even an answering echo from the walls, because the shouts just seemed to have been sucked into them. He began to feel around in the silence. The walls were soft, padded. He tried to orientate himself, searching with his hands, shifting them along an arm's length at a time. No corners. He couldn't even decipher where the door had been. A never-ending circle of cushioned pads in the blackness. His nose pressed against one, he breathed in the sweet smell of rubber like one of the glue-sniffing addicts he'd seen on the West German TV news.

Exhausted, mentally and physically, Gottfried slumped down in the middle of the freezing concrete floor. He had never felt so alone. The temporary exile to the *Jugendwerkhof* on Rügen last year had been bad enough, but nothing like this. Was this how those children felt? Was that what had driven Beate to attempt suicide? He wondered how they were. Had Irma ever acted on his suggestion about the route from Sassnitz to Sweden? Maybe that was it … Maybe the book had been discovered and traced back to him.

Sleep. Sleep. Sleep had never felt so wonderful. A release from the nightmare. He thought of Karin. He longed for her. The younger Karin. The one he'd married. How it once had been for them. Not how it had recently become, with her career taking over her whole life.

After several hours in the padded room they'd finally moved him to what appeared to be a more regular cell. A bench for a bed. A blanket. Even heating. A window, or something approximating it, constructed of translucent glass bricks. Shafts of light from the night of whichever town or city they were in entered feebly, though he could see no detail through the rippled glass.

He rolled onto his side, pulled the blanket over his head and drifted in and out of sleep.

Then light. Piercing white light again, from a square hole above the door.

Verdammt! He'd only been dozing a few minutes, then this. He counted to ten. The light was extinguished, and Gottfried turned onto his side again, doubled the blanket up. Counted to sixty. To a hundred and ten. Then the light again. Controlled from the outside. Tormenting him. On, off, on, off, but the doubled-up blanket worked and he finally managed to drift off again.

Then a metallic clang as the hatch was pulled down. A fat-faced female guard screamed through the hole.

'Hands off the blanket. Blanket off your face. Lie on your back!'

Gottfried was too exhausted to ask why, or where he was, or what he was supposed to have done.

25

Eight months earlier (June 1974).
Jugendwerkhof Prora Ost, Rügen.

I had two weeks' respite in the sanatorium, but Beate's attempted suicide had made me even more determined to find a way out of this hateful place – for myself and for her.

Today is the first of my three days in the packing room this month. We're still working on the bed contract, and as I lean down to start to fill another box I feel my neck spasm. The pain shoots down my back to my leg. I'm almost tempted to raise my hand, to try to convince Frau Schettler that the symptoms of my fifth-floor fall haven't completely gone away. But instead, I fight through it, lifting the veneered headboard and sliding it in place at the bottom of the box.

All the time, I'm calculating. Thinking. Watching.

'You're very quiet today, Irma,' says Mathias softly, to my left. 'Is something on your mind?'

I don't look at him, just shake my head. I don't want anything to disturb my concentration. I need to reach my target as soon as possible, and then exceed it. Make them think I'm a reformed pupil, that I'm knuckling down and have seen the error of my ways. That way they will watch me less. It will give me a better chance.

The frame of the box is complete. It seems a slightly crazy system to me, but then I'm not a self-build furniture designer. All the components are in one box, which is why – when fully packed – they need two of us to lift them onto the trolley. I can only imagine a truck delivers them to each home at the other end, because there is no way they would fit in a standard-sized car, and no way that one person alone could lift them.

The headboard and footboard slide into the top and bottom of the cardboard box, giving strength to the structure with the bed's sides supporting them. When constructed I imagine they will be just under two metres square, bigger than any bed I've ever seen in the Republic.

I slide the second side into the box. There's now a hollow area in the middle, where we must fit all the bed slats, the corner posts and the fitting accessories, after putting in more layers of corrugated cardboard to protect the veneer.

Glancing around to make sure all the other children are busy working, I drop the roll of packing tape onto the floor and then lean down as though to pick it up. In an instant, I place the roll upright, so it forms a small wheel, and then stand up straight again. I wait a moment, making sure no one has noticed anything amiss. Frau Schettler, at the front of the room, is looking down at her desk, checking some document or other. Mathias to my left and Maria Bauer to my right are busy packing their own boxes. I give the wheel of tape a kick, and it shoots inside the hollow of the box. It's a shot that Hans-Jürgen Kreische, the *Oberliga*'s top scorer, would have been proud of.

'*Scheisse!*' I cry.

'What's wrong?' asks Mathias, ignorant of my little piece of trickery.

'I've accidentally knocked the packing tape into the box,' I say.

'You idiot,' says Bauer. 'I'll need that in a moment to seal this one. Just reach down and get it.'

I kneel down and scrabble around for a moment. Then peer inside.

'I can't see it. It's gone right inside.'

Mathias sighs. 'Well, you need to get it otherwise we'll all fall behind target. Can't you just crawl in?'

'I'll try,' I say, sounding as reluctant as possible.

In fact, with the smooth veneer of the wood, I can slide in. I get on my back and lever myself inside. I feel the tape roll behind my head, about halfway inside. But I continue to squeeze in, taking the tape with me to the back of the box. I just wish I was thinner. Beate would have no problem and plenty of space. Mathias is thin enough but too tall, so he'd have to bend his legs slightly to get fully inside.

Then I hear Frau Schettler's voice. She's been alerted by all the commotion.

'What on earth are you doing, Irma?' I squint back towards the open end of the box, and see a pair of eyes staring back at me.

'Sorry, Frau Schettler. The packing tape's accidentally rolled inside. I'm trying to get it back.' I scratch my fingers against the veneer of the headboard for effect.

'Well, hurry up,' she urges. 'And make sure you don't damage anything.'

She moves away, and I just lie there thinking for a moment. Thinking and calculating. It's risky. Horribly risky. What would you do about air, food, drink? Going to the toilet? Yuck! But it is possible. I've proved that to myself.

I contort my arm behind my head to grab the tape roll, and then flex my heels to pull myself out of the box, centimetre by centimetre.

The heat rushes to my face as I stand back in position, and I'm breathing heavily.

'That was really idiotic,' sneers Bauer. 'If we don't reach our target, it's your stupid fault. You're so clumsy, Behrendt.' I want to say something vicious back; I want to stuff the packing tape into her ugly mouth. But instead I just apologise, look embarrassed and get on with my work.

I speed up, filling the boxes like a machine. Inside my head I'm planning and thinking. Of Sassnitz. Of Sweden. Of freedom.

26

The jangling of the phone cut through Müller's skull, which throbbed with another headache. A strong sense of déjà vu – wasn't this how it all had started ten days earlier at Tilsner's apartment? She looked at the clock. Just past seven. She'd had less than five hours' uncomfortable, broken sleep on the floor of the office. Now every part of her body ached. She yawned, covering her mouth from habit though no one was watching, and then picked up the receiver. It was Schmidt.

'Ah, Comrade Müller. I'm glad I've tracked you down,' he said. 'I tried your home but there was no answer.' Gottfried had probably turned over and covered his ears with the blankets, thought Müller, just as I was tempted to. 'We've found a few bits and pieces in the limousine. Lucky, really, because the vehicle had been pretty thoroughly cleaned. I'm testing them now.'

She forced herself to sound interested and awake. 'That's good, Jonas. What have you got?'

'Well, the most important thing is that – as we suspected – the tyre pattern matches those we found at the cemetery. Gislaveds, as I said. But there's more, Comrade *Oberleutnant*. Cleaning never erases everything, in my experience. We've found grains of what looks like sand, and some vegetable matter that I'm trying to pin down at the moment. Also soil samples and clothing fibres. I've done an initial check: some of the fibres match the girl's clothing, some don't.'

'So we know the girl was definitely in the limousine?'

'I don't think we can say that with any certainty. The fibres could have come from someone else. Someone wearing similar clothes. It's a start, though. Why don't you come along to the lab in a couple of hours? I can show you how the tests are progressing.'

Müller slowly pressed her hand to her brow, trying to push away the thud of pain. She wasn't really in any state to spend hours in a lab. Perhaps she'd be better going back to the apartment and trying to make her peace with Gottfried. But then she wasn't in much of a state for that either. 'Don't you want to get some sleep first, Jonas? You've been at it all night.'

The *Kriminaltechniker* laughed. 'This is what I joined up for, what I trained for. I think this could be our breakthrough. Shall I see you in a couple of hours?'

'OK, Jonas, OK.' Dealing with the forensic officer and what he'd found would be easier than going back to confront her husband. Müller rang off. Before she left for the police headquarters, she raided a couple of aspirin from the first-aid cupboard, and then crossed to the sink. Picking the cleanest-looking mug from the draining board, she swilled it out, half-filled it with water and then dissolved the pills and drank the mixture. Just as Schmidt needed his regular intake of sausages to function properly, she seemed more and more these days to be relying on headache pills.

By the time she reached the forensic lab, Schmidt was hunched over a microscope issuing instructions to a colleague. After repeatedly peering through the lens, he was comparing his findings with a series of reference books that the other officer ferried to him.

'Ah, *Oberleutnant* Müller. Thanks for coming. I think we have some new information for you. And can I introduce you to Andreas Hasenkamp here, from the Ministry for State Security? *Oberstleutnant* Jäger sent him to assist us.' In contrast to Schmidt's corpulence, Hasenkamp was rake-thin, with incongruous bushy sideburns on an otherwise near-bald head. Müller shook his proffered hand, while she wondered just what Jäger's definition of 'assist' meant in practice.

Schmidt ushered her towards a microscope. She could see a slide under it, which even without magnification looked like a piece of seaweed. Müller closed her left eye and squinted down the eyepiece with her right. 'OK, Jonas. It still looks like a piece of seaweed, only bigger.'

Schmidt laughed. 'Absolutely correct, Comrade Müller. What's interesting, though,' he continued, 'is the type of seaweed. Look here at this book, and then look in the microscope. Similar, no?'

Müller nodded, though she wasn't sure. 'What species is it?'

'Well, the species in the book you're looking at is *Fucus vesiculosus*, more commonly known as bladderwrack.' Müller shrugged. The Latin meant nothing to her, though she had at least heard of the common name. Schmidt had one eyebrow raised and was smiling. 'But the species under the microscope is slightly – but significantly – different, and I'm rather pleased with myself that I've spotted the variance. It's *Fucus radicans*. It looks very similar to the naked eye.' Müller noticed that Schmidt was rushing his words, barely stopping to take a breath. 'But this species is smaller, despite the magnification of the microscope. Now, you find bladderwrack all over seashores in the northern hemisphere so that wouldn't have helped us much. But you only find *Fucus radicans* in one place.'

'Where?' asked Müller.

'In the Ostsee, Comrade Müller. It's specifically adapted for the brackish waters there. Water that doesn't have as high salinity. A mixture of salty seawater and fresh water from the inflowing rivers.'

Müller frowned. 'We could be talking about the northern coast of the Republic: Denmark, Sweden, the Soviet Union – anywhere that has an Ostsee coastline.'

Schmidt's face fell momentarily. 'That's true, *Oberleutnant*. But what we're trying to do is build up a picture. It's like a jigsaw puzzle or a crossword. Once we have enough pieces fitted together, or words in their correct place, the rest of it will follow.'

The detective nodded. 'What else have you got?'

'Andreas has a sample set up on the microscope over there.' Schmidt gestured to a side table. 'Comrade Hasenkamp, perhaps you could talk the *Oberleutnant* through that?'

'With pleasure. This way Comrade Müller.' He drew up a chair for her by the second microscope. Müller looked down the eyepiece, but what she saw was meaningless to her. It just looked like a beige smudge within a brown smudge. 'What's that?'

'Yes, I'm afraid it's not as clear-cut to the untrained eye as our other sample,' said Hasenkamp. 'But what you're looking at is a sample of soil containing an undeveloped seedling from a subalpine zone.'

Müller lifted her head, and rubbed her chin. 'So from the Alps?' She sighed. 'Another very wide area.'

'Well it could be from the Alpine area, from just below the treeline. That's what we mean by subalpine. But in this case it isn't. It's from that altitude, but this type of soil combined with the subalpine seedling is only found in one place in Europe, if not the world.'

'Put me out of my misery,' said Müller.

Hasenkamp smiled. 'It's the Harz mountains.'

'But that could be the DDR or the Federal Republic?'

'Not in this case. We can pinpoint the location very accurately. The only place in the Harz that could produce a subalpine seedling like this is the Brocken, which is more than 1,100 metres high. And, of course, it's in the Republic.'

Müller visualised the mountain. She'd never been there, but she'd seen pictures at school. At its summit, the Republic's main listening station – intercepting enemy messages from the West.

'Good work, both of you,' she said. 'But the Ostsee and the Harz are hundreds of kilometres apart.'

Schmidt exhaled slowly. 'I know, Comrade Müller. I know. But I'm afraid your job is to stitch these clues together. However, don't despair. There are also the fibres, and there's a theory I'm working on there that may just take us forward.'

Müller frowned. 'What's that?'

'Oh, I don't want to say before I'm sure. I need to do some more work, but it won't take long. If you'd be so kind, Andreas and I have been working all night. A coffee and perhaps a sandwich from the canteen would help our thought processes. Would that be possible?' Schmidt grinned.

'OK, Jonas, OK. Can you show me to the canteen, Comrade Hasenkamp?' She had no faith in her own abilities to find it through the warren-like corridors of police headquarters.

'With pleasure, *Oberleutnant*. It's open on Sundays. As you know, the headquarters of the People's Police never shuts.'

27

Day Ten.
East Berlin.

As she approached her Schönhauser Allee apartment building, Müller noticed that the Bäckerei Schäfer van had finally left – the streetlight it was normally parked by was simply illuminating an empty stretch of road. The mystery of who owned the vehicle remained unsolved. Elke had checked the small bakery of the same name on Alexanderplatz, but they just sold bread and cakes in situ. They didn't even have a delivery van. Anyway, it had gone. Was she being paranoid? The strange agent who'd turned up at the Märchenbrunnen, watching her and Jäger. The attempt to kill – or at least frighten – her by whoever was driving the black car round the West Berlin ring road. Everything seemed to be closing in on her.

The sense of foreboding she felt increased further once she'd climbed the stairs to the landing outside her and Gottfried's apartment. Something was wrong. There was no noise – normally Gottfried could be heard singing along to one of his infernal western rock tracks, oblivious to what the neighbours might think. Especially at the weekend, on a Sunday evening, when he almost always stayed in the flat.

A tingling feeling in her neck prompted her to turn round. Frau Ostermann's door opposite clicked closed. *Why was she nosing about again?* And what was the smell? New paint? Had the decorators been in the lobby? On a Sunday? She touched the door just to reassure herself, even though she could see the usual old scuffmarks where the green had flaked away. Unnerved, she turned the key in the lock. It seemed stiffer than normal and as she opened the door the silence had her mind churning. Where was Gottfried? Her heart thudded in her chest as she rushed into the lounge. It was even messier than usual. Gottfried's school papers scattered over the table, a cold, half-drunk cup of coffee and a half-eaten *Brötchen*. She lifted the bread roll up, sniffing it, rolling it between her fingers. Beginning to panic, she looked for other signs of where her husband might have gone. His overcoat was still on the peg, his briefcase on the sofa and his reading glasses were on the table. It didn't make sense.

'Gottfried! Gottfried!' she shouted. No answer.

She checked the bedroom. Then the bathroom. No sign of him.

Against her better judgement, she went back out onto the landing and rang Frau Ostermann's bell. If anyone would know what had been going on, she would.

The door opened a crack, but Ostermann kept the security chain bolted.

'You didn't see my husband go out, did you, Frau Ostermann?'

'Some men came by.'

'Men? What sort of men?'

'That's not for me to say, Comrade Müller. You're the police-woman.' The woman didn't seem to want to meet her eyes.

'Were they workmen? There seems to be a smell of fresh paint, or something similar.'

'I couldn't tell you. As you know, I keep myself to myself. Will that be all?' The woman started to close the door, but as she did so, Müller jammed her boot inside. Frau Ostermann regarded it with a look of distaste.

'You're quite sure you didn't see my husband?' asked Müller, aware of the panic in her voice.

Then she heard her apartment phone ringing behind her. As she turned, Frau Ostermann immediately clicked her own door shut. Müller ran back into the apartment towards the phone, but when she reached it she made no move to pick up the receiver. Who were the men Frau Ostermann had mentioned? She was sud-denly afraid. Afraid of what the person on the other end of the line was going to say. The phone was still ringing. Müller slumped down on the sofa, and finally reached across to answer. It was Jäger.

'Karin?' he asked. There was a peculiar edge to his voice.

'Comrade *Oberstleutnant*. What can I do for you?' She tried to keep her tone light, despite her apprehension.

'We have a problem, Karin. We need to meet.'

'This evening?' asked Müller. 'I've only just got –'

'This evening. Immediately. Meet me in *Das Blaue Licht*, in Schwedterstrasse, in ten minutes' time.'

'But I've only –'

'Ten minutes, Comrade Müller. Don't be late.' The Stasi officer ended the conversation without waiting for confirmation from her. His abrupt, formal tone had done nothing to dispel her unease. She realised as she replaced the receiver that her right hand was shaking. She clasped it with her left, and gripped tighter and tighter until the pain finally overcame the tremors.

The temperature had fallen rapidly since dusk, and Müller felt the first flakes of a new snowfall melting on her face as she trudged down Schönhauser Allee and turned into Schwedter-strasse. It was almost refreshing; as with the colder temperatures, the usual Berlin smog had dissipated.

As she walked along, she tried to work out what was going on. Why did Jäger seem so angry? Was it connected to Gottfried's disappearance? Or maybe it was the damage to the Mercedes. That was the most likely reason, she told herself. Jäger had probably gone out on a limb to secure the car from the Main Intelligence Directorate – perhaps it had caused him acute embarrassment that it had now been returned badly damaged.

Or perhaps he wanted to talk to her about the evidence Schmidt had found in the limousine? The seaweed. The seedling. And then the two new breakthroughs Schmidt had made later in the day: firstly, some chalky white sand, with algae amongst it that again pointed to the Ostsee, and then, the woollen fibre. At first it seemed the few fibres that had survived the limousine's deep clean hadn't been particularly helpful. They were mostly polyester, common in all Republic fashions. But this sole woollen fibre, found late in the day, was what had got Schmidt most excited. Under the microscope, checking various books with Hasenkamp, he'd eventually managed to identify it as being from the rough-wool Pomeranian sheep. Very few of the breed remained – almost all on Rügen and the neighbouring island of Hiddensee.

So, a connection with Rügen – to the northern Ostsee coast. Perhaps she could persuade Reiniger and Jäger to allow her, Tilsner and Schmidt to go there to chase up the leads. Although Jäger didn't sound as though he was in the mood to be granting any favours. What about poor Gottfried? She couldn't go if he really was missing. Before she went anywhere, she would discover what had happened to her husband.

Schwedterstrasse itself was deserted. But as she neared *Das Blaue Licht*, the buzz of chatter, laughter and arguments grew into a roar. Müller used the reflective glass of the bar's window to check her make-up and hair, and then opened the door.

A fug of sweat, smoke and beer fumes enveloped her. Unusually for a Sunday evening, the place was packed. Müller had to fight her way through the mostly male bodies to get to the bar. If what Jäger had to say was so important, why had he asked to meet her here?

A man suddenly barged into her from the side. She stumbled as he apologised, and as she regained her footing she saw Jäger had sat himself in the snug, a small glazed side room in the corner of the bar. She fought her way through the throng – half-wishing the crowd could swallow her up – and opened the snug's door.

'Karin. Sit …' An unsmiling Jäger pointed to the chair opposite. He made no effort to get up in welcome. He had a half-bottle of schnapps ready opened on the table, from which he poured her a glass. Müller smiled, steeling herself, determined to ride out whatever problem the Stasi *Oberstleutnant* had discovered.

Jäger downed the schnapps in one gulp and slammed his glass back on the table. Müller took just her usual sip, then placed her near-full glass down too.

'I don't think you've been fully open with us, have you, Karin?' Jäger held her gaze.

'About what, Comrade *Oberstleutnant*?' Her mind raced. What was this about? All Schmidt's lab tests had been conducted in the presence of Hasenkamp, the Stasi forensic officer, so there had been no question of keeping anything from Jäger.

'About Gottfried, Karin. Your husband Gottfried.' At the sound of his name, Müller's courage evaporated. She took a deep breath, and tried to pull herself together. *Say nothing, give nothing away*.

She looked back at Jäger flatly. 'What about Gottfried?'

'Do you know where he is?'

Müller shrugged. 'It's the weekend. He may have gone to his parents. Or he could be out drinking with his mates and talking football.'

'Don't play games with me, Karin. I'm letting you run an important investigation. We both know I could have you removed just like that.' Jäger clicked his fingers.

'I'm sorry, Comrade *Oberstleutnant*.'

Jäger reached into his briefcase and withdrew a black-and-white photograph, which he passed to Müller. It showed Gottfried entering what appeared to be the doorway of a church.

'Do you know where that is?' It looked vaguely familiar, but Müller shook her head. 'What if I told you it's Gethsemane Church in Prenzlauer Berg?'

Gethsemane Church. Where Gottfried had been going for his church meetings. Both the police and Stasi knew that opposition elements were part of the congregation. She had warned Gottfried against attending, but he wouldn't be told.

Now Jäger reached into his bag again, from which he withdrew yet more photographs. He handed her the next one. It showed Gottfried, inside the church this time, in conversation with Pastor Günther Grosinski, who Müller knew was already under observation for anti-state activities.

Another photograph – this time of herself with Tilsner. On his and Koletta's bed in his flat. *Scheisse! What was this? Mein Gott!* Tilsner and her under observation, from a secret camera in his own family apartment. Courtesy of the Stasi, presumably on Jäger's say-so. It could wreck both their marriages, wreck both their careers. Clearly Werner wasn't the informer she thought he was, if the Stasi were spying on him too.

Her mind reeled, but she knew what was coming next, her hands shaking again as she reached to accept the final photograph from Jäger. There it was, the evidence. Lips locked with Werner, her hands all over him, his all over her, clearly trying to get under her *Vopo* skirt. Müller dropped the photo. She curled her fingers into her palms and dug her nails in, almost self-mutilating in an effort to stop her hands wiping the beginnings of tears from her face.

She looked up at Jäger, silently pleading.

'Your marriage is over, Karin,' he said, pointing to the final photo. 'As you yourself seem to have realised.' And then he jabbed at the photo of Gottfried with the pastor. 'But, more importantly, we cannot afford to have our leading *Kriminalpolizei* detectives consorting with enemies of the state. This has put me in a very difficult situation. Your husband is under investigation and for the time being you will not see him. It's not something I initiated but, equally, it's not something I can tolerate.'

'Can you at least tell me where he is?' she asked. Her voice sounded feeble, defeated.

'No, Karin. Not at present. In any case, you are leaving Berlin.' He reached into his bag again, and handed Müller a brown envelope. 'Railway tickets. You're booked on the early morning train to Bergen auf Rügen. Although the evidence Schmidt and Hasenkamp found is by no means conclusive, you, Tilsner and Schmidt still need to follow it up and see if it gets us any closer to identifying the dead girl. We've also had information through on the teleprinter from our local Ministry office in Bergen, which may or may not be connected: a complaint about a teenage girl that was referred to them by the People's Police. It's not much to go on, but added to the evidence Schmidt and Hasenkamp found ... well, I think it just about merits you going there. And at the present time, you being out of Berlin may be to your advantage, especially given what happened in the Mercedes last night.' Jäger paused and refilled both their glasses.

Once again, Jäger seemed to have inside information about what had gone on during their trip to West Berlin. 'I'm sorry about that, Comrade *Oberstleutnant*. Do you have any explanation for what happened?'

Jäger shrugged. 'Officially, no. But I can guess. It wasn't your fault. But I warned you when all this started – this was likely to be a difficult case. The incident in West Berlin proves it. There are people who would like this investigation shut down, closed. The official explanation for the girl's killing remains just that. Some people would prefer, I'm sure, that she is never identified; I am determined that she should be.' He met Müller's eyes and held her gaze. 'So, I hope, are you. But a People's Police detective with a husband who is engaging in anti-state activities will just give those who want the case closed more ammunition. So you will be going to Rügen for a few days. In the meantime, *Oberst* Reiniger and I will look after the case in Berlin.'

'Could I at least talk to Gottfried before I go? Or write him a letter? Something. Anything. He's not a bad man. I'm sure it's just a mistake.'

Jäger shook his head, a solemn look on his face. He was nothing like a western newsreader now, thought Müller.

'No, Karin. you will not be able to have any contact with your husband before you go. I need you to stay on the case, and that's incompatible with you being in touch with an enemy of the state. Especially one you're married to. On the way to Rügen you will have plenty of time to think about your future. Do you want to remain with the *Kriminalpolizei*, remain on this case, and perhaps in a few years' time get a promotion? Or do you want to stay with your husband, a criminal, and be thrown out of the force?'

Müller looked at the Stasi officer. In his other guise, he'd seemed so pleasant. At the cemetery, the Kulturpark, the Märchenbrunnen. She'd almost found herself trusting him. What a mistake that had been! Now she wanted to grab him. Tear at his clothes, tear at his face. Instead, she meekly put the envelope containing the train tickets into her handbag.

'You'd better get home and get some sleep. The train leaves at seven in the morning. Tilsner and Schmidt will be at the station to meet you.'

Müller cleared her throat. 'Does Tilsner know anything about this, Comrade *Oberstleutnant*?' She wasn't meeting Jäger's eyes. Instead, she stared at her hands, gripping the handle of her bag until her knuckles went white.

'About Gottfried being investigated? No, Karin, why should he?'

'I'd be very grateful if you could keep it that way, Comrade *Oberstleutnant*.'

'Of course. But let this be a warning. At this stage I intend to take no action in respect of your extramarital relations with one of your subordinate officers, but I want to emphasise how fortunate you are that I've decided to be lenient.'

Müller felt herself burning up inside. She wiped the sweat from her forehead. 'I assure you nothing really happened. It was a mistake, Comrade *Oberstleutnant*. It won't happen again.'

Jäger pursed his lips and nodded. 'Just so long as we understand each other.'

28

February 1975.
A Stasi prison, East Germany.

Morning, and natural daylight, brought Gottfried Müller some relief from the blinding electric light in the hole in the cell wall above the door, which had been turned on and off by the guards in some manic pattern throughout the night. The cell door opened briefly, and a metal washbowl was thrown inside, a hose pushed through the hatch, and then he was catching the water in it and savouring the refreshment of a first wash in twenty-four hours.

Day followed night, followed day, and no one spoke to him, told him what he'd done, or even where he was. He thought of Karin and wondered what she would know. Had she been arrested too? Had the school been told? Who would be taking his class?

On the third day the routine suddenly changed. There was no evening meal of stale bread and margarine, and no explanation why.

Night-time: light on, light off, on, off, on, off, every few seconds. He tried to get to sleep, but hunger gnawed at his stomach.

Finally, he dozed sporadically for what seemed just a few seconds at a time between the light's flashes. He was woken by the sound of keys being turned in the lock. A male guard roughly pulled him from the bed and cuffed their hands together. The metal bit into Gottfried's wrist. The guard might as well have been deaf and mute for the way he ignored all questions as they went along corridor after corridor, up and down staircases, and past red light after red light. They encountered no other prisoners and no other guards, and Gottfried could only conclude that the lights were some kind of warning system that the corridor was occupied by a prisoner – him. Finally, he was ushered into a room containing an officer in plain clothes, sitting behind a desk with a single telephone and typewriter. The guard uncuffed his wrist, and then shackled Gottfried's hands together before refastening the cuffs. He locked the door behind him as he exited, and the plain-clothes officer gestured at a stool. 'Sit, Herr Müller.'

Gottfried felt almost joyful at hearing his surname. He obeyed, and perched on the stool.

The officer looked up from the papers on his desk, and pushed his glasses back up his nose. 'I am *Major* Hunsberger. As you've probably guessed, I work for the Ministry for State Security.'

Gottfried stared back at Hunsberger. He wanted to ask so many questions. What was he supposed to have done? Why was he here? But although he tried to speak, nothing came.

'How is your wife Karin?' the officer asked.

The question momentarily confused Gottfried. Of all the things they might have asked, why were they talking about his wife? He struggled to form the words of his reply. 'I ... I ... I haven't seen her for several days.'

'No, no. I can understand that. You've been locked up here after all. But before that, how was she? How were relations between you two? Is it hard to keep a younger woman satisfied?'

Gottfried frowned – what was the Stasi man driving at? 'I don't understand. Why are you asking questions about my wife? Can you please just tell me why I'm here, get me a lawyer and release me?' He emphasised the point by slapping his hand on the table, causing the phone to jangle. Immediately, he regretted the flash of petulance. He needed to stay under control. There was no point riling Hunsberger unnecessarily.

The officer rose, wandered towards the window, then turned back towards Gottfried and held his gaze. 'You will understand quickly, Herr Müller, that *we* ask the questions here. Not you.'

'But –'

'Please let me finish, Herr Müller. I can assure you it is in your own interests. You are in a remand prison of the Ministry for State Security. You are fortunate that within less than a week, we have seen fit to interview you. That's mainly because your wife is an important detective in the *Kriminalpolizei* –'

'Yes, I know all that, but –'

'Herr Müller!' Hunsberger's sudden shout startled him. 'Sit down on the stool. Now. We have the power to keep you on remand for as long as we wish, and unless you cooperate you will be sent back to your cell, and we may not see fit to interview you for weeks … months … some people have been here years. Do I make myself clear?'

Gottfried's shoulders slumped. At the very least, he needed to know what was going on.

'I was asking you about your wife, Comrade Karin Müller. How has she seemed? How have you two been getting on?'

Where was this leading? 'We have our ups and downs – like any married couple. She's been very busy recently, because of the murder case ... It's a big thing for her.'

'Very busy, yes ... would you like to see a recent photo of your wife?'

Gottfried nodded cautiously, and Hunsberger passed him a black-and-white print. It was a photo of Karin with her deputy Werner Tilsner, lying side by side on a strange bed.

'She does look busy, doesn't she?' asked Hunsberger.

'What the hell is this, she wouldn't –'

Hunsberger handed over another photo. 'And even busier in this one, wouldn't you say? Of course you can't see exactly what her facial expression is. But her lips look ... busy.'

Gottfried stared at the photo open-mouthed. Karin and Tilsner. Together. Jaws locked in what was certainly not just a comradely kiss – their hands pawing each other. He dropped the photo to the floor.

'Is she a good kisser?' asked Hunsberger, a smirk playing on his face.

Gottfried, riled by the officer's mocking, leapt up. He attempted to strike the Stasi officer with his cuffed hands, but Hunsberger caught and gripped them tightly, making him wince with pain.

'Don't try it, Herr Müller. You'll regret it very much. Why don't you sit down there?' Hunsberger pointed at an armchair. Gottfried slumped down into it.

The Stasi officer picked up the phone and began talking rapidly into it. Then he replaced the receiver. 'You haven't eaten yet today, Herr Müller, have you? I've just ordered you some food. You will have a choice. Some of your favourite things. That will make a change from bread rolls and margarine, won't it?'

Hunsberger was smirking, rocking back on the two rear legs of his chair, his arms folded in front of him. Gottfried didn't reply. The question had been rhetorical.

A few moments later, a guard knocked on the door and brought in two plates of food, which he placed in front of Hunsberger. On the left, despite what the Stasi man had promised, more bread rolls, margarine and jam. On the right, *Gebackene Apfelringe* – Gottfried's favourite dessert, a speciality of Karin's. Apple rings in choux pastry with vanilla cream and raspberries. Something they could usually only obtain a few times a year, when raspberries were fleetingly in the shops. Gottfried could feel his mouth watering. He knew Hunsberger had seen his eyes drawn to the right-hand plate. He swallowed the saliva down.

'Just the way Karin makes it,' whispered the Stasi man, reading the teacher's thoughts. 'But first you must answer some questions, and then I will explain your choice. Look at this!' Hunsberger's tone had changed from syrupy bonhomie to ruthless efficiency in a second.

The Stasi officer handed him another photograph. Again it appeared to be from a surveillance camera, and Gottfried immediately recognised it as the sanatorium at *Jugendwerkhof* Prora Ost – somewhere he'd have been happy to never see again in his life. It showed him standing by Irma's bed, although the girl herself was obscured. He knew what was coming next – a photograph from a few seconds later. He knew it would show him kissing Irma on the forehead. But he was wrong.

'What the hell is this?' he screamed, dropping the photo back on the table. Gottfried recoiled from the image. It showed him apparently kissing a girl on the mouth, his hand mauling her breast. But the girl's face was not Irma's – it was Beate Ewert's.

'You tell me, Citizen Müller.'

Gottfried jumped up, picked the print off the table and began tearing it in two. 'This is a fake! A fake! I kissed a girl on the forehead. That girl was Irma Behrendt, whose life I'd just helped to save. But this monstrosity –' he threw the torn pieces of photo into the air, '– has been doctored to show me with a completely different girl. I certainly did not molest any of the girls.'

'The evidence says otherwise, Herr Müller. The evidence which you've just destroyed.' He bent to pick the torn pieces of photograph from the floor, and then started arranging them on the table like a jigsaw puzzle, until the image of Beate reappeared. 'But it's easy to put it back together, as you see. And we have copies.'

Hunsberger wasn't finished. He reached into a file and pulled out another set of photos. 'What I showed you in the *Jugendwerkhof* is of course very serious. But not as serious as this.' With a flourish, he passed the next photograph to Gottfried. The black-and-white print showed the teacher about to enter Gethsemane Church. 'You know where this is, don't you?'

Gottfried declined to answer. But yes, he knew. And he thought he knew when it had been taken, and suspected he knew who had taken it. That Tilsner bastard. The arsehole *had* been spying on him. Rather than look at the photo or the Stasi officer, he stared at his hands in his lap, watching the ends of his fingers shake. The next photograph was one of him with Pastor Grosinski.

'That man is under surveillance for alleged anti-state activities,' said Hunsberger. 'Yet here you are consorting with him.' Hunsberger now took two further pieces of paper from the file. They looked like official documents. He handed one to Gottfried. 'Could you read this, please?'

Article 96 of the DDR's constitution, highlighted in red marker pen. But Hunsberger read it out to him anyway from his own copy. 'This is the relevant part, Herr Müller.' He leant over and traced his finger along the red highlighting on Gottfried's copy. 'Whoever is convicted of undertaking to undermine the political or social order of the DDR can, in severe cases, be sentenced to death.'

Gottfried started to protest. 'What? I was just meeting a priest.'

'Who is going to believe you, a pervert who molests schoolgirls when they're ill in bed?'

'I didn't –'

'Silence!' Hunsberger moved the plate with the *Gebackene Apfelringe* to the centre of the desk. 'You'd better start telling us the truth, Herr Müller, otherwise it will be dangerous for you and your wife. We will question the relevant people, but it seems to me you are guilty and we will find the evidence to prove it. And the penalty, in the most serious cases, is the ultimate penalty.' Hunsberger rotated the plate of dessert so that the raspberries were under Gottfried's nose, but instead of continuing to make his mouth water, he could feel bile rising in his throat.

'Have a good look at this plate of food, Herr Müller. Before carrying out any death sentence, the prisoner is allowed to request a last meal.'

A flash of light. The entrance to Gethsemane Church. A flash of light. He and Grosinski deep in conversation. A flash of light. The photo of lips-locked Karin and Tilsner. A flash of light. The image of him kissing Beate, his hand on her breast. A flash of light. The blood-red raspberries, vanilla cream and puffed-up dough around the apple rings.

He pulled the blanket over his head, turned on his side, tried to hide from the ever-flashing light and the ever-present images. Ever since he had left Hunsberger and been led back to his cell, utterly defeated, the torment had begun again. But then came the rustle of keys, the clang of the door.

The fat-faced female guard was back. 'Hands off the blanket. Blanket off your face. And lie on your back!'

Same words. Another night. Another day. Another night. How many more before that last-ever plate of *Gebackene Apfelringe* would be brought to him? He thought of Karin. He didn't blame her for being tempted by Tilsner. He was sure that was just a mistake on her part, and he had been stupid and risked getting her into trouble, risked wrecking her career. If only he could talk to her; he was sure she would be able to clear this up and get him out of this hellish place.

29

Day Eleven.
The train to Stralsund.

Sleep last night had come fitfully for Müller, punctuated by various nightmares featuring Gottfried, Jäger, Tilsner and the girl's body on the autopsy table, all jumbled together in a montage of horror. Now, as she rocked from side to side with the motion of the train, her body craved a nap – but her brain, racing full of thoughts and theories, wouldn't let her. She glanced across at Tilsner and Schmidt on the other side of the aisle, heads slumped and snoring loudly.

Müller felt disloyal to Gottfried. Should she have refused to come to Rügen and have insisted instead that they allow her to visit him? She couldn't have done that without at least risking a reprimand.

Schmidt's progress in the lab, the clues from the car, all seemed to offer hope of a genuine breakthrough. But something nagged at her. If the limousine had been cleaned, as Schmidt maintained, why did this evidence remain? Evidence so clear-cut it almost felt as though it had been planted. If so, by whom?

The Stasi? After all, it was Jäger who was sending them up north to Rügen. But why?

She sighed and took a sip of the train coffee that Tilsner had fetched earlier from the buffet car. It was lukewarm by now, and its bitterness made her recoil. She reached for another sugar sachet and stirred it in.

The other major problem was that there were no reports of missing girls from either the Harz or Rügen – certainly none that fitted the dead girl's profile. There was just this single mysterious complaint about a teenage girl which had been referred to the Stasi. The one Jäger had mentioned in the bar. She'd even disturbed Tilsner's weekend by ordering him to go over all the files again. He'd found nothing, but had brought along the files for Müller to double-check.

She took the folders out of her bag. Three of them: one for each of the Republic's most northerly *Bezirke*: Rostock, Schwerin and Neubrandenburg. She started with Rostock, lifting it onto her lap and leafing through the pages. It was their best chance. The Rostock district included Rügen and all of the DDR's Ostsee coast.

The train rocked violently, and her coffee sloshed onto the dirty floor. Tilsner woke with a snort.

'Must have drifted off there, apologies,' he said, wiping his hand across his face. 'Mind you, you did get me to work on a Sunday.' She saw him peering over the folder she had in her hands. 'There's nothing there,' he said. 'I told you yesterday. Not a single girl matching the profile of our body.'

Müller continued to read through the files. There were older girls, taller girls, young women, men, pensioners. Many of them were marked as suspected *Republikflüchtlinge*, but Tilsner was correct – there was nothing matching the dead girl's profile.

'We need something else to go on, Karin. We need another lead.'

'What about if a girl *has* gone missing from Rügen. But it simply hasn't been reported, so it doesn't appear in these files?'

Tilsner rubbed his chin, which was now covered in several days' stubble. 'I don't see how that's possible. Surely the authorities would find out?'

Müller nodded. 'But it's not Berlin, is it? Say it was some remote farm. Maybe a domestic fight. Maybe a single parent, a farmer with a rebellious teenager. He goes loopy, strangles girl in a rage, dumps her body by the Anti-Fascist Protection Barrier in Berlin –'

'– and then goes to the trouble of shooting her in the back after she's dead, throws on a bucket of animal blood, and all to try to make out she's been shot from the West? And hires a limo in the West to try to point the finger at the authorities? And what about the rapes?' Tilsner shook his head. 'Sorry, that wouldn't make any sense at all.'

They fell silent. Müller knew he was right. She picked up another of the files and began to leaf through it. She couldn't concentrate and instead began to worry about Gottfried, before the motion of the train and Schmidt's rhythmic snoring started sending her to sleep too.

Müller slept virtually the entire remainder of the journey, and had to be woken by Tilsner just before Stralsund Hauptbahnhof

DAVID YOUNG | 201

and their change of train to Rügen, the Republic's largest island. As the new train crossed the Strelasund strait on the rail bridge from the mainland, Müller's initial impressions were disappointing. She was expecting a rural landscape, but the view was industrial – like many parts of the Republic. Only when they got further onto the island could she see the gently rolling landscape and farms that she'd imagined from her only previous visit to the Ostsee coast – the countryside she remembered from her honeymoon spent camping amongst the dunes of Prerow, further to the west. She remembered lusting over Gottfried's toned and tanned body. He didn't look like that now. The memory triggered an abrupt resurgence of guilt, and fear for her husband. Why was she thinking ill of him in his current predicament? She should instead be trying everything she could to help him. He'd been stupid getting involved with the church group, but he wasn't a bad man and the memories of their honeymoon reminded her that they had loved each other. In the early days, the early years, of the marriage.

At Bergen auf Rügen station they were collected by a *Volkspolizei* officer and taken to the local People's Police headquarters to be briefed on the arrangements that Jäger had made for them in advance.

They were led into a room at the back of the police station. '*Oberst* Drescher will be with you in a moment, Comrade Müller,' said the policeman, and left the three Berlin officers alone.

'Has Jäger sorted accommodation?' asked Tilsner.

'As far as I know, yes,' said Müller. 'That's what it said in his note with the tickets. They should be providing us with a car too.'

'Hmm. No doubt with one of their goons to accompany us everywhere.'

As Tilsner finished speaking, a side door opened, and in strode an officer in a police colonel's uniform. The three Berlin officers made to stand, but the *Oberst* waved them to remain seated.

'This is a pleasure, Comrade Müller. *Oberst* Marcus Drescher, of the Rügen People's Police. And these officers are –?'

Müller introduced Tilsner and Schmidt, and then Drescher urged them to move their chairs from the side of the room to a central desk. 'We've been told by the Ministry for State Security in Berlin to provide you with accommodation and transport, and that's something we're glad to help with. But I read about the case you're working on in *Neues Deutschland*. I thought the girl was supposed to have escaped from the West into the East?' The colonel was smirking slightly as he asked the question. 'It would appear now that that's perhaps not the case,' he continued. 'Are you now thinking the girl is from Rügen itself?'

'Possibly,' said Müller. 'Certain evidence discovered at the scene points to that, but it's just one line of inquiry we're following. However, it seems as though there are no girls missing from Rügen who match the dead girl's profile.'

'You've checked all the files?' asked Drescher.

'Yes,' interrupted Tilsner. 'I performed that fascinating task.' Müller frowned at his flippancy.

'What I was wondering,' asked Müller, 'is whether there might be anything short of a formal missing person's report that might be worth following up? You know the sort of thing: a neighbour gets suspicious about a family and reports them, or the police are called out to a domestic disturbance, or a girl's been beaten up or mistreated.' Müller already knew from Jäger that there was *something* worth following up. But she held that back initially. She wanted to test how open with his help and information the Rügen People's Police colonel was prepared to be.

Drescher shuffled forward, pulling his chair closer to the table. 'The trouble is that not all of those sorts of reports would come to us. Some would go to the local office of the Ministry for State Security, but then they would send them to Berlin, and no doubt your *Oberstleutnant* Jäger would have access to them.'

Müller nodded. It didn't look like Drescher was going to volunteer very much without further prodding. 'The Ministry has indeed informed us about one incident that was referred to them, a complaint about a teenage girl. We'd like to see any details on that, and anything else that may be relevant.' She watched Drescher's face for a hint of reaction. But he appeared as though he had nothing to hide.

'Of course, of course. I will get one of my officers to bring you the files. Off the top of my head I don't know about that incident, but the details should have been noted. You can go through them here, and then we will show you the car we're providing for you and give you directions to your accommodation. We've found you a place in one of the coastal resorts. I thought you'd prefer that to staying here in Bergen. It will be more comfortable for you, and more of a change from Berlin.'

The files were arranged month by month. They decided to look through a year's worth of entries initially. Müller took March to June of the previous year; Tilsner July to October; Schmidt started on the ones from November to the current month.

Müller leafed through the pages, quickly discarding irrelevant entries. Theft of a car. Theft of some wood. Someone who wouldn't repair their smallholding's fences so sheep kept escaping. A fight in a pub in Bergen. A fire which someone claimed had been started deliberately by a tenant to try to secure better accommodation.

'There's nothing here,' she complained. 'What about you two?'

'Nothing out of the ordinary in mine,' said Schmidt.

'Ha! This is a good one,' said Tilsner. He ran his finger under the words of the report, from left to right. 'Frau Probst of Am Hafen street in Gager rang up the People's Police station in Göhren complaining about children fishing from the pier. She said this was an anti-socialist enterprise and the police should either stop them or collectivise the activity.'

Müller sniggered. 'What was the recommendation?'

'No action required,' said Tilsner.

Müller was now on her final file, for June. The words 'no action required' drew her eyes to a similar recommendation in her file. She read through it. This was more promising. Tilsner noticed her rhythmic page-turning had paused.

'Have you got something, boss?'

'I'm not sure,' she replied. 'Maybe. It sounds like this could be the incident Jäger claims was referred to the Stasi. Citizen Baumgartner, manager of the state campsite in Sellin, attended the local police station to file a complaint after being denied access to her granddaughter. She says her granddaughter, Irma Behrendt, was injured in a fall at the closed *Jugendwerkhof* Prora Ost in May last year.' Müller shuddered inwardly at the name of the reform school. It was the one at which Gottfried had taught. Presumably just a coincidence. He hadn't mentioned a girl being hurt in a fall. She hoped the other two didn't notice her reaction – she didn't want Tilsner to know about Gottfried's stint there. She turned her attention back to the entry in the file: 'She was allowed to visit the girl in the youth workhouse when she was in the sanatorium, which was unusual, and she was very grateful. However, she was denied a follow-up visit.'

Tilsner turned the sides of his mouth down. 'It doesn't seem to amount to much, boss. What is a *closed* youth workhouse, anyway?'

'They're usually for the more problematic or rebellious teenagers, or those who've committed more serious offences. This and Torgau are the only "closed" ones – it just means the pupils are locked up there.'

'For what sort of offences? Running away from home?' suggested Schmidt.

'I think more serious than that, Jonas; maybe running away from a less strict children's home ... that sort of thing.'

'What was the recommendation?' asked Tilsner.

'No further action,' said Müller, looking at the bottom of the page. 'That's why I noticed it. It's like your child fishermen. So perhaps this isn't the one Jäger was talking about.'

'I don't know why he didn't just give us all the information himself. Why do we have to scratch around to find it all?' Tilsner looked over her shoulder. 'Hang on, it says, "please turn over".'

Müller hadn't noticed this at first. She turned the page. There was an addendum from *Oberst* Drescher. Müller read it out.

'He's written: "*Suggest we refer this complaint to Ministry for State Security*". She closed the file and turned to Tilsner.

'So it *is* the one Jäger seemed to imply was suspicious, although this doesn't actually say *why* a referral to the Stasi was necessary.'

Tilsner nodded. 'I think we need to pay Citizen Baumgartner a visit.'

30

Eight months earlier (June 1974).
Jugendwerkhof Prora Ost.

We begin our evening shift in the packing room at half past six. Everyone else who worked on drilling or cutting shifts is being allowed to watch the big game in the common room. Even though I hate what my country has done to me, what it's *doing* to me, I still want us to win. That would be such a big story and one in the eye for the Westlers. Ha! But tonight my thoughts are not really on the game.

We get to the workbench. I've got Beate to my left and Maria Bauer to my right. To Beate's left is Mathias. Every now and then I see them making puppy eyes at each other. I wonder if I should have let him in on our plan. Maybe a boy's strength would have been useful, but trying to get three of us out at the same time would be too dangerous. When I'd taken Beate aside in the communal toilets to explain it to her, she had looked scared enough. I know she is as desperate as I am to escape, even though it will mean leaving her boyfriend behind.

Then I look down at the packing materials and components and realise something is wrong. Horribly wrong. These are not double beds! It's kitchen cupboards again. Smaller boxes, smaller components. I look to my right. Bauer's are the same. To my left, though, Beate has the double bed kit we were expecting. And Mathias, too. To the other side of Mathias, an empty workstation.

I feel my skin tingling as sweat forms. *Don't panic*, I tell myself.

I put my hand up.

'Yes, Irma,' sighs Frau Schettler.

'Frau Schettler. We've got the wrong things to pack here. We've got the kitchen cabinets instead of beds.'

'Don't complain, Irma,' she says. 'Just get on with it.'

I rack my brain; I need to come up with an idea before the end of the shift. Turning my head to Beate, I wonder what she is thinking. There's a scared look on her face.

I work quickly. Box after box, ahead of target, just hoping that if I finish the kitchen cabinets, then I can ask to do more on the empty workstation, which I've seen also has double-bed parts waiting to be packed. But as I finish one cabinet, more kitchen components are wheeled to my desk in a never-ending cycle.

With less than half of the foreshortened evening shift to go, I make a last desperate throw of the dice. First I look left and right to make sure neither Mathias nor Bauer is looking. Then I run my hand under the wooden lip of the workbench, to check the chocolate bars and Vita Cola bottles we saved from weeks and weeks of pocket money are still safely taped underneath. I gently feel their shapes.

Then I raise my hand again.

'Can I go to the toilet, Frau Schettler, please?'

She purses her mouth, and breathes out slowly and ostentatiously. 'OK, Irma, but no sneaking off to the common room to see the match.'

'No, Frau Schettler, I promise.'

When I return, instead of going into the workstations from Maria Bauer's end, I enter at the empty end, next to Mathias. I move past him, between him and Beate, and then begin to whisper.

'Mathias. Move along one to your left. I need to be here.'

'Why? I want to be next to Beate.'

'Please, Mathias,' I hiss, hoping Schettler won't see the exchange and come over. 'I'll give you all my pocket money for this week.'

'All of it?' he asks, eyebrows raised.

'All of it,' I repeat. Little does he know I won't even be around to receive it. He shrugs and moves across. I see Bauer taking an interest, so I put my finger to my lips in the hope she won't give the game away. I can't believe it when she smiles back. But since my fall she has been friendlier to both Beate and myself.

With half an hour to go, I gently kick Beate's shin. That's our prearranged sign. I just hope she won't chicken out.

She raises her hand. 'Frau Schettler. I've finished. May I go and watch the game now?'

'Yes, Beate, you may.'

She makes to move off, but once Schettler has dropped her gaze back to her book, Beate ducks down under the workbench. There is a half-finished bed package that we stowed under there earlier in the shift. Maria sees it, Mathias sees it. I urge them both to keep quiet with my finger to my lips. Maria nods slightly, but Mathias is frowning.

I see Beate squeeze inside the box, sliding herself in a centimetre at a time. Accidentally on purpose, I drop the roll of packing tape and a ballpoint pen onto the floor. As I crouch down, I grab a chocolate bar and cola bottle and throw them in after her. Then I tear off two strips of tape, and seal up Beate's box, punching a couple of holes for air through the cardboard with the pen. Then I stand again, and my heart is in my mouth as I see Frau Schettler walking towards us.

'Are you nearly finished too, Irma? Maria? Mathias? Anyway, once you have finished you can all go and watch the game.' She looks down at the floor. 'I thought Beate said she'd met her target. She's left one completed box here.' She starts to reach down, as though to examine it. I feel my pulse racing.

Then Mathias pipes up. 'It's OK, Frau Schettler. Irma and I will load it onto the pallet for her, won't we, Irma?' I just nod. Schettler rises without paying the box further attention, and moves away.

Mathias and I move round to pick up the box. It's so heavy I can hardly lift it. Maria sees and comes to help. The three of us manoeuvre the box towards the trolley. My legs feel like they will give way, but we get there and lower it. We wheel it over to the pallets at the side of the warehouse and lift it onto one of them. Maria whispers to me: 'Good luck.' I grin, and I'm glad

I've made my peace with her. She wanders back to the work-bench, and I hope her change of attitude towards me is genuine and that she isn't helping in order to then turn us in. As I move to follow her, Mathias grabs my arm.

'What the hell do you think you are doing? You and Beate will get into huge trouble – and anyway, I'm not letting Beate go without me,' he whispers.

I knew something like this would happen. 'It's too dangerous to have three of us,' I hiss, my voice almost quieter than his.

He grips my arm tighter. 'You get me away in the next box, or I blow the whistle. And I need to know where we're heading.'

Scheisse. I thought Mathias was my friend, but of course he's in love with Beate. I should have thought about it. 'OK,' I say, defeated. 'The packages are exported to Sweden.'

'Sweden? Are you mad? We'll never make it to Sweden.'

Time is running out. If Mathias goes, there probably won't be enough time for me to get away, and it increases the odds of us being detected. But if I don't allow him, I know he will inform on us.

'Do you want your girlfriend to end up in Sweden without you? If not, you'll have to take the risk too.'

He doesn't answer for a moment. His eyes have an empty look. Then he glances across at the pallet where Beate is hidden. His Beate. I can see his mind is made up. He will take the risk, for her. It means I won't be going, but at least Beate will be free, with someone to help her.

Back at the workbench, and this time it is Mathias who ducks under. I just hope Maria Bauer will not feel she is being left out. I do the same thing with the tape, the chocolate and drink bottle, punch the holes with the pen and then stand upright again and raise my arm.

'Frau Schettler. Can I get one of the boys to help me with this? The wood seems heavier.' I try to laugh off my suggestion. 'Perhaps I'm tired.'

She nods. I cajole two of the boys from the other desk to come over. We bend down and lift Mathias. They pant and groan. 'What have you got in here?' one of them asks. 'It feels like lead.' We have to put the box down. Damn Mathias! He's ruined everything. But then Maria is there. 'Four of us should be able to do it,' she whispers. We try again and stagger over to the trolley. The boys return to the workbench, muttering as they go. Maria and I wheel the box to the pallet, and slide it on.

Before we walk back, she whispers in my ear. 'Mathias took your place, didn't he?' I feel tears welling in my eyes. I nod. She places her hand on my arm. The girl who bullied me so often, now showing me kindness. 'I could report you, you know that.'

I look into her eyes. She holds my gaze for a second or two, then smiles and shakes her head.

'I don't know why I'm doing this, Behrendt. There's another box at your workstation. Let's make it quickly together, and then I'll help you.'

There's a problem, though. Nearly everyone has gone to watch the end of the match. Word has got through that the Republic is winning with just minutes to go. Maria and I furiously finish the last double-bed box – hiding the slats and bedposts behind us in the pile with the others – so there is room for me to slide inside. She looks across. The other two boys are still there. There is a chance. She pushes me down. I squeeze myself inside and then feel Maria closing the end of the cardboard box, sealing it up and then punching the holes with the pen. I realise that was a flaw in our original plan: if Maria had not been here to help, how would I have sealed my box? How would I have moved it? I thank God that she is helping, but there's no chocolate or drink for me – Mathias has had my share. I hear her walking off. Then three sets of footsteps walking back. And then I feel the box I'm inside being lifted, jostled, thrown around. I try to brace my arms and legs to stop myself sliding about. I feel my lungs spasm, the urgent need to breathe as panic sets in. Why did I ever suggest this? Then a different motion, smoother. But with wheels squeaking. My box must now be on the trolley. Then I feel the box lifted again, but very briefly. I'm on the pallet.

Suddenly light shines in, from the end nearest my head. The tape's come off. *Gottverdammt!* I can see Maria and the two boys going back to their workbenches. Clearing up. Heading off to watch the end of the match. Then footsteps, and I see Frau Schettler walking towards the pallets. She seems to be checking for something. I'm sure now I will be discovered. The end of my box is almost fully open. My heartbeat thunders in my ears. Surely she will see? I close my eyes tight, not wanting to know.

Then I hear her walking away again. She must be going to raise the alarm. I risk opening my eyes fractionally, peering through the lashes. I see her pick up a roll of packing tape, cut two strips off and return. She tapes the end of my box again, without ever looking inside, and my world is plunged back into darkness.

Beate and I had, in advance, discussed what to do if the pallets didn't get moved. We would wait for a day before trying to get out. But Mathias wasn't in on those discussions, so I just pray he doesn't panic and give us away. The minutes tick by. Minutes become an hour. Then suddenly noise and light coming in through the cracks in the box. The roar of the motor, the clang of metal on metal. And, at last, the pallet is moving. I try to interpret each movement, each noise. I can hear the forklift truck driver discussing the game with another man. Maybe the lorry driver taking us to Sassnitz ... I hope so. 'What a goal,' he's saying. 'We really showed the Westlers. That'll teach them.'

The lorry noise and vibrations tell me we're on our way. For the first time, I allow myself to think that maybe this will really work. At the end of the journey, more sounds of what I guess is another forklift. I feel the box being lifted from the lorry, and see the port lights streaming through the cracks in the cardboard. And then there is stillness and quiet. The minutes pass by. An hour, then two. I start to panic. I hadn't thought of this. I try to move around, but my arms, my legs, everything is wedged in tightly. We could be here for days, weeks. In some sort of holding area at the port. We could be trapped inside. Suffocated. Starved. This was a stupid plan. A stupid, idiotic plan. I've brought us all to our deaths. I try again to turn in the box, but there isn't enough room. Instead I begin counting. The seconds. The minutes. The hours. Counting, counting, counting.

At some stage I must have fallen asleep, because suddenly I'm woken by more machinery noise, and what looks like daylight coming through the gaps. It must be morning. More work-men discussing last night's game. Then I'm on the move again. The same motion as when we were put onto the lorry at Prora, so I guess another forklift. It knocks me about; the ground is rougher. I feel the old bruises from my fall ache as I'm thrown about inside the box, pain shooting down my neck and back. But then suddenly all is stillness and quiet and I notice another kind of motion that fills me with elation. I want to shout. I want to scream with joy, but I know I must stay silent. It's an almost imperceptible rocking from side to side. From my days at the seaside at Sellin I know what it is.

The gentle sway of a boat in harbour.

31

February 1975. Day Eleven.
Rügen, East Germany.

The car the Rügen police had provided them with was a brand-new, sky-blue Trabant. Müller was aware that many citizens of the Republic waited years for one of these, despite its basic design, so she felt slightly ashamed that she was wishing they had the *Kriminalpolizei* Wartburg instead. She glanced down at the tourist map on her lap. They were just over halfway between Bergen and Sellin. She turned the map at ninety degrees, so that the two folds showing the island were pointing upwards, in their direction of travel.

'So how much further, oh expert navigator?' asked Tilsner.

Müller found a distance guide between two red marker points on the map, widened her fingers to that width, and then moved her fingers in three jumps towards Sellin. 'Six – maybe seven – kilometres? Not long now.'

Within a few minutes, they were in the outskirts of Sellin resort. By coincidence, the police had booked rooms for them in the same town as the campsite that the grandmother managed. The campsite itself – Drescher had told them – was to the southeast of the resort, in a forested area by the beach. Müller looked from right to left as they drove at walking pace along the main street, the cobbled surface rattling the Trabant. On the map, where the street met the coast, a seaside pier was marked. 'These buildings are fantastic,' she said, admiring the facades decorated with balconies and verandas.

'It's a unique architectural style,' added Schmidt from the rear of the Trabi. 'It's got its own name: *Bäderarchitektur*. You find it all along the Ostsee coast, but especially on Rügen.'

'I hope our hotel is as flash as some of these buildings,' said Tilsner.

Müller peered from side to side at the colonial-style architecture. 'It's not a hotel as such – it's a union rest house. It should be one of these. The Peace Rest House is what we're looking for.' She pointed to one of the white-balconied buildings near the seafront. 'There it is. Just there on the left.'

They parked the car round the back of the building, and then climbed out and retrieved their luggage from the boot. A freezing wind was coming in off the Ostsee, and the Trabant's heater hadn't been as efficient as the Wartburg's. Müller rubbed her hands together to try to get some warmth into them. She fancied another luxury bath to warm herself, like the one in Charlottenburg, the one before Tilsner had gone off on his mysterious trip. She'd almost forgotten that. Müller studied her deputy as he carried his bag and hers into the rest house, his ostentatious wristwatch glinting in the last rays of the winter sun. She didn't know what to make of him, but she could not help but notice the way she found herself drawn to him.

After a change of clothes, a quick wash and some mascara repair, Müller was eager to interview the grandmother. Her extended soak in the bath would have to wait. She wandered onto her balcony, which overlooked Wilhelm-Pieck-Strasse. Late afternoon, and the sun had already disappeared. Müller returned to the bedroom to put a phone call through to the state campsite reception just to check someone was there. A woman – presumably Frau Baumgartner – answered, but Müller immediately apologised, saying she'd got the wrong number, and hung up. She didn't want the grandmother to be too prepared for her police visit. Catch her unawares. They might get more information.

She pulled on her coat, scarf and gloves, then collected Tilsner and Schmidt from their room. The three police officers went down the stairs, past the receptionist, and out into the bracing Ostsee air.

They walked along the seafront, above the empty beaches, which in summer Müller knew would be packed with bodies, citizens soaking up the sun's rays, naked – the East German way. Today, though, the beach was empty, with white patches of ice where the surf had frozen.

After about ten minutes, the houses and rest homes of the resort had disappeared, replaced by row upon row of beech trees, a shroud of darkness enveloping the land right up to the cliff edge. Then the beech forest in turn gave way to a clearing, dominated by a small house, in the traditional Baltic resort architecture style, with its white clapboarding and wooden verandas and balconies. This, Müller guessed, must be where Frau Baumgartner lived, but it looked as though no one was actually camping at this time of year, with just the lights of the reception house illuminating the gloom.

From close up, Müller noticed some of the balcony's rails were missing, and not all the window shutters were complete. She went on ahead of the other two and rang the doorbell.

After a few seconds, the door was opened by a sixty-something woman in a beige housecoat. Müller couldn't help staring at her oddly coloured, silver-blue hair. She looked a little like an older Margot Honecker: the *Volksbildungsminister* – whose ministry of education included the *Jugendwerkhöfe* – had recently taken to dyeing her prematurely greying hair a similar shade.

'We've no pitches free,' the woman said, gloomily. 'I'm not opening this year until after Easter.'

'We've not enquiring about camping,' said Müller, flashing her *Kripo* ID. 'We're here about your granddaughter, Irma.'

The woman jerked her head back. 'What about Irma?'

'We need to come inside and talk to you, Citizen Baumgartner. Is there somewhere we can sit down?'

The woman's face turned a lighter shade of pale. 'It's not bad news, is it?'

'Not necessarily,' said Müller. 'But we should talk inside.'

The woman led the three *Kripo* officers upstairs from the reception area to her apartment. In the lounge, easy chairs were arranged in a semi-circle around an open fire. Frau Baumgartner took one for herself and gestured for the three police officers to take the others. As she faced the warmth of the fire, Müller felt her throat constrict from the fumes of the burning lignite.

She took her gloves and scarf off, but kept the overcoat on. Despite the fire, the room still felt chilly and damp.

'Now I gather, Citizen Baumgartner, that in June of last year you complained to Sellin police station that you'd been denied a visit to see your granddaughter in the *Jugendwerkhof* Prora Ost?'

'That's correct. Horrible place. Built as a Nazi holiday camp. The *Jugendwerkhof* is at one end, and the rest is a barracks for army construction soldiers,' said the woman, rubbing the skin of her right wrist nervously.

'Has that situation changed? Have they let you see her?'

Baumgartner shook her head sadly. 'No. The last time I saw or heard from Irma was in May last year, when I visited her after her fall. I asked again, even after I lodged my official complaint, but they told me nothing. And then the Stasi sent someone round and told me to stop asking questions.' She kept her eyes lowered, trained on a threadbare rug in front of the fire.

Schmidt tried to attract Müller's attention to something, but she waved him away, and instead continued questioning the woman.

'And is it your belief that Irma is still at the *Jugendwerkhof*?' asked Müller.

'I've no idea,' said the woman, wringing her hands now. 'She is due to stay there until she's eighteen. Or until "our family situation improves", as the authorities put it.'

Müller furrowed her brow. 'What does that mean?'

Baumgartner glanced up at a picture on the mantelpiece. It showed a woman of about thirty, with a girl aged about ten. 'That's my daughter. With Irma. It was taken about six years ago. Before it all started.'

'Before what all started?' asked Tilsner.

'Before my daughter got arrested and jailed for supposed anti-revolutionary activities, and before Irma, my granddaughter, was taken away.' Baumgartner wiped her eyes with the sleeve of the housecoat.

Müller rose to her feet, and picked up the photograph. It was hard to tell if the young girl in the picture bore any resemblance to the one found in St Elisabeth's cemetery. 'Do you have a more recent photo? Or one in colour?'

'I might have a colour one,' said the woman, getting slowly to her feet. 'But what's all this about?'

Müller sighed. 'Get me the picture first, please.' She saw the woman frown, and then open a cupboard at the back of the room. Frau Baumgartner knelt down, and then picked up a cardboard shoebox and placed it on the side table next to her, moving her knitting onto the floor in the process. Müller gave Schmidt a knowing glance – that's why he'd wanted to attract her attention: the ball of wool.

The woman started flicking through the photos in the box. 'Most of these are of my husband and me,' she said. 'From before the war. He was a Luftwaffe pilot. And before you ask: no, he didn't survive. I've been a widow for more than thirty years. It's harder and harder to keep this place properly maintained on my own, as you can probably see.' The woman pulled one of the photos from the box. 'Here we are. That's one of Irma, taken with my first colour camera. She was a happy child then, always smiling.' She handed the photograph to Müller.

The detective's eyes were immediately drawn to the girl's unruly shock of red hair. Not even the best hair straighteners and dyes could have transformed it into the straight bob of black hair on the dead girl's head, and in any case the dead girl's hair colour was natural – the pathologist's report had confirmed that. This clearly wasn't the girl from the cemetery.

'What is it?' the woman asked.

'We're looking for a missing girl. There is certain evidence that makes us think there is a link to Rügen, but the girl in question has straight, dark hair.'

'A missing girl? Are you saying you think Irma may be missing?'

'Not at all, Frau Baumgartner. Just because you haven't been permitted a visit to the *Jugendwerkhof*, there's no reason at all to believe Irma isn't still there. I'm sure she is. So it doesn't look like the girl we're looking for and Irma are connected.'

The woman fingered the buttons of her housecoat. 'Yes, but I still don't know how Irma is; I still haven't been able to see her.'

Müller leant across and laid her palm on Baumgartner's arm. 'We will be paying the *Jugendwerkhof* a visit. I will be able to check how Irma is. I cannot promise anything, but if there is anything amiss I will ask the youth services to contact you. That's all I can do.'

The woman gave a weak smile. 'Thank you.'

Tilsner interrupted the exchange. 'She still had her red hair last time you saw her, Citizen Baumgartner?'

'Yes. Yes, of course. In the sanatorium.'

'How old is she? How tall would you say she is? Is there anything else that might be useful for us to know?'

'She's sixteen now, but I can't tell you how tall she is, I'm afraid. She was lying in bed. And the time I last saw her before that, before she was taken to Prora, well … well it was two years ago.

In the children's home in Greifswald. She wasn't fully grown. She's a woman now. Well, almost.'

Müller nodded. 'And why did she end up in a closed *Jugendwerk-hof*? Surely that's only for children who've done something seriously wrong?'

Frau Baumgartner shrugged. 'My daughter was jailed – I told you – and poor Irma suffered for it, and was sent to the normal children's home. But she kept on trying to run away. Eventually they sent her to Prora.'

Tilsner leant forward in his chair. 'Was she allowed to write letters to you from the *Jugendwerkhof*?'

'Yes, I received the odd one.'

'Did she mention any friends?' probed Müller. 'Anything odd going on?'

Baumgartner raised her eyebrows. 'Friends? Yes, yes. I think she did mention one, actually. The letter should be in this same box.' She shuffled through the contents again, and then drew out a cream envelope. 'I was surprised it hadn't been censored, actually. Sometimes some of what she writes gets struck out.' Müller could see her scanning the page quickly, then turning over. 'Here it is,' Baumgartner said. 'She says she's worried about her best friend Beate – how she seems upset all the time, and Irma doesn't know why.' She passed the letter to Müller, who read it through for confirmation.

'But she doesn't mention a surname?' asked Müller. 'In any of her letters?'

'No, I'm afraid not,' said the woman.

Müller nodded, deep in thought. Then she gathered herself, and rose from the chair. She extended her hand to Baumgartner.

'Thank you very much, Citizen Baumgartner. You've been a great help.'

She felt a tap on her shoulder. Schmidt whispered: 'Comrade Müller. What about the wool?'

'Ah. Yes.' She turned back to the woman, and pointed to the wool and needles, which now lay at her feet. 'Would it be alright to have a small sample of your wool, Citizen Baumgartner?'

The woman's brow creased in confusion. 'Why ever would you want that?'

'Don't be alarmed,' said Müller. 'It's nothing to worry about. It would just help us compare against some fibres linked to our inquiries. Have you knitted anything for Irma from it?'

Baumgartner nodded. 'Yes. A jumper. She wrote and told me how thrilled she was to have it. She keeps it in her bed at night to remind her of her family and Sellin. It must be a comfort. I noticed it there in the sanatorium, on her pillow, poor girl.'

'Well, a sample may help our inquiry.'

The woman smiled, and lifted the ball of wool. 'In that case, of course. Our handmade Rügen jumpers are very popular. you know. The wool is very warm, although some people find it a bit rough. The wool is from a sheep we only get round here.'

Müller nodded. 'The *Pommersches Rauhwollschaf* – the rough wool Pomeranian sheep.'

The woman laughed. 'Absolutely right. I didn't expect you Berlin types to know that. By all means ... Here, take as much as you want.'

Schmidt took the proffered ball of wool, cut off a small section and put it in a plastic evidence bag. 'That will be sufficient for my needs, Frau Baumgartner. Thank you so much for your cooperation.'

32

Day Twelve.
Sellin, Rügen.

For Müller it had been another night of tossing and turning, constantly going over the case in her head, and then switching her attention to Gottfried, and wondering what sort of night he'd be facing. Was he in jail somewhere? Being questioned in Normannenstrasse? She resolved that as soon as she was back in Berlin, she would give his welfare the fullest attention, even if she had no idea where to begin. She owed it to him, whether or not their marriage was over, as Jäger had insinuated.

She felt stabbing pains from her throat as she awoke, her tongue sticking to the roof of her mouth. The heating had been on too high, but she couldn't see any way of controlling it, and she didn't want to sleep with the balcony doors open.

She went to the bathroom, turned on the light and examined her face in the mirror. In two weeks, she seemed to have aged five years. Maybe the days of minimal make-up were behind her. She brushed her teeth, and then washed away the taste of the toothpaste with a glass of water. Her body was urging her to go back to bed, but she knew that at this time of the day her thought processes were likely to be at their most incisive. Back in the bedroom, she put on her dressing gown and slippers, opened the curtains and then wandered onto the balcony.

An overnight hoar frost had left countless tiny crystals of ice glistening on the balcony railing. She brushed the frozen glitter off the veranda chair, and sat on the cold wood. Her teeth began to chatter, but the freezing conditions helped clear her brain. She looked down towards the end of Wilhelm-Pieck-Strasse, and the Ostsee beyond, shimmering in the morning light. The beauty of the surroundings contrasted sharply with the vicious death the girl had suffered.

The dead girl almost certainly wasn't Irma. She was sure of that now, but she was still determined to check out the *Jugendwerkhof*. If nothing else, she was curious to see where Gottfried had taught during his enforced exile from Berlin. Schmidt had examined the wool from Frau Baumgartner when they'd got back to the hotel with the microscope he'd brought with him; the fibres were an exact match. Even the dye was the same. There had to be a link. Why wouldn't they let Baumgartner see her granddaughter again? Why had Irma ended up in the sanatorium after a 'fall'? That in itself sounded suspicious. And why was this Beate crying all the time? Her tears must have been out of the ordinary, or Irma Behrendt would never have mentioned them in a letter to her Oma.

All these thoughts ran through Müller's mind like errant trains as she gazed out to sea. She could feel the material of the dressing gown under her buttocks starting to stick to the frozen

wood of the chair. Suddenly a rustling sound from the neighbouring balcony made her turn. Quickly, she drew the gown
together.

Tilsner was standing there, a pack of cigarettes and a lighter
in his hand. He took one out, lit it and took a long drag. Then he
reached across the balcony railing to offer her one. Müller was
tempted, stood and stretched her arm, then thought better of it
and thrust her hands in her pockets.

Tilsner shrugged. Then she noticed his eyeline, which was
directed at her breasts.

Looking down, she saw that the gown had flared open. She
pulled it together angrily, stomped back inside the room and
slammed the balcony doors.

After what was grandly termed an Ostsee coast special breakfast – hard-boiled eggs, stale bread and some unidentified grey
smoked fish – the three Berlin officers retraced their route in the
Trabi back towards Bergen auf Rügen. Müller's embarrassment
over the incident with Tilsner on the hotel balcony hadn't dissipated. She pointedly sat in the back and gave directions using
the map from there, leaving Schmidt to accompany her deputy
in the front of the car.

They soon reached Binz, the next resort along the coast,
northwest of Sellin. It seemed larger to Müller, but otherwise
quite similar – the same *Bäderarchitektur* as in its more southerly neighbour. Several roads veered towards the seafront, but
Müller directed them straight on – through the back of the
small town.

In just a couple of minutes, the Nazi monolith of Prora rose into view. Müller wasn't quite sure what she'd been expecting. Gottfried's description had been of a hellhole, but then he was gloomy at the best of times. To Müller, it didn't look wildly different from a very long series of Berlin apartment blocks – just greyer, and without any gaps in between. It was the location that was strange – in the middle of nowhere, obscuring what she imagined would otherwise have been a magnificent view of the wild Ostsee coast. But the fact it had been built on the orders of Hitler, to reward his Nazi subjects, sent a renewed chill through her.

'Hmm,' said Tilsner. 'I wouldn't fancy taking a holiday there. No wonder it was never used.'

'But this is the back of it, Comrade Tilsner,' said Schmidt, speaking through a mouthful of food. He seemed to have squirrelled away some extra breakfast to keep up his calorie intake. 'I've seen a book showing the artist's impression of the front; how it would have looked if it had been completed. There would have been a theatre, auditoriums and a harbour. The plans were impressive.'

Tilsner snorted. 'Don't sound too enthusiastic, Jonas. *Oberleutnant* Müller will be reporting you for your pro-fascist attitude.'

'I ... I ... didn't mean –'

'Ignore him, Jonas,' said Müller. 'He's just teasing you.'

After finding the section of the almost never-ending building which contained the *Jugendwerkhof*, Müller and Tilsner buzzed the intercom and were shown inside. Müller had told Schmidt to see if he could find a way round to the beach, to check if the sand here matched the sample found in the Volvo limousine.

The two detectives were led by a young female member of staff down several corridors, and shown to a room with a grey metal door bearing the sign: Direktor F. Neumann. Müller was aware of his reputation from Gottfried's tales of woe about the place from the previous year, so she was surprised when – as she knocked on the door – a female voice asked them to enter.

A stern-faced woman who Müller estimated to be in her early or mid-fifties greeted them with firm handshakes, and examined the *Kripo* detective's ID and the authorisation letter signed by Colonel General Mielke – the one Jäger had given Müller in the Kulturpark. The woman paid particular attention to this, as she introduced herself as deputy director Monika Richter and ushered them to sit down.

'I'm standing in for Director Neumann. He's away for a few days on another Ministry of Education project. What can we do for you?' she asked. 'We're used to having dealings with the police, but not usually detectives from the Hauptstadt.'

Müller made a mental note of the director's absence. She'd follow that up later. 'We're investigating a murder,' she said, holding the woman's gaze. With Frau Baumgartner the previous night she'd been more circumspect, wanting to tease information from the woman; but with deputy director Richter, she decided a direct approach might be better. Try to unnerve her from the start.

'On Rügen?' asked Richter. 'It's not often we get murders here on the island.'

'No, Frau Richter – in Berlin. But there is evidence to suggest the dead girl may have come from Rügen.'

Richter creased her forehead with yet more severity. 'But why is that relevant to the *Jugendwerkhof*? All our girls are accounted for. No one has ever escaped from here.'

Tilsner raised an eyebrow. 'Who said anything about anyone escaping?'

The interjection seemed to throw Richter. Müller noticed her blink repeatedly.

'There's no need to be concerned, Frau Richter,' she said. 'We just need to rule a few things out to help advance the inquiry.'

'Such as?'

'Such as how did Irma Behrendt end up in the sanatorium after a fall?'

Richter gave a sharp intake of breath, then a slightly manic laugh. 'What on earth has that got to do with your murder inquiry?'

Tilsner slapped his hand on the table. Richter flinched. 'Just answer *Oberleutnant* Müller's questions. You've seen our authorisation. It comes from the highest level.'

Müller waited, but Richter failed to say anything.

'We don't want to be here all day, Frau Richter,' said Müller. 'Tell us about Irma Behrendt.'

'She was a very unruly, unstable girl. For some reason, she climbed out of the toilet window and jumped.'

'When was that?'

Richter paused a moment as though to collect her thoughts. 'It was spring or early summer last year. May, I think.'

'And from which floor did she jump?' asked Müller.

'The fifth.'

'The *fifth*! How on earth did she survive that with mere bruising?'

Richter looked flustered now, her eyes darting from Müller to Tilsner and back. 'We did our best to help her. When we realised she was trying to get out of the window, a teacher thankfully organised a chain of children to bring down mattresses from the dorms to cushion her fall. Fortunately, the fire brigade arrived in time with their safety net and managed to catch her.'

Something didn't add up here, thought Müller. If it had simply been a case of the girl getting out of the window and jumping, how would they have had time to pile up mattresses? How would the fire brigade have had time to get in position and set up the apparatus to catch the girl? 'And who was the teacher who tried to help? Can we talk to him or her?'

'It was a him. And no. He was just here temporarily from Berlin.'

Müller heard Tilsner gasp. He'd put two and two together. She gave him a gentle kick under the table to keep him quiet. But now it was her turn to be flustered. Why hadn't Gottfried ever told her about that? Because presumably it was him whom Richter was talking about.

'So a girl attempts to jump out of a window, yet the staff have time to pile up mattresses to save her. That sounds unlikely. Also, I've seen a recent letter from Irma Behrendt. She seemed to me to be a level-headed girl. In her letter, she worries that her friend, Beate, might do something stupid. So this isn't adding up, Frau Richter.' Müller could see the tendons bulging in Richter's neck as she tried to hold herself in check. 'I think perhaps we need to speak to Irma Behrendt and Beate –'

'Ewert. Beate Ewert is her name. But I'm afraid it won't be possible to speak to them, at least not here.'

'Why's that?' asked Tilsner. 'We've already warned you about the need to cooperate with us.'

Richter, flicking her dyed-black fringe, didn't answer immediately. Instead she rose to her feet and retrieved a file from the shelf to her right. She sat down again and leafed through its pages. 'The information you want is here somewhere. Ah yes, 22 June last year.' She turned the file round to show the two detectives.

Müller sighed, but didn't bother reading the entry. 'Just tell us what it says, Frau Richter.'

The woman seemed calmer now, more in control. 'Both Irma Behrendt and Beate Ewert were transferred on that day to a special children's home in Schierke, in *Bezirk* Magdeburg.'

'Does the entry say why?' asked Müller.

Richter ran her finger under the neat handwritten note. 'The entry was by Director Neumann. It says it was felt that to help Ewert and Behrendt, due to their nervous dispositions, they should be moved to a more remote institution, with a more relaxed regime. One of their friends was moved at the same time. One Mathias Gellman. On account of his good behaviour.'

'Was her grandmother informed of the transfer?'

Richter shrugged. 'I don't have that information.'

'And what about Director Neumann? What exactly is this project he's involved with that's taken him away from his main job?' asked Müller.

Richter's face reddened. 'It's a special Ministry project in the same area to which the girls were transferred. He spends part of the time here, part of the time there. But while he's away, I'm in charge. I can give you all the help you need.'

'Do you have his phone number? His address?' persisted Müller.

Richter folded her arms across her chest. 'I'm afraid I cannot divulge that, *Oberleutnant*. You would need specific authorisation from the Ministry of Education.'

Tilsner jabbed his finger at the letter from Mielke on Richter's desk.

'That's all the authorisation we need. From the Minister of State Security.'

Richter smirked at him. 'No, *Unterleutnant*. That's where you're wrong. As I say, you would need specific authorisation from the Ministry of Education. But perhaps your connections to the Stasi can help you. By all means call Comrade Mielke himself. I'm sure he would have a hotline to Comrade *Volksbildungsminister* Margot Honecker. I would need him to clear it with her. If you can't manage to arrange that, there is nothing more I can do for you.' With a thin smile, Richter shut the folder on her desk, and rose from her seat.

'That's not quite all, Frau Richter,' said Müller. 'I want to speak to everyone who would have had contact with Irma and Beate. I want to interview their teachers, and I want to talk to any children who witnessed Irma's fall. Would that be possible?'

Richter sighed, and sat down again. 'Of course, *Oberleutnant*. But it will take some time to arrange. Could you come back tomorrow?'

Tilsner banged his fist down on the table. 'No. Not tomorrow. We're doing it now. As we said at the beginning, this is a murder inquiry. If you don't want a visit from this lot,' he pointed to the Stasi headed notepaper, 'then I suggest you start cooperating immediately.'

Richter didn't reply, but just nodded slowly. She'd attempted to bluff them once by urging them to call Mielke. This time, the two detectives had called her bluff.

The teacher in charge of the packing room – where Müller and Tilsner established Irma and Beate had spent their last shift – seemed a very different character from the *Jugendwerkhof*'s deputy director. There was a nervous timidity about Frau Schettler, but also – it appeared to Müller – a touch more humanity and caring towards the children. What the two women had in common, though, was a tendency to pause and dart their eyes around before answering questions.

'So their evening packing shift was the last time you saw the three children who were transferred?' asked Müller.

'Yes, that's right,' Schettler replied.

'How would you describe their mood?'

'They were all quite excited. I gave them permission to go and watch the match if they reached their targets early.'

'The match?' asked Müller.

Tilsner interrupted. 'It was the evening we beat the Westlers in the World Cup.'

'That's right,' agreed Schettler.

'But before that, in the days leading up to that – and before Irma's fall. How would you describe their demeanour then?' probed Müller.

'I did notice that Beate seemed upset much of the time. And that Irma was worried for her. It earned her a spell in the bunker.'

'The bunker?' asked Müller.

'It's an isolation cell. For when children have been particularly disruptive and need to be punished.' As she said this, Schettler had her eyes downcast, shame written legibly across her face.

'But going back to the night of the football match: you saw all three children leave early and go to watch the game on television? You're quite sure about that?'

Schettler paused. Müller noticed her eyes dart to the left. Then she looked down at her hands as she answered. 'Yes,' she said softly. 'I'm quite sure about that.' Müller frowned. She wasn't convinced by the woman's assertion.

'As you know, Frau Schettler, this is a murder inquiry,' she continued. 'Now it's very likely that the victim has nothing to do with this *Jugendwerkhof*, although we believe there is some sort of link with Rügen. However, if you feel able, we'd like you to look at a photograph of the dead girl. I have to warn you that she was badly mutilated. Her face, in particular, doesn't look much like a face anymore.' Schettler gasped, and clasped her hand to her chest.

Tilsner pulled the autopsy photo from his briefcase, and handed it to Müller, who in turn passed it to Schettler.

The woman sharply sucked air through her mouth, and then covered it with her hand. She dropped the black-and-white print on the table, and shook her head.

'What, Frau Schettler?'

'It's ... it's just so horrible. Seeing ... seeing someone like that,' she said. Eyes to the left again, noted Müller.

'Seeing *who* like that?'

'I'm ... I'm not sure I know what you mean,' said Schettler. 'I've not seen this girl ever before in my life.' She pushed the photo back towards Müller, turning her head away.

'You're quite sure of that?' asked Tilsner.

The woman gave a small nod, but didn't meet either of the detectives' eyelines.

'I'm sorry we had to do that, Frau Schettler. But I hope you understand why,' said Müller.

Schettler again jerked her head up and down, but kept her eyes fixed on her clasped-together hands, not wanting to look at the photograph again. Picking the photo up, Müller and Tilsner rose from their chairs and said their goodbyes.

They walked back to the Trabant via the exercise yard where Irma had nearly fallen to her death. It seemed bizarre to Müller that the girl had only been saved in part due to the quick thinking of her husband Gottfried. Something was horribly awry there, thought Müller. Caring hero one moment, then enemy of the state just months later. It made her all the more determined to help him. Surely if she took the story about his bravery to Jäger he could intervene?

'What do you think, boss?' asked Tilsner. 'We seem to be back to square one if it was neither of those girls.'

'What I think, Werner, is that they're lying.'

'Who?'

'Richter and Schettler for starters. Possibly for different reasons, but they were both lying. However, if Schettler was lying about the photograph, that's easy to disprove. We know it's not Irma, but I think it's still worth checking with Beate's relatives. And at least we have a name now. We can get one of the relatives to look at the photographs, and the body.'

'But according to Frau Richter, both girls are supposedly alive and well in this home in Schierke. Shouldn't we check there first?'

Müller knew he was right. A check with the home would be simple enough. They could probably put the call in from the People's Police office in Bergen. They started to wander back towards the car. When they reached the main gate, they buzzed the intercom for the staff to unlock it automatically and let them out. Müller took one last glance back up at the fifth floor, from where Irma had fallen. What sort of a place would drive a girl to jump to what would have been – if it hadn't been for the intervention of her husband and the fire brigade – an almost certain death? It didn't bear thinking about.

Schmidt had already set himself up in the back of the Trabant, examining some sand he'd obtained from the beach.

He looked up from the microscope as the two detectives climbed into the car. 'It wasn't that easy ... Nearly got myself arrested by the People's Army. They were OK once I showed my

ID, but I had to get the sample from a slightly different section of the beach.'

'But does it look like it matches the sample from the Volvo?' asked Müller.

'Yes, Comrade Müller. I'm pretty sure it does, but I'll need to do some more detailed analysis in the lab once we're back in Berlin. What about you two? Any progress?'

'I think so, Jonas,' said Müller. 'I think so.'

Tilsner started the engine. 'Where to, boss?'

'Let's go to the People's Police headquarters in Bergen. From there we can wire or phone Jäger to get him to ask for authority to interview Neumann. We can also contact the children's home in Schierke to check if the children actually are there as Frau Richter claims. And we need to track down Ewert's parents – if they're not in jail – and have them examine the body.'

Tilsner killed the engine again. 'Hang on a minute, I've got an idea.' He reached under the dashboard and opened the glove compartment. 'Aha. Good.' He pulled out a small book, covered in red plastic. Müller read the cover. *Deutsche Demokratische Republik Verkehr*: a road atlas for the entire country. Tilsner was examining the index at the back. 'Where did she say that children's home was?'

Müller consulted her notes. 'A village called Schierke, in *Bezirk* Magdeburg.'

'Map 11, square C,' said Tilsner. He leafed back to map 11, near the front of the book, and then traced his finger down to square C. He squinted at the page for a moment, and then shouted excitedly. 'There!' Müller looked to where he was pointing and saw the corresponding village name. Then Tilsner moved his finger about a centimetre to the northwest: the Brocken, the highest mountain in the Harz, and the only one with subalpine soil.

As soon as the three of them arrived back in Bergen auf Rügen and the People's Police office, Müller knew something was wrong. Two uniformed officers were waiting for them, and escorted them directly to Drescher's office.

The People's Police colonel failed to stand as they entered the room, and didn't ask them to sit. He looked up from the documents on his desk with a stern face, and addressed Müller.

'I'm afraid you three will have to go back to Berlin immediately. I have been given instructions by the Ministry of the Interior.'

Müller started to protest. 'We just need to telephone –'

Drescher held up his hand. 'I don't think you understand, Comrade *Oberleutnant*. This isn't a request, it's an order. You have –' Drescher glanced down and read from the document on his desk '– "exceeded the terms of your inquiry".' He looked up and held her gaze. 'And I have been instructed to provide two officers to accompany you on the train journey back to the Hauptstadt, to make sure you go directly to the People's Police administration building there.'

'Are we under arrest?' asked Tilsner.

'Not at this stage,' replied Drescher. 'But you will be if you don't comply.'

33

Eight months earlier (June 1974).
At sea.

My temporary joy at feeling the swell of the sea in harbour soon gives way to terror. In effect, I am trapped in little more than a makeshift coffin, and so too – presumably – are Beate and Mathias. Panicking will not help. But Beate is more fragile. I have no way of communicating with her even if, as I hope, she's on board like me.

After perhaps a couple of hours of machinery noise – I assume this is the ship being loaded – the background sounds and motion change. A low hum begins, and the box vibrates. The motion of gentle rocking becomes ferocious lurching. My only comfort is that this must be the open sea. I feel as though the chipboard panels enclosing me could break at any moment, so violent is the motion. The airflow is minimal from the holes punched in the cardboard with the pen. All I can smell is my own sweat, and the sharp sweetness of urine where I've wet myself. Beate and I had deliberately cut our food and liquid intake in the days before the escape attempt to the bare minimum, but the body's functions cannot be completely stopped. At least Beate and Mathias had their smuggled bottle of cola and chocolate bar; nothing to eat or drink for me.

As each wave crashes into the boat, as the vessel slams into the next trough, I feel a corresponding spasm of nausea. Saliva pools in the insides of my cheeks. I manage to swallow the first retch down, but then bile erupts from my mouth. I fight to spit it out. To breathe. I'm choking. Finally the attack subsides, but the stench is worse.

I don't dare break out of the cardboard tomb, not until we've reached port on the other side of the Ostsee and the waves have subsided. As hour follows hour, that possibility diminishes. I have no guarantee that we are even heading for Sweden. Or the West. What if this ship is taking a consignment to the Soviet Union? I feel sure I would be dead long before we reached there. Through thirst, suffocation or choking on my own vomit. Why did I ever take any notice of those markings in the book from Herr Müller?

At some point the weather changes, because it becomes slightly calmer. A gentle rocking, only slightly more pronounced that when we'd been in harbour. The blackness inside the cardboard box heightens my awareness. Every noise, every creak of the boat, is amplified and dances around my head. Every hair on my body detects the tiniest movement.

Sleep comes in fits and starts, but I try to fight it because that moment between sleep and wakefulness is so terrifying. Not knowing where I am, not knowing what will happen: a deafening uncertainty.

Something, though, has gone wrong in my calculations. I have no watch. I have no clock. But this journey was supposed to take just a few hours. I'd managed to glean that information from the *Jugendwerkhof* library. We have already been at sea for more than a day. My mind can't be playing that many tricks.

All of a sudden, the rocking of the boat calms completely. The motion now is barely perceptible above the vibrations and hum of the motor. We must have reached Sweden at last. Hope courses through me once more. We've made it!

I push at the end of the box above my head, hearing the packing tape tear off. A dim light enters. I want to try to squeeze out before unloading begins, in case this isn't Sweden, in case it isn't even the West. I brace my arms and legs against the veneered chipboard panels that form the box walls, and push, sliding forward centimetre by centimetre. I get my head out, my shoulders. By a stroke of good fortune my pallet seems to be at the end of a row, with my head by the open side. I can only imagine what it would have been like if I'd been trapped in the middle of the pile of boxes. It's another stupid flaw in the plan, I realise, of which Mathias and Beate could be the victims. Trapped, suffocated and starved – all thanks to me.

I push again and get my arms far enough out that I can cling onto the edges of the box. I try to force my head round to see how high up I am in the pile of boxes. More good luck. Just one box away from the bottom of the pile. I wriggle out further and stretch one hand down to the steel floor of the boat's hold, to support myself as I struggle to free the rest of my body. A thud. Pain in my head from where it hits the floor. But I'm out.

I slowly move myself to a standing position. I have to grab onto the sides of the boxes because my legs feel like jelly. And the smell. I don't want to think about the smell and my damp clothing.

And then I hear a voice – barely more than a whisper – calling for Beate. It's Mathias. I see him coming down the gap between the pallets, towards me. I want to cry with joy, I want to hug him, but he pushes me away.

'I'm worried,' he says. 'I can't find Beate. I'm not sure she's even here.'

'She must be. We've both made it. Why would her box have been split off from the rest?'

'You're right. Let's look again.'

We split up and check the piles of boxes methodically. The rows go on and on. I realise how lucky we've been. This is several days' output from the *Jugendwerkhof* that must have been stored out in the yard, or at Sassnitz harbour, before being shipped. That could have been us waiting in a holding area, and slowly starving to death; instead, our boxes were loaded within hours, in less then a day. But what if Beate's hasn't been?

I start on another row, whispering Beate's name, still without any luck. I daren't raise my voice in case we alert the crew, and in case we're not in the West after all. I notice the engine motors are still running. There is a very faint rocking motion. For some reason we are still moving.

'Beate, Beate,' I whisper up and down the boxes of yet another row. Then I hear something from the top of a pile. 'Irma, Irma.' An answering cry. I call back as loudly as I dare: 'Beate, don't worry. We'll have you out in a moment. Just stay calm.'

I run to the edge of the row to try to see Mathias. I hiss at him and gesture. Finally he sees me, and comes running. His breath is as foul as mine, panting in my face. 'Up there,' I say, pointing to the top of the pile of boxes. 'Right at the very top, I think. That's what it sounds like.'

He finds energy that I know I no longer have, and clambers like a monkey up the side of the boxes. Around twenty of them, stacked in a criss-cross pattern to strengthen the pile. I see him scrabbling with the topmost boxes, trying to move them to one side.

'She's under here ... a couple of boxes down,' he calls to me. 'But I can't lift them on my own. You'll have to come up and help me.'

I try to follow the same route he used, surprised at my own strength, the urge to save my friend driving me on.

'Hurry up,' he whispers, stretching his arm to help pull me the last metre or so. 'Her voice sounds very weak.'

We crouch on top of the pile. Mathias counts to three and then we both lift the top box, and move it over. Beate's voice is louder now, and we realise this is her box, the second one down. Mathias rips the cardboard end, flinging the pieces to the floor. After a nerve-wracking wait, Beate's head slowly appears. But there is no way to get down. No way to get out without falling. She has been face down in her box, whereas I'd been on my back.

'Stay there,' shouts Mathias. 'Don't try to get out any further. You'll fall.' He moves to the neighbouring box, and starts to tear off the cardboard from the top of Beate's. Together, we lift the headboard and then, centimetre by centimetre, pull Beate out.

She slumps into his arms, exhausted. He's kissing her, cuddling her, telling her he loves her, and I feel an intense stab of jealousy. She's my friend, it was my plan, and yet he's making out he's her saviour. Mathias, the boy who was quite happy to steal my rightful place. I begin to hate him.

Once we've slowly helped her down to ground level, I do get my hug from her. I do get my congratulations. And strangely, it makes me feel slightly better that Beate stinks as badly as I do, that she looks a complete mess.

'Oh Irma,' she says. 'I cannot thank you enough. It was horrible, horrible in there. I thought we would never get out alive.'

I stroke her sick-covered hair. 'I'm sorry I put you through it.'

'No, no,' she says. 'Never be sorry. I will always be grateful to you, Irma, always. You don't know what they did to me in that place. You don't want to know, I promise you.' She begins to sob.

'Shhh,' I hush her. 'Shhh. It's OK now. It's OK.'

But as I'm stroking her hair, I realise the motors are still running. We still haven't reached our destination.

'Where do you think we are?' I ask Mathias.

'I *know* where we are,' he says. 'At least I think I do. There's an exit from the hold there.' He points to a red sliding door. 'I've already been up to take a look.'

'Well, tell us where we are then. It's not Sweden, is it?'

But he won't say. He grabs Beate by the hand, like the star-crossed lover he is, and urges me to follow. As we run through the door, I can see daylight coming down the stairwell. We huddle round the first porthole and look out. The daylight blinds my eyes for an instant, and then I adjust. The glass is smeared and dirty and at first I can't make much out, except that we seem to be travelling up a river or something, because I can see cars and buildings on the bank side. Then I see a factory sign. In German. My heart sinks.

'We're not still in the Republic, are we?' I ask.

'No, no,' he shouts over the din of engine noise. 'Look at the cars.'

I stare. I'm not sure of all the makes. I see Volkswagen Beetles. Bigger luxury cars. But not a Trabant, not a Wartburg in sight.

Then road signs. Rendsburg, Kiel, Hamburg.

The West!

I feel the rush of joy through my whole body.

We have reached the West. Never to see *Jugendwerkhof* Prora Ost again. No more Richter. No more Neumann.

I turn to Beate and hug her to me. Her smile is as wide as mine. I know we are best friends for life.

34

February 1975. Day Thirteen.
East Berlin.

On their return to the Hauptstadt, Müller had expected to be immediately summoned to either the Stasi or the People's Police headquarters – but instead the three officers were split up, and Müller was escorted back to her apartment and told to stay there overnight, and not to try to contact anyone. She knew better than to disobey, after her requests to speak to Jäger were met with silence. When she asked to see Gottfried, she received a similar response.

Now she and Tilsner were sitting in two chairs, next to each other, opposite a table in a large room at the Keibelstrasse police headquarters. Schmidt had no doubt been allowed to return to the forensic lab, safe in the knowledge that – if there had been wrongdoing – he was simply following her orders. Behind the table, arranged in a line, sat five male officers who, from their differing shades of grey-green and olive-green uniforms, looked to Müller to be a mixture of Stasi and People's Police. They introduced themselves but Müller found her concentration wavering.

The only one she knew was the one she recognised: her police superior, *Oberst* Reiniger, and even he seemed to have a more serious expression than usual. He refused to meet Müller's eyes.

After the introductions, the middle officer of the five, a grey-haired man in his late fifties with black-rimmed spectacles, was the first to speak. 'We've summoned you here to make it clear to you that you are both being removed from the missing person's inquiry into the girl found dead in St Elisabeth's cemetery. *Oberst* Reiniger –' the officer gestured to his left, towards the end of the table, '– fully approves of this decision.' Reiniger gave a small nod, as the more senior officer continued. 'That means you are to make no further inquiries about the girl. You have in any case already exceeded the agreed remit, putting the People's Police and Ministry for State Security in a position of some embarrassment. This is a serious matter, and will be investigated, and the outcome will be made known to you in due course. In the meantime, *Unterleutnant* Tilsner, as you were acting under the authority of *Oberleutnant* Müller here, you may return to your official duties and await further instructions. *Oberleutnant*, for the moment you will remain here.'

Müller looked across at her deputy. He'd made no move to stand, and instead cleared his throat, and looked to be about to launch into a speech in their defence. Reiniger pulled him up short.

'That means now, Comrade Tilsner.'

'But Comrade *Oberst*, we were given the authority to do what we did by –'

'*Now*, Tilsner,' barked Reiniger, his face turning red.

Tilsner scraped his chair back, gave an apologetic shrug towards Müller, and then marched out of the room, slamming the door behind him.

Müller ignored Reiniger's warning look. 'What *Unterleutnant* Tilsner was about to say was that we were given the authority to ask the questions we did, and go where we did, by Ministry for State Security *Oberstleutnant* Klaus Jäger.'

'We have no record of that,' said the officer in the centre of the table. 'And *Oberstleutnant* Jäger has been removed from the case too.' Müller tried to disguise her shock at this news. 'And for you, *Oberleutnant*, things are more complicated. As well as exceeding your authority, I gather you're aware by now that your husband stands accused of anti-state –'

'I haven't been allowed to see my husband.'

'We will see about rectifying that.'

The chairman of her inquisitors gave a questioning glance to his right, the opposite side to Reiniger, where an officer in the olive-green uniform of the Stasi gave a small nod. 'You will be allowed an accompanied visit to your husband. But you have to understand that his activities – if proven – are incompatible with the husband of an officer of the People's Police. So, should you be allowed to continue with your career once our inquiry is over, it will be on the understanding that you obtain a divorce. In the meantime, you too may return to your office, and wait for *Oberst* Reiniger to assign you new duties.'

'So I'm being removed from the Mitte Murder Commission?'

'No. Not for the time being. But – as I said – the missing person's inquiry in connection with the body of the girl at

St Elisabeth cemetery is being taken away from you. You should do nothing – I repeat *nothing* – more in connection with the case. Do you understand, Comrade *Oberleutnant*?'

Müller nodded. She felt numbed. Was this the beginning of the end of her police career? Perhaps – back at the graveyard when this had all started – Tilsner had been right. They never should have become involved in this case. But Jäger hadn't really given them any choice.

'You can go back to the office now, *Oberleutnant*,' said Reiniger. 'I will speak to you later today about your new duties, and about arranging a visit to your husband.'

Müller stood and saluted, then turned on her heels. All she could think of was the poor girl in the cemetery, her eyeless sockets and the pathetic black nail 'varnish'. As she closed the door on the five officers, she wondered if anyone would bother – or dare – to challenge the official account of the girl's death, now that she and Jäger had been conveniently removed from the equation.

35

Day Thirteen.
East Berlin.

Müller stared up at the grim buildings that housed the Stasi headquarters, after being summoned there from the office in Marx-Engels-Platz just an hour after leaving the meeting in Keibelstrasse. On all sides, pebble-dash beige concrete walls towered above her, with darker bands of brown highlighting some of the floors – at least twice as high as Prora, maybe more. Was Gottfried being held in one of these rooms? That's what she'd perhaps naively assumed. But she was wrong: the tall, sharp-faced Stasi captain who'd met her at the check-point – *Hauptmann* Schiller – was planning on taking her on a car journey.

She followed the Stasi officer to rows of parked cars in the central courtyard. He went to one of them, and opened the door for her. It was a Volvo. *Of course.* Müller ducked inside. Leather seats, the smell not unlike the Mercedes they'd used to go to

West Berlin. She hunched herself into the seat as Schiller opened the driver's door and climbed in.

After driving through unfamiliar eastern parts of the Hauptstadt, they came to another checkpoint, and Schiller again flashed his ID as a guard peered in through the window.

Once they were waved through, Schiller finally broke the silence. 'You're privileged, *Oberleutnant*,' he said. 'This is a restricted zone. Even for a *Kriminalpolizei* officer like yourself. You won't find it on any street maps of the Hauptstadt.'

On their right, she saw a watchtower at the corner of a four-metre high wall, topped with barbed wire. It looked like a section of the protection barrier, although this was several kilometres further east. 'Here we are,' said Schiller.

The Stasi captain again showed his pass and the gates to the compound opened. Schiller parked the Volvo in the courtyard, turned the engine off and then gestured to Müller to follow him inside.

Their footsteps echoed down a series of corridors – a labyrinth she knew she would have no way of negotiating without someone to guide her. Every few metres there were gates of steel bars, with some sort of control lighting system. *Green on, red off*. Müller wondered what it meant when the lights were switched the other way.

Towards the end of a particularly long corridor, Schiller stopped at a door on the left and knocked. A male voice commanded them to enter.

A middle-aged man with a round face and too obviously dyed black hair stood up as they entered, rubbing his eyes and then replacing his spectacles. Schiller performed the introductions.

'*Oberleutnant* Müller, this is *Major* Hunsberger. He's in charge of the investigation into your husband, Gottfried.'

The Stasi major ushered them to sit. 'I'm pleased to meet you, *Oberleutnant* Müller, though I wish the circumstances were more pleasant. In a moment we will bring your husband in to see you, but there are a few things we need you to look at first.'

Müller nodded, but said nothing.

Hunsberger reached into the pile of papers on his desk, and drew out a selection, which he placed in front of him, smoothing out the pages. He pushed his glasses back up his nose again, and brandished one of the documents between his thumb and forefinger. 'What we have here is a signed request from your husband Gottfried to terminate your marriage.'

'*He* wants to divorce *me*?'

'That's correct,' said Hunsberger. 'I believe you have already been briefed about our surveillance pictures showing you with your deputy, Werner Tilsner. We, of course, had to show those to your husband.'

Müller felt a sudden coldness inside. She breathed, slowly, deeply. Struggling for air.

'He requests a divorce on the grounds of your adultery.'

She held the Stasi officer's gaze. 'I didn't commit adultery. Those photographs are not what they seem. This is outrageous!'

Hunsberger ignored her denial, but paused a moment. 'However,' he continued, placing the document to one side, and instead picking up a photograph, 'it doesn't suit our purposes for the divorce to be initiated by him. We simply wanted to demonstrate to you that your marriage has no future. I think you'd agree with me there. And while you were away in Rügen, we received new evidence. This.' Hunsberger thrust the photograph under her nose.

Müller recoiled in shock. She immediately recognised the girl in the photo from the pictures reluctantly supplied by the *Jugendwerkhof* deputy director: it was Beate Ewert. Here she was with her eyes closed, the back of a man's head in view, his hand on her teenaged breast. Hunsberger handed her a second photo, from a slightly different angle. Now, from the side of the man's face, she could clearly see it was Gottfried, kissing the girl on the mouth. *No!* This couldn't be true. These photos had to be fakes. She swallowed repeatedly, fighting the urge to be sick. Hands shaking, she turned the photos face down.

Now it was Schiller's turn to speak. 'I'm sorry we had to show you these, Comrade *Oberleutnant*. The girl is only fifteen. You know what that means from your police legal training?'

Müller nodded. 'Section 149 of the Republic's criminal code,' she said in a quiet voice.

'Exactly, *Oberleutnant* Müller,' said Hunsberger. 'In the event a victim's moral immaturity is exploited, then the perpetrator is guilty of a criminal act. But irrespective of the criminality or not, is this really the sort of man to whom you wish to be married?'

Schiller joined the fray now. 'If so, *Oberleutnant*, I'm afraid you will have to resign from the force immediately.'

Müller felt as though her whole body was collapsing in on itself. She couldn't believe this was something Gottfried would do; yet now those pictures were indelibly etched on her brain. Shocking images. If she accepted them as fact, she knew she had to accept that she had married a pervert. She and Gottfried had their problems, and their marriage had long been teetering on the edge of breakdown, but surely he wouldn't have stooped to that?

With tears beginning to pool in her eyes, she raised her head and looked first at Schiller, then Hunsberger. 'I need to talk to him first. Whatever evidence you have, whatever photographs you have, I need to hear it from him. You must at least allow me that.'

The two Stasi officers looked at each other, then Hunsberger nodded. 'We will let you see your husband now.'

They seemed content to leave her alone in the interrogation room until Gottfried was brought to her. But judging by what had happened so far – the photographs she'd been shown – she was under surveillance anyway.

She fiddled with the buttons on her jacket as she waited. What she'd seen – Gottfried molesting Beate – it didn't bear thinking about. It was scarcely credible. And yet the evidence was there.

As Gottfried was finally brought into the room by one of the guards, she found herself moving back in her chair towards the window, edging away. He hadn't looked up, and his cowed demeanour indicated that he believed he'd been brought in here for another bout of questioning. She noticed a bruise on the side of his face. Apart from that, his skin was deathly pale, his eyes sunken into their sockets. Finally, as the guard cuffed Gottfried's hands together, her husband raised his head.

'Karin!' he said, clearly shocked at her presence. She didn't react, just continued to stare at him. Part of her wanted to reach out to him, to hug him close, to give him comfort. Part of her wanted to tear his hair out. How could he have done such a thing? Gottfried had always been so considerate, so attentive to her needs. The first time they'd made love he had immediately sensed that she'd been damaged, that she needed tenderness. Yet the photographs now in the hands of the Ministry for State Security told a very different story.

'Karin, they've done a terrible thing to me. To us. The photo of me with the girl. You know it's faked, don't you?'

Müller shook her head, sadly. 'Why would anyone fake that, Gottfried? How could anyone fake a photograph like that?'

'Please, Karin. Believe me. You must believe me. You know they've done it – you saw the fakes they made of you kissing Tilsner,' he continued. 'I know I've been very suspicious and possessive, but in my heart I know you wouldn't do that to me.' Müller said nothing, and Gottfried continued, a half-crazed look in his eyes. 'I knew it couldn't be true, but they made me sign a document asking for a divorce. At first I believed it must be true, but then they showed me the doctored photo of me with Beate. It's disgusting. It never happened. What are they trying to do to us? Can't you do something?'

Müller closed her eyes for a few seconds, and clasped her hands tightly together in an attempt to stop them shaking. She didn't know what to think. Everything just seemed to be falling apart. Did she believe him? He was obviously capable of deception: the condom packet hidden on top of their wardrobe in the apartment was sufficient evidence of that. She gave a long sigh. 'And the photograph of you at the church with the Pastor? That's a fake too, I suppose?'

She watched her husband's head drop to his chest.

'No,' he said, his voice barely a whisper. 'I shouldn't have done it. I put you in an embarrassing position. I'm sorry.' Then he lifted his head again, his eyes still full of paranoia. 'I didn't even visit Beate in the sanatorium; it was Irma, her friend. They've doctored the photograph, just like with you and Tilsner –'

Müller felt the moisture gathering in her eyes. Gottfried tried to reach out to her, but she pushed his hand away. 'The photo of Tilsner and me is accurate. It's what happened,' she said flatly.

She saw in his eyes, his expression, that he felt she'd betrayed him. All of a sudden, the fight seemed to go out of him. He slumped in his chair.

'They've asked me to sign the divorce papers –'

'– no, no, please Karin, please help me, I –'

'I don't know what to think,' said Müller. She met his eyes and stared hard into them. 'If what you say is correct, it calls into question the very methods of the Ministry for State Security. So be careful what you say out loud, whatever you believe.'

'But will you help me?'

'I don't know. I don't even know if I can. I'm just an *Oberleutnant* in the People's Police – people far more senior than me are in charge.'

'Please, Karin. Please. I swear to you I'm telling the truth.'

Gottfried got down on his knees. She tried to pull him to his feet, and then bent to whisper in his ear. 'I don't know if I can help you, but I will try. But if it turns out you're lying, and if that ends my career –' She didn't complete the sentence. Instead, she gently moved his chin up, so he had to meet her eyes. In doing that, she felt his weakness, felt that he was a broken man and felt that they still had some connection, no matter how badly it had been strained.

'Guards,' she shouted. The guard waiting outside the door unlocked it and strode in. 'Please take this prisoner back to his cell.' She turned away from Gottfried, and stared out of the window.

'Karin! Karin!' he shouted. 'At least get someone to examine the photographs.' She didn't turn round. Not until she heard the metallic clang of the door being closed. Then she picked up the black-and-white prints that Hunsberger had left on the desk, and rang for Schiller to escort her out.

As Schiller drove past the barrier that signalled the edge of the restricted area, he asked Müller where she wanted to be taken. She thought about it for a moment. In many ways, she didn't want to go back to the flat – it would seem cold, empty, lonely, and in her current mood she wasn't sure she could cope with it. The only way she would survive this would be by throwing herself into her work, so maybe she should go to the office. But the empty apartment would have to be faced some time.

'Take me to Schönhauser Allee, please.'

36

Day Fourteen.
East Berlin.

If Jäger had indeed been moved to another department, he didn't seem to have lost any of his power, because he was still able to order a Ministry of State Security motorcycle messenger to deliver a summons to Müller for a meeting.

She found herself on the same tram she'd taken to the Märchenbrunnen, but this time, instead of getting off at the Friedrichshain People's Park she continued her journey towards the outer suburbs of the Hauptstadt. Jäger wanted to meet in another park, but further out, in Weissensee – at the boathouse of the actual Weisser See from which the area took its name. When she reached it, she saw the Stasi lieutenant colonel in a small boat, rowing towards the shore. He stood and steadied the craft alongside the jetty, and then held out his hand. She took it, stepped in and sat on the bench opposite him.

When she tried to greet him, he mouthed a 'shhh', and continued to row silently towards the centre of the lake. Only when they were equidistant from each shore did he pull in the oars and begin to speak.

'I'm sorry for having to meet in another out-of-the-way place,' he said. Then he drew in a slow breath. 'Things have got significantly more complicated.'

Müller nodded. 'You know Tilsner and I have been taken off the case?'

'Yes. I'm sorry if it's caused you problems. That wasn't the intention, though I warned you at the start that it wouldn't be straightforward.'

'And I understand you've been reassigned, too?'

'Yes ... and no. In our Ministry, people are always trying to pull strings, get one up on each other. In some ways, that's what this is all about. But I can't tell you more at present.'

Müller wiped her hand across her face and kept her eyes closed for a second. Then gave a long sigh. 'To be honest, being taken off the case is the least of my worries.' She paused. 'I wanted ... I wanted to talk to you about my husband.' Jäger nodded slowly. 'I need you to help him, to see if there is some way you can get him out of jail.'

Jäger placed the handholds of the oars in the rowlocks again, and gave a couple of pulls to stop the boat drifting back to shore. Müller trailed her finger in the icy water. It felt so fresh, so clean. The exact opposite of her life at present.

'If I did that,' he said, 'what could you do for me?'

Müller looked him in the eyes. 'What do you want me to do?'

'Have you still got the letter of authority I gave you? The one signed by Mielke himself?'

She knitted her brow. Despite having to appear before the panel of senior officers, despite her career hanging by a thread, she knew she still had it. She patted her jacket pocket. 'Yes. But what good is that now? I've been taken off the case.'

'Don't lose that letter. You will almost certainly still need it; I want you, and Tilsner, to continue to help me, to continue to work with me.'

'On the investigation into the killing of the girl?'

Jäger nodded.

'But I would be risking being thrown off the force for good. My career would be in tatters.'

The Stasi lieutenant colonel shrugged. 'That's the price, I'm afraid. If you want me to help your husband, you need to help me. Don't worry about Tilsner. He won't be a problem. He owes me.'

'Owes you? Owes you how?'

'Let's just say we go back a long way. So Tilsner will help, but I need you too.'

She held her head in her hands, thinking of Gottfried's pathetic pleas in the Stasi jail, the revolting photographs that she hoped must be fakes. But what if they weren't? She raised her head, and looked directly at Jäger, his western newsreader visage unperturbed and unreadable. How much did it matter to him? Why did this case matter to him? Could it be as simple as his somehow feeling personally moved by the image of the girl in the cemetery? The girl could have been his daughter. She could have been Müller's daughter.

She breathed out slowly. 'Alright,' she said finally. 'But please don't let me down.'

'I will do my best, Karin. I can promise you that much. But I cannot promise you that the outcome will be favourable. Your husband is in serious trouble.' He began to row again, this time in a circular pattern, the splashing as the tips broke the surface feeling almost sacrilegious to Müller in the way it disturbed the eerie calm of the dark water. 'Now,' he said, after a few moments. 'Fill me in with everything you found out on Rügen.'

Jäger said nothing as she talked, and gave little away in his facial expression, simply continuing to row round in a large circle, using the right oar to do most of the work, occasionally trimming with the left if they started to drift from the centre of the lake. His lack of reaction made Müller wonder if none of this was news to him – as if she was simply confirming information he already knew, or at least suspected. His concentration seemed to be as much on the rest of the lake, and the shoreline, as on her – his eyes scanning the handful of people strolling at the lakeside. Was the agent from the Märchenbrunnen among them?

'That's about it,' she said, as she came to the end of her update.

Jäger rested the oars on the rowlocks again, and held her gaze. 'So do you think this is all connected to the dead girl in the cemetery?'

She held her palms outwards, and shrugged. 'I just don't know. The clues in the car all pointed to Rügen or the Harz, but they all seemed terribly convenient.' She stared hard at him. 'As though they could have been planted.' Jäger's face didn't change from its neutral expression – if he knew it was all a set-up, he wasn't revealing that to her. 'Of course, it could all just be coincidence,' she continued. 'If the teenagers are safely at the home in Schierke, then it takes us no further.'

'I can check the Ministry of Education records. But what is written there is simply that. I will try to track Neumann down. Do you have photographs of him and the children?'

'The children, yes. We got some from the *Jugendwerkhof*, and others of Irma Behrendt from the grandmother. But she has natural red hair. The girl in the cemetery is not her. The other girl, though, Beate Ewert –'

'You think it could be her?'

'It's a possibility, yes. Although, as I said, the *Jugendwerkhof* staff insist she's safe in Schierke. And the murdered girl's face was so badly mutilated no one on Rügen was able to identify her.'

Jäger started to row back to the lakeside. She noticed him glance warily at a figure seated outside the Milchhäuschen café. Jäger seemed to deliberately change course after spotting the man.

'This is useful information, Karin. We already had suggestions – from our own inquiries – that this case was perhaps linked to the Ostsee coast, somewhere. It makes sense. I will see what I can find out about the whereabouts of the children, and let you know. I will also see if I can trace Ewert's parents, and try to get one of them to identify the body in the morgue.'

He steadied the boat by the jetty, jumped out and then held its rope taut with one hand, while helping Müller climb out with the other.

She looked into his eyes. 'And you won't forget my husband, will you?'

'No, Karin, but sorting that out – if indeed I can – may take some time. It won't be overnight.'

'Is there a number on which I can reach you?'

As they started to walk back to the park exit, he shook his head. 'No, wait to hear from me in the usual way. With a sealed telegram. There are still some Ministry of State Security messengers I can trust.'

37

Eight months earlier (June 1974).
On board the cargo ship.

My delight at reaching the West is starting to wear thin. Mathias and Beate continue to whisper sweet nothings to each other and share meaningful glances. While Beate regularly makes the effort to talk to me, I can see that – to Mathias – I am nothing. Just the thorn between two roses. But if it hadn't been for me, neither of them would have escaped.

We take turns to make occasional forays to the porthole on the stairwell, but the canal we're travelling down seems tens of kilometres long.

None of the crew come down here to the hold. Why would they? As far as they're concerned, all that's here is hundreds, thousands of cardboard boxes full of self-assembly beds. But we still think it's safer not to venture beyond the bounds of the stairwell – despite our hunger, despite our thirst.

We sit in the near-darkness of the hold, listening to the hum of the engines and the creaking of metal, with our backs slumped against the pallets of cardboard boxes. A small shaft of daylight illuminates Mathias's face for a moment, and I see it fused to Beate's.

'Should we check the porthole again?' I ask. 'To see where we've got to?'

Mathias sighs, and pulls his lips free.

'You go if you must, Irma. It will give Beate and I a few moments of privacy.'

Beate gives him a playful slap. 'Mathias!' she says, but the scolding is only mock-scolding.

'Will you come with me, Beate?' I ask, hopefully.

'OK. In a moment,' she says. I watch Mathias turn her face back to his. The faint sound of lips and tongues duelling makes me feel slightly ill.

My legs feel shaky as I stand. Whether it's the effects of lack of food, lack of water or just plain old seasickness, I'm not sure. I head to the stairwell and the porthole on my own.

Sitting there, watching the occasional house or car glide by, I worry about why I feel so sad. Wasn't this what I wanted? To leave the Republic behind? To leave the horrors of the *Jugendwerkhof* for good? But I suppose I expected I would be doing it with my best friend, that it would be a huge adventure. It's not quite worked out like that. I feel lonely, jealous and just a little afraid.

The sun is starting to set, and in the last rays of the evening, everything on the canal side is thrown into sharp contrast. It all looks so clean, so new, compared to the Republic. And now we're entering another town. From the lights, the cranes, the warehousing, it appears to be a port. I have no idea where, but I guess it is still West Germany. Any signs I do see are still in German.

The vessel slows and the hum of the engines dies down. Is this it, have we arrived? I rush down the stairwell to tell Beate that we should get ready, that we should try to jump on the quayside before any officials can stop us.

I hear it before I see it, as I move quietly back into the hold. Mathias panting rhythmically. Answering breaths from Beate. I stand, rigid, in the shadows. Watching. I feel rage, jealousy, confusion.

I don't think they've seen me. I retreat to the peace of the stairwell, climb the two flights and slump down once more by the porthole, more alone than ever. The engine noise and vibrations have increased again. Lights still shine through the dusk on the shore, but they're further away now, dancing up and down in the porthole. I clutch my stomach as the boat hits a wave, or trough; I'm not sure which. We're at sea again. Nausea takes hold, but there's nothing left in my stomach to regurgitate. No, no, no! *Surely we can't have got so near to the West to then be denied our escape?*

We seem to be hugging the shoreline, because the lights never completely disappear, a continuous galaxy of western freedom, each one signalling a family home, a business, a street where the Republic has no influence – where its rules count for nothing. That's what I assume, anyway. That's what I hope.

In less than an hour, the motion of the ship has calmed – just a gentle rocking and a steady hum that slowly lulls me to sleep.

I wake with a start, shivering from the cold, disorientated, the hunger from days without food gnawing at my stomach. Thinking

I'm back at the *Jugendwerkhof*, trying to push my body further into Oma's hand-knitted *Strickpulli*. Already June, but summer stubbornly refusing to arrive. The engine noise has changed, the sea – if it is still the sea – a flat calm. Outside the porthole, it's now a black sky, but the lights are brighter, closer. Cranes tower up like giant metallic daddy-long-legs, throwing irregular-shaped shadows across a port. Floodlit ships at the quayside, being unloaded, even at this time of night. Where? I try to find a sign, scanning from left to right. Then I see it in white lettering on a blue-and-red background – a huge notice lit up above a warehouse: *Hamburger Hafen- und Lagerhaus-AG*. We've reached Hamburg! All of a sudden, the shroud of sadness and jealousy I've been wallowing in lifts, and I'm running down the stairs, the metal clanging and echoing under my footfall.

I enter the hold, see Mathias and Beate sleeping in each other's arms, and I shake Beate awake.

'We're here. We're here,' I shout. 'It's Hamburg. Quick. Let's get ready.'

The two lovebirds stand up, and rub their eyes simultaneously. Then they embrace, but this time I try to fight the jealousy back, and Beate pulls me in for a group hug. She whispers in my ear: 'I'm so proud of you, Irma, this is all thanks to you.' She squeezes me tight, and we are best friends again.

Mathias looks slightly awestruck, and I realise my hope that he might take control is misplaced. It will be down to me again.

'I think we need to find our way up on deck,' I tell them. 'We need to find food, drink. Somewhere to stay. I have an aunt near Nuremburg. In Fürth. Maybe we could make our way there?'

Mathias shrugs, looks glum. 'We don't have any money, clothes or anything. How would we get there?' But I'm not going to let his pessimism deter me. Even Beate tells him to stop being such a misery.

'The authorities will help us. They are used to receiving *Republikflüchtlinge*. They must be.'

I urge them to follow me up the stairwell. We have no plan of the boat, no idea which door leads where. I just know that somehow we have to find out where the crew disembark; we must hide near there till the gangplank connects the ship to shore, and then fade into the night.

Up another flight of stairs, and we hear noises. Shouting. Hatches opening. I try to pull down the handle on the door, but I'm not strong enough. Mathias adds his hand, and together we manage to open it. I urge him back, behind me, and open the door just a crack. I'm not sure if this is a German ship, and, if so, whether it's from the East or the West. If it's from the East, the risk is that there will be guards on board, but all I can see is seamen unwinding giant ropes to tether us to the quayside.

Their shouting dies down. The ropes look taut. The engine noise has been cut, and there is no motion to the boat. We must have safely docked. I give a tiny wave of my hand to the other two, beckoning them as I start to move out of the doorway and along the deck. We maintain our crouching position as we run, heading towards the lights of the bridge. Then I see it. The gangplank. Men in green uniforms coming aboard. Darker green than in the Republic.

We've been spotted. I urge Beate and Mathias back towards the stairwell to the hold to try to hide. But Mathias just stands his ground and grabs Beate as she tries to follow me. I see her pleading to me with her eyes. Then I turn and run. Out of the corner of my eye I see the West German uniforms follow as Mathias points me out. Panting, I swing back round the corner of the opened door to the stairwell. I clatter down as fast as I can, jumping steps, colliding with the metal walls. I hear dogs snarling behind me, their barks echoing through the bowels of the ship.

In the hold, I find my opened bed box; I squeeze inside backwards, holding my breath to try to avoid the stench of sick and sweat, and then try to pull the cardboard flaps together to conceal myself. But the dogs sniff me out, and stand there barking, as though they're howling my name. I see the cardboard flaps open, and a female face framed by a green beret stares back at me. I read the badge on her lapel as I try to control my rapid breathing. The word *Bundesgrenzschutz* in white on green. I look at her face again. She's smiling kindly.

'Welcome to the *Bundesrepublik Deutschland*,' she says, and I begin to cry.

38

February 1975. Day Fourteen.
East Berlin.

Müller took her shoes off and rested her feet on her office desk, rubbing gently where her boots had chafed at her toes. Since being summoned to the meeting in front of the panel of senior officers in Keibelstrasse, Reiniger had given her and Tilsner a list of mundane jobs to do: petty theft, a flasher, criminal damage. All involved legwork that would usually be the preserve of some uniform or other. But so far no actual disciplinary action had been taken against them. She'd been hoping for some speedy news from Jäger about Gottfried's welfare, but perhaps that was unrealistic.

In the outer office, she saw Tilsner studying the teleprinter intensely, as it spewed out information in its slightly irregular way – a burst of a sentence, then nothing for several minutes till more came through. She could hear the clatter of printing resume, then saw Tilsner beckon.

'Boss!' he shouted. 'Here, now. Look at this.'

She jumped up, still in bare feet, and ran through to see what had caught his attention. She peered at the printout that Tilsner was pointing to, but he seemed determined to tell her what it said in any case.

'Big development, boss. You know you wanted me to check out the children's home in the Harz with the local police? Well that was more of a problem than it sounded. The phones are down due to the snow. Anyhow I radioed them at Wernigerode. Turns out they were trying to get through to us too.'

'Why?'

'They wouldn't say over the radio link. Said they'd telex it. And here it is. Another body's been found. Same as before. A teenager again. Only this time next to the inner German border in the Harz, rather than by the Berlin Wall. But that's why they wanted to let us know. Same sort of thing. Made to look as though the victim had escaped to the East from the West, and then been shot in the back from the West. They obviously read about the original case in *Neues Deutschland*, saw that you were the lead detective, and clearly weren't aware that we'd been ordered off the case.'

'Surely they'd have run it past one of their superiors, wouldn't they? Then they'd have found out we'd been pushed aside.'

Tilsner shrugged. 'It's the country. Back of beyond in the Harz. That's why you get all these superstitious tales of witches dancing in the forest, and that sort of rubbish. So no, thankfully they think we're still the team in charge.'

'And what do we know about the body? What age, what sex is the victim?' asked Müller, conscious that she was sounding almost as excited as he was, and mentally chastising herself for it. The age-old moral dilemma for a homicide detective: it often takes a second murder to solve the first.

'Teenager again – this time a boy, around the right age – between fifteen and seventeen.'

Müller breathed in deeply. 'We need to go there to check it out. And we could call in on the children's home at Schierke at the same time, to see whether those teenagers – if they're still alive – truly are there. The trouble is, there's no way Reiniger will let us. Not while I'm under investigation for supposedly exceeding my authority.'

Tilsner cocked his head to the side. 'I thought you said Jäger wanted us back on the original case?'

'Yes, but not openly.'

'Reiniger seems to do his bidding though. I don't know what sort of hold he has over him – there seems to be something.' Müller remembered what Jäger had said: that *Tilsner* owed him. There were too many secrets in this case. Too many lies. She wasn't sure what or who to believe.

The bell at the office front door rang. Both looked around for Elke, expecting her to answer it, then they realised it was too late in the evening and she'd already gone home. Tilsner went instead.

As he opened the door, Müller could see behind him it was the motorbike messenger from the Ministry of State Security, the one who regularly delivered Jäger's messages. Tilsner took an envelope from him, closed the door and then brought it to Müller.

She broke the red wax seal, emblazoned with the Stasi's emblem: the Republic's flag, flying from a rifle held up by a muscular arm. And then tore open the envelope and began to read:

You and T must go to Harz. Latest killing there may be linked. Three Rügen teens are in Schierke home according to Ministry of Education records in Berlin. Please check this when in Harz. Reiniger cannot explicitly approve but he agrees. Do not contact him, just trust me. I will back you if any problems with Ministry. I have found Ewert's mother, so will be taking her to morgue. Will contact you once you're there via Wernigerode Volkspolizei. Good luck. KJ.

KJ. Klaus Jäger. How had he heard about this new Harz killing before they had?

'Well?' asked Tilsner expectantly.

Müller realised she'd just been standing there, thinking things through, worrying that the latest development could be part of an elaborate set-up by the Stasi lieutenant colonel. 'Jäger's saying we should go to the Harz. He already knows about the new body.'

Tilsner whistled through his teeth. 'It figures, I suppose. He's got his fingers in lots of pies.'

'And I gather you two go back a long way?' Müller held Tilsner's eyeline, challenging him.

He dropped his eyes, and scuffed his left shoe on the floor, as though kicking an imaginary stone. *Embarrassment or guilt?*

'I suppose he told you that, did he? It's not something I want to talk about.'

'Why not?'

Tilsner raised his eyes. 'Ask him,' he said, an edge to his voice. 'He's not as clean as he makes out. I'm not even sure we can trust him.'

Müller said nothing, just lifted Tilsner's cuff and pointed to the watch.

'It's a nice watch,' he said. 'I like good watches.'

Müller shrugged. 'I was just wondering, Werner –'

'Wondering what?'

'When Jäger said you two went back a long way, was that all the way to Stasi school?'

Tilsner sneered at her, turned his back and appeared to study the teleprinter again.

'You'd better get the Wartburg ready,' she said. 'It'll need snow chains. And you might need to go home and pack a case.'

He turned, his face still grim after the argument. 'We're not going tonight, are we? There's been a huge dump of snow in the Harz; it's sleeting here and the roads will be awful.'

Müller imagined the teenager's body, lying in a snow-covered Harz forest. And the poor girl from St Elisabeth's cemetery, who they still hadn't identified, with her ragged black cape and pathetic attempts to mimic black nail varnish.

'Yes,' she said. 'We need to leave as soon as possible. Time may be running out.'

39

Day Fourteen.
East Germany.

A mixture of rain and sleet hammered against the windscreen of the Wartburg, as they drove southeast through the outskirts of the Hauptstadt towards Bohnsdorf to join the motorway system. Tilsner leant forwards in the driver's seat, wiping away condensation from the inside.

'Can't see a thing,' he complained, narrowly missing a broken-down motorbike at the side of the road, swerving at the last minute.

'If you can't see, then slow down, or stop,' she warned.

'I thought we were in a rush to view this boy's body?'

'We are. But I'd rather get there alive.'

Ever since Magdeburg, the snow had started settling on the road, slowing their progress. Müller could now see cloudlets in front of her face each time she breathed out. As the road climbed towards Blankenburg, she felt the tyres start to slip from under them.

'*Scheisse*,' said Tilsner. 'Time for the chains.' He pulled his gloves on, wiggled his fingers to warm them and then got out of the car. No traffic seemed to be passing. No one else was stupid enough to travel in this, thought Müller. It took Tilsner about fifteen minutes of manoeuvring the car, centimetre by centimetre, fiddling with the chains, before he was back inside, shivering.

'Can you warm my hands up?' he asked, resting one on her thigh, his teeth chattering.

'No,' she said. 'I don't want to start any of that stuff again. Think of your children.' But as she said it, she knew it was only partly true. It might just be a physical thing, but it was there – and she wasn't sure how long she'd be able to resist.

Tilsner stared into her eyes. 'Don't lay that on me. I might not be a good husband, but I try to be a good dad.'

Müller took his hand and placed it firmly back on the steering wheel. 'Let's just get there as soon as possible.'

It was almost another hour's laborious driving to Blankenburg, at little more than walking pace. When they finally got to the edge of the town, with its medieval buildings, Tilsner sighed. 'Nice place, but I've had enough.'

Müller grimaced. 'It's only another fifteen kilometres or so to Wernigerode. And I thought you said the police there had arranged accommodation?'

'They have, but I'm shot. Would you like to drive the rest of the way?'

Müller didn't answer.

'I'll take that as a no. OK, we need to find rooms here then, and call the Wernigerode police and apologise. I'm sure they'll understand.'

Müller woke in the early hours in the middle of a dark dream. It featured Beate Ewert, Gottfried, Richter, Jäger and her – all at Prora. She'd suddenly become a girl again. Jäger was the director of the home. One of the teachers was making a grab for her, reaching for her breast, and – as she saw his face – she realised it was Gottfried. She tried to fight him off, push him away. Then Prora was replaced by the police college, but she was still struggling with a man. Not Gottfried, no it was *him*, it was … He wouldn't release her until she pushed with all her strength, holding something sharp in her hand. And then she was awake, sweating, throwing off the heavy mountain blankets. The perfect darkness initially disorientated her. For an instant she was still at the college, in his room with the lights off. Then she remembered. She remained bolt upright for a few seconds, heart thumping in her chest, and switched on the bedside lamp.

She went out onto the landing, to the guesthouse's shared toilet, and then to wash her hands. She jumped back slightly as she realised Tilsner was already there, drinking a beaker of water and admiring himself in the mirror. He saw her reflection, smiled and turned around.

'You couldn't sleep either, I guess? Do you want to come and join me?'

For an instant, the idea seemed attractive. A warm muscular body to hold her, to protect her from her dreams in this nightmare murder case. But she knew she ought to resist the temptation. If she didn't, they'd be finished as a partnership. It couldn't carry on if they became embroiled in a serious relationship, and surely that's what would happen if she said yes. But she doubted he'd leave his wife and kids, and she wasn't ready to become someone's mistress.

She smiled, shoved him out of the way and began washing her hands.

'That's a no then, is it?'

She just laughed, and returned to her own room.

40

Day Fifteen.
East Germany.

The snowstorm had abated overnight, and by the time Müller and Tilsner set off in the Wartburg, the ploughs had cleared the route to Wernigerode. A journey that might have taken more than an hour or longer the previous night was completed by Tilsner in around twenty minutes. The sun had broken through the clouds, and Müller needed her sunglasses as she admired the scenery to the left-hand side of the road: dazzling white snow softening the angles of the spruce forests of the Harz.

The local *Kriminalpolizei* were expecting them, and for the next part of their journey to the site where the boy's body was found, they followed the Wernigerode *Kripo* officer and his assistant, in a virtually identical Wartburg. The police captain – with a rhythmical name of *Hauptmann* Baumann, and a ruddy mountain complexion – had briefed them that the body had been found close to the border zone, in the forest a few metres from where Fernverkehrsstrasse 27 came to a dead end. The road was chopped in two there by the inner German border.

A few hundred metres past Elend, the police car in front stopped, and Baumann got out and came to speak to them. As Tilsner wound open the driver's window, Baumann leant down, his muscular arm resting half in, half out of the vehicle, looking to Müller a bit like the bough of a tree. Solid, dependable, she thought; they would be safe with Baumann.

'You'll need to put the snow chains on from here onwards, *Unterleutnant*. It hasn't been ploughed. The road's rarely used except by border troops. Anyone else has to have a special permit.'

Müller leant across Tilsner. 'Would that include Franz Neumann, the *Jugendwerkhof* director we asked you to investigate?'

Baumann slapped his oversized gloved hands together in the cold. 'It would. But we haven't found any trace of him in this area. And the children's home at Schierke has no record of the three teenagers who were supposed to have been transferred there.'

'So how come all the records show they *were* transferred?' asked Tilsner.

The *Kripo* captain sighed and shrugged. Then he clapped his glove against the Wartburg's windscreen, shaking the car on its suspension springs. 'We can talk about all that back at the office. First you must get your snow chains on, so we can show you the site of the body.' He walked back towards the car in front, opened the boot and started to remove his chains. Tilsner mirrored his actions for their own vehicle.

When he was back in the car, and they'd begun to follow the Harz officers again, Tilsner turned to Müller. 'Neumann obviously faked those records in Rügen,' he said.

'Yes,' agreed Müller. 'But somehow he also seems to have altered state records in the Department of Education. Or else someone helped him to do that. We need to find him, and fast. Jäger said he would send a picture through to Wernigerode. We need to ask them about that when we've finished here.'

As they continued to carefully follow the Wernigerode officers, the two detectives could see tracks in the snow on the road ahead, presumably where the police had been back and forth, sealing the area, taking photographs, removing the body.

After about three kilometres, the tracks came to an end – the road blocked by a red-and-white barrier. Baumann pulled over and parked, and Tilsner followed. The *Hauptmann* and his assistant, *Unterleutnant* Vogel, walked back to Müller and her deputy, who themselves climbed out.

'It's about fifty metres into the forest, just there.' Baumann pointed to where the snow had been trampled into a makeshift path by the repeat journeys of various police officers; their boot prints disappeared down an old forest track. He saw Müller examining the snowy ground. 'The footprints all belong to us, I'm afraid.' Baumann strode off with Vogel alongside him, and Müller and Tilsner immediately behind. 'However, my officers were very careful not to disturb the tracks they did find. They made sure they photographed them before they could be contaminated.'

'What sort of tracks?' asked Müller.

'Tyre tracks.'

'Have you identified the make of tyre?' asked Tilsner.

Baumann glanced at his young *Unterleutnant*. 'Any progress on that, Comrade Vogel?'

'No,' admitted Vogel, scratching the tight dark curls of his hair. The younger detective was a stark contrast to his superior. While Baumann was all agrarian ruggedness, Vogel looked slightly out of place – almost like a younger Gottfried, thought Müller. As though he should still be at university. 'We haven't been able to find a matching pattern,' said the *Unterleutnant*. 'To be honest, we were hoping you lot from Berlin might be able to help with that.'

Baumann nodded his giant head. 'That's partly why we contacted you, Comrade Müller. We'd read about your case in *Neues Deutschland*. This seems, on the surface, to be a similar killing.'

'But the tyre tracks at our site weren't mentioned in that report,' said Müller.

Baumann shrugged. 'Nevertheless, there are similarities I'm sure you can help us with.'

The two local detectives started walking down the track again, with Müller and Tilsner following. In a few metres, they came to a small clearing. Sunlight streamed through overhead, throwing sharp, knife-like shadows from the spruce trees; the shadows appeared as sentries, standing guard over the small patch of ground. The purity of the forest had been violated here, thought Müller, just as the sanctity of St Elisabeth cemetery had been violated in Berlin. The difference was that here the West Berlin traffic noise was replaced by virtual silence. There was the odd howl of what Müller assumed were guard dogs at the border – but far more distant and irregular than in the Hauptstadt.

'Do you have the photographs of the body?' asked Müller.

Vogel reached into a grey canvas bag he carried over his shoulder and produced a series of black-and-white prints, enclosed in cellophane. He handed them to Tilsner, who divided them approximately in half, and in turn handed one half-pile to Müller.

Müller's first photo showed the body as discovered by a local forest worker. The teenager had been left in a similar position to his female counterpart in Berlin: on his front, facing east. Bullet holes in the back. A bloody T-shirt. Broken and twisted leg. There was nothing to confirm this was Mathias Gellman – the face had again been badly mutilated, but Tilsner had already established in his initial radio conversation with Wernigerode the previous day that his physical characteristics matched.

'Here, boss,' said Tilsner, drawing her attention to one of the photos from his bundle. 'Training shoe footprints, apparently running away from the direction of the border.' She held up the photographs against the real-life background, comparing the two, trying to imagine the scene. It was all depressingly, disturbingly consistent.

Whoever had done this was capable of pure evil.

They had to find him. Stop him.

Before he killed again.

41

Eight months earlier (June 1974).
Hamburg, West Germany.

The female customs officer convinces me that her dog is harmless, and I agree to come out of the self-assembly-bed box. She helps me get my shoulders free, and then slides me out. I can see her recoil slightly from the smell, but her dog leaps up, licking my face, until she orders it to heel.

I follow her up the stairwell and out onto the deck.

'You must have had a horrible journey,' she says as we walk along the deck to the gangway. 'How long were you on the boat?'

'I'm not sure,' I reply. 'It felt like days. Maybe it was only a couple?'

She looks me up and down and sniffs, a faint hint of distaste in her face. 'You must be hungry.'

I laugh. 'Hungry, thirsty and filthy. I'm looking forward to my first western drink, my first western meal and my first western bath.'

She steps to one side, as a male officer joins us. 'We're taking you to a hostel while we process everything,' he says. 'You'll get a meal there, something to drink and you can wash. We'll provide you with a change of clothes.'

I can see that on the quayside a green *Bundesgrenzschutz* minivan is waiting, its blue light flashing and motor running. A male officer leads me down the gangplank, and the woman with the dog follows behind. They seem friendly enough, seem to want to help. At the bottom of the gangplank, there's just an instant where I could make a run for it if I wanted to. But why would I want to? I'm here, on western soil at last.

I climb aboard the van. Mathias and Beate are already there, holding hands on one of the bench seats. Beate smiles, and squashes up to let me sit next to her. But Mathias won't meet my eyes.

'What's the matter?' I ask him. 'Aren't you happy to be here?'

The journey through the port and into the city is one of excitement. The shop signs fascinate me, with their flashing coloured lights. It's the same feeling I used to get as a young child on Christmas Eve in Sellin, at Oma's – that tingling feeling, waiting for Oma to ring the bell and open the locked door to the room with the presents and tree inside. What would *der Weihnachtsmann* have brought me this year?

Beate is just as elated. 'Can you take us to see the Reeperbahn?' she calls to the driver.

There's an exchange between the driver and a suited official, who I guess is also with the *Bundesgrenzschutz*, but in plain clothes. The besuited man nods, and turns to us smiling. 'We will drive past it. You can't get out though, not until we've processed you at the hostel.'

Beate and I giggle. But Mathias is stony-faced, miserable. What's wrong with him?

'We can't go down the main bit of the Reeperbahn,' the suited man calls back from the front. 'It's pedestrianised. But you'll be able to see some of the nightlife.'

In a few minutes, we're there. Beate and I look left and right, pointing things out to each other. There are young girls in tiny miniskirts on the corners. I'm not sure if they're prostitutes or just dressed to look sexy. And there are nightclubs, and burger bars. It's so different from the Republic, and this – though I almost want to pinch myself to believe it – is my new home. I wonder whether Fürth, where my aunt lives, is as exciting.

All too quickly, we leave the bright lights behind, and now seem to be in the suburbs. All the road signs are different, all the shop signs are different, all the cars are different. Schools, hospitals, petrol stations, supermarkets: the same, yet different. As though someone has lifted up an East German town, coated it in bright paint, added lots more traffic and people, and then dropped it down in another part of the world. For a moment I think of the *Jugendwerkhof* and those I've left behind. I feel sorry for the ones who showed me kindness. Herr Müller, Frau Schettler, even Maria Bauer. Once a sworn enemy, yet she had helped me to escape. But then I think of Richter, and Neumann, and thank God I'm no longer there.

Beate grips my hand as we turn into some sort of barbed wire-topped compound. Maybe she's scared this is the West German equivalent of Prora Ost. But the female officer with the dog smiles reassuringly at us, and the dog itself is barking and wagging its tail in the back of the van, as though it knows it's home.

We're taken straight to the canteen, urged to sit down, and then the officers and the suited man are all helping us; they're fetching us Coca-Colas, crisps, bowls of hot soup, which seem out of place given the season. I feel as though I could eat as much as they're able to put in front of us. Beate and I slurp the soup noisily, then break off bread from the rolls, dip it into the meaty broth and stuff it into our mouths. Even Mathias seems to have thawed slightly and is eating as eagerly as us.

'I don't want to ever drink Vita Cola again,' I say, even though it was a luxury in the East, for which we saved up our pocket money.

'Or eat Spreewald pickles,' says Beate.

'Or Nudossi,' adds Mathias. And then I feel slightly sad again, because Nudossi – when we occasionally got it for breakfast in Prora – was a real treat. I can almost taste the memory of the nutty chocolate spread.

As soon as we finish the soup, suit man grabs our bowls, and nice woman officer is back with the next course. Currywurst with chips, the steam rising from each hot plate. I just look at mine for a moment, then lean down and breathe in the spicy aroma, letting the saliva gather in my mouth – savouring the smell. Then I cut a slice of wurst, add it to a few chips on my fork, dunk it in the curry sauce, add some tomato ketchup and thrust it in my mouth. There's too much, the curry gets up my nose and I splutter it all out again onto the plate.

'Yuck!' exclaims Beate, laughing. 'Don't they teach you any manners, you Ostlers?' She winks at me. Even Mathias grins.

After our meal, we don't have to clear away our plates; the officers tell us to leave them as they are, and direct us to our bedroom and the showers on the first floor.

There are two sets of bunk beds in the room, and I realise with surprise that Mathias will be sharing with us. I know I won't get much sleep tonight now, because the two lovebirds will be noisily entwined. Oh well. Even the thought of that is not going to dampen my spirits.

Then Beate and I are in the showers, spraying each other, shampooing each other's hair, washing each other's backs. And I realise, in our nakedness, that we are not so very different. Being in the West has made me feel more beautiful, more confident. Yes, I've got curly red hair. But I'll get it cut, in a fashionable western style. Yes, I'm overweight. But I can go on a diet. Yes, Beate is absurdly pretty, but here in the West there will be lots of pretty girls, all with the latest fashions and make-up, and she will have to start again. So we are not so very different. And we are friends. She smiles at me, and we hug under the shower spray, the water cascading over our faces. Two very happy girls who are free at last – the very best of friends until our dying day.

In the middle of the night, I hear Mathias hiss Beate's name. I see her shape climb down from the top bunk above me, and move to his bed – the bottom bunk of the opposite set. She climbs in, and at first they are just whispering very quietly together. I toy with the idea of asking them to be quiet, but I don't really care. They are happy, they are together, why shouldn't they whisper to each other? And even when the bed starts rocking and creaking, even when Beate starts shamelessly calling his name, even when he is grunting on every thrust, I cannot work up any anger. I just lie, and listen, and dream of the West and of one day finding a boyfriend of my own – someone who will take me as I am; someone who will cherish my curly red hair, my determination, my sense of adventure. The attributes that have helped both Mathias and

Beate win new lives in the West. Because I know they could have never done it without me. It was my plan. And it worked.

The next day – over breakfast – the officers begin what they call 'processing'. I expect it's to provide us with our new West German passports, maybe some Deutschmarks. Perhaps they will give me train tickets down to Fürth to my aunt's. I don't know, and I don't really care. I don't look at the paperwork, just sign where they want, knowing that I am free.

Then we're in the van again. The three of us, and the same officers, and the same suited man. I try to catch the female officer's eye, but she's looking down at her hands with a slightly sad demeanour. Oh well, I guess people still have their troubles in the West. Maybe she's had an argument with her husband.

Beate and I are still holding hands childishly as the van sets off, out into the Hamburg suburbs again, and onto the autobahn. Sleek luxury cars overtake us at lightning speeds. We take the A7 towards Hanover. Beate and I start singing *Hänschen Klein*, clapping along; Mathias puts his hands over his ears. I glance again at the female officer, but find her eyes wet with tears. She looks away.

Beate shouts at suit man: 'Are you taking us all the way to Irma's aunt in Fürth?' Because although our geography of the Federal Republic is not good, we both know that's the way we're heading. He just shakes his head, but doesn't enlighten us further.

At Hanover, we turn onto the A2 and see the signs to West Berlin. Well, that wouldn't be such a bad place to end up. The words to *Hänschen Klein* run around my head, even though we've stopped singing it aloud:

> *Hänschen klein ging allein*
> *In die weite Welt hinein.*
> *Stock und Hut stehn ihm gut,*
> *Ist gar wohlgemut.*

I don't get as far as the second verse. By then, the motion of the van and the roar of the autobahn have lulled me to sleep.

What wakes me is Beate, tugging at my sleeve. 'Look,' she says, pointing at what appears to be a border crossing. I frown. There's a tense atmosphere inside the van. Suit man is gathering papers together. Dog woman is looking at me vigilantly, but with a set face. Even the dog seems alert, ears pricked, panting next to his mistress.

'Where are we?' They don't answer. I look at Mathias. He gives a sly little smile. 'Do you know, Mathias?' He just shrugs.

Something isn't right, but we're waved through the crossing. Maybe we're at the entrance to West Berlin. Beate holds my hand, but this time tightly, nervously.

Then I see the sign: '*Herzlich Willkommen in der DDR.*'

I jump to my feet, trying to drag Beate with me, but Mathias is holding her back. I let go and try to open the van door. The dog starts barking, straining at its leash. Suit man is shouting; dog woman is trying to grab me. The other male officer pins me down before I can get the door open. What sort of nightmare is this? 'Get off me,' I shout. 'I don't want to go back, I won't go back.' Dog woman is trying to shush me gently, but the other officer has his hand over my mouth. I try to bite him.

'*Miststück!*' he screams, but doesn't let go.

And then we're at the DDR checkpoint. *Grenztruppen* rush to the van, handcuffing the three of us. Beate and I are snarling like wildcats.

'Mathias, do something,' shouts Beate, hoping he will be her knight in shining armour. But he is strangely subdued. Unresisting. Almost as though he wants to go back. And then I realise. He does! The *Arschloch*. He didn't want to escape from the DDR. He just wanted to be with her. To keep her, trap her with him, like a butterfly pinned in a frame.

I'm still screaming, trying to kick the border troops, but they put us in arm locks and march us to the checkpoint building. I wrench my head round to look back at the van, and the West German border officers who have betrayed us. I can't believe it; dog woman seemed so nice. She is crying, shouting at suit man, and then she holds my gaze, and I see her mouth: 'Sorry.'

The three of us are taken into a room at the side of the checkpoint, and I see the back of a man's head in a swivel chair, facing away from us.

The chair swivels round, and I hear Beate scream.

But there he is, a manic grin creasing his horrible scarred face, and lifting his black eyepatch slightly out of place.

Director Franz Neumann, of *Jugendwerkhof* Prora Ost.

42

Wernigerode might have been out in the provinces but its police headquarters put Marx-Engels-Platz to shame. The *Kripo* team here were housed in a smart modern block – sharing offices with the rest of the town's *Volkspolizei*. Baumann and Vogel even had a special room reserved for their inquiry.

Scanning the photographs pinned to one wall, Müller noticed the tyre track patterns. As in Berlin, the *Kriminaltechniker* here had produced a negative image of the tracks found in the snow. Müller felt the hairs stand up on the back of her neck. She waved Tilsner over.

'Look familiar?' she asked.

'*Scheisse*.'

'Gislaved. I'm almost certain,' she whispered.

Vogel noticed the two Berlin detectives staring closely at the image. 'Do you recognise them?'

Müller nodded. 'They're from a Swedish tyre. Fitted to Volvos.'

The Wernigerode *Unterleutnant* immediately understood – Müller saw it in the pallor of his youthful face. She was confused. Surely someone couldn't have hired the wedding limousine from West Berlin again? And brought it all the way here, to the Harz? That would be madness. And how would they have negotiated the narrow forest track? A car perhaps, but not a stretch limousine.

Vogel had ushered Baumann over.

'The tyre tracks,' he said. 'They're from a Volvo. Do you understand what that means, Comrade Baumann?' Baumann had a blank look on his face. 'It's almost certainly from a car assigned to a government official.'

'*Verdammt!*' exclaimed Baumann.

'Or a Stasi official,' added Vogel.

'Did your *Kriminaltechniker* measure the wheelbase?' asked Tilsner.

Vogel leafed through his notebook. 'I'm not sure. But he was categorical it was from a saloon car. Quite a large saloon, but definitely a saloon. And he was adamant he'd never seen that tyre pattern before.'

Tilsner nodded thoughtfully.

Baumann slumped down in a chair. 'I could tell this one was going to be trouble. If it had been a hundred metres or so further west we could have left it to the border troops. Now it looks like we'll have to inform the Stasi. Usually they leave us to our own devices, which – to be honest – is how I prefer it.' He eyeballed Müller. 'Is that why this Stasi *Oberstleutnant* is involved? He's faxed through a photograph of this Neumann fellow. Most of the phones are down due to the snow, but the fax is still working.'

'Can you bring it to me?' she asked.

Baumann walked over to a desk, opened the top drawer and picked out two pieces of paper.

The first was the faxed photograph, and as he handed it to Müller, she immediately felt a sense of dread come over her. She wasn't sure why. Perhaps it was the black patch over Neumann's left eye, or the scar that ran down his cheek. He certainly looked capable of the killings, but Müller knew that looks were almost always deceptive.

Something else nagged her about the poor-quality faxed photo – a sense of familiarity, although she was certain she'd never met the man before.

Baumann coughed. Müller looked up, and saw him proffering the second faxed sheet. She took it.

It was a terse note, telegram-style, faxed from notepaper headed with the Ministry for State Security emblem, addressed to her.

Went to basement at Charité with mother. Confirmed as B.E. Good luck with the investigation. KJ.

Less than two lines of text, and just two initials instead of her name. *B.E.* After days without a proper face, without a name, the dead girl in the cemetery suddenly had one; the one Müller had suspected ever since the visit to *Jugendwerkhof* Prora Ost: Beate Ewert, Irma Behrendt's best friend. Beate, the one who'd found life so unbearable in the youth workhouse. As Baumann and Vogel looked on quizzically, she handed the note to Tilsner. Her deputy shook his head, a grim expression on his face, and then gave it back to her. As Müller held the note between her fingers, she stared at her unpainted nails. And tried to picture Beate. In her last happy moments. Colouring in her nails with a black felt-tip pen.

If the circumstances of the Harz killing gave Müller and Tilsner a sense of déjà vu, that was heightened still further two hours later in the mortuary at Wernigerode Hospital. The pathologist, one Dr Eckstein, looked as ancient as his surroundings and tools, white hair sprouting from his ears and nostrils. To Müller, he looked like he'd probably done the exact same job in the Nazi era, possibly even in the Weimar Republic.

His actual findings were remarkably similar, and so was the rigmarole they had to go through to get a ringside seat for the autopsy. Once again, the provisions of the Order on Medical Post Examinations were haughtily quoted, but here, Baumann's local connections seemed to hold sway. When the *Hauptmann* explained that the Berlin detectives might be able to shed some light on the difficult case, Eckstein agreed to allow all four detectives to witness his examination of the body.

Just as Feuerstein had in Berlin, Eckstein demonstrated why the bullet wounds had almost certainly been inflicted post mortem.

Müller nodded. 'Our killing in Berlin was exactly the same, Comrade Eckstein.'

The pathologist looked slightly taken aback, but then went on to explain how blood had been applied to the body and clothes from the outside, only he'd already gone one step further in analysing the blood from the clothes.

'I could tell straight away something didn't look right, so I tested the blood from the T-shirt before we started the autopsy.'

'And?' asked Müller.

'And it's from an animal,' said Eckstein.

'Same story in Berlin again, Doctor,' said Tilsner. Müller noticed the sharp looks from Baumann and Vogel. Clearly they weren't best pleased that the Berlin detectives had withheld information from them.

Eckstein gave a heavy sigh. 'I can see it's going to take quite a bit to impress you city types. However, that's not the whole story.'

'What do you mean?' asked Tilsner.

'As I say, I could tell from the shape of the cells under the microscope that the blood was from an animal, not a human. A cat, in fact. And then I managed to run some tests using isoenzyme analysis of the red blood cells.'

Müller could see the pathologist was enjoying bamboozling them with science, and drawing out his moment of drama. 'What I'm trying to say,' continued Eckstein, 'is that the blood is from a very special moggy: *Felis silvestris*, the European wildcat. And this was a particularly pure beast; its forebears hadn't been fraternising with any local village cats.'

'What does that mean?' asked Müller.

'It means the blood was obtained from an animal in a relatively remote location.'

Baumann stepped forward at this point, turning to Müller. 'The Brocken. A colony resides there on the slopes. We're often getting ramblers claiming they've sighted a leopard or a lion.'

'They must be pretty short-sighted,' joked Tilsner. 'Anyway, I thought the Brocken was a restricted zone.'

'It is,' agreed Baumann. 'And the main colony of cats is thought to be inside that zone, but occasionally one or two stray outside.'

Müller nodded thoughtfully. More evidence pointing to the highest mountain in the Harz, but hardly conclusive.

The mortuary assistant tried to pass the pathologist a saw to begin opening the body cavity, but Eckstein waved him away and continued to discuss the case. 'Do we know who the victim is?'

'We're not certain, but we have a good idea,' replied Müller. It wasn't the entire truth. The receipt of the faxed note from Jäger had removed what little doubt Müller had left as to the boy's identity. She retrieved her briefcase from a chair at the back of the room and pulled out some pieces of paper. 'These are the dental records from a *Jugendwerkhof* on the island of Rügen. If the boy is who we think he is, they should be a match.' Out of the corner of her eye she could see Baumann and Vogel frowning. More information she should already have passed to them.

Eckstein studied the sheets. Then, with his hands protected by rubber gloves, he eased open the boy's jaw and asked the assistant to angle a spotlight to highlight the inside of the buccal cavity. Unlike the girl in Berlin, his teeth were still intact. 'I'll take a full cast of the teeth later, but from a superficial examination I'd say you have the right boy.' He waved Müller forwards. 'See here, this gap in the lower dentures. On the right-hand side of his jaw, or left as you're looking.' Eckstein was rubbing his finger on the empty gum. 'Two teeth are missing: the second premolar, and the first molar.'

'That's nothing to do with the cause of death, then?' asked Müller.

'No, no, *Oberleutnant*. I should think perhaps he was involved in a fight a year or two ago, something like that. The teeth became cracked and rotten as a result.' He let the mouth close, and picked up the dental records again. 'The reason isn't given here, but the missing teeth are. So you can be fairly certain you have the right boy. What's his name?'

'Mathias Gellman. Aged fifteen at the time he disappeared. Now sixteen,' said Tilsner.

Eckstein nodded, then began examining the rest of the exterior of Mathias's naked, mutilated body. As he dictated his observations to his assistant, Eckstein said something which left all four detectives bemused.

'Your case in Berlin. I assume it was murder?' he asked.

'Yes,' replied Müller. She felt a small flutter in her stomach.

'Well, I can tell you this isn't, at least I don't think so. Even before I begin any incisions I can tell you that it looks as though this boy died as the result of a fall. Of course, he may have been pushed, but there's no bruising consistent with a struggle.'

He began pointing to lesions on Mathias's torso and limbs, and finally to one on his forehead. 'This is probably what did for him. He's hit his head on a hard stone surface at the end of a fall of some three to four metres I'd say, so perhaps just one flight of stairs. I won't be able to confirm this until I have opened the skull, but I don't think you all need to stay for that. It's not a spectator sport I'd recommend.'

'So he died from a blow to the head? Couldn't it have been from a blunt instrument? *After* he was pushed downstairs?' asked Müller.

Eckstein shook his head. 'The head injury is not consistent with that, *Oberleutnant*. This appears to me to be a fairly simple case of cranio-cerebral trauma after a fall down stairs. Albeit the stairs were stone stairs. And that he hit his head on a hard, angular rock at the bottom of his fall. I managed to retrieve some grit fragments from the wound. I will analyse them and give you the results later.'

'What will that tell us?' asked Tilsner.

Müller glared at her deputy. 'It may help us locate where he died, because it clearly wasn't in the middle of the forest where the body was found. And that may lead us to Neumann. We've accounted for two of the three missing teenagers. Let's try to find the other while she's still alive.'

Soon afterwards, Eckstein ushered the four detectives from the mortuary, insisting he needed peace to continue with the rest of the procedure.

Once back at Wernigerode People's Police headquarters, Müller was informed that Reiniger was trying to get through to her on the police radio. The connection was poor and Reiniger's voice barely cut through the static.

'*Oberleutnant* Müller,' he said, in a formal tone. 'You and *Unterleutnant* Tilsner must return to Berlin immediately. I never gave you permission to leave the Hauptstadt in any case. Furthermore, I regret to inform you that your husband is having charges brought against him. They include undermining the political or social order of the Republic, exploiting the moral immaturity of a minor for the purposes of intercourse or similar acts and, most seriously, in respect to your current investigation, the –'

The two-way radio that Müller was using in the police station side office crackled and cut to static.

'*Oberst* Reiniger. Could you repeat that please? I'm afraid the line is very bad.'

'He is being charged with murder. The murder of the girl found at St Elisabeth's cemetery. As I believe you now know, that girl has been identified as Beate Ewert, the girl you have seen in compromising photographs of your husband.'

All of a sudden Müller felt breathless, as though she might faint. She found it difficult to believe the photos of Gottfried with Beate were genuine, but she certainly couldn't accept he was a murderer. And Mathias's body had been dumped while he was in jail, so clearly he couldn't be directly responsible for that. What game was Reiniger playing? She wondered if Schmidt had yet been able to analyse the photograph of Gottfried in the sanatorium, the one her husband insisted had been doctored – his last plea to her before they parted in the interrogation room at Hohenschönhausen.

'Until your divorce is finalised you are still married to a suspect, now charged, in this investigation. So you are being suspended and must return to –'

She remembered Jäger's pledge to back her. She patted the letter of authority from Mielke she still carried in her inside jacket pocket. It gave her the courage to take a gamble. 'Hello, *Oberst* Reiniger. I'm unable to hear you. I'm afraid the line has gone again. I haven't been able to hear any of this conversation.' In fact, Reiniger's voice was clearer than at any time in the exchange. He was telling her that the suspension was effective immediately and had been approved at the highest level at Keibelstrasse. Her only defence was in the lie. '*Oberst* Reiniger. If you can hear me, I'm afraid I cannot hear you.' Reiniger kept on repeating what he'd just said, the anger in his voice mounting, but Müller still insisted the reception was too bad, and finally terminated the conversation.

43

Day Fifteen.
Wernigerode, East Germany.

Back at the incident room at the Wernigerode People's Police headquarters, Müller and Tilsner sat down with Baumann and Vogel to take stock of where they were. Müller didn't reveal to the others any of her conversation with Reiniger. She ran her hands backwards through her hair, with her elbows resting on the table. They would need to work quickly. If Reiniger had been able to get through on the radio once, he would surely try again – and given what he'd said, would almost certainly order her arrest.

Leaning back in his chair, Tilsner sighed. 'We need to find Neumann. But if he's not at the children's home at Schierke, and if he's not on Rügen, where do we start?'

Müller picked up a pen, and tapped it on the desk. 'We must be missing some clue. Either Neumann or someone else has led us here so far. All the evidence in the car, when it had apparently been steam-cleaned ... it was just too staged. Too easy. He or they want us to find them.'

'So what do we do?' asked Tilsner.

The phone rang, and Vogel went to the side of the room to answer it. Müller knew it meant that phone communications had been restored. She ought, therefore, to ring Reiniger back in Berlin. But she wasn't going to.

'The phones are back on then?' she asked.

'Not exactly,' said Baumann. 'Some local lines, yes. But phone lines to Berlin and the rest of the country are still down. There's some fault with an exchange near Blankenburg.'

He began to spread out a large-scale map of the Brocken area on the table. 'Maybe the wildcat colony is significant? Most of the sightings have been around here.' Müller followed his finger to a section of the map where the narrow-gauge railway which led to the Brocken summit swung out to the west.

'That's very near to the border defences, isn't it? Is the public allowed there?'

'Only with special permission,' said Baumann. 'But for the local farm workers and foresters that's not so difficult to obtain.'

'And what about the Brocken itself? Isn't that heavily patrolled?' asked Tilsner.

Baumann nodded. 'That's correct, Comrade Tilsner. There's a company of border troops barracked in the railway station at the summit.'

The three detectives looked up from the map as Vogel returned to the table. 'That was the forensic pathologist, Dr Eckstein, on the phone.'

'And?' asked Baumann.

'He's managed to analyse the grit from the boy's head wound under a microscope. Says it might help us. Apparently it's *Bleiglanz*.'

Baumann shrugged. 'That means nothing to me, Comrade Vogel.'

'It didn't to me, *Hauptmann*, to be honest.' Vogel looked down at his notebook. 'But Dr Eckstein explained it's lead sulphite or galena. It's the ore you get lead from, but silver deposits are often found in the same vicinity.'

Müller rubbed her forehead. 'And why does he think that might help us?'

'Well, as you could probably tell, Comrade Müller, the good doctor's been around the block a few times. He says in the old days there used to be silver mines dotted throughout the Harz. A lot of the area's wealth came from silver mining.'

The four detectives looked back at the map, searching around the Brocken area to see if there were any marks signalling an old mineshaft, anywhere where Neumann might be holding Irma Behrendt.

Tilsner suddenly tapped the map.

'There. Heinrichshöhle. Right near the Brocken summit. That's a cave!'

Baumann put his reading glasses on to examine the map more closely. 'No, Comrade Tilsner,' he snorted. 'Take another look. It's Heinrichs-*höhe* not *höhle*. That's a mountain, not a cave.' Müller smirked as she saw Tilsner's face redden.

Lifting the map towards her slightly, she pointed out two small black rectangles a couple of kilometres east of the Brocken summit.

'What are they?' she asked Baumann.

'They look like ski huts. They provide shelter to anyone trapped up there when conditions turn nasty – like now.'

'It's worth investigating those, isn't it?'

Baumann shrugged. 'We could, but we're dealing with an area surrounding the summit of ... what? Twenty square kilometres? Maybe more. And anyway it's getting late, the road beyond Schierke hasn't been ploughed yet, but it may have been by tomorrow morning. I suggest you go back to your lodgings and get a meal and some sleep, and then meet again here first thing tomorrow morning.'

Tilsner seemed subdued during their meal at the guesthouse, perhaps embarrassed by his *höhe/höhle* slip in front of the others. They barely said a word as they sipped their soup, other than Tilsner suggesting it might actually be better for her to try to contact Jäger again. But then Jäger didn't know that – officially – they were once again off the case. Worse than that, Müller was supposed to be suspended. By tomorrow, no doubt Reiniger would have sent someone to arrest her.

Before finishing his main course, her deputy announced he was off to bed for an early night. There were no other guests in the restaurant, so Müller was left alone with her thoughts. She'd hoped by now she might have heard something positive from Jäger about Gottfried. Instead, the communication from Reiniger seemed to be pointing the other way: that things were getting worse for her husband, not better. The accusations against him were preposterous, but the best way of disproving them was to find the real killer. Somewhere near here were Neumann and the one remaining teenager from Rügen, Irma.

As soon as the phone line to Berlin was once again operational, Müller vowed to ring Schmidt, and see if he'd got anywhere in his examination of the incriminating photographs. That's if she got the chance before Reiniger ordered her arrest.

Before going up to her room, she visited the wooden-panelled sitting room. The bookshelf in the corner, below the portrait of Erich Honecker, contained several books on the Harz area, but what Müller was looking for was a map. A map on a larger scale than the one at the police office, with more detail.

She found the maps on the bottom shelf, piled horizontally; they were being used as a bookend. Müller leafed through them until she found what she wanted: a folded sheet of yellowing paper, with a forest-green and black front cover. *Harz Wanderkarte für Wernigerode und Umgebung.* She sat down in an armchair next to the coffee table, and spread the map out carefully. The paper was brittle, and Müller suspected the map dated back to the Nazi era, possibly before. There was no border barrier marked in the valley to the west of the Harz's highest peak. *It was illegal to have this, surely?* In Berlin, this would have meant confiscation, possible arrest. Here in the mountains, they seemed to do things differently.

Looking around the room, she spotted what she wanted on the mantelpiece: a magnifying glass. She rose to retrieve it, and used the convex lens to enlarge the detail of the map. She concentrated on the Brocken, and the area that Baumann had pointed to. It took her a couple of minutes before she saw it, hidden in the forest, just a few hundred metres from where she knew the border ran: a circle, possibly just a millimetre in diameter, with a solid black rectangle alongside.

She looked at the map's key, tracing her finger down it, feeling her breath coming in short, sharp bursts.

Near the bottom, she found a small black circle with a white centre. She knew what it would say alongside, and she was correct. *Stillgelegten Schacht*. Disused shaft.

44

Müller found herself regularly waking and going over the case in her head throughout the night. If Neumann had dumped Mathias's body near the state border just beyond Elend, if it was he who'd daubed the boy's T-shirt with wildcat blood, then surely he still had to be in the area. The subalpine seedling pointed to the Brocken. The lead ore in Mathias's head wound did, too. What perplexed her, though, was why one teenager's body had been dumped in the Hauptstadt, the other left here in the Harz. It made little sense.

Throwing the heavy duvet aside, Müller got up, walked along the landing and went to the toilet. She didn't do it particularly quietly or subtly, banging the toilet lid down after herself. Maybe she wanted him to hear. Maybe she wanted another early-hours encounter in the washroom.

As she wiped her hands on the towel after washing them, she heard his footsteps on the creaking floorboards of the landing. She could hear his breathing behind her. Then warm air on her ear.

'Couldn't sleep again?' Tilsner whispered. Then his teeth nibbled her earlobe, she felt his strong arms envelope her and she backed against his growing erection. She felt him lifting the back of the nightdress, his fingers in the waistband of the western knickers she'd kept from the West Berlin assignment. Easing them down. She grabbed his wrists to stop him, and turned.

She raised her index finger, and put it to his lips, rubbing it up and down fractionally to feel the resistance of his stubble. 'Not here,' she whispered. 'My room.'

An early breakfast found them smirking at each other. Müller felt no shame, and it surprised her. As far as the authorities were concerned, she was a single woman now – her husband an enemy of the state, a pervert and a murderer. But although she'd just been unfaithful, she wasn't prepared to completely give up on Gottfried just yet.

So what about Werner Tilsner? She looked up as he stuffed a piece of *Brötchen* into his handsome mouth. He was married with kids. Should she feel guilt about that? But he was the one who'd made the marriage vows to Koletta, not her, and she hadn't exactly had to do much seducing.

Tilsner took a last sip of coffee, and wiped his mouth with his napkin. 'Ready, beautiful?'

She nodded. 'But it's Karin, or boss to you, please. *Unterleutnant.*'

Kitted out in the warmest clothes they could find, Müller and Tilsner made their way in the Wartburg to Wernigerode police headquarters. At the entrance to the car park, Vogel stood smoking a cigarette, as though waiting for them.

Tilsner wound the window down. Vogel blew the smoke out to the side, then leant his head into the car.

'A little warning,' he said. 'I wouldn't come in here if I were you. And today's joint reconnaissance exercise up the Brocken is off.'

'Why's that?' asked Tilsner, frowning.

Müller saw Vogel flick his eyes towards her.

'*Oberleutnant* Müller here. The Stasi have asked us to detain her.'

'What?' shouted Tilsner. 'But we're investigating this case on the highest authority, of the Stasi. Show him, Karin.'

Müller reached into her jacket pocket and withdrew the letter of authority, signed by Mielke. Tilsner handed it to Vogel.

The young officer shrugged. 'I don't understand; this appears genuine. Can I take it to show Comrade Baumann?'

Müller stretched her hand out for the document to be returned. 'No, I'm afraid not, Comrade Vogel. But once we're back later today you can take a photocopy.' She grabbed the letter, refolded it and placed it carefully back in her pocket.

'In any case, *Hauptmann* Baumann doesn't like being told what to do by the Stasi, and tries to keep out of their way whenever possible,' Vogel continued. 'But if you cross his path, especially in the police station, he'll have to act. So I'd stay out of the way. And if you want to go up to the Brocken you'll need to go on your own. The road's been cleared now. Oh, and here's something you left behind last night.' Tilsner took the proffered papers and examined them. Authorisations to enter the Brocken restricted area, dated from the previous day.

'Much appreciated, *Unterleutnant* Vogel,' said Tilsner, grinning.

Vogel nodded, a serious expression on his face, and walked off.

Before he started the car, Tilsner turned to Müller. 'What's all that about the Stasi?'

Müller wouldn't meet his eyes. 'It's Reiniger. He's suspending me because they've charged Gottfried with murder, and a whole heap besides.'

Tilsner didn't reply at first, and had a strange expression on his face. Almost as though he looked slightly guilty – maybe because of their night-time liaison. *Perhaps he's not the super-cool player he thinks he is.*

'Was that what the radio call was about?' he finally asked.

'Exactly. And now, because I've ignored an explicit instruction, he's ordered my arrest. I claimed I couldn't hear him due to the poor reception.'

'So do I take over?' asked Tilsner.

'No, Werner. You don't. You start the car. And you drive. To the Brocken.'

Tilsner grinned. 'Yes, boss.'

45

Three months earlier (December 1974).
A forest in East Germany.

Six months have passed, but Neumann's expression when he turned round in his chair is still imprinted on my brain. Even though now I see his mangled face nearly every day, even though I want to tear it open again along his ugly scar, the image I always see is the way he looked when that chair swivelled round, and all my hopes and dreams were snuffed out in an instant.

I am still alive, but it's a living death. Six months down here in the near blackness of the mine. I never dreamed there was anywhere worse than *Jugendwerkhof* Prora Ost. People whispered about Torgau, of course. But I cannot believe that even the *Jugendwerkhof* at Torgau could be worse than this.

What about Mathias? What does he think as he works with me in this freezing underground hole, hacking away at the rock loosened by Neumann's explosives? It's his job to load the trolley with the rock scraped out by the others. We're not sure who they are. About four or five muscular, thick-set men alternately guard the compound and work at the rock face.

My job is to wheel the trolley back along the level and the old rails, round the corner by the stone steps, to the bottom of the shaft. I'm not sure what we're digging out, or why.

Mathias says he's been cheated, but he won't tell me why. All I know is that he and Beate no longer speak. The great love affair is well and truly over.

I jump back as part of the roof loosens. The dust stings my eyes, attacks my lungs. Already when I'm above ground I spend most of the time coughing up my guts, but my worst nightmare is that we get buried alive, or that there's an explosion. I remember from school lessons years ago about gas, and mines, and canaries. We have no canaries here.

I get my shovel, and spoon the fallen debris into the trolley, and then push it along the rails, iron groaning against iron.

Oh, Mathias, I think, you poor boy. Your lover doesn't want you, and the people you thought were your friends have deserted you. Hah! Serves you right. Because as well as remembering Neumann's expression at the *Grenzübergang*, I remember the look on Mathias's face. For him it was no surprise that we were being taken back to the Republic. Oh Mathias, Mathias. You've got it coming to you. Just you wait. And if I ever get the chance, even the slightest opportunity, then Neumann has it coming to him too. But it's not just Neumann. There are the others who work down the mine and guard us. And then a couple of high-ups, very high-ups. Not many, but certainly at least two. People's Army officers – stripes aplenty, and stars on their interwoven gold epaulettes.

I force my aching arms to tip the trolley until it empties its contents into the bucket. Then I pull on the rope to alert Beate at the top of the shaft. The rope tautens and the bucket finally lifts as she uses the pulley system to haul it up.

Beate. The pretty one. She gets the easy job above ground, but I'm not jealous, because now I know the hell they've put her through. The big secret she would never tell me at Prora Ost, and the reason for her tears each night. After we'd been here in the mine for three months, she finally told me.

It was the field trip when it all began. The evening field trip to the Soviet base at Gross Zicker on Rügen – part of our re-education programme, showing us the brave Soviet servicemen defending us against fascist and capitalist aggression. I remember at the time thinking it was odd that only girls were allowed to go, but put it down to the fact that – other than in the workshop and at mealtimes – we weren't really allowed to mix with the boys anyway.

It wasn't much of a field trip. We got a quick tour of the facilities in the bus. Then we were taken into a large room, where we were given a talk and shown a film by one of the Soviet officers – a German coastal border force officer translated, although we could understand some Russian from our school lessons.

At the end of the talk, they announced that the group was to be split into two for the remainder of the field trip. Another Soviet officer walked down the rows of chairs and nodded towards certain girls, who were told to stand and move to the front of the room. There were fifteen of them – fifteen of the prettiest. Though there were around forty in total; so not exactly a fifty-fifty split.

Then a senior German officer entered the room, and walked up and down that line of girls. Ten were sent back to their seats, five remained. Those five weren't just pretty, they were beautiful, and they included Beate. I put up my hand to ask if I could go with my friend, but the officer laughed cruelly, and told me not to be so insolent.

The chosen five were marched away. We didn't see them again that night. The remaining thirty-five of us were sent back on the bus to the *Jugendwerkhof*. Beate's bed remained empty. And the next day her tears began.

Mathias's shout from the end of the level brings me back to the present. 'Irma. What are you doing? There's stuff waiting here to be cleared.'

What am I doing? I am sitting here, on my arse, on the cold stone by the bucket, which Beate has now lowered again, watching occasional flakes of snow helicopter down to the bottom of the shaft.

With a sigh I get to my feet. I wheel the trolley back along the rails, round the corner by the stone steps and back down the level towards Mathias. To fill it up once more.

As I say, Beate reminded me of the Gross Zicker visit about three months ago, give or take a day, or a week. They're all pretty meaningless down here, though we count them at night upstairs in the old silver-mine house, scratching marks on the timber walls. But she didn't reveal everything. She let me think about it all for a few weeks; how being ugly red-headed Irma perhaps wasn't so bad after all.

At night, though, as we tried to get to sleep next to each other, chained to the floor, lying on lumpy, stinking old mattresses, I would nag her to tell me more.

Finally she did.

From the lecture room where we'd been shown the film, Beate had been taken down corridors with the other four girls, until they reached another large room. There the German officer had directed them to rails of party frocks, boxes of stockings and underwear, rows of fancy shoes. They were shown showers at the side of the room, fresh fluffy towels. And on one table, bottles of opened champagne, stemmed flute glasses and canapés. The girls were told to shower and then pick whatever clothes they fancied. They were going to a party.

'I was so excited. So excited, Irma. I felt like a young woman, I felt special. Not like an awkward *Jugendwerkhof* girl,' she whispered to me as we lay in the pitch-black of the mine house.

'We got out of the showers and dried ourselves. I was a bit embarrassed because the German and Soviet officers were lounging at the side of the room, sipping champagne and watching. I wrapped myself in the towel and moved over to choose some clothes. The German had his eyes on me; he came across and handed me a dress. I took it and asked him to turn away again. There was a stand-up mirror. As I shuffled into the dress, I admired myself. I really did look good, like a princess. And then the German officer came up behind me, looked over my shoulder into my eyes. He was old, old enough to be my grandfather. But as he zipped me up, he gently stroked my back and I shivered. Then he led me over to where the Soviet officer was drinking champagne. "Doesn't she look gorgeous?" he said, in German. The Russian nodded, passed me a glass of bubbly and then offered me something to eat – little pieces of bread and toast, covered with fishy black beads. I asked him what it was. "Caviar," he said. "Only the best for girls like you."'

She broke down in tears again and – although I prompted her – that was all I would learn that night.

For the next few days, Beate didn't want to talk anymore. But eventually I managed to persuade her to open up again. In the dark one night, with Mathias able to hear everything if he wanted, Beate continued her story. She didn't seem to mind that Mathias could listen in. He was nothing to her now. They never spoke. There had been a huge shouting match one night, and then that was it. I had my own suspicions about Mathias Gellman, pretty-boy Mathias. He didn't hold any attraction for her now.

Beate continued: 'All five of us were standing around, drinking champagne. You can imagine, it went to our heads quickly. I think I was the oldest at fifteen. The other four were all fourteen. That's what makes it so sick. But they, like me, were caught up in the moment.

'The officers brought us all military-style overcoats – to cover up our pretty dresses – and then led us out into the night, to a quayside where a boat was waiting, all lit up. I wasn't nervous. If anything, going on a boat trip seemed even more exciting.

Imagine the contrast between that and daily life in the workshop at the *Jugendwerkhof*.

'We set off. The water was quite calm. That bit of the Ostsee is protected by Rügen. The boat was quite a powerful speedboat, I'm not sure what type. Maybe it belonged to the Soviet navy. Anyway, I could see we weren't going out towards Sweden. We were staying in the lee of Rügen, hugging the coastline. I could see lights to our right-hand side.

'After a few minutes, the boat's motor slowed, and we glided in towards a jetty on a small island. I now know that island to be –' Beate had to pause as she swallowed back her sobs. '– to be … Vilm.'

Vilm! I knew of it, I was sure. Maybe Oma had told me once. Important people from the Republic holidayed in Sellin. But I'm sure she told me once they also went to Vilm.

I tried to calm Beate. She was shaking with tears again.

'Are you OK, Beate?' asked Mathias, from the other side of the room.

'Shut up, pig,' she spat towards him. 'You're just as bad as the rest of them.' I stroked her hand, trying to calm her down. She was my friend. I had loyalty to her. Not to him.

'Anyway, we reached the island, where there were men waiting to escort us. One of them took my arm, walked me from the jetty to a low building. And inside it was laid out for a banquet. It was so exciting. The meal was fantastic – food I've never had before. Lobster, goose, meringue.

'I'm sure you can guess how the evening ended, though. The man I was with, well I'm sure I recognised him from the government. It wasn't Honecker. It wasn't Mielke. But it was someone in the second rank. He said he could get me out of the *Jugendwerkhof*. Get me back in a normal school. Let me take my *Abitur*. Get me a place at university. And all the time, under the table, he was moving his fingers up the inside of my thigh. I'm so ashamed that I didn't stop him, but you know what it's like in Prora Ost. This was a chance to get out. To escape ...

'And then he took me to his bedroom. He ripped the pretty dress off, the one I liked so much. He forced me down on the bed. And he took me. Again, and again, and again.'

I was holding Beate's hand so tightly, I thought I might break one of her bones. I wanted her to know I was there for her, that it wouldn't happen ever again. But really, I was powerless. She was powerless.

She gave a little sob. 'But did he help me get out of the *Jugendwerkhof*? Did he keep all his promises? Well, you know the answer. I was back there, and crying every night. So you see, Irma, I owe you a lot for helping me to escape. I'm so, so glad you got me away from the *Jugendwerkhof*. I owe you my life, and I will never forget.'

I was the one who was crying now. I couldn't help it. I was pleased for her, of course, if she was happier. But for myself? No. I hated it there, and I hated our slavery here. In fact, for me, here was worse – we didn't even know where we were, or the significance of our digging.

46

February 1975.
A forest in East Germany.

Christmas has gone. New Year has gone. We might have lost count with our days scratched into the wood, but they were no different to any other days. Mathias still shovels the rock into the trolley, the rock that the guards, or miners, or whatever they are, dig from the rock face. I still trolley it to the shaft, and Beate still lifts the bucket to the surface. But we are not mining silver ore for Neumann's private fortune, I know that, because there is a pile of slag by the top of the shaft – the debris we've removed from the mine – and it just stays there, and grows and grows. So what are we doing? Neumann won't tell us. He just says it's a special project approved by the Ministry of Education. Sometimes he's not even here. He comes and goes, but always there is someone guarding over us, gun at the ready.

So nothing much has changed. Except for Beate's mood; she seems elated. Then, one night, she confides in me. She whispers to me on the mattresses, stretching so she can get right up against my ear, straining against the metal chains that bind our legs each night. That way Mathias won't be able to hear.

'I've found out where we are,' she says.

'Where?' I whisper back.

'The Harz mountains. Right by the inner German border. The foothills of the Brocken. It's the highest mountain in this region. That's why there's so much snow outside.'

I turn this new information over in my mind for a few seconds: we're digging a tunnel, right by the border. I try to picture which way the sun sets in relation to the direction of the level underground. West. The level must be heading west. But that doesn't make any sense at all. We escaped to the West. We were ordered back to the East, under what Neumann claims is a legal repatriation agreement for anyone under sixteen. So the *Bundesgrenzschutz* officers had just been following orders. No wonder dog woman had looked so upset. Though how they came on the boat to find us straightaway no longer seems a mystery: Mathias must have betrayed us, that's the only explanation I can think of. And now we are digging our way back to the West? Madness! I can't believe the tunnel is for us.

Beate wonders why I haven't said anything. 'Did you hear me, Irma?' she whispers again.

'Yes, but why's that got you so excited? We're still being held as slaves.'

She squeezes my hand hard. 'I've been invited to another party – Neumann says it's going to be like the ones on Vilm.'

I don't understand. Why is she looking forward to it?

'And I've worked it out. Who had sex with me. On Vilm. I knew his face was familiar. I saw it again yesterday in a copy of *Neues Deutschland* that one of the guards had left on the breakfast table. He's going to be at the party being held at the top of the Brocken. And he's invited *me*. He's a real, proper high-up. His name's Horst. Horst Ackermann. He's about as high as you can get without being a government minister. He's a colonel general, in the Ministry for State Security.'

'The *Stasi*? Oh be careful, Beate. You cannot trust them.'

'Don't be silly. I'm sure this time if I play along I will be able to convince him to free us, to keep his promise about the *Abitur*, about everything. Don't you see, Irma? It's a chance. I'll try to persuade them to help you, too, and then all this will be over, and we will be free.'

I stroke her hand and shush her.

'Be careful, Beate. Be very careful. I hope you know what you're doing.'

Of course I should have stopped her, should have known it was lunacy for her to get back into the abusive relationship that had made her so unhappy – but I didn't.

Beate Ewert and I were sworn friends for life, yet I allowed her to dress up in her short, black witch's outfit for the fancy dress party, and helped her ink in her nails with a black felt-tip pen borrowed from Neumann. I kissed her on the cheek as she went, half wishing I could go with her, despite now knowing what went on at these 'parties'.

That was the last time I ever saw her.

47

March 1975. Day Sixteen.
The Harz mountains, East Germany.

'Is it sensible to be doing this on our own, boss? Don't you think we need back-up?' asked Tilsner as they drove away from the Wernigerode People's Police station car park.

'We don't have any option,' said Müller. 'If we ask Baumann, he'd have to arrest me.'

They lapsed into silence, Müller grateful to be wearing sunglasses to protect against the snow glare and any lingering embarrassment from the previous night's lovemaking.

On each side of the road they passed old mine workings and quarries cut into the forest. Müller could imagine that in summer they might be an eyesore, but now the snow softened the landscape, giving it an Alpine feel. They followed the same route as they had the previous day, but then instead of carrying on further west towards the border, they turned northwest towards the Brocken. The road here was covered in snow. Tilsner stopped the car and pulled over. 'I'd better put the chains on as a precaution. According to the map, the road climbs another hundred metres or so towards Schierke.'

'I didn't realise it would be this bad,' said Müller as Tilsner climbed out. She opened the passenger window and called to him. 'We're going to need skis, aren't we?'

Tilsner got back in for a moment to move the Wartburg a few centimetres forward so that he could attach the snow chains. 'It's a winter sports training village. We should be able to get skis and boots from the sports club if we show our police passes. But that will be a risk if Reiniger's already sent people after us.'

Müller frowned, and rubbed her gloved hands together to ward off the mountain chill. 'From the map, it didn't look as though we could go all the way to the mine in the car. We'll have more chance with skis. It's a risk we'll have to take.'

If they had been put on a wanted list in the Republic, then – possibly due to the adverse weather conditions – the police bulletin clearly hadn't reached Schierke. As soon as they showed their *Kripo* IDs, the staff at the sports club were all over them trying to help, excited about why Berlin detectives were engaged in an operation in their village. Müller knew, though, that even if the phone lines weren't working properly yet, the network of gossip would be. Someone at the club would be a Stasi informer, and their whereabouts would soon be known.

With the cross-country skis firmly attached to a roof rack borrowed from the club, they used the antiquated map Müller had confiscated from the guesthouse to navigate the road up towards the Brocken.

Reaching a plateau in the road, Müller signalled for Tilsner to pull over. He turned off the motor of the Wartburg, and for a few moments Müller sat alongside her deputy in silence, enjoying the reprieve from the car's vibrations. She turned around to check that they weren't being followed, and then both of them soaked in the view through the windscreen towards the heights of the Brocken. It almost looked like the opening of a feature film. Dotted across the mountainside were pine trees loaded with snow, their branches drooping from the weight; at the summit, a collection of aerial spikes aimed into the sky like needles, as though trying to puncture the azure above. Surrounding them, the globes of the listening station – the Republic's eyes and ears trained on the capitalist world outside.

The old mineshaft and neighbouring buildings were still some two kilometres distant, down a hill track to their left, heading for the border. They would have to ski the rest of the way – the Wartburg's snow chains wouldn't cope, and even a four-wheel drive would struggle. Müller, born and brought up in a winter sports village – though further south in Thuringia – had no qualms about negotiating the route down through the forest. But she suspected Tilsner's claims of skiing proficiency might just be the bluster of the boastful.

As she opened the car door, freezing air laced with the scent of the spruce trees blasted her face. The skin on her cheeks tightened, pores closing in defence. It was such a contrast to Berlin's daily smogs. She stood, then stamped the hired langlauf boots in the snow. Tilsner was out of the car too, stretching his arms and slapping his hands together. He freed the skis from the roof rack, fumbling in the cold. Müller hadn't got her gloves on yet, and the metal of the bindings froze to her palms as Tilsner handed her the skis.

'I don't like the feeling of this at all,' he said. 'There's just the two of us, in totally unfamiliar terrain. You did bring your gun, didn't you?'

Müller already knew it was safely there in its holster, but just to show him she dropped the skis on the ground, felt under her jacket for the Makarov and nodded.

'What about wire cutters?' he asked.

'There are some in the boot.'

Müller watched as he went round the car, first ducking into the driver's side for something. He spent a couple of minutes there, and then looked up furtively at her as he moved round to the rear of the vehicle, as though he'd hoped she hadn't been watching. *What was he up to?* I'm on my own in this, she thought. Because he's as likely to turn me in as anyone. Maybe this case just wasn't worth it. Why did the girl, Irma, matter so much to her? But if she gave up now, what hope had she of Jäger keeping his part of the bargain, in trying to help Gottfried?

Finally, Tilsner nodded to indicate he was ready.

Müller set off first, skating on the flat to pick up speed, digging in her poles and pushing out each ski, sliding the left then the right to leave a herringbone pattern behind her. Then she brought her legs together and crouched into a schuss as the track headed downhill. It reminded her of winter skiing holidays with Gottfried in the early years of their marriage, near her Thuringian home of Oberhof. He'd been hopeless, falling over every few minutes. But still determined to have a go, and try to keep up with her, because he knew how she loved the snow.

She could hear the swoosh of Tilsner's skis close behind; his claims of skiing ability justified – Gottfried certainly wouldn't have been able to keep pace at this speed. The pine trees flashed by on either side for several hundred metres. Then Müller realised she couldn't hear her *Unterleutnant* anymore. She added a couple of turns to try to slow down, but the track had steepened.

She was losing control.

Suddenly, pain knifed through her shins.

Time slowed as she tumbled over and over in a mass of snow, her body buffeted as she spun head over heels, trying to dig her hands into the snow to stop her fall. Then a crack. Her head smashed into a tree trunk, the pain now overwhelming.

Müller strove for consciousness, as though she was underwater and fighting her way to the surface. But the knifing from her legs and the agony of her head were like hands pushing her back down. She felt her right leg, her trousers torn, her shin soaked with something. She brought her hand up to her face. Blood. There must have been a tripwire stretched across the track, and she'd skied straight into it.

Then her face grew cooler as a shadow moved across her vision, between her and the winter sun. Tilsner had come to rescue her.

She focused. It wasn't Tilsner. It was a man she didn't recognise, camouflaged in white, with a gun pointing right between her eyes.

48

Days went by. Now it was Neumann himself who'd taken over from Beate at the top of the shaft. I asked him outright what had happened to her, but he wouldn't meet my eyes. Said she'd been taken ill ... wasn't up to the demands of the work here ... she'd been moved to another children's home. Lies. All lies.

Neumann has started looking increasingly mad. His one good eye has a wild, haunted look to it; the eyepatch on the mangled side of his face is dirty; his hair's unkempt, and whenever he speaks to me he's always fidgeting.

Now it's just Mathias and me in the old mine house, I've deigned to talk to him more. Otherwise the nights in the darkness would be unbearable. We lie and talk and wonder what's happened to Beate. We've given up marking the days on the side of the wall. All I know is that it's February. Both Mathias and I are sixteen, and if we'd waited until now before escaping from Prora Ost, then the evil repatriation agreement for under-sixteens wouldn't have been applicable. We'd now be free in the West. But we didn't know about it back then, in the *Jugendwerkhof* – at least Beate and I didn't. Maybe Mathias knew, and that was why he was so ready to jump in the bed boxes and take part in my hare-brained plan – my crazy plan that nearly worked.

One day, Mathias notices something about the level. There's a small slope. Upwards. Neumann must have been setting the dynamite charges in a slightly different place each day. We don't know what it means. We still do our tedious slave jobs: the goons digging out the loosened rock, Mathias loading it, me pushing the trolley along the rails of the level, round the corner by the stone steps, and tipping its contents into the bucket, which Neumann hauls above ground.

Each day, we're worked to exhaustion. Only then can we climb the dozen or so steps hacked into the rock to take us to the part of the shaft where the vertical ladder starts.

As Mathias and I are lying on our mattresses, on opposite sides of the room, I ask him what he meant when he said they had 'cheated' him.

'You'll hate me for it if I tell you,' he says.

'Try me.'

'They made an agreement with me, in Prora Ost.'

'What agreement?'

'That if I kept a close watch on people, if I secretly reported on them, then when Beate and I turned sixteen, we would both be allowed to return to regular school, to leave the *Jugendwerkhof*, and to take our *Abitur*. They promised me that we could go to university, and that we'd be assigned a flat together. Our futures would be mapped out.'

'Did Beate know about that?' If she had, then her submission to Ackermann's perversions had been totally pointless.

'No. I didn't dare tell her.'

I don't reply for a moment, thinking through the implications of what he's just told me.

'You probably hate me now, Irma, don't you?'

I still don't say anything initially.

'I know what they are capable of, Mathias,' I reply after a few moments. 'I can't agree it was right what you did, but no, I don't hate you.' But what I say to him out loud does not necessarily reflect my true thoughts.

'Thank you, Irma,' he says. 'That means a lot to me. Goodnight.'

'Goodnight, Mathias.' In a few moments, he is snoring, perhaps comforted in his sleep by my words. But my mind is racing. If he was reporting on us, what was he reporting and to whom? Did he know about Beate being forced to go to the parties on Vilm? Did he take part in –?

The last thought ... I stop myself thinking. It's too horrible to contemplate.

We don't get a chance to continue the conversation at breakfast the next morning. Neumann and his goons are watching us closely. But I've been doing more thinking overnight. There is more I want to ask Mathias.

I wait till we're climbing the ladder down the shaft; Mathias is a few rungs below me.

'Psst,' I hiss. 'There is just one thing I don't understand. Why did you want to escape with us, if you felt they were going to look after you in the East, and let you leave the *Jugendwerkhof*?'

He doesn't answer me until we reach the intermediate platform. Then he turns towards me, as I tackle the last couple of rungs. I see his face thrown into angular relief by the dim light of the mineshaft. He's no longer the pretty boy he was. Months of working here, underground, in the dust and grime, have taken their toll.

'I couldn't bear to be parted from her, Irma. I knew she wanted to go to the West. I hadn't told her about the informing – she would have hated me for it. So I had to go with her, there and then.'

I hold his gaze. He looks down at his feet. There's something he's not telling me, and I think I know what it is. I've suspected it for some time now.

'Your last bit of informing,' I say, and I'm sure he can hear the hatred and anger that fills my voice. 'That was on the ship, wasn't it? When you said you'd already been above deck?'

He won't look up at me. He's too ashamed. 'Yes,' he says, his voice barely above a whisper.

'You had them radio the Republic.' He nods, almost imperceptibly. 'And they told you about the teenage repatriation agreement, didn't they?' No reaction. 'Didn't they, Mathias?'

Another tiny nod.

'And I've a good idea who it was you were telling in the Republic. It was the Stasi, wasn't it? They recruited you in Prora, didn't they?'

'I'm sorry, Irma. I'm so, so sorry.'

I pause for a moment to let it all sink in. But I'm not going to let him off the hook. 'Why did you do that, Mathias? Why turn us in when you and Beate were so close to winning your freedom together?'

'Because I knew there was a good chance we would fail. And even if we didn't, with us being minors I knew it was likely we would be sent back to the East. And then –'

'Then what?'

'Then those hopes of getting out of the *Jugendwerkhof*, getting a place at university. Starting a life with Beate. They would all be in ruins.'

It all makes sense now. Why the *Bundesgrenzschutz* officers were already waiting at the quayside in Hamburg; they weren't just checking the boat on the off-chance. They'd been tipped off, by people in the Republic. And they in turn had been tipped off by Mathias Gellman. Mathias Stasi spy Gellman. Working for the same organisation that had made sure my Mutti ended up in prison; the same organisation that had made sure I was separated from Oma, and dumped in hateful *Jugendwerkhöfe*.

'You're a bastard, Mathias. A complete and utter bastard and I will never, ever forgive you.'

'I'm sorry,' he mumbles again, and then turns to negotiate the steps. Flashing in my brain are the images of Beate, the *Jugendwerkhof*, the elation at seeing the lights of Hamburg.

Happy images of me and Mutti and Oma on the beach as a young girl. They close in on me, taunt me, and as Mathias takes his first step down, as he's momentarily off balance, I push.

He falls.

His scream ends with a sickening thud at the bottom of those steep, slippery stone steps.

Every action has an equal and opposite reaction. You see, I do remember some things from school.

49

February 1975.
The Harz mountains, East Germany.

I murdered Mathias Gellman, but no one will ever know.

Neumann hears the argument, hears the scream. He comes clambering down the ladder with a torch. I stand frozen to the spot, unable, or unwilling, to go to help.

'He fell,' I say.

Neumann brushes past me and runs down the steps, his torch beam leaping up and down, until it settles on Mathias's head. An ugly open gash, and blood discolouring the stone floor of the mine. Neumann feels for a pulse. Starts mouth to mouth. All in vain.

While his goons continue to hack away at the rock face further along the level, he gets me to help him carry the body and haul it into the ore bucket, and then uses the pulley system to take Mathias to the surface.

I just sit at the top of the steps, thinking of dog woman and her kindly face ... The short-skirted girls on the Reeperbahn ... The drink of Coca-Cola and the currywurst and chips ... The ketchup ... And the bloodstains by Mathias Gellman's head.

50

March 1975. Day Sixteen.
The Harz mountains, East Germany.

Müller looked at the black metallic tube pointing at her forehead, then moved her gaze a fraction to the gloved finger resting on the gun's trigger.

She raised her eyes to those of her captor, who stared back from inside the hood of a white camouflage jacket. For some reason, the gloved finger did not move.

Instead, they both heard the crack of a tree branch some fifty metres back up the track. Müller and the man both turned towards the noise – the movement sending a flash of pain up from her injured legs. She saw her chance and tried to reach under her jacket for the Makarov pistol, but the guard was too quick for her, squeezed her arm and forced her to drop the weapon, kicking it away down the slope. As he did so, she made a grab for his gun, but he pulled her tight to him, and pressed the weapon to her temple. Müller felt herself gag – partly through panic, partly through the stench of his unwashed body.

'Don't move. Stay completely still,' he hissed into her ear. Then he shouted back up the track, towards the noise in the trees. 'Come out, with your hands up! Otherwise I'll shoot her.'

For a moment there was no answer, and then Müller heard Tilsner's voice. Despite the freezing metal of the gun barrel pressing into the side of her head, she felt relief flood through her.

'*Kriminalpolizei!* You're under arrest,' her deputy shouted from behind the cover of the pine trees. 'Drop your gun and release her.'

Müller's captor kept her firmly gripped, jabbing the gun barrel even harder into the side of her head. 'Tell him to drop his gun and come out,' he whispered urgently. Müller stayed silent. He yanked her arm up behind her back. 'Tell him. Now!' Müller still refused to speak, not wanting to undermine what little advantage Tilsner may have.

Trying to ignore the pain in her arm, she started to squirm away, but her captor tightened his grip still further, forcing her arm up and back until she thought she would black out. 'I'm losing patience,' he hissed, jabbing the gun at her temple. She saw him about to squeeze the trigger.

Tilsner shouted out again. 'Release her! I won't give you another warning.'

While the guard concentrated on keeping his hold on her, Müller lifted one leg and kicked back with her ski boot into his shin. Surprised, his grip loosened for an instant, and Müller forced herself sideways into a bank of snow, creating enough space between them to give Tilsner a safe target, praying that he would grab his opportunity.

Up the slope, Tilsner stepped out and aimed. The same instant, the man swivelled and raised his gun arm. A flash from Tilsner's weapon. Then two cracks, microseconds apart, echoing through the mountains and trees.

The man fell forward into the snow, crimson discolouring the back of the white army ski jacket where the bullet had passed through his body. No sound came from him, no movement. She turned her head to look back up the slope, to congratulate her *Unterleutnant*, to thank him for saving her life. But Tilsner, too, lay in a crumpled heap in the snow.

Müller dragged herself up the incline towards him, the snow and her injuries slowing her progress, pain pulsing from her leg wounds. He was calling her name. *He's still alive.* But the voice was faint, and growing fainter.

Müller finally reached him, and knelt in the snow. She ripped off her scarf and held it to his chest as blood pumped out.

'Karin ... K-K-Karin,' he gasped, trying to reach up and touch the side of her face. His arm fell back.

'You'll be alright, Werner. You'll be alright.' But even as she said it, the blood soaking into her scarf told her otherwise. She tried to remember her first-aid training, but all she could think of was not wanting to lose him.

'I'm s-s-s-sorry, Karin. So sorry.'

'You've nothing to be sorry for. You're a hero of the Republic. You saved my life.' She brought her mouth towards his. Wanting to kiss him. Breathe life into him. Anything.

Tilsner tried feebly to push her back. 'S-s-s-sorry –'

His attempts to form words stopped.

She felt for a pulse – it was still there, faint, but still there. She looked up and down the slope – how could she get help? They'd been stupid to come without Baumann or Vogel who at least knew the terrain. She'd been stupid. Tilsner had said they needed back-up. Now he was lying here, dying, and she couldn't help him.

She was so beside herself she only half-heard the engine of the Soviet Gaz as it approached from the valley, its four-wheel drive able to cope with the gradient in a way that the Wartburg couldn't have done – even with snow chains. When she finally looked up from Tilsner's body, as life seeped from it, and found not one, but two guns pointing in her face, she was almost beyond caring.

The bumps in the track sent jolts of pain through Müller's tenderised frame. She knew these people were her captors, not saviours, but she had pleaded with them to do something to help Tilsner. Finally the two gunmen had lifted her dying deputy's body into the back of the Gaz. Müller closed in on herself – desensitised by the blindfold they'd wrapped tightly over her eyes, numbed by grief over Tilsner. She knew he wasn't going to survive. It was almost as though the object of her mission, to rescue the remaining girl, had become irrelevant. All she could think of was Werner, and what might have been.

The vehicle finally came to a halt. Müller urged the men to attend to Tilsner, but they ignored her and instead she was dragged from the back of the Gaz–69 and forced to stand upright, while he lay dying inside. She winced from the brightness of the snow as her blindfold was removed, and then felt the jab of metal in her back as she was pushed forward. To the side of the track, sheltered by the pines, she saw an old wooden shed. This must have been the building she'd seen on the map, next to the mineshaft. Its windows – if that's what they were – were shuttered closed, and snow had drifted halfway up the building's sides. One of the men, his face half-hidden by a scarf, pulled back the wooden beam that was holding the door closed, and then his accomplice shoved Müller inside.

In one corner, hunched into her woollen, filthy *Strickpulli*, her face bruised and reddened, a teenage girl looked up at Müller with a mixture of what seemed to be hope and longing. It was Irma Behrendt, struggling to stand against the weight of her chains. Despite the bruising, despite the emaciated face, Müller recognised her as the last of the three teens who had supposedly been transferred from the Rügen *Jugendwerkhof* in May last year. Her red hair was tangled and dirty, but she was alive: the sole survivor of the three. Müller's captors tied her to an iron pillar next to the girl, and lashed the detective's wrists together.

As the guards left, and barred the door closed behind them, Müller turned to the teenager.

'Irma,' she whispered. The girl turned in shock, wondering how this woman knew her name. 'We will survive, Irma,' continued Müller. 'We have to. When the local police realise I've disappeared they will look for us.'

The girl just continued to stare, shafts of light from the gaps in the decaying timber walls highlighting her matted red hair and her emaciated features.

'Who are you?' she finally asked.

'Police *Oberleutnant* Karin Müller. I'm married to Gottfried Müller – he used to teach at your *Jugendwerkhof*.'

'And you've come to rescue me?' The girl snorted, sounding half-delirious, staring at Müller's tightly bound hands. 'You haven't done a very good job.' She laughed. Then she grew serious. 'Have you any news of Beate?' Müller tried to give nothing away. But her silence, and the way she dropped her eyes, spoke for themselves. 'She's dead, isn't she?'

Müller gave a long sigh, but her lack of an answer was enough for Irma. The girl began to scream, high-pitched, terrible wails. Müller would have covered her ears if she could. Instead she tried to shush Irma gently, but to no avail. The girl was slumped forward, but the shuddering of her body told Müller that her tears were still falling.

'We will be OK, Irma. I'm sure we will.'

But though she spoke with confidence, she didn't expect the girl to take the words at face value. Müller didn't even believe them herself.

51

Müller was left alone with Irma overnight, their hands untied, their legs shackled to the floor, with just filthy damp mattresses and blankets as bedding. She held the girl's hand. She knew that wasn't just to give the teenager comfort. Müller herself needed that connection with living flesh and blood. Irma was asleep, breathing heavily – more accustomed to her captivity than Müller was. The detective tossed and turned as far as her shackles and injuries would allow. Each time she tried to move, the stabbing pains from her legs reminded her of the crash into the tripwire.

In the darkness, she thought of Tilsner. There was nothing she could do for her deputy. She didn't know his precise fate, but when they'd been bundled into the Soviet 4x4, she was conscious that he was already in his death throes. Her prospects – and those of the girl she was trying to save – didn't seem much better. Whoever had captured her and the girl she was certain it must be someone connected to Neumann and the *Jugendwerkhof* on

Prora. Although the guards to this hideout had worn snow camouflage dress similar to that of the Republic's People's Army, this was no formal arrest.

What of Gottfried? As far as she knew, he was still incarcerated by the Stasi, unless Jäger had fulfilled his part of the bargain and had somehow got him free or reduced the charges he faced. She'd missed her opportunity to help him. She should have acted earlier. Why hadn't she asked Schmidt to examine the photos of Gottfried and the murdered girl straightaway and give her an immediate assessment of her husband's claims that they were fakes? Now she was helpless, and couldn't believe she or Irma were going to get out of here alive, or that she would ever see Gottfried and their Schönhauser Allee home again. She remembered what had been done to Beate, before and after death, and shuddered.

Neumann – if he *was* behind all this – still hadn't made himself known to her. As she dozed, the faxed photograph of his mangled face with its sinister eyepatch replayed in her head, forcing her back awake. Was he even here? And if so, what was he up to?

Irma grunted, and turned in her sleep, as much as the iron leg shackles would allow. She let Müller's hand drop as she did, and now the detective felt even more alone. Perhaps Irma had been right to mock her attempts at rescuing her. It was true. She hadn't done a very good job.

When she awoke, daylight was streaming through the cracks in the timber of the shed in which they were being held.

She turned towards Irma, and found the girl was already looking at her, smiling.

'You know, in a funny way,' said the girl, 'I'm pleased you're chained up here next to me.' Her face darkened. 'After Beate ... after Mathias ... I was getting lonely.'

Müller took her hand again. 'Don't worry, Irma, we will get out of this mess. We will escape.'

Irma shook her head. 'Believe that if you want, but there is no escape. Even if we get out of here, we're still in the Republic.'

Müller didn't reply.

Irma snorted. 'It's OK for you, anyway. You're one of them. You're part of the system. You try living in a closed *Jugendwerkhof*. Then you would see why so many people are desperate to leave this shitty little country.' Müller dropped her gaze. She didn't want to admit the truth of what the teenager was saying. It struck too close to what she had always believed in.

The girl turned away, and stared up at the ceiling, where the half-rotted timbers of what Müller assumed was the mine house struggled to support the ancient roof. 'You realise we escaped, don't you? The only three children to have ever escaped from *Jugendwerkhof* Prora Ost.'

Müller frowned. 'I thought you were transferred? Moved out by Neumann.'

Irma laughed. 'No, we escaped. In the furniture packs. And we got to the West, before we were betrayed.'

'Betrayed?'

'Yes. By Mathias. You know he's dead, don't you?'

Müller nodded. She reached over and took the girl's hand again, stroking it gently. 'I'm sorry, I'm truly sorry, Irma. He was your friend too.'

'Hah!' Irma spat. 'Friend? He was no friend of mine. He was besotted with Beate, but even she saw through him in the end. Mathias Gellman betrayed us, to the Stasi. They recruited him to spy on the children, and the teachers. And he did, to try to make his own life easier. When we were on the boat, when we were nearly in the West, he persuaded the crew to radio the authorities in the East, and they persuaded their counterparts in the West to send us back. The little shit was an informer. I'm glad he's dead.'

Müller said nothing, shocked that the Stasi recruited children – it was the first she'd ever heard of it. She wasn't sure if she believed it, but then she wasn't sure what she believed anymore.

'And do you know what else, Mrs Berlin Detective? I killed Mathias. I murdered him. I pushed him down those steps. So what are you going to do about that? Arrest me?' Irma started laughing like a maniac, laughs that after a few moments devolved into sobs. 'You can't arrest me, can you? Because you're as powerless as me in this shithole of a country.'

Müller tried to grab the girl's shoulders, to hold her, to calm her. But Irma violently shrugged her off, and turned to face the wall.

52

Day Seventeen.
The Harz mountains, East Germany.

The door swung open and two guards in snow camouflage over-alls entered. They unlocked the chains that bound Müller's and Irma's legs, and then prodded the two females with their rifle barrels out of the mine-house door. Müller shouted at them, say-ing she was injured and couldn't walk quickly, and asking what had happened to her deputy. They wouldn't reply. They were taken some fifty metres through ankle-deep snow, further into the forest, in the opposite direction to the inner German border.

'This is where their lair is,' whispered Irma. One of the guards gave her an extra sharp prod with his weapon for daring to speak.

Hidden in the trees, camouflaged by undergrowth and snow, steps led down to what appeared to be some sort of underground bunker. Like the mine house, it looked to Müller as though it had seen better days, but with its thick sealed metal doors, secured by release wheels, no one was going to be able to find them. 'I think it was built by the Nazis,' whispered Irma as they entered the concrete complex. 'They take us here for a shower once a week. You're lucky to get one on your first day. But I warn you, there's no hot water. It will be freezing.'

As she showered, Müller examined her wounds. It was her legs she was most concerned about: the broken flesh was bruised, inflamed. Pain flashed from the wound as the water hit, forcing Müller to grit her teeth. She knew she needed hospital treatment, probably stitches. She glanced over at Irma who pulled a face, then smiled.

'Your leg doesn't look too good,' she said. 'Try to insist they take you to hospital. It might be a way out.'

'What about you?' Müller shouted over the noise of the shower spray.

'If you get out, you can come and rescue me. But do it properly next time, with some back-up. Not in the amateurish way you tried this time.' She smirked at the detective.

Müller turned away, feeling herself redden at the comment.

Clean clothes – shapeless unisex track suits and T-shirts – had been left on the side for them. Once they were dressed, the guards took them to another underground room. Wood panelling covered the walls, and the furniture was traditional Harz farmhouse style. A touch of luxury that couldn't mask the underlying odour of damp and earth.

Breakfast was laid out on a table: fresh rolls, cheese, ham, coffee. It was as good as the one at the Wernigerode guesthouse.

Minutes after they'd started eating, the door opened.

'It'll be Neumann,' whispered Irma.

But it wasn't. At least to Müller it wasn't.

Because as she looked up from her coffee, standing before her with the good side of his face in profile – but greyer, thinner, more unkempt – was a man who she'd vowed, years before, to never set eyes on again. Now she knew why the faxed photo Jäger had sent to Wernigerode had seemed strangely familiar – even though she thought she hadn't recognised the man portrayed in it. Here, from a different angle, she did.

The flash of recognition took Müller's thoughts back to the police university. The lecturer – a senior detective on secondment – who'd befriended her. Offered to help her up the career ladder. To smooth her path into the *Kripo*, as long as she agreed to the police's version of the casting couch. She'd resisted, even though there was something in him – at that time – that she found attractive. Perhaps it was just a power thing: that he did have the ability to kick-start her career. Now she felt nausea well up. She closed her eyes for a moment, trying to wipe the memory: him plying her with vodka, pressing himself against her, the foul smell of his breath only partially hidden by alcohol fumes, and then how he'd held her down, ripped off her clothing, thrust himself into her. How she'd been helpless as he grabbed her wrists, the pain tearing her insides as flesh tore against flesh, and then – just as he was about to finish – how he'd relaxed his grip in the ecstasy of the moment, and she'd smashed the vodka bottle against the table and jammed it in his face.

'Aren't you going to say hello, Karin? I've waited a long time for this reunion.'

She heard Irma gasp. 'You know Neumann?'

'Oh yes, she knows me, Irma. Intimately. We've even had a child together. That's if you can call a twenty-week foetus a child. A twenty-week foetus that she killed. Was it a girl or a boy, Karin? Did you ever find out?'

Müller felt as though the whole room was spinning. She swallowed, but gave no answer, her eyes fixed on her shaking fingers as they gripped the table for support. She wished that she was back at the apartment on Schönhauser Allee. Taking out the baby clothes. Stroking them. Comforting herself.

'I've never had the chance to have another child, Karin. Who would want to marry someone with a face like this?' He stroked the scar tissue under his eyepatch. 'You killed my only one. My only son or daughter. And my facial injuries and the scandal from you claiming I raped you – a claim which was patently untrue – meant I had to leave the force. They offered me a job in charge of the *Jugendwerkhof* under a new name. That or face trial. It wasn't much of a choice. You cost me my job, and the chance of a child. You ruined my life. But I still felt some tie to you, despite your betrayal. I wanted to see you again. Now I'm not so sure it was a good idea.'

Müller looked up, and could see tears welling in the remaining eye of the man she knew as Walter Pawlitzki – a man now known as Franz Neumann, lately director of the *Jugendwerkhof* Prora Ost.

'Have you been able to have other children, Karin?'

She forced herself to try to give nothing away, but knew he could probably see the pain, the longing, in her expression. As time slowed, she could see Irma watching the exchange intently, fingering her sharp metal meat knife.

Pawlitzki drew up a chair, and sat next to them at the table. Müller tried to catch Irma's eye, hoping the girl wouldn't do anything stupid. Müller knew that the former police university lecturer – the former *Jugendwerkhof* director – would have ensured the guards were ready to respond instantly should either of them try to attack him.

Müller drew in a deep breath, and held her former lecturer's one-eyed gaze. 'Did you murder Beate Ewert?' she asked.

Pawlitzki rocked back in his chair, laughing.

'It's not a laughing matter,' screamed Irma, her hand tightening round the knife handle.

'Put that down, Irma. Immediately. Otherwise I will call the guards back.' The girl's grip loosened. 'All I know is that Beate went to the party on the Brocken, and then on to Berlin. If you're saying she's dead, I certainly didn't kill her. Can you say the same about Mathias, Irma?' The girl lowered her gaze.

'So what happened?' asked Müller.

'Why do you think I know what happened to her? And even if I did, would I really tell you that, Karin? You, a detective for the People's Police of this good Republic.' Pawlitzki took a bread roll, broke a piece off and began to butter it. 'What I will tell you is that the problem arose when Beate recognised the photograph of the esteemed Joint First Deputy Minister for State Security in a copy of *Neues Deutschland* that one of the guards stupidly left on the breakfast table here.' He kept his eyes on both of them, as he reached across to the breakfast-room's magazine rack. 'Here it is.' He handed the paper to Müller. 'The joint deputy boss of the Stasi, *Generaloberst* Horst Ackermann.' Pawlitzki paused, and put the piece of bread roll into his mouth.

'I've heard of him,' said Müller, turning the newspaper face down. If they got out of here alive, she didn't want Irma to recognise the Stasi general and try to take her own revenge. All the time, with half an eye, she was looking round the room, wondering if there was a way to escape. But she also wanted to hear what Pawlitzki had to say.

'He was guest of honour at the winter fancy-dress party on the Brocken. It was actually he who asked Beate to attend. He thought she was still in the *Jugendwerkhof*, but as until recently I've been able to go back and forth between Rügen and the Harz, I still got the message he sent to Prora.'

'The sick bastard,' screamed Irma. 'And you just served her up to him on a plate.'

'I was just following orders, Irma.' Pawlitzki looked down at his hands. Müller noticed they were shaking, and his voice sounded almost tearful. 'It's not something I'm proud of. But it's how this Republic is run.' He tried to compose himself, folding his arms across his stomach. 'And as far as I know, they went back to Berlin. But it's Ackermann you need to find, not me. And good luck with that. I don't think you'll get very far trying to arrest the deputy head of the Stasi.'

Something in Pawlitzki's expression told her that he was still withholding information, that he knew more than he was letting on.

'How do I know you're not just lying to save your own skin?'

Pawlitzki sighed, and took a sip of coffee.

'What reason do I have to lie?'

Müller watched him place his coffee cup down, reach under his coat and draw out a gun. She recognised it immediately: a Walther

PKK – a *Polizeipistole Kriminalmodell*, easily concealed for under-cover work, and the inspiration for her own Makarov. He fingered the gun lovingly.

'Whatever I tell you, you won't be telling anyone else. I tried to do my best by the three teenagers, but when they were handed back by the West Germans, I had to intercept them at the Helmstedt autobahn crossing. I was under orders to make sure they told no one about their escape or their methods, and more-over that they were in no position to make allegations against Comrade *Generaloberst* Ackermann. Helping our work here was a necessity. I'm sorry it hasn't turned out as intended.'

Irma stood up now, and made a move towards Pawlitzki. Mül-ler held her back as she launched her invective. 'Don't claim you're sorry. You treated us like shit in Prora and you've treated us even worse here.' She aimed a globule of spittle at Pawlitzki's face.

As he wiped it off, deathly calm, Müller asked about Mathias. 'Why did you try to make out that Mathias's death was murder? What was that all about? Why try to make it look like the killing in the cemetery in Berlin?'

'Because I'd seen that case in the papers, I wanted to lure you here. I knew a similar killing would do just that. That you would be sent to investigate. Despite what you did to me, I still have feelings for you, Karin. These last few years, I've thought about you almost every day. The things we did –' Pawlitzki was sweating now, even though the temperature in the bunker was cool. He wiped his brow with the back of his sleeve as he con-tinued to talk at machine-gun speed. 'I knew that if I faked Mathias's death to look like Beate's murder, the local police would ask you for help. Presumably that's why you're here?'

'I'm here because I was captured by your guards, the same guards who shot my deputy. But if I have my way you will be arrested, and face ultimate justice.'

Pawlitzki shook his head, fingering his gun, a look of disappointment at her answer clouding his face. 'It won't happen, Karin. Don't you see? They couldn't afford for any of this to come out. It would undermine the very fabric of the regime.' He leant back in his chair again, wiping the hair back from his forehead. 'In any case,' he said, lifting the gun and then releasing the safety lever, 'as I've already said, you're not going to be around to arrest me. But I've got to hand it to you, you've followed my clues well.'

'Your clues?' asked Müller.

'In the lim—'

'I thought you said you had nothing to do with the body in the cemetery?'

Müller could see his confusion. He'd let something slip that he hadn't wanted to, in his attempts to boast about how clever he'd been. But then Pawlitzki shrugged. 'You're not leaving here, and I am.'

'Well, if I'm never getting out of here alive, there's no harm telling me what all the digging in the mine is for ...'

Pawlitzki sucked his teeth, uncertainty etched across his face. 'It's a tunnel. Ackermann and the others involved in abusing the girls wanted an escape route. We're already under the border, going upwards. Just a few more metres and we'll be through. And, believe it or not, I didn't want to leave without seeing you again. I think about you still, you know. Your body ... your *smell*.' His thin smile caused a wave of nausea to run through her, and he frowned. 'But now you're here, I can see that's not going to happen. So it will have to be the other way. What is it they say, an eye for an eye? Well, I need paying back with more than just an eye for what you've done to me. You turned me into this monster.' He lifted his eyepatch, and Müller expected to recoil in horror. But this wasn't like the bloody, ripped mess of Beate's eye socket in the cemetery. The skin was pale, healed – more like the smooth skin on the girl's hands.

Müller realised the man was crazy, but their best chance was to keep him talking, to use his warped feelings for her to their advantage.

'I'm sorry,' she lied.

'Sorry? Sorry doesn't do it, I'm afraid.'

She moved closer to him, still keeping eye contact, and then placed her right hand on his arm. He looked down at where their two bodies joined once more, his distorted face creased in confusion and indecision. Müller thought she saw something else in his Cyclops-like eye. Was it lust? Some sort of crazed love? It was something to cling onto: a possible last chance for herself and Irma.

Still holding Pawlitzki's arm lightly, she began talking in a soothing voice. 'I can understand what a burden this must have been to you. And we're not so very different. My own marriage is in trouble. I'm about to be kicked out of the police force. I've no reason to stay in the Republic any more than you. What I did to you was awful, I can see that now. And I do think of you too – of us –' She moved her face closer to his. At the same time, with her left hand behind her back, directly in Irma's vision, she made a tiny stab with her finger into her back. Müller continued to move in, as though to kiss him, even though the thought disgusted her. Even the memory of kissing him disgusted her. Her abortion disgusted her. The rape that led to him losing his job disgusted her. But in his good eye, she could see his longing, his need. They only needed an instant.

At that moment, Irma jumped up. Before Pawlitzki could change his mindset and retrieve his gun, Müller grabbed both of his arms and Irma plunged the meat knife into his neck. All the force from muscle built in months of slavery concentrated into one blow. Pawlitzki went white with shock, blood pumping from the wound.

He fell back, trying to stem the blood flow with one hand. 'Guards,' he shouted. There were responding noises and shouts outside the room, but then the sounds of automatic gunfire.

A plain-clothes officer burst in through the door. Another round of automatic fire into Pawlitzki's abdomen, chest and head, finishing the job Irma had started. He slumped back. Müller looked up in shock as another man entered the subterranean room.

Jäger!

Everything was unfolding so quickly, Müller struggled to make sense of it. She was about to say something to the Stasi lieutenant colonel when she saw the first officer raising his gun arm, aiming towards Irma. She screamed 'No! No!' at Jäger, but the *Oberstleutnant* made no effort to stop the gunman. Müller in that instant leapt across to shield the girl with her body.

She saw the flash, felt bullets tear into her flesh. Only then did she hear Jäger's cry of 'Hold your fire!'

53

March 1975.
Hohenschönhausen, East Berlin.

Gottfried Müller had tried to keep count of the days in his head, but with the constant yet irregular flashing of the light at night-time, he'd pretty much lost track. Ten days, eleven, two weeks … he had no clear idea.

His visit from Karin had been the one thing he was clinging to. Surely she would help him? But a strict coldness gripped his heart as he recalled her guilty expression when she'd admitted the photographs of her entwined with Tilsner were genuine. And there had been the second bout of questioning. It didn't seem to be the fake photographs they were interested in anymore … Instead they'd been focusing on Pastor Grosinski. Saying he'd been spying for the West. And that Gottfried had been passing him information, information about the police, his wife, her latest murder case. That, they said, constituted spying in itself … Helping a foreign power to undermine the Republic.

It was madness, absolute madness. But in his tiredness, his hopelessness, his utter fatigue, Gottfried wasn't entirely sure what he'd agreed to. It was true – he *had* talked to the pastor about his marriage, and about the murder case. But that was merely meant as an example of the problems Karin and he faced. Her obsession with her work. But when they'd thrust the papers in front of him, he wasn't sure what it was he'd actually been forced to sign.

The sound of keys being turned in the lock startled him. Was this it? Would they just take him into a yard somewhere and shoot him? It was the same guard who'd taken him to the two interviews with Hunsberger. Gottfried tried to cling to the bed, but the guard roughly grabbed his hands, forced them together and cuffed him.

'No!' he screamed. 'I haven't done anything. It's all a mistake.' The guard yanked him to his feet, but Gottfried was too weak to resist. Then he was prodded in the back, and forced to walk into the corridor. The red lights, doors, the clanking and clanging of metal. Finally, the garage with blinding floodlights, where he'd arrived the first day. And there it was again: the prison on wheels in which he'd been transported here.

'Where are you taking me?' he shouted as another guard arrived; both guards tried to push and pull him into the small van. Finally, he gave up, stopped resisting and let them do with his body whatever they wanted.

He was shoved into one of the tiny cells in the back of the vehicle, forced to crouch once more in the darkness – the too-small cell that stank of piss and shit, his body unable to stretch out, crushed against the sides, the floor and the roof.

Then the engine started, and Gottfried readied himself to endure a reprise of his journey all those long days and nights ago. He didn't know where they were taking him then, and he didn't know now. Acceleration, deceleration. Stop. Start. Banging him about just like before. Was he being taken to another jail? Or did a far worse fate now await him?

54

Day Seventeen.
The Harz mountains, East Germany.

Müller grabbed her left arm and squeezed to try to stop the flow of blood. At the instant the officer had fired, Jäger had stuck out his arm, pushing the barrel away fractionally – enough so that she just caught a glancing blow. Müller knew she had been lucky.

She felt Irma under her, moving. Alive.

Jäger stepped towards them.

'Don't touch me,' Müller screamed. 'Or her.' She'd trusted him … Those intimate meetings at the Kulturpark, the Märchenbrunnen, the Weisser See. Yet an instant earlier, Jäger would have quite happily allowed Irma to be shot dead.

The Stasi *Oberstleutnant* backed off. He began issuing new orders to the plain-clothes officer – presumably a Stasi agent allied to Jäger's faction. From outside, Müller could hear more gunfire, more screams and the sounds of explosions.

'Are you OK?' whispered Irma, shuffling to try to get comfortable under the weight of Müller's body.

'Yes, are you?' asked the detective. She felt Irma's head nod behind her, felt the grip from the girl on her good arm.

Jäger moved out of the room, issuing more orders, and then suddenly – in front of her face – there was the friendly giant smile of *Hauptmann* Baumann, and behind him, *Unterleutnant* Vogel. *Kripo* officers like herself; people she felt she could trust.

'I'm only moving away from her if you guarantee she won't be harmed,' she said to Baumann.

He nodded. 'You'll both be OK. I give you my word.' He unwrapped a bandage handed to him by Vogel, and wound it tightly round the flesh wound in Müller's arm. 'We need to get you to hospital as soon as possible.'

'She has to come with me. Don't let Jäger near her,' she said, fiercely.

Vogel helped Baumann to lift Müller up. The junior officer smiled too. 'We will look after you both, *Oberleutnant* Müller.' Then Baumann knelt down to comfort Irma and double-check that she was unharmed.

Müller glanced at Pawlitzki's crumpled body in the corner of the room. The second former police colleague shot dead in less than twenty-four hours. At least, she assumed Tilsner must be dead.

'Have you found Werner?' she asked Vogel.

He lowered his eyes, and nodded slowly. She didn't have to ask if he was dead. She could see it in Vogel's expression.

'He's being taken to hospital. But it doesn't look good.'

Müller breathed in sharply.

'So he's still alive?'

'Don't get your hopes up,' said Vogel. 'There was a faint pulse, that's all.'

Vogel and Baumann were true to their word, escorting Müller and Irma to the hospital so she wouldn't have to have anything to do with Jäger for the time being. As they helped her climb the few steps to the surface, Baumann explained what the bunker was – a forward command post linked to Hitler's development of V2 rockets in the latter days of the war. Müller – in her groggy state – only partly took it in. She knew the main V2 production site after it was moved from the Ostsee coast had been further south in the Harz, near Nordhausen, but she guessed it made some sort of sense. As they got back to the mine house, Müller saw bodies scattered around, their white camouflage clothing besmirched with crimson, lying in the snow between the trees. Smoke and dust rose from the mineshaft itself, presumably the aftermath of the explosions she'd heard. Were they sealing Pawlitzki's putative escape route?

The two local *Kripo* detectives drove Müller and Irma in a four-wheel-drive vehicle back up the forest track. Her head swivelled round as they passed the site where Tilsner had been shot. And then she saw the terror and confusion in Irma's face and reached out to hug her, wincing from her injured arm as she did so.

'Shhh,' whispered Müller. 'It will be alright now. It's over.'

Irma looked up at her, a defeated expression in her face. 'For you, perhaps. You will be going back to your secure job in the police force.' Müller wasn't as sure as the girl was that her career wasn't over. After all, she'd defied Reiniger and broken rule after rule. 'For me it's not over,' continued Irma. 'I will be going back to the *Jugendwerkhof*. That, or a prison, and I cannot believe there is much difference.'

Müller held the girl's gaze as the police vehicle bumped along the snow-covered forest track. 'I won't allow that to happen. I promise you,' she said.

At the top of the track, as they reached the plateau, Müller scanned the side of the road, looking for the Wartburg.

Baumann must have seen her searching for it in the rear-view mirror. 'Your car's a write-off, I'm afraid, Comrade Müller. They burnt it out and pushed it over the side. That's what alerted us to everything.'

Müller frowned, rubbing her bandaged arm gingerly. 'And was Jäger with you?' she asked.

'No,' said Baumann. 'Jäger and his Stasi men were already down there. We arrived just as the fun was starting.'

'So who alerted Jäger?' asked Müller, perplexed. Although Pawlitzki had partially filled her in on his side of the story, there was still much she didn't understand.

'We don't know, Comrade Müller. You'll have to ask him that yourself.'

55

Day Nineteen.
The Harz mountains, East Germany.

Müller and Irma stayed in Wernigerode Hospital for two days. Müller insisted on a private room, with a twenty-four-hour guard provided thanks to Baumann and Vogel pulling strings at the local People's Police headquarters. She also insisted on keeping her Makarov at her bedside.

The doctors were more concerned about the leg wound from the tripwire than her arm, which they maintained was little more than a graze.

She looked across at Irma, sleeping in the next bed. And then she ran her fingers lightly over the trigger of the gun, as though to reassure herself it was still there.

Irma was suffering from shock and mild malnutrition. After a day, the doctors said she was well enough to be discharged, but Müller overruled them; the girl was staying with her. When they tried to disagree, she called in Dr Eckstein. The senior pathologist concurred with her. The more junior members of staff evidently revered him even though his speciality was the dead rather than the living.

What of Gottfried? She still had no news of him, and her best hope – Jäger – was someone she no longer wanted to deal with. She remembered Schmidt and the photos, and asked the nurse if she could use the telephone in the office. Irma would surely be safe on her own for a few minutes, wouldn't she? Müller made sure the People's Police guard knew where she'd gone.

The nurse ushered her into the ward office. Müller closed the door behind her and dialled Schmidt's number at Keibelstrasse. When he answered in the forensic lab, Müller had a hard job making out what he was saying over the crackles and interference.

'Sorry we haven't been in touch, Jonas. Things have been a little difficult. You know those photos I gave you before I left Berlin – the ones of my husband? What did you make of them?' she asked, shouting to try to make herself heard.

Schmidt shouted back, and Müller had to move the earpiece away from her head a fraction to avoid being deafened. Yet it was still hard to decipher his words.

'The prints of your husband outside the church in Prenzlauer Berg and meeting the pastor look perfectly genuine to me, I'm afraid, Comrade Müller.'

She sighed. 'I thought they would be, Jonas. I was more interested in the ones taken in the *Jugendwerkhof.*'

'Ah well, there your suspicions, and your husband's claims, proved absolutely spot on.'

Müller felt a lightness in her chest. 'Go on, Jonas. What do you mean?'

'The photos are fakes. I can prove it quite easily. They've been made from two different negatives, from surveillance photographs taken at different times. You can tell by the shadows.

Both photographs were taken during the daytime – the shadows are from natural light. The room appears to face due west, so, looking at maps of Rügen, I would say it was at the back of the Prora complex.' Müller tried to picture the scene. It seemed to make sense from what she remembered of the road map and the layout of the *Jugendwerkhof.* 'But the ones of Beate were taken around midday or early afternoon. She has her back to the window and the water jug throws a shadow to her left,' continued Schmidt, 'yet the ones of your husband in the sanatorium were taken in the late afternoon or early evening, because his shadow is directly behind him, at almost ninety degrees to the window.'

Müller felt the tension drain from her body. She closed her eyes for an instant. Gottfried had been right. How had she ever doubted him? Maybe, just maybe, they did still have a future.

'Are you still there, Comrade Müller? The line is very bad.'

'I'm still here, Jonas. I heard all of that. Thank you so, so much.' She breathed in and out slowly. 'You've no idea what it means to me.'

'That's a pleasure, Comrade Müller. I don't like it when people tamper with the truth, and I don't suppose you do either. I'm glad to have been of assistance. Especially on such a ... delicate matter.'

'Well, I'm extremely grateful to you, Jonas. But I need you to do something else for me. If those photos go missing, I may not have the proof I need that my husband is innocent, so I'd like you to write up your findings and give a report and copies of the photos to –' She paused. Who could she trust? Could she trust anyone? It was *Oberst* Reiniger who'd said her husband was being charged with murder. He was the one who needed to know the photos were fakes. 'Send them to Reiniger. And tell him they're from me. Do a second copy of the report and photos and send them to me at my flat. And do a third and post them to someone you trust implicitly. Just in case, Jonas. I'm sure you understand.'

'That will be a pleasure, Comrade Müller. And how, may I ask, is the investigation progressing?'

Müller thought of all that had happened. About the three teenagers, Tilsner, even Pawlitzki. Schmidt didn't need to know – at least not yet. 'We're on the right track, Jonas. And your forensic work helped get us there. It's not quite over yet, but soon, I think.'

'That's good to hear, Comrade Müller. Keep safe, and I look forward to seeing you when you are back in Berlin.'

After ending the phone call, Müller returned to see the same nurse. Was there any way, she wondered, of finding out where a particular patient had been transferred to, and his condition? The nurse looked doubtful, but Müller gave her the name she wanted checking on anyway: People's Police *Unterleutnant* Werner Tilsner. A few minutes later the nurse returned with her answer. She hadn't been able to obtain any information about anyone of that name. What did that mean? Had Tilsner been transferred somewhere secret? Or worse, did the health service have no record because her deputy hadn't survived?

When she got back into the ward, the police guard smiled at her, and she saw that Irma was still sleeping peacefully. Müller decided she could afford to make one further phone call: to Jäger. He'd ordered her not to call him, but she wasn't going to play by his rules any longer. She asked the nurse if she could use the office once more.

The notepaper on which she had Jäger's Normannenstrasse office number shook slightly in her strapped-up left hand, as she picked up the receiver, held it with her chin in the crook of her neck and dialled with her good arm. The sense of foreboding she'd felt so many times during this strange case now returned as she waited for Jäger to answer. Finally, he did.

'So, Karin. You're recovering well, I hope,' he said.

'I'm still in some pain. But yes, I'm OK. I expect to be well enough to leave the hospital tomorrow and return to Berlin. With Irma.'

'Yes, she is one of the matters we need to deal with. But what do you want to talk about first?' he asked. Müller didn't trust his tone. It was back to the friendliness of their several clandestine meetings, and that worried her.

'Gottfried. My husband. You must know now that the murder accusations don't hold up?'

'That's true. I apprised the investigators of that. I kept my promise to help you.'

'And that the photographs of him abusing Beate were faked?'

'Yes, Karin. But the photographs of him meeting dissidents in the church were genuine, so nothing has changed in terms of you and him. We cannot have you married to an enemy of the state. I've done what I can to help you in respect of your husband, but if you wish to remain in the *Kriminalpolizei* you will have to sign the divorce papers.'

'And what of my suspension? What about me disobeying Reiniger's orders?'

'Did you disobey him, Karin? That's not what he's reported. He's said the phone lines were so bad that you were unable to hear him.' Müller pictured her police colonel. He'd always protected her. He was the one who had originally promoted her, let her lead the Mitte murder squad; the first female detective to be given that level of responsibility in the whole of the Republic. Now he seemed to be letting her off the hook. 'But there is a condition to you not facing any disciplinary charges. You will have to, as I said, divorce your husband. Gottfried has already signed the papers. You just have to add your signature.'

'Can I see him first?' asked Müller.

'No. That won't be possible, I'm afraid, Karin.'

'Why? Is he still in jail?'

'No, Karin. He's been released. The murder charge and sexual deviancy charge have been dropped. I said I would help you, and I have.'

Müller frowned. 'But then why can't I see him? I don't understand.'

Jäger sighed at the other end of the line. 'In the circumstances, the best outcome for all concerned was to accede to your husband's request to leave the Republic. He has gone to West Germany, with our blessing. The remaining charge will lie on file. He won't be welcomed back.'

The news hit Müller like a blow to the stomach. She gasped, and had to grip the table to steady herself. 'When did this happen?'

'Just these last couple of days, while you've been in hospital in Wernigerode, Karin.'

Müller felt a coldness in the core of her body.

'So you will sign the papers?' asked Jäger.

Images flashed through Müller's head. All the good times. The lovers' meetings at the Märchenbrunnen. The way he used to be able to make her laugh at the smallest thing. Gone, all gone. But maybe it had gone as soon as she slept with Tilsner. Maybe it had gone earlier, at the start of all this, that drunken night with Tilsner that somebody – the police or the Stasi – had surreptitiously filmed.

'Karin?' prompted Jäger.

'Yes,' she said, in a quiet voice, trying to hold back the tears. 'Yes, I'll sign the –'

An urgent knocking on the glazed office door stopped her midsentence. She looked up to the see the alarmed face of the nurse.

'The girl,' she said, breathlessly. 'She's gone.'

'What?' exclaimed Müller, dropping the receiver. She ran back to the ward, with the nurse following behind her. Another nurse and a woman in a different uniform who Müller assumed must be the ward sister were stripping the bedding from Irma's bed. The People's Police guard was nowhere to be seen.

'Where's she gone?' Müller screamed.

'There's no need to take that tone, Comrade,' said the sister. 'She was discharged by a senior official. It's all above board. The official ordered the policeman to leave too.'

Müller checked she had her gun in her holster and raced to the lift. From the lights, she could see it was occupied and on its way down to the ground floor and the exit. She raced down the stairs, each jolt sending pain shooting from her injured left arm, and knifing up from her legs. Adrenaline kept her going. She reached the ground floor just as the lift door opened. But Irma and the 'official' were nowhere to be seen; instead, a white-coated doctor emerged.

'Have you seen a teenage girl with red hair?' she shouted. The doctor shook his head. She scanned the corridor. No one. She ran out into the car park, looked left and right, her heart pounding in panic, but there was no sign of Irma anywhere. Knowing that each second counted, Müller ran back, panting, to the third floor. The sister and second nurse were still calmly making the bed.

'I don't know why you're so worried,' said the sister, as she swept her hand over the undersheet to iron out the creases. 'The man had all the correct papers. He was very senior.'

'What was his name?' demanded Müller.

'Oh I can't remember that. It'll be in the records. Wait a moment and –'

With her good arm, Müller reached into her pocket for the cutting from *Neues Deutschland* taken from the paper Pawlitzki had shown her: the one Beate had seen on the breakfast table in the bunker by the mine.

She thrust the picture of Horst Ackermann, the deputy head of the Stasi, in front of the sister.

'Was this him?' she shouted.

'Yes, yes. I told you he was senior. I couldn't say no to –'

Müller immediately ran to the office, yanked a nurse out of the way and then dialled Jäger again. As she explained the situation, the Stasi lieutenant colonel – usually the model of control – sounded as panicked as she was.

'*Verdammt!*' he screamed down the line. 'We'd put out an alert to prevent him crossing any of the Republic's borders. We should have warned the hospital too.'

'I think I know where he will be heading,' replied Müller.

'But I gave instructions for that tunnel in the mine to be blown up.'

'He doesn't know that, though, does he?' said Müller. 'I'm going there now.'

'Be careful, Karin. He's desperate. I'll ask the local People's Police to give you back-up and order the border guards to co-operate, but don't go in gung-ho like last time. You know how that turned out.'

56

Day Nineteen.
The Harz mountains, East Germany.

I suppose I'd always expected to be returned to the *Jugendwerkhof.*
Ever since the West Germans handed us back to Neumann at the
motorway crossing point, then I thought I would eventually be
going back to Prora Ost. But I didn't expect to be back here, at
the rock face of the mine level, digging amongst the dirt and dust,
coughing and sweating. Barely able to breathe.

I'd been half-asleep in the hospital, and couldn't really understand what was happening. There was an important-looking
man standing by the bed, urging the sister to dress me quickly.
I said I didn't want to go, that I wanted to wait for the friendly
policewoman. The sister said this man from the Ministry was in
charge of me now.

Now he's here next to me. In the semi-blackness. The only
light, a dim yellow from his torch, propped up on the floor.
When I saw his eyes as he rushed me out of the hospital into his
four-wheel drive, there was a familiar look to them. They had
that same mad glint of desperation that Neumann's one good eye

displayed in the bunker by the mine, just before I stabbed him in the neck. That's what this Republic has done to me: turned me into a killer. Two victims in as many months.

I said I would get Neumann at some stage, and I did. This other man digging beside me, panting because he's not as fit as me, not as used to the work, if I get the chance, well he'll be next. He's got a gun. But I've got a shovel. All I will need is an instant. I've shown that already.

57

Day Nineteen.
The Harz mountains, East Germany.

When Müller, Baumann and Vogel reached the mineshaft, they found it closely guarded by border troops. Their commanding officer insisted no one had tried to get through their cordon.

'In any case, explosives were laid in the level on Sunday immediately after the incident, Comrade *Oberleutnant*. The tunnel has collapsed. No one would be able to get into it.'

Müller frowned. She was sure her hunch was correct. Jäger had thought the same in their phone call: that Ackermann would try to escape to the West by using the tunnel under the border. If she was wrong, then they had no idea where Ackermann and Irma had gone, only that he was presumably planning to use the girl as some sort of bargaining tool. But Müller doubted such a plan would succeed. Even Jäger's faction of the Stasi had been all too ready to liquidate the teenager. Jäger's quarry was Ackermann; he couldn't care less about Irma. Somehow Müller had to find her, to save her.

Müller eyeballed the officer. 'I understand what you're saying, Comrade *Leutnant*. Nevertheless, I would like to go down the shaft to see for myself.'

The border guard nodded. 'You will have to be accompanied by my men, and they will go ahead of you to check for safety. It seems pointless, though. As I say, the tunnel is blocked off. But we're under instructions to be of assistance to your inquiry, so on your own head be it. Will you be OK with that arm?' he asked, gesturing towards her sling.

Müller nodded, then climbed down the shaft after the two border guards chosen to accompany her. Baumann and Vogel followed. Müller negotiated each rung with precision, gripping one side of the ladder with just her right arm, edging down bit by bit, trying to ignore the pain from her injuries.

The two guards lit up the stone steps with their torches, and after the group of five descended, they turned into the level.

As the torchlight illuminated the rails, Müller could see the parallel lines of iron disappear into the jumble of rocks that now blocked the mine level. The pile of stone reached from floor to ceiling. Müller moved towards it, but one of the guards held her back.

'It's not safe further than here, I'm afraid, Comrade *Oberleutnant*. The tunnel has been reinforced to this point so that we could check it was properly blocked up. It's a temporary measure. In the coming days we will secure stronger explosives, and blow up the whole shaft and complex. No one will be using this again.'

Müller's mind raced. Ackermann and Irma couldn't have got through here. So if they weren't here, where the hell had they gone?

She started to say something, but was shushed by Baumann.

'Listen, Comrade Müller. Did you hear that?'

The five held their collective breath. The two guards extinguished their torches, perhaps hoping the darkness would concentrate their powers of hearing.

'There!' whispered Baumann.

This time Müller heard it. It was very faint, but it was definitely there. A rhythmic thud. Again and again. Then silence. Then it started again. Thud, thud, thud.

'What do you think it is, *Hauptmann*?'

'I can't be sure, of course,' replied Baumann. 'But my best guess is that's the sound of someone digging.'

Müller listened once more. The thudding resumed.

The border guards still wouldn't let them near the collapsed rock wall and seemed in no hurry to investigate whatever the digging sounds were. They assured the *Kripo* officers that they would scale up the urgency of acquiring more powerful explosives, to destroy the whole complex. If anyone was at work in the mine, they would be blown to smithereens.

The three detectives had no option but to retreat back above ground.

Müller looked at Baumann in desperation. 'What can we do now? We've got to save that girl somehow.'

Baumann glanced towards the border guard lieutenant. 'I don't think you're going to be able to persuade him to re-open the tunnel. He's dead set on simply blowing the whole thing up.'

Müller nodded. But there had to be *something* they could do.

'Is it worth looking at that map again?' asked Vogel.

She frowned. 'Which map?'

'*Hauptmann* Baumann and I managed to get hold of an old map of the mine workings from the local library. That day we came up here trying to find you. It's more detailed than the one you had.'

'Where is it?' asked Müller.

'In the Gaz.' The three of them ran back to the four-wheel drive, parked at the side of the forest track. Vogel retrieved the map, and after wiping the vehicle's bonnet with his gloves, spread it out on top.

'We're here,' he said. 'By this shaft and mine house. But as you can see, originally there were other shafts leading down to the mine too.' He pointed at three different circles, dotted throughout the forest.

'How do we know they connect with our mine?' asked Baumann.

Vogel flipped the map over. On the reverse side, there were sectional drawings of the mine. 'Bear in mind this is more than a hundred years old. The border guards most probably will have found all the old shafts and blocked them off to prevent anyone trying to do what Neumann and Ackermann have attempted.'

'To dig under the state border, to the West?' asked Müller.

'Exactly.' Vogel started tracing his finger along the tunnels and shafts of the sectional drawing. 'There are two possible shafts that may link up. One is a hundred metres or so that way.' Vogel pointed into the forest, downhill towards the border. 'The other's about fifty or so metres in the opposite direction, up towards the Brocken.' The uphill route looked steeper, more treacherous.

Baumann dived into the four-wheel drive, and brought three torches out. He handed one to Müller. 'Have you got your gun?' She nodded. 'Then I think it's best you and Vogel take one of the shafts; I'll try the other. You've only got one good arm. Vogel here will be able to help you.' The *Unterleutnant* smiled at Müller.

'Should we ask the border guards to come with us?'

Baumann shook his head. 'They weren't exactly helpful down the main shaft, were they? If there is a way in, we don't want them stopping us.' The three of them studied the map and sectional diagram one last time, trying to memorise potential routes, then set off in opposite directions: Baumann uphill, Müller and Vogel towards the downhill shaft.

Müller had to cling onto the junior officer with her good arm as they negotiated the rocks, snow and tree trunks. They clambered from tree to tree, gradually making their way down the slope to where the shaft ought to be. At first they didn't spot it, then Müller pointed to a low, circular wall, with a rusting grille on top.

'It looks like it's been sealed,' she said.

Vogel gave the grille a tug. It moved slightly, but didn't give way. He picked up a rock, and crashed it down on one side of the grille. Then, squeezing between a tree and the shaft top to gain leverage, he pulled once more. A groan and crash and it came away in his hands, throwing him backwards.

Switching on her torch, Müller shone it down the shaft. 'There's a ladder,' she said, then reached down and pulled at it with her uninjured arm. 'Seems secure.'

Vogel gently moved her aside. 'I'd better go first, *Oberleutnant*, then I can help you if you get into trouble.'

Müller wasn't sure how far down they climbed into the blackness. The shaft was freezing cold with a dank, fetid atmosphere. Vogel descended more quickly than her, until she realised from the motion of his torch that he'd reached the bottom.

Once Müller caught up with him, she saw they had a choice of two passageways to crawl down. Vogel trained the torch beam down one of the tunnels. 'This way,' he whispered. 'At least, I hope so.'

First it was the sounds she heard: the 'thud, thud, thud' from the other side of the rockfall, only now the sound was sharper, louder, echoing down the level they were crawling through. They turned their torches off as a precaution. As Vogel turned a corner, she saw a new flicker of light. Then their level opened out to head height. They stretched for the first time for several minutes, Müller rubbing her left arm. As they moved further towards the thudding sound, the light grew stronger. The tunnel they were in reached a junction. Vogel stopped, peered his head round the corner and then immediately drew it back. She saw the silhouette of his arm beckon her. Then he whispered in her ear.

'They're at the end there. About twenty metres away.'

As he pulled back, Müller moved ahead of him, flattening herself against the end of the wall of their tunnel, right at the junction with the main level. Then she edged her head to the side slightly, so that her left eye could see down to where the pair worked. It was the flaming shock of Irma's hair she saw first, then, alongside, Ackermann's bald pate shining in the torchlight.

She drew out her Makarov and released the safety catch. Behind her, she could hear Vogel doing the same.

Simultaneously, she saw another flash of light, from the tunnel on the other side of the main level. But Ackermann and Irma, busy side by side, hadn't noticed. The light grew stronger, then Ackermann heard something, turned and picked up his gun, aiming it towards the tunnel from where Müller assumed Baumann was about to emerge.

'Careful, he's seen you,' she shouted.

Ackermann swivelled, aiming the gun towards her.

'Drop the weapon, Comrade Ackermann!' shouted Baumann. 'You're under arrest, suspected of the abduction and murder of Beate Ewert.'

Ackermann started to lower his gun arm, but as Baumann stepped out, Müller saw him turn and raise it again. A twin flash of light and then a double crack of gunfire, as she and Vogel raced down the tunnel, pistols aloft. Baumann was hit and fell, and in the confusion as Ackermann turned his aim towards Müller, she saw the glint of steel, a dull thud and anguished cry as Irma used all her force to crack her shovel blade against Ackermann's head. The Stasi general slumped forward, blood welling from his head wound.

Müller shouted: 'No, Irma!' But the girl continued to rain blows down on the Stasi general's skull, the same repetitive rhythm he'd forced her to use in his futile attempt to dig an escape route. Müller forgot about the pain in her bad arm as she grabbed the girl. The teenager dropped the shovel, and clung to the detective, sobbing in her arms. Müller had wanted Ackermann alive. To face proper justice. But as his body twitched in its death throes, she knew that wasn't going to happen.

She swung her torch back down the level, to where Vogel cradled Baumann's oversized head. Müller almost couldn't believe what she was seeing in the dim torchlight. Baumann had seemed larger than life, solid, dependable. But as Vogel looked up into her eyes, his own glistened in the torch beam. He slowly shook his head. His *Hauptmann* – the mountain detective who looked more like a farmer – had investigated his last case.

58

Day Twenty.
East Berlin.

On her return to Berlin, Müller was immediately summoned to a meeting with Jäger at the Märchenbrunnen. She tried to suggest an alternative venue to avoid the reminders of her and Gottfried, but Jäger would have none of it.

He was sitting in his usual place, in front of the still-closed fountains. But the scene looked different, less magical: most of the snow had melted.

'How's your arm?' he asked, glancing at it.

'Getting there. But I feel utterly exhausted.'

'You've been through a lot.'

Müller thought of Baumann's body, lying in the mine, killed by a senior member of Jäger's own Ministry for State Security. She pictured Beate's mutilated body at the cemetery, at the start of this strange investigation. Yes, she'd been through a lot, but she'd got off lightly.

'How's Tilsner? Can I go and see him?'

'If you wish, of course. But he's on a life support system at Charité Hospital. He won't realise you're there. They don't know if he'll pull through or not.'

'What about Ackermann? Will there be an official explanation of his death? Do we know that he was our killer?'

Jäger rubbed his chin, staring out into the distance, as though he hadn't heard her.

'*Oberstleutnant* Jäger?' Müller prompted, as he continued his silence.

Finally, Jäger sighed, and got to his feet. He held his hand out to Müller to help her up.

'Come,' he said. 'I will show you something.'

Jäger drove north through the outskirts of the Hauptstadt, and kept driving, still in a northerly direction through the surrounding Brandenburg forest. The darkness of the trees almost reminded her of the Harz, except here the terrain was flatter. Müller wasn't sure where they were going – wondered if perhaps they were going as far as Rügen and the Ostsee coast – but after about forty minutes, Jäger turned off the main road.

At a barrier, he showed his pass and was waved through. They were in some luxury complex in the centre of the forest, with streets laid out in a regular pattern and low-rise cream-coloured buildings with red-tiled roofs. All the surrounding lawns and bushes were carefully manicured. It was like something Müller had never seen before – a total contrast to the historic towns of the Harz, although those too were surrounded by trees on all sides.

'I can see you're impressed, Karin. Ordinary citizens of the Republic don't often get a chance to visit here. Consider yourself honoured.' He smiled at her.

He pulled the car up outside one of the buildings, and Müller could see the grounds were closed off with red-and-white tape, with People's Army soldiers standing guard. Jäger opened the door for her, showed his pass to the soldiers, and they went inside. The house itself was modern, functional. It was a little how Müller imagined people in the United States of America must live. What was this place, and why had Jäger brought her here? She began to feel slightly alarmed.

Jäger guided her into one of the rooms.

'This was Horst Ackermann's study,' he said. 'It will now be reallocated, of course.' He gestured for her to sit on a chair in the corner, while he took the leather swivel seat at the desk; he then turned towards her and held her gaze.

'I owe you an explanation. And I'm sure you want to know for certain that our killer has been disposed of. He has.' Jäger handed her a copy of *Neues Deutschland*.

She started to read the front-page story. The headline alone was enough to tell her what Jäger wanted her to know.

GENOSSE ACKERMANN KILLED IN CAR CRASH

She didn't even bother to read the rest. 'So no mention of what he did to that poor girl?'

Jäger shook his head. 'Nor what Irma did to him. That would not reflect very well on the Ministry for State Security. But we can be sure he was the killer and the rapist. Forensic teams have found Beate Ewert's fingerprints in this house. Fibres from her clothing, even some scraps of the black witch's cape she wore to the fancy-dress party on the Brocken. They obviously came back here afterwards.'

'And she believed that by going to the party, by cooperating with Ackermann, he would finally get her out of the *Jugendwerkhof*?'

Jäger shrugged. 'Maybe. With all the players except Irma being dead, we're never going to find out. We found the acid used to disguise her identity. We've found pliers with dental remains on, presumably used to pull her teeth out. And we found these.' Jäger swivelled the chair back towards the desk, picked up a brown envelope and then turned again and handed it to Müller. She opened it and shook out its contents. Photographic negatives. She held them up to the light of the window.

'They're the original surveillance photographs from the sanatorium at the Rügen youth workhouse. Ackermann and Pawlitzki, working together, seem to have used them to mock up the photographs of your husband. We found both their fingerprints on them.'

Müller replaced the negatives, then handed the envelope back to the Stasi lieutenant colonel. She didn't want them. It was part of her history now. A part she wanted to forget.

'What about the Volvo limousine? I still don't understand why that was used?'

'We're not sure who dumped the body. We think it was Neumann – or Pawlitzki if you prefer – using Ackermann's limo. Ackermann had an identical one to the one at the West Berlin hire place; he would use it on visits to the western sector. Visiting prostitutes – though why he needed to go to the West to do that, I don't know. There's plenty this side of the barrier, including – by the way – Beate Ewert's mother. That's how her daughter ended up in the *Jugendwerkhof* system. Her mother was considered an unsuitable role model. Anyway, Ackermann regularly swapped the two cars round. We're not sure why. We don't even know if the hire company ever realised which car was which.'

Müller frowned. 'But if he could do all that, why did he and Neumann need to dig the tunnel in the mine? He could have simply defected at any stage.'

'The tunnel must have been their last resort. One he had to use when he finally realised we were onto him, and when we'd sealed the Republic's borders. That was why the initial investigation had to be headed by you, a People's Police detective, rather than anyone in the Stasi. We didn't want him to realise he was being investigated by members of his own Ministry.'

'And what about all the convenient geographical clues?' asked Müller.

Jäger shrugged. 'I don't really understand that myself. All I know is that they fitted in with the rumours we'd heard about illicit activity on the part of Ackermann: the parties involving underage girls on Rügen. We knew three of them had gone missing. The rumours reached another of the Ministry's deputy heads: Markus Wolf, head of the Main Intelligence Directorate. He decided the bad apple at the top of the pile had to be removed – but, as I said, we couldn't have Stasi agents investigating Stasi generals.'

Müller frowned. 'Maybe what Pawlitzki claimed about the clues was the case, then?'

'What was that?'

'That he wanted to lure me there. That he knew I would be investigating the case.'

Picking up a pen, Jäger seemed to make a note of what she was saying. Unless he was just doodling on the pad. She couldn't quite see. 'That's possible, I suppose. You were the Mitte murder squad head.'

'Were?' asked Müller, alarmed.

'We may have a new role for you,' said Jäger, twirling round on the seat like a young boy with a new discovery.

'I don't want a new role.'

He smiled at her. 'Don't reject it out of hand. I'll let you know more about it in due course.'

There was something else left unanswered, which Müller needed to know. 'What will happen to Irma?'

Jäger gave a long sigh, then clicked the end of the pen and placed it down. 'She will have to return to the *Jugendwerkhof.*'

'No!' interrupted Müller. 'She's not going back there. I won't allow it.'

Her outburst seemed to leave Jäger unperturbed. 'I don't see that you have any choice in the matter,' he said. 'She is under the care of the Ministry of Education, not the *Volkspolizei.* She is very fortunate not to be facing a murder charge.'

'There are no witnesses. Neither Vogel nor I would testify against her. Surely you cannot be so cruel as to send her back to that godforsaken place?'

Jäger looked at her sternly. 'Careful, Karin. I've already done a lot for you, made sure you aren't facing any disciplinary charges. Why should I go out on a limb over this, and why do you care?'

'It's just those girls ... they could ... they could be –'

'Your daughter? The one you aborted?'

His words were like a stab to Müller's heart. 'How ... How do you know about that?'

'It's the Ministry for State Security's job to know about people. Especially those working for it. That's one of the reasons you were chosen for this case. You had a very personal reason to make sure those involved were brought to justice. The other reason, of course, is that you're young, inexperienced, slightly out of your depth.' Müller knew she ought to feel anger at the slight, but she'd long suspected Jäger hadn't recruited her on the basis of ability. 'Your youth made you vulnerable, malleable. More willing to do what I required.'

Müller slumped forward in her chair, trying to shut out what he was saying. She'd removed her sling the previous day when she'd gone down the mine, and hadn't put it back on. But the wound in her arm still hurt as she held her head in her hands.

A small smile played on Jäger's face. He didn't seem like the affable western newsreader now. 'However, turning back to Irma Behrendt's future, there may be another way,' he said. 'We might be prepared to let Irma stay with her grandmother at the campsite in Sellin. Her mother is due for release from jail shortly, isn't she?'

'I think that's right.' Müller no longer trusted anything Jäger said or did.

'I will have to speak to Irma first,' he said. 'She will have to agree to certain conditions. But yes, it might be possible to meet both your wishes and our needs at the same time.'

He rose from the chair. 'I think that just about concludes things here. Why don't I take you to see Tilsner?'

59

March 1975.
East Berlin.

As she looked through the window of the door into the intensive care unit, Müller was shocked by the number of tubes attached to her deputy. His face was partially covered with a breathing mask, and the surrounding flesh was horribly pale. She was about to push open the door when Jäger reached out his arm to stop her and gestured with his eyes to the side of the room.

There sat Koletta – his wife – and his two children. They wouldn't welcome her. Koletta would blame her for leading her husband into danger, even if she knew nothing of Müller and Tilsner's intimacy. She backed away, and slumped on a seat in the corridor outside. Jäger sat down next to her.

'He's a good officer. For you ... and for us,' he said.

Müller wasn't sure how Jäger would expect her to react, whether he thought she would be surprised. But she wasn't. She'd guessed some time ago, although she could not have guessed whether the arrangement was official. What Jäger was saying was simply confirmation. She shrugged, as though it didn't matter to her.

Jäger smiled. 'Who do you think radioed to tip us off from the Brocken when you insisted on setting off on your lunatic mission with just two officers and two guns? If he hadn't, you wouldn't be standing here now, and I would be attending a double funeral.'

'Was that what he was doing when he went off on his own in West Berlin?' she asked.

Jäger nodded. 'He needed to pick up some documents for a little industrial espionage racket we were running.'

She sighed. 'He's still a good man. He's someone you'd want on your side rather than the enemy's.'

'A good man. I'd agree. And a good photographer.'

Müller felt the blood drain from her face. She turned towards the Stasi *Oberstleutnant*, her brow furrowing. 'But you said it was Pawlitzki and Ackermann who faked those pictures of Gottfried with the girl.'

Jäger laughed. 'That's right. Tilsner's interest was in photographing churches.' Müller gasped, but Jäger wasn't finished. 'But why he provided pictures to the Ministry for State Security from his own apartment is more of a mystery. Perhaps he had a personal reason for wanting your marriage to come to an end?'

It was the final straw for Müller. She grabbed Jäger by the lapels of his coat. 'You bastard,' she spat.

He smiled, and loosened her fingers. 'Careful, Karin. After all that's happened it would be unfortunate if you found yourself on a disciplinary charge after all.'

She got up, straightened her coat and stomped off down the corridor without a backward glance. The *Arschloch*! She'd gone along with his little games, done her best, but she wasn't playing them anymore.

When she reached her apartment block on Schönhauser Allee, she saw the Bäckerei Schäfer van had returned to its usual place. That was probably Jäger's doing too. In the lobby, she stopped to pick up her mail: three letters – two official-looking ones and one with a West German postmark.

Her legs weighed her down as she climbed the stairs to the apartment. Frau Ostermann's door clicked open when she reached the landing. The infernal woman had probably been watching out for her.

'Frau Müller,' she said. 'Is everything OK between you and your husband? I haven't seen him around much recently.'

Müller turned to the interfering woman. 'Is that any business of yours, Citizen Ostermann? I don't think it is, is it?'

The woman snorted, and clicked her door shut again, retreating inside. Once the door closed, Müller shot her the *Mittelfinger*. She wasn't in the mood.

Müller entered the flat with a heavy heart. It would be quiet enough for Ostermann from now on. Because there was just her. On her own.

She closed the apartment door and slumped on the sofa, the exhaustion of the last few days and weeks catching up with her. Placing the two official-looking letters on the coffee table, she tore open the West German postmarked one, half-suspecting who it was from. She could feel tears begin to prick her eyes, but tried to fight them back as she read the typewritten letter, dated from two days earlier:

Heilbronn,
Federal Republic of Germany

Dear Karin

I'm sorry it had to come to this, and I am sorry I didn't
get a chance to see you before I left. You'll know by
now that those photographs from the reform school
were fakes. But apart from that, after what you told
me about you and Tilsner, the deal they offered me to
leave the Republic was too good to turn down.

That does not mean that I do not think of you with
affection. I still do. We had a lot of good times together.
But I always felt there was something missing from
your life – some big sadness – and I was never able to
compensate for that fully. Perhaps you will manage to
find someone else who will.

Anyway, this is just a very quick note to say there
are no hard feelings on my part. I would hope one day
that I will be able to visit you and that we can remain
friends at least, and that you will remember me fondly.

I'm hoping that I may be able to land a job quite
quickly, despite the poor unemployment situation in
the West. Good maths teachers are in short supply,
and there's a position I'm going to see about tomorrow
in Bad Wimpfen – a small town near here in a pretty
spot on the River Neckar. It's all quite exciting, if a little
frightening.

Don't think badly of me.

At the end of the typing, the only piece of handwriting: his name, Gottfried, and a single 'X' for a kiss.

Karin ignored the other two letters. Instead, she went to the bedroom and reached up to the top of the wardrobe for the key. Then she sat on the end of the bed and turned the drawer lock.

Sometimes just stroking the clothes would be enough to comfort her. But not today. She got out the two sets of baby clothes, one blue and one pink, and arranged them carefully side by side on the bed. She stroked them as the tears fell. Because Pawlitzki hadn't been cheated of one son or daughter – he'd been cheated out of one of each: a boy and a girl. Twins that, if she'd continued with her unwanted pregnancy, would have put an end to her police career there and then.

The twins that she knew she could never replace.

Oberleutnant Karin Müller had lost her babies, lost her husband and didn't know if her deputy would survive his injuries. But she had saved a young girl's life. She hoped Irma Behrendt would now find happiness and make the best of her second chance.

60

March 1975.
Ostseebad Sellin, Rügen, East Germany.

I'm so excited. Over the past few years – years of utter misery –
this is the day I've been waiting for, and I know Oma feels just
the same. Our little gathering is quite small. Some people in the
town still do not want to be seen with us. I suppose I can understand that. But those of us who are here have dressed in our best
clothes, put on our finest make-up, even polished our shoes.

In the last week, I've been helping Oma make the small campsite house look attractive once more. Repainting the front in
brilliant white that sparkles in the spring sun. And then helping
her bake the cakes and make the paper decorations. It won't be
long until Oma will open for the season, at Easter, and she has
promised that if trade is good, I can have a job looking after the
campsite, earning my own money at last. Not the pathetic pocket
money at the *Jugendwerkhof,* but a proper wage, albeit a small one.

The front doorbell rings. We shush each other and giggle, trying but failing to keep quiet. Laurenz – Frau Brinkerhoff's son –
gives me a look of encouragement, and a smile. I blush under his

gaze. He's asked me out next week, to the cinema in Göhren, up the road. My first proper date. I'm so nervous.

The bell rings a second time. I can see the shadow of someone through the knobbly-glazed front door. Before I open it, I check my new hairstyle in the hall mirror and brush my fringe out of my eyes.

As I pull the door open, and see her, I'm already speaking: 'I'm sorry we don't have any spaces free. We're not open for the season yet.'

I see her face crease in confusion.

'I ... I ... haven't come to camp here,' she stutters. I know she's wondering who this new girl is at the door. Finally, I see her look again at my red hair, at the colour of my eyes. She realises who I am, and that I'm joking.

'Irma!' she cries. 'Is it really you?' I just nod, and she hugs me – tighter than she's ever hugged me before. I can't speak because I know that then the tears will fall, and won't stop. She breaks the hug, and pushes me back slightly to take another look. She strokes my face. 'You're so beautiful. What's happened to you? My beautiful, beautiful girl.' The tears are flowing down her face freely. She is thinner than I remember. She has more lines and wrinkles, probably more than she should at her age. The years in jail have taken their toll.

But she is Mutti.

My Mutti.

She is home. And I know that in accepting *Oberstleutnant* Jäger's arrangement, I have made the right choice.

61

March 1975.
A forest near East Berlin.

The Stasi officer was disorientated by all the deliberate false turns and stopping and starting inside the Barkas van; for the prisoner, it would be even worse. He would have little idea, if any, of their location. The officer knew they were somewhere on the outskirts of the Hauptstadt, but no more than that. He was fully aware of the job he had to do, but not how it fitted into the larger picture; he didn't even know what the prisoner was guilty of. But for them to be here, for him to have been assigned this task, it would have to be something serious. It was usually espionage: undermining the Republic, helping the fascists and counter-revolutionaries in their attempts to destroy the socialist state of workers and peasants.

He listened as the guards dragged the prisoner out of the van and tried in vain to shut out the noise of the screams, the protestations, the terror. Of course, very occasionally there would be a late intervention. Or the ritual would be followed to the very edge of the precipice, before it was suddenly aborted and the prisoner taken back to whichever jail he had come from. Usually a 'he'. Not always, but usually. An extreme form of *Zersetzung*, of psychological terror: the last trick in the arsenal to try to break them, to get them to confess.

This, though, was not *Zersetzung*.

The moment was near. He shuffled his hands into the white gloves, which wouldn't stay white for long.

He picked up the case and – crouching – made his way out of the van.

They were in a forest clearing, surrounded on all sides by spruce trees, the air fresh and crisp, a welcome contrast to the Hauptstadt's pollution and smog.

The officer adjusted the gloves, bent down and clicked open the aluminium case. The weapon was already prepared, checked, oiled. He'd done all that back at Hohenschönhausen.

Kneeling in front of him on the forest floor, constrained in a straitjacket and held by a guard on each side, the prisoner was quieter now. No more screaming, no more protestations of innocence through the heavy fabric of the hood that covered his head.

The officer loaded the gun, released the safety catch and then held the barrel against the back of the prisoner's skull. The accused tried to flinch away, began shouting unintelligibly through the close-knit material. But it was too late now.

The officer paused for a moment as a bird chattered overhead to allow the solemnity of the occasion to settle on the forest, to allow the condemned his last thoughts.

Then he squeezed the trigger.

EPILOGUE

March 1975.
The island of Rügen, East Germany.

The woman's eyes darted around the handful of people in the café, never resting for more than a moment, moving on before any return gaze could challenge her. Where was he? This was the correct meeting place, she had made sure she was on time, but none of the customers here carried the package that was the agreed signal. She glanced down at her watch. He was ten minutes late already. She resumed her surreptitious observation: watching, but not wanting to be watched.

Were any of the others in the café informers? The waitress who'd just brought her coffee – the one with the painted-on, over-blacked eyebrows and a sour, Pomeranian farmer's-wife demeanour. She looked like a loyal party type. Or the unshaven man in the grey fishing sweater, sitting in the corner nursing a beer even though it was not yet midday. He hadn't drunk a drop of it. She'd noted that.

The woman rubbed her hands together as though the chill of an Ostsee Easter had invaded the inside of the salon. In fact – under a portrait of a middle-aged man in horn-rimmed spectacles – an open fire crackled and spewed smoke, as though suffering indigestion from its meal of low-grade coal. She brought the coffee to her lips: the edge of the cup trembled against them, so that some of the liquid spilled. The woman smiled ruefully to herself. So careless.

She checked her watch once more, and then looked up again at Comrade Honecker's portrait. She had the sensation he was watching her too, from behind the glass of the frame. For the last few years he and his ilk had held her captive, like a bird in a cage. A chief jailer with a network of helpers, who she knew were carefully trained to spy on people like her.

The woman was indeed being watched, but not by anyone in the café. Her observer was concealed by the shadow of a white wooden veranda on the opposite side of the resort's main street. A slender figure, with an angular face barely visible inside a tightly drawn hood, seemingly busy sweeping the building's entrance, but concentrating on watching the coffee shop, not the motion of the brush.

The hooded figure's gaze became more alert as a man in an overcoat and suit approached, carrying a bouquet of spring flowers. There was something distinctive about them. They were too early for Rügen island flowers. The blooms seemed to attract the woman's attention. She rose from her seat, hurriedly threw a couple of marks on the table and then rushed to join the man outside. Her face lit up as they embraced. Almost a look of love, but the hooded figure didn't think that was what it was.

They moved off, walking up Wilhelm-Pieck-Strasse, past piles of cleared snow from the unseasonal blizzard just days earlier, the stems of the flowers bending in the bitter wind. They strolled towards the sea and the cliff steps that would take them down to the Seebrücke, with its wooden legs stretching out through the ice-cold water.

After a few moments, the figure on the veranda followed, keeping pace a few hundred metres behind the couple. The figure stopped at the telescope at the top of the cliff, the one used by children to watch passing ships in the summer. However, anyone checking the angle of the telescope would see it trained not out to sea, but to the end of the wooden pier. There the couple still talked, standing by a lamp post thickly iced with frozen sea spray. Winter's grip clinging on until spring finally arrived.

After a few moments, the figure moved to a yellow public call box, just a few metres away.

A finger turned the dial, calling a Bergen auf Rügen number.

In Bergen, the Ministry for State Security operator heard the caller ask for *Hauptmann* Gerd Steiger.

'Can I ask who's calling?' asked the operator.

In the call box, the figure drew back her hood and ran her fingers through her newly styled red hair.

'Tell him it's Wildcat. Tell him the subject has made contact.'

The girl with the angular looks waited for Steiger. She wondered if she was doing the right thing, but she was sure she was. That was the price of her freedom; the payment to avoid being sent back to the *Jugendwerkhof*. To be allowed to live with her grandmother.

To spy on her own mother.

After all, that was what she was.

Like Mathias before her.

A spy.

An informer.

A Stasi child.

GLOSSARY

Ampelmann	Little green/red man with hat at pedestrian crossing lights
Arschloch	Arsehole
Bäderarchitektur	Resort architecture
Bezirk (pl *Bezirke*)	East German district or region
Brötchen	Bread roll
Bundesgrenzschutz	Federal border guard – the first police force permitted in West Germany after WW2
Der schwarze Kanal	Notorious East German propaganda television programme
Eingaben	Petitions
Gebackene Apfelringe	Baked apple rings
Generaloberst	Colonel general
Gottverdammt	Goddamnit
Grenztruppen	Border guards

Grenzübergang	Crossing point in the Berlin Wall or inner German border
Hänschen klein	*Little Hans* (name of a famous children's song)
Jugendliche	Youth; teenager
Jugendwerkhof (pL Jugendwerkhöfe)	Reformatory (literally 'youth work yard')
Kaufhaus des Westens (usually abbreviated to *KaDeWe*)	West Berlin department store
Kriminalpolizei	Criminal police
Kriminaltechniker	Forensic officer
Kripo	Criminal police (short form)
Leutnant	Lieutenant
Neues Deutschland	Daily party newspaper
Oberleutnant	Lieutenant or first lieutenant
Oberliga	First division of the East German football league
Oberst	Colonel
Oberstleutnant	Lieutenant colonel
Ostler	Slang word for an East German (after 1989, called an *Ossi*)

Ostpolitik	Normalisation of relations between West and East Germany in the early 1970s
Ostsee	Baltic Sea
Republikflucht	Movement of people from East Germany to the West
Republikflüchtlinge	Escapees (people who escaped or left East Germany)
Scheisse	Shit
Seebrücke	Pier
Unterleutnant	Second lieutenant
Volkspolizei	People's Police
Westler	Slang word for a West German (after 1989, called a *Wessi*)

AUTHOR'S NOTE

This novel is a work of fiction, but some of the story is inspired by true events – in particular the way the Stasi recruited young people. It is estimated that by the time the Berlin Wall fell in 1989, around six per cent of the Stasi's 173,000 unofficial collaborators were under the age of eighteen. Recruitment of youths began in the 1970s and gathered pace in the 1980s. You can find out more in the book *Stasi Auf Dem Schulhof* by Klaus Behnke and Jürgen Wolf.

The favoured method of execution in East Germany was the guillotine up until the mid-1960s and from then on a bullet in the back of the head. The death sentence was not abolished until 1987. In 1982, the head of the Stasi, Erich Mielke, was quoted as saying that Stasi operatives should 'execute if necessary, even without trial'. You can hear those chilling words as part of the exhibition at the Museum in der Runden Ecke, the old Stasi HQ in Leipzig.

Although the *Jugendwerkhof* featured in this book is fictional, the 'closed' *Jugendwerkhof* at Torgau was notorious for sexual and physical abuse of the children there. One harrowing first-hand account comes from Heidemarie Puls, who was an inmate in the

1970s. Her book, *Schattenkinder hinter Torgauer Mauern*, provided some of the background inspiration for this novel. The only *Jugendwerkhof* on Rügen was shut down in the 1950s. However, Prora itself is still there and makes for an interesting visit.

The idea of Neumann and Ackermann's fictional escape tunnel was inspired by one built for East German leader Erich Honecker. He had a fifty-metre escape route built under the Berlin Wall in the event his people turned against him. Like my fictional Ackermann, he never got the chance to use it.

The island of Vilm does exist and was used by the East German political elite. The story of sexual abuse set there in this novel is, however, entirely fictional, as is the fancy-dress party on the Brocken. The Soviet base at Gross Zicker on Rügen described in this book is fictional, but there was a base nearby at Klein Zicker (since dismantled).

I have no evidence that the children of *Jugendwerkhöfe* were involved in making furniture for the West. Political prisoners of the Stasi were however used to produce items of IKEA furniture in the 1970s and 1980s. This included the well-known Klippan sofa. In November 2012, the head of IKEA Germany, Peter Betzel, made a formal apology to a roomful of former prisoners after a report by auditors Ernst & Young confirmed that IKEA managers were aware of the practice.

The plotline of the repatriation agreement for under-sixteens derives from a fascinating story on the internet called 'Flight to Freedom', told by a former American serviceman, Thomas Pucci. Thomas and his friend Harry Knights witnessed a fourteen-year-old boy escape near the 'Doppel housing area' in Berlin one day in the mid-1970s. Harry even took photos. But although the boy successfully evaded the death strip and reached the West, Thomas says he was taken into custody by the West Berlin authorities. Three days later, according to newspaper headlines, he was returned to the East under the terms of the 'agreement'.

Sending Stasi agents to the West to get a hire car back to the East for forensic tests did actually happen in a murder case from 1977 related to me by Dr Remo Kroll, author of *Die Kriminalpolizei im Ostteil Berlins (1945–1990)*. The Stasi did have a special homicide division and would become closely involved if the suspect was related to the ruling party, the SED (Socialist Unity Party). And they did sometimes take over criminal investigations from the *Kripo* – Dr Kroll cites the example of the 1986 murders of babies in a Leipzig hospital.

Finally, although party leaders did occasionally parade in their Volvos, more often than not they would be watching the parades themselves on a raised podium, Kremlin-style – so Karin's memory from the twenty-fifth anniversary parade was a little authorial licence for the sake of the plot.

I hope you enjoyed reading the novel as much as I enjoyed writing it, and that it will encourage you to visit the eastern part of Germany, where the ghost of the dystopian world that was the DDR is still very much evident – but disappearing fast.

For more background, please see my website: www.stasichild.com

ACKNOWLEDGEMENTS

This novel was written for the inaugural Crime Thriller Creative Writing MA at City University, London. Special thanks to my fellow students for their invaluable help and suggestions, particularly Stephanie Broadribb, Rob Hogg, James Holt, Philip Horswood, Kylie Morris, Seun Olatoye, Rod Reynolds, Jody Sabral, Laura Shepherd-Robinson and Emma Tuddenham. As I write, two of us have obtained publishing deals (with, I'm sure, more to follow), one has won the Debut Dagger and several have secured literary agents.

Also many thanks to my tutors – Claire McGowan, Laura Wilson and Philip Sington – for their suggestions. Philip's novel *The Valley of Unknowing* – set in Dresden in the 1980s – was far and away the best fictional account I read during my research.

For sharing his experiences as a child in Sellin, Rügen, and for reading my first draft, I'm very grateful to Oliver Berlau of the BBC World Service. I spent a fabulous research trip in Sellin in April 2013, staying just off Wilhelmstrasse (Wilhelm-Pieck-Strasse in DDR times) and that – together with Oliver's recollections – inspired the Rügen parts of the book. Thanks also to Stephanie Smith for her valuable comments on the first draft.

For their help with explanations of DDR policing I'm indebted to former detectives Siegfried Schwarz and Bernd Marmulla, and to Jana Reissmann and Thomas Abrams for very kindly helping with interview translations. Many thanks, too, to Ronald Schulz-Töpken of the Berlin Police Presidency, Remo Kroll and former East Berlin police officer Kerstin Krüger.

Also a big thank you to the organisers of the international Yeovil Literary Prize. My shortlisting and third prize there was the first step towards publication.

Last, but not least, without my agent Adam Gauntlett and his colleagues at Peters Fraser & Dunlop (especially Rachel Mills, Naomi Joseph and Jonathan Sissons) this book might never have seen the light of day. I was thrilled when it was bought for Bonnier UK by Mark Smith, and am very grateful for the improvements suggested by my editor and publisher at Twenty7, Joel Richardson. All remaining errors are – of course – solely down to me.